Horatio R. Palmer

Palmer's Class Method of Teaching the Rudiments of Music

Horatio R. Palmer

Palmer's Class Method of Teaching the Rudiments of Music

ISBN/EAN: 9783337390112

Printed in Europe, USA, Canada, Australia, Japan

Cover: Foto ©Andreas Hilbeck / pixelio.de

More available books at **www.hansebooks.com**

PALMER'S CLASS METHOD

OF TEACHING THE

RUDIMENTS OF MUSIC

BY

H. R. PALMER, Mus. Doc.

AUTHOR OF "PALMER'S THEORY OF MUSIC," "PALMER'S PIANO
PRIMER," "PALMER'S PRONOUNCING POCKET DICTIONARY
OF MUSICAL TERMS," AND UPWARDS OF THIRTY
OTHER POPULAR MUSICAL WORKS

THE JOHN CHURCH CO.,

CINCINNATI.   NEW YORK.   CHICAGO.

A WORD TO TEACHERS WHO USE THIS BOOK.

THE work is not arranged in chapters or lessons, for the reason that some classes will progress much faster than others. The teacher should determine what points he will cover during a given lesson, and study them well. He should never go before his class without spending from *one* to *three* hours in studying the lesson he is to give. No matter how well he knows the lesson, he should always go to his class fresh from his study. The teachers who are wielding the best influence to-day, and those who are to be the greatest teachers of the future, are they who are willing to take pains in preparing their work.

Many, having misunderstood our meaning as expressed in Note 28, page 20, think that we intend to inculcate the idea that the class must not read in any other than the C key until " almost the entire theory of musical notation " has been taught ; but if Note 95, page 61, is carefully read it will be seen that we not only urge the early practice of reading with Do on other degrees, but have prepared a large number of exercises for that purpose. There are excellent reasons why the teacher should, as soon as short and long notes have been explained, take the class over to the first two exercises in the G key (114 & 115, page 36), go up to Sol, call that a new Do, and after explaining the hold, read and sing both exercises by syllables without beating (as quadruple measure has not yet been introduced). Also No. 150, page 55, take Fa as a new Do, sing without beating, give a short

3

note the time of one pulse, and a long note the time of two pulses. This may be done once or twice during each lesson, in various keys, avoiding exercises which involve points not yet explained, and always being careful to give each new Do its proper pitch. To do this, teachers should provide themselves with a fork or pipe (pitched on C) which tone they will always call "our old Do," with which they can compare the efforts of the class, and from which any new Do can be found by the process explained at Note 293, page 196.

An excellent adjunct to the teacher's outfit is a Mason & Hamlin *Baby Organ*, which costs only $27, and can be folded and carried in one hand. It has a pure but powerful tone, and may be used in small country choirs to good advantage.

To the noble army of teachers, (now upwards of 5,000) who have adopted the term "CANCEL" in the place of the pernicious term "NATURAL" the author hereby extends hearty congratulations, and sincere thanks. He would bespeak their kind aid in changing the name of sharp Sol (Si) to Sil, (pronounced *Seel*), the good and sufficient reasons for which are given in Remark 3, page 163.

Teachers will undoubtedly be pleased with our further change by the use of the syllable Ta instead of La for all special work,—first because La is so prominent as the name of one of the tones of the Scale, and second, the palatal sonant quality of the L, makes it less effective for *attack* than the syllable Ta.

In the author's class Text book GRADED STUDIES, (published by The John Church Co., price 60 cents,) reference to this CLASS METHOD is made continually; in fact they are intended to accompany each other, the CLASS METHOD for the teacher, and GRADED STUDIES for the pupils.

If the teacher's time is limited, and he can only give a short term (ten lessons for example) he may find it convenient to omit certain exercises and form his course according to the time at his disposal. However, whether his course be a long one or a short one, he will find it better economy of time to follow the general order as laid down in this volume.

A new set of Modulators has been published as follows:—PALMER'S SCALE MODEL for Primary classes and kindergartens; MODULATOR No. 1 giving three keys; MODULATOR No. 2 showing seven keys with their sharps, flats and letters; and MODULATOR No. 3 showing the thirteen major keys and the thirteen minor keys, with the sharps and flats printed in colors. See advertisement at the end of this volume.

The author has been greatly assisted in the preparation of the Junior Grade of this work by Mr. L. S. Leason, whose extended experience in teaching this Method, and whose unusually analytical mind have been of great service throughout this grade. Many of its best points would undoubtedly have been overlooked because of the severe pressure upon the writer's time, had it not been for the thoughtful care which Mr. Leason has bestowed upon this part of the work.

H. R. PALMER.

PARK HILL–ON–HUDSON,
NEW YORK CITY, *April 20th*, 1896.

PALMER'S
CLASS METHOD OF TEACHING
THE
RUDIMENTS OF MUSIC.

INTRODUCTORY REMARKS.

NOTE 1.—The teacher remarks to the class that all present will be considered as beginners, that all will be expected to comply with every request he may make. that although some may have studied music previously, they must regard themselves, for the time being, as beginners, and by answering questions, and otherwise complying with his requests, they will encourage the younger members. He also remarks that in learning to sing, as in learning to talk, we depend very largely upon imitation. The child hears its parents speak the little words it is trying to learn hundreds of times before it can place its vocal organs in the proper position to pronounce them, so in learning to sing we listen to tones produced by the teacher, and try to imitate them.

THE SCALE.

§ 1. TEACHER. "Listen!" (Sings the tone C, syllable Ta.)

NOTE 2.—The teacher should give *a* the sound it has in the word father, taking care that the tone is *pure*, neither too long nor so short as to be abrupt—also being careful that the position in which he stands is such as he would wish to have imitated, namely, the body erect and the shoulders thrown slightly back.

§ 2. Tr. "All sing that tone." (They sing.)

Note 3.—They make the effort, and are more or less successful. After allowing them to repeat it a number of times, he asks them to listen, and produces the tone D, to the syllable *Ta*, as before, and says:

§ 3. Tr. "Did I sing the tone you sang, or a new tone?" Class. "A new tone."

§ 4. Tr. "Sing the new tone." (They sing.)

§ 5. Tr. "Sing the tone you learned first." (They sing.)

§ 6. Tr. "Sing the new tone." (They sing.)

Note 4.—Practice these tones until all are quite familiar with them.

§ 7. Tr. "The name of the first tone is One, and the name of the second tone is Two. If I ask you to sing One, what tone will you sing?" (They answer by *singing* One.)

§ 8. Tr. "If I ask you to sing Two, what tone will you sing?" (They answer by *singing* Two.)

§ 9. Tr. (Sings the tone E and asks:) "Did I sing One, Two, or a new tone?" Cl. "A new tone."

§ 10. Tr. "All sing the new tone." (They sing.)

§ 11. Tr. "Following the order in which we named the first two tones, what shall we call this new tone?" Cl. "Three."

Note 5.—The teacher should allow the pupils to practice these three tones at some length, after which he calls upon them to sing One, Two, and Three. He then requests them to listen, and sings the tone F, and says :

§ 12. Tr. "Did I sing one of the tones you have learned, or a new tone?" Cl. "A new tone."

§ 13. Tr. "Sing the new tone." (They sing.)

§ 14. Tr. "What shall we call the new tone?" Cl. "Four."

Note 6.—Practice these four tones upward and downward thoroughly.

§ 15. Tr. "Sing One." (They sing.) "Sing Two." (They sing.) "Sing Three." (They sing.) "Sing Four." (They sing.)

Note 7.—He requests them to listen, and sings G to the syllable *Ta* as before.

§ 16. Tr. "Did I sing one of the four tones you have learned, or a new tone?" Cl. "A new tone."

§ 17. Tr. "Sing the new tone." (They sing.)

§ 18. Tr. "What would be a good name for this new tone?" Cl. "Five."

Note 8.—Practice these tones thoroughly before proceeding farther.

§ 19. Tr. "Sing One, Two, Three, Four, Five." (They sing.)

§ 20. Tr. (Sings A.) "Did I sing one of the five tones you have learned, or a new one?" Cl. "A new one."

§ 21. Tr. "Sing it." (They sing.)

§ 22. Tr. "What will you name the new tone?" Cl. "Six."

§ 23. TR. "Sing One, Two, Three, Four, Five, Six." (They sing.)

§ 24. TR. "Listen!" (He sings the tone B.) "Did I sing one of the six tones you have learned, or a new tone?" CL. "A new tone."

§ 25. TR. "Sing it." (They sing.)

§ 26. TR. "Name the new tone." CL. "Seven."

§ 27. TR. "Sing One, Two, Three, Four, Five, Six, Seven, and then add a new tone."

NOTE 9.—They naturally will add Eight to those already learned.

§ 28. TR. "Following our order of naming, what shall we call this new tone?" CL. "Eight."

§ 29. TR. "What tone naturally follows Seven?" CL. "Eight."

§ 30. TR. "Seven is called the *leading* tone, because it leads to Eight. What is Seven called?" CL. "The leading tone."

§ 31. TR. "Why?" CL. "Because it leads to eight."

§ 32. TR. "These eight tones form what we term the Diatonic Scale, which is the foundation of the entire musical structure. As soon as you shall have learned all that can be learned concerning this scale and its surroundings, you will have learned all that *can* be learned about music."

NOTE 10.—After practicing the scale carefully, ascending and descending, the exercise may be varied by reqesting the pupils to "sing One twice; Two twice; Three twice, etc., throughout the scale, ascending and descending." This may be followed by asking them to "sing One three times; Two three times. etc., pausing to take a deep breath after every third tone."

RESPIRATION.

NOTE 11.—The teacher should exercise great care in the first lessons with regard to the correct manner of using the respiratory organs, as well as the vocal organs ; instructing his pupils that the breath should be taken by direct action of the diaphragm, abdominal and intercostal muscles, thus relieving the throat and lungs of unnecessary effort, which only tends to weary and weaken them.

ITALIAN NAMES OF THE TONES.

NOTE 12.—Having learned the tones of the scale, the teacher will inform the class that we commonly follow the Italian plan of giving each tone a name.

§ 33. TR. "The Italians call One, Do ; Two, Re ; Three, Mi ; Four, Fa ; Five, Sol ; Six, La ; Seven, Ti ; and Eight, Do."

NOTE 13.—The most prominent American teachers have united in the effort to change the seventh syllable (*Si*) to *Ti*, for the following good and sufficient reasons, viz. : 1st, It is the name of a pitch (C) ; 2d, it is the name of sharp Five, which leads to Six ; 3d, it is the name of Seven of the Major Scale, thus unnecessarily over-burdening our nomenclature with the anomaly of giving the same name to three different things. a predicament which is greatly to be deprecated and which would not be tolerated in any other exact science. By changing the seventh syllable to *Ti*, and sharp Sol to Sil, (Seel), the difficulty has been entirely overcome.

§ 34. TR. "What is the new name for One ?" CL. "Do." TR. "Two ?" CL. "Re." TR. "Three ?" CL. "Mi." TR. "Four ?" CL. "Fa." TR. "Five ?" CL. "Sol." TR. "Six ?" CL. "La." TR. "Seven ?" CL. "Ti." TR. "Eight ?" CL. "Do."

§ 35. Tr. "Are One, Three, Five, and Seven odd or even numbers?" Cl. "Odd."

§ 36. Tr. "What are the new names for the *odd* members of the scale?" Cl. "Do, Mi, Sol, Ti."

§ 37. Tr. "Are Two, Four, Six, Eight odd or even numbers?" Cl. "Even."

§ 38. Tr. "What are the new names for the even members of the scale?" Cl. "Re, Fa, La, Do."

Note 14.—The teacher should be careful to have the pupils pronounce these syllables correctly, informing them that one of the objects in applying different names to the tones is that we may practice the several vowel-sounds, giving the long sound of *o* to Do ; the long sound of *a* to Re ; the long sound of *e* to Mi ; *a* as in *far* to Fa, etc.

The Modulator.

Remark 1.—The Modulator is such a wonderful help in teaching the *relationship of tones* (which is the foundation of all music, whether vocal or instrumental) that a few words of explanation here are important. It is about nine and a half feet long by seven wide, to be hung in the class-room so that all can see it. It has thirteen columns; one for each key. The central column is much broader than the others, and represents the C key. All black characters on the Modulator represent diatonic tones ; all characters in carmine (red) show the intermediate tones whose tendency is upward, called *sharps ;* all characters printed in gas-light green indicate those intermediate tones whose tendency is downward, called *flats.*

It is so made that the intervals are pictured to the eye by accurate distances, so the beginner can *see* the difference between minor and major seconds, and major and minor thirds. The fourths, fifths, and, in fact, all the intervals, are thus pictured to the eye of the pupil; Every teacher of experience knows that among his greatest difficulties is that of the teaching of intervals, and that the perplexity disappears as soon as the pupil fully *comprehends* the intervals. Just here is where the Modulator is of such great advantage, as the distances are all set before the eye in such a manner that a clearer and more intelligent idea can be gotten in a single lesson from the Modulator than in a whole term of lessons without it.

The Modulator is published in four styles, viz: A SCALE MODEL, one column, no flats or sharps; No. 1, Three columns, no flats or sharps; No 2, Seven columns, with flats, sharps and letters; No 3, Showing thirteen major, and thirteen minor keys, with flats and sharps in colors. See advertisement, page 326.

§ 39. TR. "The difference in pitch between any two tones is called an *Interval*. What is an interval?" CL. "An interval is the difference in pitch between any two tones."

§ 40. TR. "The interval from any tone to the next, up or down, is called a *Second*. What is it called?" CL. "A Second."

§ 41. TR. (Pointing to Do Re in the middle column of the Modulator.) "What is the interval from Do to Re?" CL. "A second." TR. (pointing.) "From Re to Mi?" CL. "A second." TR. "From Mi to Fa?" CL. "A second." TR. "From Fa to Sol?" CL. "A second." TR. "From Sol to La?" CL. "A second." TR. "From La to Ti?" CL. "A second." TR. "From Ti to Do?" CL. "A second."

§ 42. TR. "The second Do Re (pointing) is the same as the second Re Mi. Now let us examine the second Mi Fa (pointing)—is it smaller or greater than Do Re?" CL. "Smaller."

§ 43. TR. "Yes, the second Mi Fa (pointing) is only half as great as the second Do Re. Small seconds are called *minor seconds*. What are they called?" CL. "Minor seconds."

§ 44. TR. "Large seconds are called *major seconds*. What are they called?" CL. "Major seconds."

§ 45. TR. "Sing as I point. (Pointing to Do Re.) What interval did you sing?" CL. "A major second." TR. (Pointing to Re Mi.) "What interval did you sing?" CL. "A major second." TR. (Pointing to Mi Fa.) "What interval did you sing?" CL. "A minor second."

NOTE 15.—The teacher proceeds thus till the pupils are familiar with all the seconds of the scale.

SKIP OF A THIRD.

§ 46. TR. "What is the interval Do Re?" CL. "A second."

§ 47. TR. "From any tone to the next but one is called a *Third*. What is it called?" CL. "A third."

§ 48. TR. "What, then, shall we call the interval Do Mi?" CL. "A third."

§ 49. TR. "Sing Do Re Mi." (They sing.) "Sing Mi again." (They sing.)

§ 50. TR. "Sing it once more and remember how it sounds." (They sing).

§ 51. TR. "Sing Do." (They sing.) "*Now* sing Mi." (They sing.)

§ 52. TR. "What tone is between Do and Mi?" CL. "Re."

§ 53. Tr. "What tone did you skip?" Cl. "Re."

§ 54. Tr. "We call this interval a third. What do we call it?" Cl. "A skip of a third."

§ 55. Tr. "Sing Do Re Mi Fa." (They sing.) "Sing Fa again and remember how it sounds." (They sing.) "Sing Do." (They sing.) "Sing Mi." (They sing.) "Sing Re." (They sing.) "Sing Fa." (They sing.)

§ 56. Tr. "What tone is between Re and Fa?" Cl. "Mi."

§ 57. Tr. "What tone did you skip?" Cl. "Mi."

§ 58. Tr. "What do we call this interval?" Cl. "A third."

Note 16.—Introduce the skips Mi Sol, Fa La, Sol Ti, and La Do in the same way the skips Do Mi and Re Fa were introduced.

Note 17.—After having thoroughly practiced the skips of thirds, ascending and descending, separate the class into two divisions. Ask each division to sing the scale ascending and descending, without repeating upper Do; Division No. 2 commencing after No. 1 has sung Do and Re, so as to form a duet.

Note 18.—Ask one division to sing the scale ascending and descending without repeating upper Do, while the other division sings descending and ascending without repeating lower Do.

Note 19.—The teacher should invent ways like the above to keep the class interested in practicing the scale. Too much importance cannot be attached to this feature, as all future progress and musical development depend upon a thorough knowledge of tone relationships.

Chord Practice.

§ 59. Tr. "Sing Do." (They sing.) "Sing Mi." (They sing.) "Sing Sol." (They sing.) "Choose one of these tones and sing it."

Note 20.—The result will be that some will sing Do, some Sol, and some Mi.

§ 60. Tr. "Now choose a different tone— either of the three—and sing it." (They sing.)

Note 21.—The result will not be so satisfactory as before, inasmuch as the low voices will probably sing Sol and the high voices Do, thus leaving Mi out entirely.

§ 61. Tr. "Let me choose for you. All the gentlemen sing Do; these ladies (indicating those who sit in certain seats), sing Mi; all the other ladies sing Sol." (They sing).

Note 22.—The result will be much more satisfactory.

§ 62. Tr. "When two or more tones are performed simultaneously the effect is called a *Chord*, and a chord is named from its lowest tone, hence the chord of Do consists of what three tones?" Cl. "Do Mi Sol."

Spelling and Pronouncing Chords.

§ 63. Tr. "Sing Do Mi Sol." (They sing.) "This singing of the members of the chord separately is called *spelling the chord*; when the three are sung simultaneously it is called *pronouncing the chord*."

§ 64. Tr. "Spell and pronounce the chord of Do."

Note 23.—They sing Do, then Mi, then Sol, after

which they sing the three simultaneously, when the effect will be as follows:

NOTE 24.—The teacher, standing before the class with his hands elevated so all can see them, places the index finger of his right hand on the point of the fourth finger of the left hand and says:

§ 65. TR. "A chord can be formed by taking any tone of our scale as fundamental, skipping its second (here, with the index finger of the right hand he bends down, or *shuts up*, the third finger of the left hand), singing its third he places the index finger on the end of he middle finger of the left hand), skipping the fourth (bending down, or *shutting up*, the first finger of the left hand), and singing the fifth (placing the index finger on the end of the thumb)."

NOTE 25.—At this point the left hand is held before the class, and appears with the fourth finger, middle finger and thumb open, and the first and third fingers shut.

§ 66. TR. "What tones form the chord of Re?" (Again he points to the open fingers while the class answers). CL. "Re Fa La."

§ 67. TR. "What tones do we skip?" (He points to the closed fingers as they answer.) CL. "Mi and Sol."

§ 68. TR. "Spell and pronounce the chord of Re." (They sing :)

§ 69. Tr. "Following the same plan, what tones will form the chord of Mi?" Cl. "Mi Sol Ti."

§ 70. Tr. "Spell and pronounce the chord of Mi." (They sing thus :)

§ 71. Tr. "Still continuing our plan, what tones will form the chord of Fa?" Cl. "Fa La Do."

§ 72. Tr. "Spell and pronounce the chord of Fa." (They sing :)

Note 26.—The practice of chords must be confined to these four until after the EXTENSION OF THE SCALE has been introduced, several lessons hence.

Note 27.—At close of the first lesson the teacher may introduce a simple but pleasing song, of moderate compass, stating that he desires to test their musical ability, by asking them to sing a song entitled, etc. Having committed the song to memory previously, the teacher renders the first stanza in good style, while the pupils listen—after which he sings the first line and asks them to imitate him. When they can sing it well he teaches them the second line in the same manner ; then requests them to connect the two, after which he presents the third, and so on to the end, calling their attention frequently to their pronunciation, and teaching them to exercise great care in enunciating the consonant elements and vowel-sounds. The following song, composed by I. B. Woodbury, and newly arranged for this work, will be found suitable.

The Old Oak Tree.

dwells in his som - bre sol - i - tude.
mands the..... mind at her own good will. She
wend - ed...... forth with their voic - es loud. 'Twas
-His is the strength that de - fies the storm, As it
leads mine.. back to the hap - pier time, To...
dear, me - thinks, for ... there were heard The..
danc - es a - round his state - ly form; 'Tis
fair - er ..... scenes and a sweet - er clime, When I
warb - ling.... notes of many a bird; They

then that he laughs like a king in his glee, For a
wan-der'd a-lone in my child-hood free, And..
came from the glen, o'er the hill and the lea, A.....

dar - ing ... chief is the old oak tree.
sought me a nook by the old oak tree.
trib - ute to pay to the old oak tree.

REFRAIN.

Is the old oak tree, Is the old oak tree, For a
By the old oak tree, By the old oak tree, And..
To the old oak tree, To the old oak tree, A....

ABSOLUTE PITCH.

NOTE 28.—The teacher, immediately upon calling the class to order, should test their capacity for remembering the pitch of the tones, which were learned in the previous lesson, by asking them to sing Do, without singing himself, and taking care that no instrument shall be used in their hearing. This is an important point in our system, and we wish teachers to notice particularly, that we commence with the key of C, and do not leave that key until it is perfectly understood ; that almost the entire theory of musical notation is taught while the class is studying that key ; that when we leave it we explain to them how far we have gone from it, thus keeping uppermost in the minds of the pupils that each tone has a certain pitch which never changes. One of the worst features in all the systems of musical notation which we have examined is, that the respective authors have not held to any particular key in the first exercises, but have commenced with Do on the first line, then on the first space, etc., etc., in many instances giving them all the same pitch, thus failing to inculcate in the minds of the pupils the fact that each line and space represents a tone which is always the same. The authors of the systems alluded to claim that by changing the location of the scale frequently the pupils learn to read in the different keys more readily, but this cannot be, for, by the frequent changes the pupils are confused as to a definite pitch, and what confuses the pupil retards his progress. Thus we see that not only nothing is gained, but very much is lost by not holding to one key until it is perfectly understood.

The first attempt of the class to sing Do will undoubtedly amuse them very much, as each will produce a different pitch, but if the teacher immediately checks their mirthfulness, and bids them repeat the effort once or twice, all the ladies and part of the gentlemen (the tenors) will almost surely bring their voices together upon a tone two or three degrees too high. He tells them they are incorrect and draws upon their judgment still further by asking whether they think the tone they produced was too high or too low; after which he gives them the correct pitch and proceeds with the lesson. Many times during the progress of the lesson, he should stop, and ask them to sing Do. Especially at the commencement of each lesson he should proceed in the same way, never failing to commend the individual, or that part of the class at least, which is nearest correct, and after a few lessons he will have the satisfaction of hearing them sing C, upon the first request, and without a dissenting voice.

NOTE 29.—Always review thoroughly the last lesson before commencing a new one.

NOTE 30.—We cannot emphasize too strongly the fact that all future development of the class, musically speaking, depends on the thoroughness with which they have learned the tones of the scale and their relationships.

NOTE 31.—When they can sing the tones accurately and without much hesitation, he proceeds to call for any tone which may occur to his mind, gradually proceeding to the most awkward order of succession which he can invent. If a well-tuned piano or an organ is accessible, it will be found a valuable practice to play the tones within the compass of the octave and have the pupils give the syllable names as he plays, after which he chooses some simple tune or exercise, the compass of which does not extend below One, or above Eight, and which moves in even time, and asks them to learn it, singing the tones as he calls for them.

The following melody would answer the purpose:

NOTATION.

§ 73. Tr. "As you are now well acquainted with the tones of the scale, it seems necessary that we agree upon a system of signs for them."

Note 32.—An interesting exercise may be given at this point by the teacher placing several articles on a table before him, such as a handkerchief to represent Do; a hat to represent Re; a book to indicate Mi, etc.; or if such articles are not at hand, he may point to the piano for Do, blackboard for Re, table for Mi, chandelier for Fa, window for Sol, etc., requesting them to sing the tones as he points to their representatives. In this way he can have the class repeat the exercise given at the close of Note 31, without calling for the tones orally, thus showing the necessity for a musical notation.

BUILDING THE STAFF.

§ 74. Tr. "We have signs or characters called notes, which, when placed in different positions indicate the tones of the scale. They are made thus." (Places a quarter note on a short line.)

Note 33.—In writing exercises on the board, the teacher should never stand between the class and the writing. Always manage to write at arm's length, so to speak; especially is this important when they are singing an exercise. The teacher should have a pointer long enough to enable him to stand well to one side.

§ 75. Tr. "When the note is placed on a short line, it indicates Do. What tone have I indicated?" Cl. "Do."

§ 76. Tr. "Sing as I point." (Points to the note and the class sing Do.)

§ 77. Tr. "What tone did you sing?" Cl. "Do."

§ 78. Tr. "How did you know you were to sing Do?" Cl. "Because the note is placed on a short line."

Note 34.—The class should be encouraged to abbreviate their answers. The teacher should explain that while the last answer is entirely correct, still all will understand what is meant if they reply, "Short line."

Note 35.—It will be observed that we have adopted the plan of calling tones by their *syllable names*, rather than to insist upon speaking of them by their numeral names. If any teacher prefers the old, and almost universally used plan of always *speaking* of tones by their numeral names, he can, of course, use it; but it will be a serious disadvantage both to himself and to the class. There is no good reason why tones should not be called by their syllable names both in speaking and in singing.

§ 79. Tr. "A note above the short line indicates Re." (Places the note above the short line.)

§ 80. Tr. "What tone is indicated?" Cl. "Re."

§ 81. Tr. "Sing as I point." (Points to the notes and they sing Do Re.)

§ 82. Tr. (Draws a long line and places a note upon it.) "A note upon the long line indicates Mi. What tone is indicated?" Cl. "Mi."

NOTE 36.—The class should practice the tones as the teacher points, after each new representation.

§ 83. TR. "Where shall we place a note to indicate Fa?" CL. "Above the long line."

§ 84. TR. "How shall we represent Sol?" CL. "Draw another long line."

§ 85. TR. "Where will La be represented?" CL. "Above the line."

§ 86. TR. "How shall we represent Ti?" CL. "By another line."

§ 87. TR. "Where shall we represent upper Do?" CL. "Above the line."

NOTE 37.—The teacher now draws two more long lines and says:

§ 88. TR. "It is frequently necessary to have five long lines. The five lines together with their spaces are called a *staff*, and each line and each space is called a *degree*. The names of the degrees are : short line (added line below) ; space below ; first line, first space ; second line, second space ; third line, third space ; fourth line, fourth space ; fifth line, space above ; added line above."

NOTE 38.—The teacher should have the class practice naming the degrees as he points to the lines and spaces, in order that they may be able to readily distinguish the degrees upon which the notes are placed.

NOTE 39.—Inasmuch as blackboards with one side painted black without staff are seldom met with in more remote places, the teacher may omit the last fourteen sections, and proceed as follows, using a board with two staves.

§ 89. TR. "When a note is placed on a short line it indicates Do." (Places a note upon the added line below.)

§ 90. TR. "What tone is indicated?" CL. "Do."

§ 91. TR. "Sing as I point." (Points to the note and the class sing Do.)

§ 92. "What tone did you sing?" CL. "Do."

§ 93. "How did you know you were to sing Do?" CL. "Because the note is placed on the short line."

§ 94. TR. "When the note is placed on the space below the long lines it indicates Re." (Places a note on the space below and says:) "Sing as I point."

NOTE 40.—After exercising upon Do and Re some time, he says:

§ 95. TR. "When the note is placed upon the first of these long lines it indicates Mi." (Places a note on the first line and proceeds as before.)

NOTE 41.—The teacher goes through with the entire scale as above (stopping to practice after each new representation), after which he asks questions something as follows:

§ 96. TR. "Where is Do represented?" CL. "On the short line."

NOTE 42.—The teacher may explain the term *added line*, and use that term if he chooses.

§ 97. TR. "Where is Re represented?" CL. "On the space below the long lines."

NOTE 43.—The teacher remarks that brief answers are better, therefore if they answer the above question with the two words "Space below," it will be sufficient.

§ 98. Tr.　"Where shall I place a note to indicate Mi?"　Cl.　"First line."

Note 44.—The answer to the above question will probably be "First of the long lines," or "Lowest long line." For the sake of brevity the teacher instructs them to answer "First line."

§ 99. Tr.　"What tone is represented by the first space?"　Cl.　"Fa."

§ 100. Tr.　"On the second line?"　Cl. "Sol."

§ 101. Tr.　"If I wished to indicate La where should I place a note?"　Cl.　"Second space."

§ 102. Tr.　"If you should see a note upon the third line, you would know it to indicate what tone?"　Cl.　"Ti."

§ 103. Tr.　"Where is upper Do represented?"　Cl.　"Third space."

§ 104. Tr.　"Are Do, Mi, Sol, Ti, represented by lines or by spaces?"　Cl.　"By lines."

§ 105. Tr.　"If Do is represented by a line, Mi, Sol, and Ti will also be represented by lines; and Re, Fa, La, and upper Do by spaces."

Note 45.—Have them read (not sing) as the teacher points, with Do represented by other degrees than the short line, showing that if Do is represented by a space, Mi, Sol, and Ti will also be represented by spaces, and Re, Fa, La, and upper Do will be represented by lines.

Note 46.—The teacher should question the class frequently on these points during the next few lessons, thereby preparing them for the change of keys.

Note 47.—After having the class sing the tones as the teacher points, until they are quite familiar with them, ask Division No. 1 to follow the right hand, and No. 2

the left, while the teacher points to notes which will form a duet.

First Exercise.

Note 48.—An exercise may now be introduced in the following manner :

§ 106. Tr. "I have in my mind a tune (or exercise) which I wish to represent, and you may dictate to me where the notes shall be placed. The first tone is Do ; where shall we place the note to indicate it ?" Cl. "Short line."

§ 107. Tr. "The next tone is Mi ; where shall I place the note ?" Cl. "First line," etc.

Note 49.—He goes through the exercise in this way, when it will appear as follows :

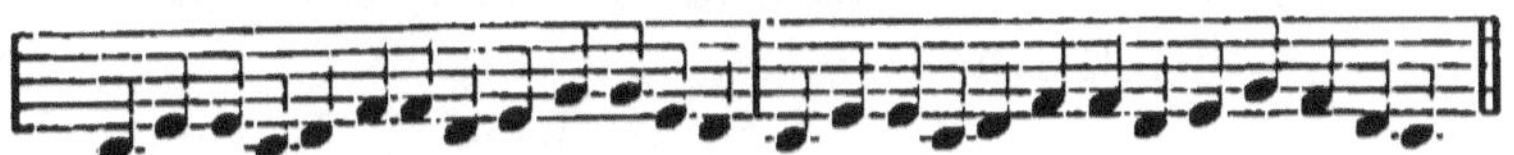

The teacher commences at the beginning and questions them as follows :

§ 108. Tr. "What tone is indicated by the first note ?" Cl. "Do."

§ 109. Tr. "Sing the tone indicated by that note." (They sing.)

§ 110. Tr. "What tone is indicated by the next note ?" Cl. "Mi," etc.

Note 50.—When he is sure that they understand the exercise perfectly, he will request them to sing as he points, and thus slowly proceed in order from the first note to the last, seeing to it that they do not give a false intonation to any of the tones. And here I would remind the teacher that he should not fail to impress upon the minds of the pupils that correct position and manner of breathing are among the all-important requisites of a good vocalist. He should also carefully observe every tone which they produce, and correct the slightest tendency toward a thin or nasal quality, giving frequent examples of false and good tones, insisting always upon their producing a full, round, and resonant tone. In order that he may the more closely observe their singing, he should never sing with them, nor allow them to sing with him.

A variety of exercises may now follow the last, introduced in a similar manner.

First Book Exercise.

Note 51.—The teacher should carefully observe Note 28, after which he requests them to turn to page 9 in the text-book,* and look at Exercise No. 1. Questions may be asked as follows :

§ 111. Tr. " Where is the first note placed ? " Cl. "Short line."

§ 112. Tr. " What tone does it indicate ? " Cl. " Do."

§ 113. Tr. " Where is the next note placed ? " Cl. "Space below."

§ 114. Tr. " What tone is indicated by the next note ? " Cl. " Mi."

§ 115. Tr. " How do you know ? " Cl. " Because the note is placed on the first line."

§ 116. Tr. " Sing the tone indicated by the first note." (They sing Do.)

---

* The text-book referred to is Graded Studies. When any other text-book is used, exercises corresponding to those referred to should be selected ; and if the book does not contain suitable exercises it is suggested that some of these exercises may be transferred to the board.

Note 52.—The teacher should be careful as to his expressions. A very common error is to ask the class to sing this *note* or that *note*, or to say, when pointing to a note, "Sing this tone ; " thus mistaking the *sign* for the *thing signified*. He should remember, and teach his class, that a *note* cannot be *sung*, neither can a *tone* be *seen*. He should contract the habit of saying, when pointing to a note, "What tone is indicated by this note?" "Sing the tone indicated," etc., etc. ; thus making his instruction intelligible. There is a feeling on the part of many scientific men that music is nothing but a bundle of inconsistencies, and the loose, bungling manner in which many teachers impart their instruction has contributed largely to that feeling.

§ 117. Tr. "Sing the tone indicated by the next note." (They sing Re.)

§ 118. Tr. "What tone is indicated by the next note ?" Cl. "Mi.'"

§ 119. Tr. "Sing it." (They sing.)

§ 120. Tr. "Sing the tone indicated by the next." (They sing.)

§ 121. Tr. "The next." (They sing.)

§ 122. Tr. "The next." (They sing.)

§ 123. Tr. "What tone did you sing ?" Cl. "La."

§ 124. Tr. "How did you know you were to sing La ?" Cl. "Second space."

Note 53.—Practice the whole exercise in this way :

Rule for Applying Words.

§ 125. Tr. "We have a rule for singing by words, namely, *Apply one syllable of the words to each note of the music*. What is the rule ?" (They repeat the rule in concert.)

§ 126. Tr.   " What tone do you apply to the word My ? "   Cl.   " Do."

§ 127. Tr.   " What tone do you apply to the word Days ? "   Cl.   " Re."

§ 128. Tr.   " Of ? "   Cl.   " Mi."

§ 129. Tr.   " Praise ? "   etc.

Note 54.—He proceeds in this way to the end of the exercise, after which they sing by words.

The Close.

§ 130. Tr.   " We have a character which indicates the end of a piece of music, which we call a *Close*. It is made thus."   (Draws two broad bars perpendicularly across the staff.)

§ 131. Tr.   " We also have a character called a *Double Bar*, which is frequently used at the end of a line of poetry."   (Writes a double bar.)

§ 132. Tr.   " Look at Exercise No. 2.   Do you see a close at the end of the staff ? "   Cl.   " We do not."

§ 133. Tr.   " In such cases you will go directly to the next staff and sing until you come to the close.   Where is the close of this exercise ? "   Cl.   " At the end of the second staff."

§ 134. Tr.   " What is the name of the first tone ? "   Cl.   " Do."

§ 135. Tr.   " The next ? "   Cl.   " Do."

§ 136. Tr.   " How do you know ? "   Cl.   " Short line."

§ 137. Tr.   " The next tone ? "   Cl.   " Re."

§ 138. Tr.   " The next tone ? "   Cl.   " Re."

§ 139. Tr. "How do you know?" Cl.
Space below."(And so on to the end.)

Note 55.—Question them as to the other tones of the
exercise (what they are, and how they know) and then
give them practice it by syllables and by words.
Note 56.—The teacher should always question the
class, as above, before singing a new exercise.

PRONUNCIATION.

Note 57.—The teacher should pay strict attention to
their pronunciation, and should also see to it that they
do not *draw the words together*, but speak them promptly
and intelligently.

RULES FOR BREATHING.

§ 140. Tr. "We have four rules for taking
breath while singing ; two positive, and two
negative rules." (See Note 364, page 246.)

FIRST POSITIVE RULE.

§ 141. Tr. " *We may always take breath at
punctuation marks.* What is the first positive
rule?" (They repeat it.)

SECOND POSITIVE RULE.

§ 142. Tr. " *We may, if necessary, take breath
after words which are emphatic.* What is the
second positive rule?" (They repeat it.)

FIRST NEGATIVE RULE.

§ 143. Tr. " *We may never take breath between the syllables of a word.* What is the
first negative rule?" (They repeat it,)

SECOND NEGATIVE RULE.

§ 144. TR. "*We may never take breath aft[er] words which are not emphatic.* What is t[he] second negative rule?" (They repeat it.)

NOTE 58.—The teacher should oblige the pupils to [re]peat these rules frequently.

NOTE 59.—Practice all the exercises which invol[ve] these ideas, always questioning the class thoroughly [be]fore beginning to sing.

MEASURES, COUNTING, AND BEATING.

NOTE 60.—If the teacher is not convinced that the c[ommon] definition of measure (a space between two bars) is wrong, it is hoped that he will hold himself "open [to] conviction" long enough to read the following explan[a]tion, when he will doubtless be converted to the n[ew] definition, viz.: that a measure is a *group of strong a[nd] weak pulses*. and is represented by the space between t[wo] bars, and that the bars have no significance except [to] show where the strong pulses are.

And here I wish to add a few words with regard [to] definitions. In not a single instance have I found [a] Dictionary consistent with itself: *e.g.*, *sound*, which [is] correctly defined as "anything audible," is frequen[tly] used as synonymous with *tone*, which is "any sound [of] which pitch is perceptible." Richard III. did not e[x]claim: "An animal! an animal! my kingdom for [an] animal!" he wanted a specific animal whose name w[as] *horse.* All horses are animals, but all animals are n[ot] horses. So all tones are *sounds*, but all *sounds* are n[ot] *tones.* A tone is a specific sound. Neither is it go[od] sense to go back to the dawn of music and show th[at] *tone* has always been used as the name of "the *inter[val] between* two tones." We may admire Abraham's fait[h] but we don't care to use his plow. Simply because usage is *old* is not a sufficient reason for retaining it.

So, too, *tones* and *notes* are almost hopelessly tangle[d]

His low *notes* are good," "Her high *notes* are thin,"
re usual with many writers who should know better.
. *note* is for the eye, not for the ear; a *tone* is for the
ar, not for the eye ; we cannot see a *tone* nor hear a
ote. "Her high *tones* are good," "His low *tones* are
ad," tell the truth, and do not pain those who are striv·
ıg to be accurate.

Again, *measure*, *bar*, and *time*, are badly mixed.
Play such a *bar*," meaning "play such a *measure ;*"
Written in triple *time*," meaning in "triple *measure*,"
re usual expressions.

Scale and *key* are also confounded. "Written in such
scale," meaning "in such a *key*," is not uncommon.
. *scale* is the simplest little exercise that can be written
r played in a key ; it must follow its simple order,
ʼhile a key is "a family of tones bearing a fixed rela-
on to each other," its tones may be in any order and
et be in the key.

And so, with all controverted points, let us not be con·
ınt with anything short of correctness. *Thinking* mu-
cians are striving for a uniform use of the terminology
f our loved science, "a consummation most devoutly
ɔ be wished ;" and it was with an earnest desire to as·
st in bringing about such consummation that the pres-
ɑt work was undertaken.

§ 145. Tʀ. "Listen!" (Counts *one*, two ; *one*,
wo ; being careful to let the voice fall at
two.")

§ 146. Tʀ. "How many times did I count
ne, two ?" Cʟ. "Twice."

§ 147. Tʀ. "Class count *one*, two, twice."
They count.)

§ 148. Tʀ. "Which was the stronger count
r pulse, one or two ?" Cʟ. "One."

§ 149. Tʀ. "Which was the weaker count or
ulse ?" Cʟ. "Two."

§ 150. Tʀ. "A group of strong and weak

pulses is called a measure. What is a measure?" CL. "A measure is a group of strong and weak pulses."

§ 151. TR. "Listen! (Counts four measures.) How many groups or measures did I count?" CL. "Four."

§ 152. TR. "Class count four measures." (They count.)

§ 153. TR. "Count five measures."

NOTE 61.—While they count, the teacher sings Ta to each count, pitch G, beginning after they have counted one measure. His tone should be firm so that all may hear him.

§ 154. TR. "How many measures did you count?" CL. "Five."

§ 155. TR. "How many did I sing?" CL. "Four."

§ 156. TR. "How many Ta's did I sing in each measure?" CL. "Two."

§ 157. TR. "How many Ta's did I sing altogether?" CL. "Eight."

§ 158. TR. "I will now represent these eight Ta's." Writes as follows:

♩ ♩ ♩ ♩ ♩ ♩ ♩.♩

§ 159. TR. "How many notes have I written?" CL. "Eight."

§ 160. TR. "Does this note (pointing to the first note) represent a strong pulse, or a weak pulse?" CL. "A strong pulse."

§ 161. TR. "This one (pointing to the second note); this one; this one (skipping about).

NOTE 62.—Of course they will be puzzled, not being able to tell without reckoning slowly from the beginning.

§ 162. TR. "I will indicate the strong pulses by marks like these." (Makes the bars, when the exercise will appear as follows:)

| ♩ ♪ | ♩ ♪ | ♩ ♪ | ♩ ♪ |

§ 163. TR. "These marks are called bars, and they are used to show the strong pulses. What are these marks called?" CL. "Bars."

§ 164. TR. "For what are they used?" CL. "To show the strong pulses."

§ 165. TR. "Yes, bars always show the strong pulses; they have no other meaning."

§ 166. TR. "How many measures are there in this exercise?" (Pointing to the board.) CL. "Four."

§ 167. TR. "Sing the exercise by syllable Ta, while I count. Begin after I have counted one measure." (They sing.)

§ 168. TR. "You may now count while I sing. I will begin after you have counted one measure." (They count and teacher sings.)

§ 169. TR. "Now all sing the exercise by syllable Ta, and count *one*, two, at the same time. After I have counted one measure you will begin." (The effort results in failure of course.)

§ 170. TR. "You see that you cannot count one, two, and sing *Ta*, *Ta*, at the same time; still it is necessary that they should go together. We will substitute motions of the hand for the counting. When we would say *one*, let the hand drop; when we would say *two*, let the hand rise."

§ 171. TR. "What count does this motion indicate?" (Drops the hand.) CL. "One."

§ 172. TR. "What does this motion indicate?" (Hand rises.) CL. "Two."

§ 173. "Indicating the counts by motions of the hand is called beating. What is it called?" CL. "Beating."

NOTE 63.—Explain that a beat is a sudden motion of the hand at the beginning of a pulse.

§ 174. TR. "Beat and count four measures." (Many start with the wrong motion.)

§ 175. TR. "Do we begin counting with *two* or *one?*" CL. "With one."

§ 176. TR. "Then what motion should we begin with?" CL. "Downward."

§ 177. TR. "Then the hand must be ready to fall when we say *one*. Hereafter, when I say *Ready* bring the hand up."

§ 178. TR. "Ready!"

NOTE 64.—The teacher should bring his hand up at the word "*Ready*," and wait until all hands are up, looking deliberately around to see if all have complied. Many will not have their hands up. The teacher drops his hand and asks:

§ 179. TR. "What does *Ready* mean?" CL. "Hands up."

§ 180. TR. "Ready!" (After scanning the class to see if all are ready, he says:)

§ 181. TR. "Beat and count a few measures. Begin!" (All start with him.)

§ 182. Tr. "Now we can sing this exercise (pointing to the board) by Ta, and count with our hands at the same time."

Note 65.—Practice the exercise several times, being careful that the correct motions are given, and that the strong and weak pulses are well defined, after which the teacher says :

§ 183. Tr. "Open your books at page 10, and look at No. 12. Does the first note indicate a strong pulse or a weak pulse ? " Cl. "A strong pulse."

§ 184. Tr. "Which motion of the hand must we give to the strong pulse ? " Cl. "Downward."

§ 185. Tr. "What is a measure ? " Cl. "A measure is a group of strong and weak pulses."

§ 186. Tr. "How do we distinguish the strong pulse ? " Cl. "By the bars."

Note 66.—Practice the exercises which follow in the text-book.

Class Tactics.

Note 67.—The teacher should discipline the class in beating time, by allowing them to beat a few measures, without singing. They should always commence with the *downward* motion, and in order that all may commence at the same instant the teacher should oblige them to raise the hand at the word " *Ready*," and when he sees their hands up, he may say " *Commence !* " or " *Count !* " when all will start at once. They should beat and count one measure before singing an exercise. Too much importance cannot be placed upon this point, as it is one of the most essential elements of good chorus singers that they be ready to commence, not only at the first word, but are prepared to give forcible utterance, if necessary, to the first consonant sound.

It is very desirable that the teacher should be able to perfectly control the regularly recurring pulsations in the minds of the pupils. This may be done in various ways, usually by a sharp stroke of the hands on the first strong pulse of each measure.

The necessity for something of this kind will become apparent when it is remembered that no two persons can possibly keep time together without some outward indication of the recurrence of the pulses. A body of superior musicians, if set to beating, could not keep together thirty seconds if all should close their eyes, and there was no outward indication of the pulse-points ; then how much greater is the necessity of some such outward indication with a class of beginners who have never had their attention called to regular pulsations. The objector may say that the class should be kept together by looking at the leader, but when the pupils are fully occupied with the book, the rhythm is lost sight of in a certain degree, and a slight stroke will recall their attention to the pulsations without interfering with their reading.

For the first few lessons the teacher should exaggerate the strong pulses, but as soon as the class can keep together he should abandon the strokes except when they waver, giving the pupils to understand that whenever they do hear them they may know they are out of time.

The Tie.

Note 68.—The teacher writes four measures thus:

§ 187. Tr. "How many measures have I written?" Cl. "Four."

§ 188. Tr. "Sing the exercise by syllable Ta." (They sing.)

§ 189. Tr. "Count and beat while I sing,

and observe whether I sing correctly." (He sings and connects the two pulses in the second measure.)

§ 190. Tr. "Did I sing correctly, or incorrectly?" Cl. "Incorrectly."

§ 191. Tr. "In which measure did the error occur?" Cl. "In the second measure."

§ 192. Tr. "How was it wrong?" Cl. "You connected the two pulses."

Note 69.—The word *connected* is what the teacher wants from the class, as no other word expresses the error so well. If some one does not speak the word, it would be well for the teacher to pretend that he has heard it, and quickly nodding in that direction say :

§ 193. Tr. "Yes, I connected the two pulses in this measure (pointing). I wish the class to connect them, and will indicate it by a curved line (making the line) which is called a Tie. What is the curved line called?" Cl. "A tie."

§ 194. Tr. "How many notes does the tie connect in this instance?" Cl. "Two."

§ 195. Tr. "Sing the exercise." (They sing.)

§ 196. Tr. "This tie (pointing) represents the connecting of how many pulses?" Cl. "Two."

§ 197. Tr. "How many beats will you give the tone?" (still pointing.) Cl. "Two."

§ 198. Tr. "Sing the exercise again and see if I can puzzle you." (He steps quickly to the other end of the board, so as not to obstruct their view, and *while they are singing*, ties the notes of another measure. This may be repeated until he has placed ties over the notes in all the measures.)

§ 199. Tr. "What is the rule for applying words to music?" Cl. "Apply one syllable of the words to each note of the music."

§ 200. Tr. "We have a rule for applying words in case of a tie; listen, and repeat the rule after me. 'Apply one syllable of the words to as many notes as are connected by the tie.' What is the rule?" (They repeat it.)

§ 201. Tr. "Look at No. 14. How many ties are found in this Exercise?" Cl. "Three."

§ 202. Tr. "In which measures are they found?" Cl. "In the second, fourth, and last measures."

§ 203. Tr. "What is the rule for applying words in the case of a tie?" (They repeat the rule.)

§ 204. Tr. "Sing No. 14." (They sing.)

The Long Note.

§ 205. Tr. "We have a note which represents the connecting of two pulses. I will erase the two notes and the tie in one of these measures and write the new note thus."

Note 70.—After he has erased the notes and tie and placed a half note instead, he asks:

§ 206. Tr. "How many pulses does this note represent?" (Pointing to the half note.) Cl. "Two."

§ 207. Tr. "How many pulses does this note

represent ?" (Pointing to a quarter note.) CL. "One."

§ 208. TR. "Hereafter we will call this note (pointing to a quarter note) a SHORT NOTE. What is it called ?" "CL. "A short note."

§ 209. TR. "And we will call this note (pointing to the half note) a LONG NOTE. What is it called ?" CL. "A long note."

§ 210. TR. "How many beats should the short note receive ?" CL. "One."

§ 211. TR. "How many beats should the long note receive ?" CL. "Two."

§ 212. TR. "Look at the next exercise. How is the first measure filled ?" CL. "With two short notes."

§ 213. TR. "How is the second measure filled ?" CL. "With one long note."

§ 214. TR. "A long note represents the connecting of how many pulses ?" CL. "Two."

§ 215. TR. "How is the third measure filled ?" CL. "Two short notes."

§ 216. TR. "Fourth measure." CL. "One long note."

§ 217. TR. "Fifth, Sixth, and Seventh measures each ?" CL. "Two short notes."

§ 218. TR. "The last measure ?" CL. "One long note."

§ 219. TR. "Sing the exercise." (They sing.)

NOTE 71.—All the exercises which involve the long note should be carefully practiced, first by syllables, then by words, frequently reminding them of the proper position, pure tones, correct enunciation, etc. It will be found a good plan to pass quickly to the back part of the room, *while they are singing* an exercise, and as soon as they have finished it, ask them to "rise and face this way," thus bringing the *back seats in front*, so to speak. In this way the teacher can become better acquainted with the ability of all of his class, and those who, as will be found in all classes, are disposed to take the back seats for fun, will find that the teacher is "*able to sit up and notice things*," and consequently, they will be more likely to pay strict attention, and work harder. He should lose no time, always passing back and forth *while the class are singing*. After they have begun an exercise he will have ample time to go and take his position before they can finish it.

The Slur.

Note 72.—One of the very worst things a teacher can do is to announce to his class what he is about to do, or what he intends to do next, or what he is to say or explain next. He should never tell what he is going to do, but *do it*.

§ 220. Tr. "Give attention to the board." (He writes an exercise thus :)

§ 221. Tr. "How many measures have I written?" Cl. "Four."

§ 222. Tr. "Sing the exercise by Ta." (They sing.)

§ 223. Tr. "Listen, and observe carefully, while I sing, and see whether you can detect any mistakes." (Sings and slurs the two tones in the first measure.)

§ 224. Tr. "Did I sing it correctly, or incorrectly?" Cl. "Incorrectly."

§ 225. TR. "In which measure did the error occur?" CL. "In the first measure."

§ 226. TR. "How was it wrong?" CL. "You connected the two pulses."

NOTE 73.—Having given prominence to the word "connected" in a similar exercise a short time before, some bright pupil will be sure to earn the teacher's approbation by recalling and using it again. The teacher should nod encouragement to such a pupil, or in that direction, and proceed.

§ 227. TR. "Yes, I connected these pulses. I wish the class to connect them, and I will indicate it by a curved line (making the slur), which, in this instance, is called a *Slur*. What is it called?" CL. "A slur."

§ 228. TR. "This curved line is called a slur if the connected notes are on different degrees of the staff, as in this instance (pointing), and it is called a *tie* if the connected notes are on the same degree (pointing to the notes in the last measure of the exercise on the board, under which he has drawn a tie). The rule for applying words is the same in cases of the tie and slur. What is the rule?" CL. "Apply one syllable to as many notes as are so connected."

§ 229. TR. "Sing the exercise."

NOTE 74.—While they are singing the first measure the teacher quickly slurs the notes in the second measure, when the exercise will appear thus:

He should now erase the tie in the last measure and write words under the notes, when the exercise will ap. pear thus :

§ 230. TR. "Repeat the rule for applying words in cases of the tie and slur." CL. "Apply one syllable of the words to as many notes as are so connected."

§ 231. TR. "What tones will you sing to the word joyful?" "CL. "Do Re Mi Re."

§ 232. TR. "Sing the exercise." (They sing.)

§ 233. TR. "Turn to No. 22."

§ 234. TR. "Sing the exercise by syllables, without regard to the slurs." (They sing.)

§ 235. TR. "What tones will you sing to the word *joyful?*" CL. "Do Re Mi Re."

§ 236. TR. "Bells?" CL. "Do."

§ 237. TR. "Are?" CL. "Do."

§ 238. TR. "Ringing?" CL. "Do Do."

§ 239. TR. "Merry?" CL. "Re Mi Fa Mi."

§ 240. TR. "Voices?" CL. "Re Re."

§ 241. TR. "Singing?" CL. "Do Do."

§ 242. TR. "Sing Do." (They sing.)

§ 243. TR. "After beating the silent measure, sing the exercise by words." (They sing.)

NOTE 75.—After practicing this and other exercises until all are familiar with the slur, the teacher next introduces.

Seven Below.

§ 244. Tr. "Sing the scale ascending and descending without repeating upper Do." (They sing.)

§ 245. Tr. "There is another scale below this one, and all can sing three or four of its higher tones thus : (The teacher sings Do Ti La Sol of the lower octave.) All sing those tones." (They sing.)

§ 246. Tr. "Where is lower Do represented?" Cl. "Short line."

§ 247. Tr. "Where shall we place a note to indicate Ti below?" Cl. "On the space below the short line."

§ 248. Tr. "This space (writing the note) is called the second space below. What is it called?" Cl. "The second space below."

Note 76.—The teacher should explain that lower Do is *One* to everything above it, and *Eight* to everything below it. Practice all exercises which involve *Seven Below*.

The Scale Above.

§ 249. Tr. "Sing the scale ascending." (They sing.)

§ 250. Tr. "There is a scale above this one, and all can sing three or four of its lower tones, thus : (the teacher sings Do Re Mi Fa of the Scale Above.) All sing those tones." (They sing.)

§ 251. Tr. "Where is upper Do represented?" Cl. "Third space."

46

§ 252. Tr. "Where shall we place a note to indicate Re above?" Cl. "Fourth line."
§ 253. Tr. "Mi?" Cl. "Fourth space."
§ 254. Tr. "Fa?" Cl. "Fifth line."
§ 255. Tr. "Sol?" Cl. "Space above."

Note 77.—The teacher reminds them that upper Do is *Eight* to everything below it, and *One* to everything above it, and also reminds them that as upper Do is represented by a space, Mi and Sol *above* will be represented by spaces, and Re and Fa by lines.

Practice all the exercises involving Two, Three, and Four above.

The Short Rest.

Note 78.—The teacher writes four measures of quarter notes on second line, and says:

§ 256. Tr. "How many measures have I written?" Cl. "Four."
§ 257. Tr. "Sing the exercise." (They sing.)

Note 79.—It is very important that the class always begin an exercise by beating a silent measure. See Note 67.

§ 258. Tr. "Listen, while I sing, and observe if I sing correctly, or incorrectly." (Sings and passes the first pulse of second measure in silence.)
§ 259. Tr. "Did I sing correctly, or incorrectly?" Cl. "Incorrectly."
§ 260. Tr. "In which measure did the error occur?" Cl. "In the second measure."
§ 261. Tr. "Which pulse of the measure was wrong?" Cl. "The first."

§ 262. Tr.   "How was it wrong?"   Cl. "You did not sing it."

§ 263. Tr.   "Yes, I remained silent during the first pulse, and wish you to do the same.   I will cancel the note thus."   (Drawing a line obliquely through the first note in the second measure.)

§ 264. Tr.   "Sing the exercise."   (They sing.)

§ 265. Tr.   "Repeat it, and see if I can puzzle you."   (While they are singing, he steps quickly to the other end of the board, so as not to obstruct their view, and cancels a note here and there in advance of them, which will keep them on the alert.)

§ 266.   "When we remain silent we are said to rest.   We have characters which indicate silence, called *Rests*.   I will now erase these short notes and their cancel-marks, and replace them with rests."

§ 267. Tr.   "Sing the exercise as it now appears."   (They sing.)

§ 268. Tr.   "Turn to No. 31.   How is the first measure filled?"   Cl.   "One short note and one short rest."

§ 269. Tr.   "How are each of the following six measures filled?"   Cl.   "One short note and one short rest."

§ 270. Tr.   "How is the eighth measure filled?"   Cl.   "One long note."

§ 271. Tr.   "How is the ninth measure filled?"   Cl.   "A short rest and a short note."

§ 272. Tr.   "How are each of the following

six measures filled ? " Cl. " One short rest
and one short note."

§ 273. Tr. "How is the last measure filled ?"
Cl. "One long note."

§ 274. Tr. "Sing the exercise." (They sing
this, and other exercises which involve the short
rest.)

Skips.

Note 80.—Too much importance cannot be attached
to the aid to be derived from the Modulator in showing
the skips. The mind of the pupil is most powerfully
impressed by what really becomes an object lesson, the
various distances (intervals) being portrayed to the eye
in such a manner as to give a clear and definite understanding in a comparatively short time.

The skips of a third should be reviewed at this point,
as explained at Sections 46 to 58, and skips of a *fourth,
fifth, sixth,* and *octave* should be explained in the same
general manner before practicing No. 36.

§ 275. Tr. "Look at No. 36. How is the
first measure filled ? " Cl. "With two short
notes."

§ 276. Tr. "How is the second measure
filled ? " Cl. "One short note and one short
rest."

§ 277. Tr. "How is the third measure
filled ? " Cl. "Two short notes."

§ 278. Tr. "What syllables are they ? " Cl.
"Mi, Do."

§ 279. Tr. "What is this skip called ? "
Cl. "A skip of a third."

§ 280. Tr. "What skips are indicated in the
fifth, sixth, and seventh measures ? " Cl.
"Skips of a third."

§ 281. TR. "What skip is indicated at the eleventh measure?" CL. "Skip of a fourth."

§ 282. TR. "At the nineteenth measure?" CL. "A skip of a fifth."

§ 283. TR. "At the twenty-seventh measure?" CL. "Skip of a sixth."

§ 284. TR. "At the thirty-fifth measure?" CL. "A skip of an octave."

LONG REST.

NOTE 81.—The teacher writes four measures, the second being filled with two short rests, and after the class have sung the exercise, says:

§ 285. TR. "We have a rest which indicates a silence of two pulses, called a *long rest*. I will place it here instead of these short rests." (Erasing the short rests and writing the long rest.)

§ 286. TR. "How many beats do we give the long rest?" CL. "Two."

§ 287. TR. "Sing the exercise." (They sing.)

§ 288. TR. "Look at exercise No. 38. What kind of rests are in the eighth and fifteenth measures?" CL. "Long rests."

§ 289. TR. "Sing the exercise." (They sing.)

NOTE 82.—The teacher should spend a few minutes at the beginning of each lesson with *chord practice* and Modulator. The following exercise, which is intended to foreshadow the change of keys, should be dwelt upon until, after a few lessons, the class can be taken out to the key of six sharps and back to the key of C, without losing the pitch.

Modulator Exercise.

§ 290. Tr. " Sing as I point." (Points to Do, Re, Mi, Fa, Sol in the C column.)

§ 291. Tr. " What is the second, Sol Fa?" (pointing to those syllables.) Cl. " A major second."

§ 292. Tr. " What is the second, Do Ti?" (pointing to those syllables in the G column.) Cl. " A minor second."

§ 293. Tr. " Sing Sol." (Pointing to Sol in the C column, and while they are singing, let the pointer glide deliberately across to Do in the G column.)

§ 294. Tr. " Sing it again and call it Do." (They sing.)

§ 295. Tr. "Sing as I point." (Pointing to Do, Ti, Do in the G column, and while they are singing the last tone he draws the pointer deliberately back to Sol in the C column and says :)

§ 296. Tr. " Sing as I point." (Pointing to Sol, Fa, Sol.)

§ 297. Tr. " What is the second, Sol Fa?" Cl. " A major second."

§ 298. Tr. What is the second, Do Ti?" (pointing to G column.) Cl. " A minor second."

§ 299. Tr. " Sing as I point." (Pointing to Sol, Fa, Sol, C column, followed by Do, Ti, Do, G column, and *vice versa*, repeating many times, until they can sing these intervals accurately.)

§ 300. Tr. " Sing as I point."

Note 83.—The teacher goes from Do in C column, step by step, class following, up to Sol and across to Do in G, and up and down the scale of G, within moderate compass, and back to Do in C column by way of Fa in G column. If they should come out below the pitch, it will probably be owing to the lack of a sufficiently minute comprehension of the difference between the major second, Sol Fa in C, and the minor second, Do Ti in G. The teacher should call their particular attention to it, and repeat the exercise with reference to beginning and ending in exact pitch. They may not be able to do this at first, but if the teacher always begins with the correct pitch and compares at the end of the exercise, he will have the satisfaction of seeing a marked and steady improvement from time to time.

Melody and Harmony.

Note 84.—Explain that a single succession of tones is called a *Melody;* and that when two or more parts are sung at the same time, they produce *Harmony.*

The Brace.

§ 301. Tr. "The brace is used to connect two or more staffs, and generally indicates the number of parts which are to be sung simultaneously."

Note 85.—Practice exercises involving the brace.

Male and Female Voices.

Note 86.—The teacher announces that the subject of the following explanation is of such a difficult nature that unless he has the close attention of the class he may fail to make it clearly understood. He should not tell *what* he expects to do, but simply say that their close attention is required.

§ 302. Tr.   "Gentlemen   remain   silent."
(Teacher sings Do, second space Bass staff and
says :)

§ 303. Tr.   "Ladies sing that tone."   (They
sing a tone just an octave above, of course.)

§ 304. Tr.   "You did not sing the tone I
sang ; I will repeat it and you may try again."
(As before, they sing an octave above.)

§ 305. Tr.   "Again you sang incorrectly.
While you supposed you were singing the same
pitch, you were really singing a tone an octave
higher than the one I sang.   Moreover, there is
not a lady in the room who *can* sing the tone I
sang.   I will now undertake to demonstrate this
fact.   Ladies sing your tone and sustain it softly, while I sing the scale ascending.   There is a
point at which our voices will come together :
as soon as you perceive that they are together,
raise your hand, both ladies and gentlemen."

Note 87.—The teacher sings the scale ascending slowly and distinctly, and at Eight his voice is so restrained
and merged into the tone which the ladies are holding
as to be imperceptible, when many hands will be raised.
If all are not yet convinced, the demonstrations may
proceed in a variety of ways, *e.g.*, the teacher standing
with a book before his face, requests all to raise their
hands when they perceive that he is singing (ladies
sustaining lower Do, as before).   When he sings *One*
all hands will be raised, but when he sings *Eight* few,
if any hands will be raised.   Should he suspect that
any are being guided by the muscles of the upper part
of the face, he can operate these muscles without singing, and thus catch them.   If necessary to demonstrate
farther, the following will be found effective.   Again
the ladies sustaining Do, he asks all to raise hands

when he *ceases* to sing, commences with lower Do, and slurs to upper Do (skip of an octave), when most of the class will think he has stopped singing, and raise their hands.

§ 306. Tr. "Ladies sing your tone again." (They sing.)

§ 307. Tr. "Gentlemen sing the same tone." (All who thoroughly understand the subject will sing Eight, but many will probably sing One. This may be corrected by asking the ladies to sustain their tone, while the gentlemen sing the scale ascending and thus their voices may be brought together.)

§ 308. Tr. "Gentlemen sing Eight." (They sing.)

§ 309. Tr. "Ladies sing the same tone." (Some of the less careful ones will probably sing Eight, but a majority will sing correctly, thus showing that they have mastered the subject.)

§ 310. Tr. "All who understand from these experiments that the gentlemen's voices are an octave lower than the ladies' voices will raise their hands." (All hands will probably be raised.)

§ 311. Tr. "Yes, what is a low tone for ladies is a high one for gentlemen ; the difference between the two voices being an octave."

§ 312. "Ladies sing your tone again." (They sing.)

§ 313. Tr. "Where shall I represent that tone?" Cl. "Short line."

§ 314. Tr. "Ladies sing as I point." (Points

to the note he has written on the short line, and they sing lower Do.)

§ 315. Tr. "Gentlemen sing as I point." (Points to the same note. Most of the gentlemen will probably sing correctly, but some of the less careful ones may sing lower Do.)

§ 316. Tr. "If the gentlemen sing the tone represented by the short line, will they sing *One* or *Eight?*" Cl. "Eight."

§ 317. Tr. "If the ladies sing the tone represented by the short line, will they sing *Eight* or *One?*" Cl. "One."

§ 318. Tr. "Ladies sing as I point." (Points to short line. They sing.)

§ 319. Tr. "Gentlemen sing as I point." (Points to short line. They sing.)

Note 88.—The teacher should here write the scale from short line to third space, and proceed.

§ 320. Tr. "All sing as I point." (Points to Do Re Do ; Do Re Mi Re Do.)

§ 321. Tr. "Begin again, and ascend the scale, gentlemen will stop when they must." (Some of the gentlemen may accompany the ladies as high as Four or Five. The ladies proceed to Eight, and return to One, where the gentlemen all join them.)

§ 322. Tr. "All sing as I point." (Points to Do, short line.)

§ 323. Tr. Where shall we place a note to indicate Ti below?" Cl. "Below the short line." (Writes.)

§ 324. Tr. "Sing as I point." (Points to

Do Ti Do, and they sing, after which he draws a long line and writes La and says :)

§ 325. Tʀ.   "Sing as I point." (Points to Do Ti La.)

§ 326. Tʀ.   "Sing Sol below."   (They sing).

§ 327. Tʀ.   "Where shall we place a note to indicate   Sol?"   Cʟ.   "Below the long line." (Writes.)

§ 328. Tʀ.   "Sing as I point." (Points to Do Ti La Sol.)

§ 329. Tʀ.   "Gentlemen sing Fa."   (They sing.)

§ 330. Tʀ.   "How shall we represent Fa?" Cʟ.   "Draw another long line." (He draws the line, writes Fa, and says :)

§ 331. Tʀ.   "Sing as I point." (Points to Do Ti La Sol Fa.)

§ 332. Tʀ.   "Gentlemen sing Mi." (They sing.)

§ 333. Tʀ.   "Where shall we place a note to indicate   Mi?"   Cʟ.   "Below the line."

§ 334. Tʀ.   "Sing as I point." (Points to Do Ti La Sol Fa Mi.)

§ 335. Tʀ.   "Gentlemen sing Re."   (They sing.)

§ 336. Tʀ.   "How shall we represent Re?" Cʟ.   "Draw another line."   (Draws the line, writes Re, and says :)

§ 337. Tʀ.   "Sing as I point." (Points to Do Ti La Sol Fa Mi Re.)

§ 338. Tʀ.   "Gentlemen sing Do."   (They sing.)

§ 339. Tʀ.   "Where shall we represent Do ?" Cʟ.   "Below the line."

§ 340. Tr. "Sing as I point." (Points to Do, short line, and descends the scale).

§ 341. Tr. "Gentlemen, sing Ti below." (They sing.)

§ 342. Tr. "How shall we represent Ti below?" Cl. "Draw another line." (He draws the line, writes the note, and says :)

§ 343. Tr. "Sing as I point." (Points to Do Ti.)

§ 344. Tr. "Gentlemen sing La." (They sing.)

§ 345. Tr. "Where shall we represent La?" Cl. "Below the line."

§ 346. Tr. "Sing as I point." (Points to Do Ti La.)

§ 347. Tr. "Gentlemen, sing Sol." (They sing.)

§ 348. Tr. "How shall we represent Sol?" Cl. "Draw another line." (Draws the line, writes, and says :)

§ 349. Tr. "Sing as I point." (Points to Do Ti La Sol La Ti Do.)

Note 89.—The exercise on the board will now appear thus :—

§ 350. Tr. "How many staffs have we formed?" (Pointing to the two staffs). Cl. "Two."

§ 351. Tr. "Is the lower staff (pointing) for

ιdies or for gentlemen?" Cl. "For gentle-
ιen."

§ 352. Tr. "Is the upper staff (pointing)
ιr gentlemen or for ladies?" Cl. "For
ιdies."

Remark 2.—If obliged to use a blackboard with the
ιffs already painted upon it, the teacher must omit the
ιove thirty sections and proceed as follows:

§ 353. Tr. "Sing as I point." (Points to Do,
ιort line.)

§ 354. Tr. "Where shall we place a note to
present Ti below?" Cl. "Below the short
ιe." (Writes.)

§ 355. Tr. "Sing as I point." (Points to
ιo Ti.)

§ 356. Tr. "Where shall we represent La?"
ι. "On the fifth line."

§ 357. Tr. "Sing as I point." (Points to Do
ι La.)

§ 358. Tr. "Sing Sol." (They sing.)

§ 359. Tr. "Where shall we represent it?"
ι. "Fourth space."

§ 360. Tr. "Sing as I point." (Points to Do
ι La Sol.)

§ 361. Tr. "Gentlemen sing Fa." (They
ιng.) Tr. "Where shall we represent Fa?"
ι. "Fourth line."

§ 362. Tr. "Sing as I point." (Points to Do
ι La Sol Fa.)

§ 363. Tr. "Gentlemen sing Mi." (They
ιng.)

§ 364. Tr. "Where shall we represent Mi?"
ι. "Third space."

§ 365. Tr. "Sing as I point." (Points to D
Ti La Sol Fa Mi.)

§ 366. Tr. "Gentlemen sing Re." (They
sing.) Tr. "Where shall we represent Re?"
Cl. "Third line."

§ 367. Tr. "Sing as I point." (Points to D
Ti La Sol Fa Mi Re.)

§ 368. Tr. "Gentlemen sing Do." (They
sing.)

§ 369. Tr. "Where shall we represent Do?"
Cl. "Second space."

§ 370. Tr. "Sing as I point." (Points to D
short line, and descends the scale.)

§ 371. Tr. "Gentlemen sing Ti below?"
(They sing.)

§ 372. Tr. "Where shall we represent it?"
Cl. "Second line."

§ 373. Tr. "Sing as I point." (Points to D
Ti.)

§ 374. Tr. "Where shall we represent La?"
Cl. "First space."

§ 375. Tr. "Sing as I point." (Points to D
Ti La.)

§ 376. Tr. "Gentlemen sing Sol." (They
sing.)

§ 377. Tr. "Where shall we represent Sol?"
Cl. "First line."

§ 378. Tr. "Sing as I point." (Points to D
Ti La Sol La Ti Do.)

§ 379. Tr. "How many staffs have we?"
(Pointing to the two staffs.) Cl. "Two."

§ 380. Tr. "The staff for ladies' voice
(pointing) is marked thus." (He writes the so

›rano clef, but must not call it the soprano staff, ›ecause the term soprano has not yet been de- ined.)'

§ 381. Tr. "Which voices sing from this staff?" (Pointing to upper staff.) Cl. "Ladies' voices."

§ 382. Tr. "The staff for the gentlemen's voices (pointing) is marked thus." (He writes the bass clef without giving its name.)

§ 383. Tr. "Which voices sing from this staff?" (Pointing.) Cl. "Gentlemen's voices."

§ 384. Tr. "Look at No. 43. Which voices sing from the upper staff?" Cl. "Ladies."

§ 385. Tr. "Which voices sing from the lower staff?" Cl. "Gentlemen."

§ 386. Tr. "What tone is indicated by the first note?" Cl. "Do."

§ 387. Tr. "Ladies, sing your first tone." (They sing.)

§ 388. Tr. "Gentlemen, sing your first tone."

Note 90.—This thought being so new, many of the gentlemen will probably sing an octave below; if so, they may be corrected in the following manner:

§ 389. Tr. "Gentlemen, does the first note indicate your upper Do, or your lower Do?" Cl. "Upper Do."

§ 390. Tr. "Go up through the chord of Do to your first tone." (They sing.)

Note 91.—After practicing No. 43 several times, the teacher calls attention to No. 44 and asks:

§ 391. Tr. "Is this written for gentlemen or for ladies?" Cl. "For gentlemen."

§ 392. Tr. "Ladies, if you were asked to sing the first tone of this exercise, which is written for gentlemen's voices, would you naturally sing the tone represented, or a tone an octave higher?" Cl. "A tone an octave higher."

§ 393. Tr. "With this understanding, the ladies may sing with the gentlemen from their staff, as they have heretofore been singing with you from your staff."

Note 92.—The teacher should again review the four chords already learned, and introduce the chords of Sol, La, and Ti as follows:

Chord Practice Continued.

§ 394. Tr. "What tones will form the chord of Sol?" Cl. "Sol Ti Re."

§ 395. Tr. "Spell and pronounce the chord of Sol?" (They sing thus:)

§ 396. Tr. "Spell and pronounce the chord of Sol in the lower octave." (They sing as follows:)

§ 397. Tr. "What tones form the chord of La?" Cl. "La Do Mi."

§ 398. Tr. "Spell and pronounce the chord

)f La in the lower octave." (They sing as fol-
ows :)

§ 399. TR. "What tones form the chord of
Ti?" CL. "Ti Re Fa."

§ 400. TR. "Spell and pronounce the chord
f Ti?" (They sing as follows:)

NOTE 93.—Great care must be taken with the dimin-
hed chord, on account of the tendency to sing the low-
st tone (Ti) too high. After a few minutes' drill, how-
ver, the teacher will have the satisfaction of hearing
ie chord *stand as still* as any of the other chords.

NOTE 94.—Here should be introduced the *resolutions*
tones, viz., the tendency after singing 7 is to sing
"When tones progress (move) according to their
atural tendency they are said to *resolve*, hence 8 re-
lves 7, 3 resolves 4, 5 resolves 6, and 1 resolves 2."
fter asking the class to "Sing 7 and resolve it," "Sing
and resolve it," "Sing 6 and resolve it," "Sing 2 and
solve it," they are requested to—

§ 401. TR. "Spell, pronounce, and resolve
ie chord of Ti." (They sing as follows:)

NOTE 95. — At No. 40 will be found an exercise
hich is very important; viz., the practice of *reading*
ith Do on other degrees than C, in order that the class

may not become anchored to the C key
this kind will be found frequently inters]
out the method, and should be thorou
There can be no objection to holding th(
key during the introduction of most of
principles, providing they are not allowe
there is no other position for Do; in fact
manifest advantages, among which may
the idea which is peculiar to this method
class is never permitted to sing in one ke)
reading in another, thus establishing th(
lute pitch. Classes taught by this meth(
few lessons, sing the pitch C accurately,
strument, and this point will hereafter t
important, inasmuch as all first-class inst
have now adopted the International pi
tions per second for the A above middle
as the class knows nothing about any of
the C key as yet, these exercises (like 4(
sung, but should be read both backwar
many times. Here let us remind the tea
the first lesson, or at the beginning of the
every subsequent lesson, he should be car(
any instrument played upon, or tones stru
ing of the class, for a half-hour before the
lesson, and that as soon as he has call
should ask the class to " sing the Do th
last time." He will be surprised to see
will come to the true pitch, and after c(
effort with the instrument he should inf
they are expected to commit that tone to
they can sing it at any time and und(
stances. The third lesson, and from th
have the satisfaction of hearing them si
pitch with scarcely a dissenting voice. 'I
this idea will be appreciated when one gra
that if they can establish *one tone accurate*
any other tone from a process of recko
taught in future lessons.

Triple Measure.

§ 402. Tr. "What is a measure?" Cl. "A
measure is a group of strong and weak pulses."

§ 403. Tr. "Listen!" (Counts, 1, 2, 3, being
careful to accent the first pulse.)

§ 404. Tr. "How many pulses are there in
this measure?" Cl. "Three."

§ 405. Tr. "How many strong pulses?" Cl.
"One."

§ 406. Tr. "Which is the strong pulse?"
"The first."

§ 407. Tr. "How many weak pulses?" Cl.
"Two."

§ 408. Tr. "Which are they?" Cl. "The
second and third."

§ 409. Tr. "A measure consisting of one
strong pulse and two weak pulses is called
Triple Measure. What is it called?" Cl.
"Triple measure."

410. Tr. "How many pulses has the measure we first learned?" Cl. "Two."

411. Tr. "How many strong pulses has
it?" Cl. "One."

412. Tr. "How many weak pulses?" Cl.
"One."

413. Tr. "A measure consisting of one
long pulse and one weak pulse is called
Double Measure. What is it called?" Cl.
"Double measure."

414. Tr. "In beating triple measure, the
strong pulse is indicated by the downward motion, as in double measure. The second pulse is

indicated by a motion to the left, and the thir
pulse by an upward motion. I will place a dia
gram of these motions on the board." (Write
thus :)

NOTE 96.— Most conductors nowadays beat trip
measure down, *right*, up.

§ 415. TR. "How many pulses has trip
measure?" CL. "Three."

§ 416. TR. "Triple measure is indicated b
the figure 3 placed at the beginning of the e
ercise."

§ 417. TR. "Turn to exercise No. 48. Wha
kind of measure?" CL. "Triple."

§ 418. TR. "How do you know?" C
"Figure 3."

§ 419. TR. "How is the first measur
filled?" CL. "With three short notes."

§ 420. TR. "How are each of the first seve
measures filled?" CL. "Three short notes."

§ 421. TR. "How is the eighth measu
filled?" CL. "One long note and one sho
rest."

§ 422. TR. "Sing the exercise." (They sing

THE DOTTED LONG NOTE.

NOTE 97.—The teacher writes two Triple measu
thus :

§ 423. Tr. "How many measures have I written?" Cl. "Two."

§ 424. Tr. "Sing the exercise." (They sing.)

§ 425. Tr. "Beat while I sing, and notice if I sing correctly or incorrectly." (He sings, connecting the three pulses in the second measure.)

§ 426. Tr. "Did I sing correctly or incorrectly?" Cl. "Incorrectly."

§ 427. Tr. "Which measure was wrong?" Cl. "The second."

§ 428. Tr. "How was it wrong?" Cl. "You connected the three pulses."

§ 429. Tr. "I wish you to connect the three pulses in the second measure. We have a note which represents the connecting of three pulses; it is called a dotted long note. I will erase the short notes and write a dotted long note instead."

§ 430. Tr. "The long note (pointing to a half-note which has been written previously) represents the connecting of how many pulses?" Cl. "Two."

§ 431. Tr. "The dotted long note (pointing) represents the connecting of how many pulses?" Cl. "Three."

§ 432. Tr. "The dot increases the value of the note how much?" Cl. "One-half."

§ 433. Tr. "How many beats will we give to the dotted long note?" (Pointing.) Cl. "Three."

Note 98.—Practice the exercises which involve the dotted long note, asking the usual preliminary questions.

The Dotted Long Rest.

§ 434. Tr. "We have a rest which indicates a silence of three pulses ; it is called the Dotted Long Rest. I will erase the dotted long note and insert its corresponding rest. How many beats will we give to the dotted long rest?" Cl. "Three."

Note 99.—Practice the exercises involving the dotted long rest.

Quadruple Measure.

§ 435. Tr. "Listen!" (Counts one quadruple measure, accenting firmly.)

§ 436. Tr. "How many pulses are there in this measure?" Cl. "Four."

§ 437. Tr. "How many, and which are the strong pulses?" Cl. "Two, first and third."

§ 438. Tr. "How many, and which are the weak pulses?" Cl. "Two, second and fourth."

§ 439. Tr. "A group of four pulses is called quadruple measure. What is it called?" Cl. "Quadruple measure."

§ 440. Tr. "Quadruple measure is indicated by the figure 4."

§ 441. Tr. "The motions in beating quadruple measures are down for the first strong pulse ; left for the first weak pulse ; right for the second strong pulse, and up for the second reak pulse. I will place a diagram on the oard." (Writes thus :)

§ 442. Tr. "What motion (pointing to the ownward stroke of diagram) do we give to the rst pulse ?" Cl. "Down."

§ 443. Tr. "To the second ?" (Pointing.) Cl. Left."

§ 444. Tr. "To the third ?" Cl. "Right."

§ 445. Tr. "To the fourth ?" Cl. "Up."

Note 100.—Ask the class to beat and count alternate-, the different kinds of measure, until they can change 'om one to another as the teacher may call for them. hen, ask one division to beat and count double meas· re, and the other triple measure (accenting firmly), and atch the teacher while he beats double measure with e left hand, triple measure with the right, and counts uadruple measure simultaneously.

Note 101.—Practice exercises involving quadruple easure, with the usual preliminary questions.

The Repeat.

§ 446. Tr. "Dots placed in the spaces at the ft of a bar indicate a repetition, or in other ords, that the preceding passage is to be sung gain."

Note 102.—Practice exercises involving Repeat.

The Whole Note.

Note 103.—The teacher writes two quadruple measures of quarter-notes.

§ 447. Tr. "How many measures have I represented?" Cl. "Two."

§ 448. Tr. "What kind of measures are they?" Cl. "Quadruple measures."

§ 449. Tr. "How do you know?" Cl. "Figure 4."

§ 450. Tr. "Sing the exercise." (They sing.)

§ 451. Tr. "Listen while I sing it." (Sings and connects the four pulses in the second measure.)

§ 452. Tr. "Did I sing correctly or incorrectly?" Cl. "Incorrectly."

§ 453. Tr. "Which measure was wrong?" Cl. "The second."

§ 454. Tr. "How was it wrong?" Cl. "You connected the four pulses."

§ 455. Tr. "I wish you to connect the four pulses in this measure. (Pointing.) We have a note which represents the connecting of four pulses. I will write it here instead of these short notes. (Erasing the quarter notes and writing the whole note instead). Sing the exercise." (They sing.)

§ 456. Tr. "How many pulses does this note represent?" (Pointing to the quarter note.) Cl. "One."

§ 457. Tr. "What is its name?" Cl. "Short note."

§ 458. Tr. "How many pulses does *this* note represent?" (Pointing to the half note.) Cl. "Two."

§ 459. Tr. "What is it called?" Cl. "A ong note."

§ 460. Tr. "How many pulses does *this* note represent?" (Pointing to the dotted half-note.) Cl. "Three."

§ 461. Tr. "What is it called?" Cl. "A lotted long note."

§ 462. Tr. "How many pulses does *this* note represent?" (Pointing to whole note.) Cl. "Four."

§ 463. Tr. "We have had the short note, the ong note, the dotted long note, and now we lave a still longer note, which shows the necesity for seeking other names for these notes."

The Correct Names of Notes.

§ 464. Tr. "How does this note (pointing o a quarter note) compare in length with *this* ne?" (Pointing to whole note.) Cl. "It is ne quarter as long."

Note 104.—If the class should reply "*one fourth*" inead of "*one quarter*," the teacher can draw the correct rm from them by asking, "What is the other name for fourth?" They will reply, "A quarter."

§ 465. Tr. "Hereafter we will call this (pointig) a quarter note. What is it called?" Cl. A quarter note."

§ 466. Tr. "How does this note (pointing to ie half note) compare in length with *this* one?"

(Pointing to the whole note.) Cl. "It is one half as long."

§ 467. Tr. "What then, would be a good name for *this* note?" (Pointing to the half note.) Cl. "A half note."

§ 468. Tr. "Hereafter we will call it a half note. What is its name?" Cl. "A half note."

§ 469. Tr. "How many half notes (pointing) are required to equal this note?" (Pointing to the whole note.) Cl. "Two."

§ 470. Tr. "Two halves make a what?" Cl. "A whole."

§ 471. Tr. "What, then, would be a good name for *this* note?" (Pointing to the whole note.) Cl. "A whole note."

§ 472. Tr. "Hereafter we will call it a whole note. What is its name?" Cl. "A whole note."

§ 473. Tr. "The whole note (pointing) represents how many pulses?" Cl. "Four."

§ 474. Tr. "The half note (pointing) represents how many pulses?" Cl. "Two."

§ 475. Tr. "The quarter note (pointing) represents how many pulses?" Cl. "One."

§ 476. Tr. "What, then, shall we call this note?" (Pointing to the dotted half note.) Cl. "A dotted half note."

The Fraction.

§ 477. Tr. "What kind of measure have we here?" (Pointing to the exercise on the board.) Cl. "Quadruple."

§ 478. Tʀ. "How do you know?" Cʟ. "Figure 4."

§ 479. Tʀ. "What kind of a note represents each pulse?" (Pointing to a quarter note.) Cʟ. "A quarter note."

§ 480. Tʀ. "A quarter note is indicated by the figure 4 when placed as the denominator of a fraction. The fraction is always placed at the beginning of a composition ; its numerator shows the number of pulses in the measure, and its denominator names the pulses, *i.e.*, shows what kind of a note is reckoned to each pulse. The fraction is read thus : Four (pointing to the numerator) quarter notes (pointing to the denominator) or their equivalent will fill a measure." (Pointing to a measure.)

Nᴏᴛᴇ 105.—The teacher writes several fractions on the board such as $\frac{2}{4}$, $\frac{3}{4}$, $\frac{4}{4}$, etc., and, pointing to the first says :

§ 481. Tʀ. "Read this fraction." Cʟ. "Two quarter notes or their equivalent will fill a measure."

§ 482. Tʀ. "As short answers are desirable, if you say 'two quarter notes will fill a measure,' I will understand that you mean 'two quarter notes *or their equivalent* will fill a measure.'"

§ 483. Tʀ. "Read these fractions." (Pointing to the other fractions on the board.)

Nᴏᴛᴇ 106.—The teacher should always point slightly in advance of their reading ; thus. when they read "Three" his pointer should rest on the numerator, and when they read "quarter notes" the pointer should rest on the denominator, and when they read "will fill a measure" the pointer should rest on a measure.

§ 484. Tr. "What kind of measure is indicated here?" (Pointing to the figure 2.) Cl. "Double measure."

§ 485. Tr. "How do you know?" Cl. "The numerator of the fraction is 2."

§ 486. Tr. "What is the beat-note?" (Pointing to the figure 4.) Cl. "A quarter note."

§ 487. Tr. "How do you know?" Cl. "The denominator of the fraction is 4."

§ 488. Tr. "Read the fraction?" Cl. "Two quarter notes will fill a measure."

Note 107.—The teacher should question the class or triple measure and quadruple measure in a similar way and then ask them to turn to No. 58-60.

§ 489. Tr. "What kind of measure is indicated?" Cl. "Quadruple measure."

§ 490. Tr. "How do you know?" Cl. "The numerator of the fraction is 4."

§ 491. Tr. "What is the beat-note?" Cl. "A quarter note."

§ 492. Tr. "How do you know?" Cl. "The denominator of the fraction is 4."

§ 493. Tr. "Read the fraction?" Cl. "Four quarter notes will fill a measure."

§ 494. Tr. "How is the first measure filled?" Cl. "With four quarter notes."

§ 495. Tr. "How is the second measure filled?" Cl. "With one whole note."

§ 496. Tr. "How many beats will we give the whole note?" Cl. "Four."

Note 108.—Practice exercises involving the whole note.

§ 497. Tʀ. "Look at No. 63. What kind of measure is indicated?" Cʟ. "Triple measure."

§ 498. Tʀ. "How do you know?" Cʟ. "The numerator of the fraction is 3."

§ 499. Tʀ. "What is the beat-note?" Cʟ. "A quarter note."

§ 500. Tʀ. "How do you know?" Cʟ. "The denominator of the fraction is 4."

§ 501. Tʀ. "Read the fraction?" Cʟ. "Three quarter notes will fill a measure."

§ 502. Tʀ. "Is the first measure full?" Cʟ. "It is not full."

§ 503. Tʀ. "How many pulses does it lack of being full?" Cʟ. "Two."

§ 504. Tʀ. "Is the last measure full?" Cʟ. "It is not full."

§ 505. Tʀ. "How many pulses does it lack of being full?" Cʟ. "One."

§ 506. Tʀ. "Would these two fractional parts equal a complete measure?" Cʟ. "They would."

§ 507. Tʀ. "When a tune begins with a fractional part of a measure it must end with a fractional part, and such two fractional parts must equal a complete measure?"

§ 508. Tʀ. "If we begin beating with a full measure, how many beats will pass in silence before we begin to sing?" Cʟ. "Two."

§ 509. Tʀ. "Which beats would pass in silence?" Cʟ. "Down and left."

§ 510. Tʀ. "With which beat should we commence singing?" Cʟ. "The up beat."

§ 511. Tr. "Let us sing the exercise. Begin beating with a full measure and commence to sing when the hand rises. *Ready*—what does ready mean ?" Cl. "Hands up."

§ 512. Tr. "*Ready*—beat, *one, sing.*" (They sing.)

Classification of Voices.

Note 109.—The teacher writes a large note on middle C (short line) about the middle of the board, and asking the ladies to sing as he writes, he represents the tones as high as G (space above). Then asking the gentlemen to sing as he writes, proceed from middle C downward and to the left as far as first space below, when the exercise will appear thus:

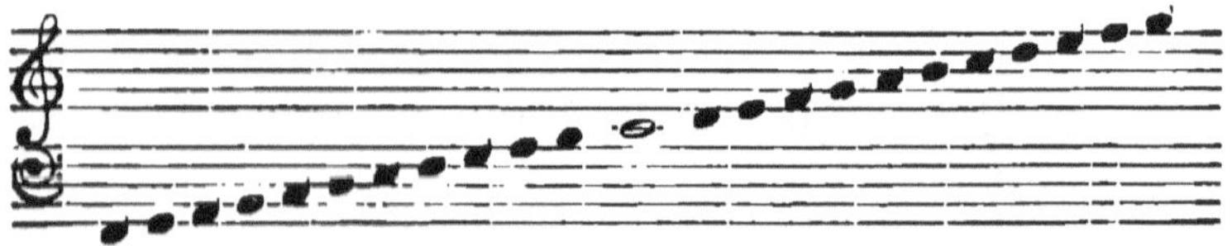

§ 513. Tr. "This exercise represents the average vocal compass. The middle tone (pointing to large note C) is common to all, and is called the Great Central Tone. The ladies can sing as many tones above it as the gentlemen can sing below it. What is it called?" Cl. "The great central tone."

§ 514. Tr. "Ladies who can sing high and cannot sing low are called Soprano Singers ; the average compass of their voices is shown by the notes inclosed in this curved line."

Note 110.—The teacher places his chalk pencil on the highest note, and the index finger of his left hand on middle C to guide his pencil in its sweep, and draws a curved line, thus :

§ 515. TR. "Ladies who can sing low and cannot sing high are called ALTO SINGERS. The average compass of their voices is shown by the notes inclosed in this curved line."

NOTE 111.—The teacher places his pencil on C, third space, and his finger on G, fourth space Bass staff and draws a curved line, when the example will appear thus :

§ 516. TR. "Gentlemen who can sing high and cannot sing low are called TENOR SINGERS. Their usual compass is shown by this curved line."

NOTE 112.—Beginning at G, second line, Soprano staff, draws an under-curve to C, second space Bass staff, thus :

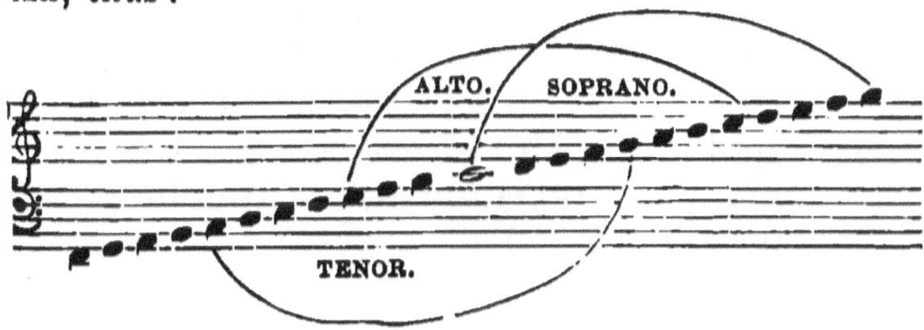

§ 517. Tr. "Gentlemen who c
and cannot sing high are called]
Their usual compass is indicated b
line."

Note 113.—The teacher draws an un
middle C to the lowest note, when the ent
appear thus:

The Compass of Voices Illu

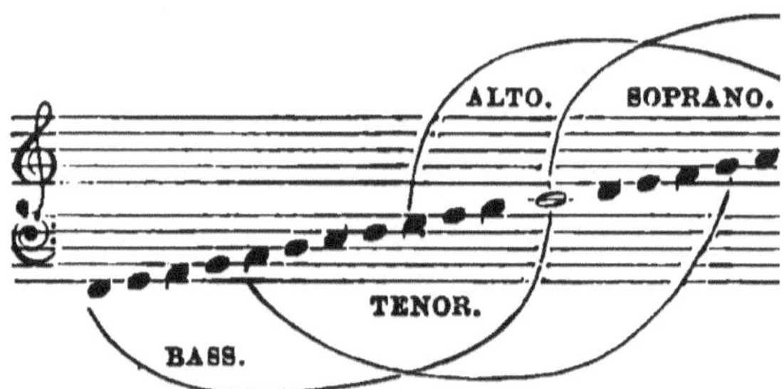

§ 518. Tr. "The proper way
which part you should sing wou
teacher to test each voice separatel
would require the time of several
we must accomplish it in a few m
dies sing as I point; all who can
tones more easily than they can
tones should sing Soprano; and al
who can sing the low tones more ea
can sing the high tones should
(Points from middle C slowly up to
note, and, returning deliberately,
down to the lowest tone of the alto

§ 519. Tr. "All the ladies who
should sing Alto please rise, and ren
until you are counted." (Appoint
take the count.)

§ 520. Tr. "Sit." (They sit.) "Now all those who think they should sing Soprano please rise." (They rise and are counted.)

§ 521. Tr. "Gentlemen sing as I point; all who can sing the high tones more easily than they can sing the low ones should sing Tenor, and all those who can sing the low tones more easily than they can sing the high tones should sing Bass." (Points from C, second space Bass staff up slowly to the highest tone of the Tenor compass and, returning deliberately, proceeds down to the lowest tone in the exercise and says:)

§ 522. Tr. "All the gentlemen who think they should sing Tenor please rise." (They rise and are counted.)

§ 523. Tr. "All those who think they should sing Bass rise." (They rise and are counted.)

Plan for Seating a Choir.

Note 114.—After the classification of the voices the different parts will be seated according to the following diagram:

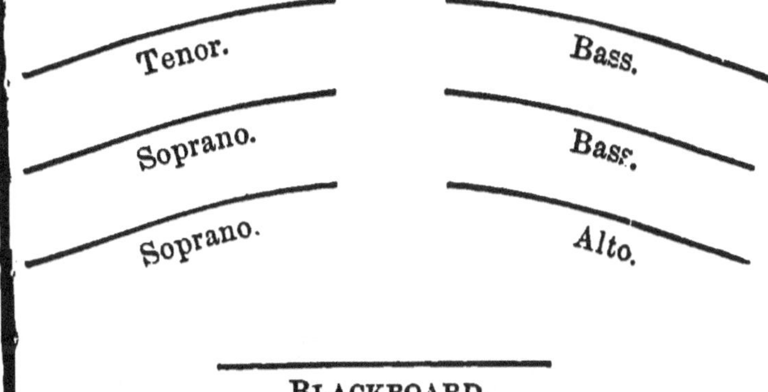

BLACKBOARD.

§ 524. Tr. "The Tenori (Tenors) will occupy *these* seats (designating certain seats at his left); the Bassi (Basses) will occupy *these* seats (designating certain seats on his right). The Alti (Altos) will take *these* seats, and the Soprani (Sopranos) will sit here (indicating). Now all take your places."

§ 525. Tr. "Give attention to the board. What is the tone called which all voices have in common?" (Pointing to the large note.) Cl. "The Great Central Tone."

§ 526. Tr. "Which voices sing from the staff bearing this character?" (Pointing to G clef.) Cl. "The ladies' voices."

§ 527. Tr. "This character is called the Soprano clef. What is it called?" Cl. "The Soprano clef."

§ 528. Tr. "It shows that The Great Central Tone is represented by the short line below (pointing), Soprano and Alto voices sing from the staff so arranged."

§ 529. Tr. "Which voices sing from the staff bearing this character?" (Pointing to the F clef.) Cl. "The gentlemen's voices."

§ 530. Tr. "This character is called the Bass clef. What is it called?" Cl. "The Bass clef."

§ 531. Tr. "It shows that The Great Central Tone is represented by the short line above (pointing), and that the Bass voices sing from the staff so arranged."

§ 532. Tr. "We have a third clef called the Tenor Clef which shows that The Great Cen-

TRAL TONE is represented by the third space.
(Writes the C clef and places a large note in third
space.) What is its name?" CL. "The Tenor
clef." (See new tenor clef, page 156, read foot-
note).

§ 533. TR. "Which voices sing from the staff
so arranged?" CL. "Tenor voices."

NOTE 115.—Explain that the Tenor singers read from
the Tenor staff exactly as they did from the Soprano staff,
upon which some wise pupil will ask, or want to ask, why
the Tenor part is not written on the Bass staff as the Alto
part is written on the Soprano staff. The reply is that
many of the tones of the Tenor part lie above the Great
Central Tone, and would require too many added lines
to represent them.

§ 534. TR. "Turn to No. 46. What is the
first character used?" CL. "The Brace."

§ 535. TR. "How many staffs does the brace
connect?" CL. "Four."

§ 536. TR. "Which part sings from the
highest staff?" CL. "Soprano."

§ 537. TR. "Which part sings from the staff
below the Soprano?" CL. "Alto."

§ 538. TR. "Which part sings from the lowest staff?" CL. "Bass."

§ 539. TR. "How do you know?" CL. "It
bears the Bass clef."

§ 540. TR. "Which part sings from *the next
the lowest* staff?" CL. "The Tenor."

§ 541. TR. "How do you know?" CL. "It
bears the Tenor clef."

§ 542. TR. "In what kind of measure is this
piece written?" CL. "Double measure."

§ 543. TR. "How do you know?" CL. "The numerator of the fraction is 2."

§ 544. TR. "What is the beat-note?" CL. "A quarter note."

§ 545. TR. "How do you know?" CL. "The denominator of the fraction is 4."

§ 546. TR. "Read the fraction?" CL. "Two quarter notes will fill a measure."

§ 547. TR. "Is the first measure full?" CL. "It is."

§ 548. TR. "With which pulse do we commence to sing?" CL. "First."

§ 549. TR. "What tone is first in Soprano?" CL. "Mi."

§ 550. TR. "What tone is first in Alto?" CL. "Do."

§ 551. TR. "What is the first tone in Tenor?" CL. "Sol."

§ 552. TR. "What is the first tone in Bass?" CL. "Do."

§ 553. TR. "Sing the first tone of your several parts, beginning with Do, and going through the chord of Do to your places." (They sing.)

§ 554. TR. "When two different notes of a part occupy the same pulse they are called CHOOSING NOTES and the singer is free to sing either. As a general rule sing the one which is best adapted to the compass of your voice."

NOTE 116.—The teacher should explain that when four parts are sung simultaneously, it is called four-part harmony, Quartet or chorus. That three part harmony is called a Trio ; and that two-part harmony is called

Duet ; and that a melody sung by a single voice is called a Solo.

NOTE 117.—Explain that to save space four parts are frequently printed on two staffs and called a *compressed score*. Compare the space occupied by No. 46 with that of No. 47. Practice exercises to No. 47 inclusive.

CHORD OF THE SEVENTH.

§ 555. TR. "I now wish to form a chord which differs from those we have learned, inasmuch as they consist of *three* tones each, while the new chord has *four* tones."

§ 556. TR. "Spell and pronounce the chord of Ti again, and in the pronunciation I want the Altos to sing Ti, the Tenors to sing Re, the Soprano will sing Fa as usual, and the Bass remain silent." (They sing.)

§ 557. TR. "Now spell and pronounce it again and I will ask the Bass to join us, singing Sol in the pronunciation." (They sing thus :)

§ 558. TR. "We thus have a four-fold chord founded upon Sol, and in order to distinguish it from the three-fold chords we add the name of its largest interval. From Sol (pointing to the notes on blackboard) to Ti is a third ; from Sol to Re is a fifth ; and from Sol to Fa is seven degrees or a seventh, hence this is called the chord of the Seventh of Sol."

§ 559. TR. "What tones form the chord of the Seventh of Sol ?" CL. "Sol Ti Re Fa."

§ 560. Tʀ. "Spell, pronounce, and resolve the chord of the Seventh of Sol." (They sing as follows, the Bass singing Do in the resolution.)

Technical Terms.

Noᴛᴇ 118.—The time has now arrived when it is necessary to give technical names to the tones. This is done as follows:

§ 561. Tʀ. "Scientific musicians of all languages have adopted a set of names for the members of our scale, which are called ᴛᴇᴄʜɴɪᴄᴀʟ ᴛᴇʀᴍs. To One and Eight they have given the name Toɴɪᴄ; Two they call Sᴜᴘᴇʀ-Toɴɪᴄ; Three they call Mᴇᴅɪᴀɴᴛ; Four, Sᴜʙ-Doᴍɪɴᴀɴᴛ; Five, Doᴍɪɴᴀɴᴛ; Six, Sᴜʙ-Mᴇᴅɪᴀɴᴛ; Seven, Sᴜʙ-Toɴɪᴄ."

Noᴛᴇ 119.—The teacher now writes these names upon the blackboard, in the following order:

8. Tonic.
7. Sub-Tonic.
6. Sub-Mediant.
5. Dominant.
4. Sub-Dominant.
3. Mediant.
2. Super-Tonic.
1. Tonic.

After practicing these until they are familiar, the teacher says:

§ 562. Tʀ. "Hereafter we will apply these terms in naming our chords. The chord of Do will in future be called what?" Cʟ. "The chord of the Tonic."

§ 563. Tr. " The chord of the Tonic consists of what tones ? " Cl. "Do Mi Sol."

§ 564. Tr. " The chord of the Super-Tonic consists of what tones ? " Cl. "Re Fa La."

§ 565. Tr. "The chord of the Mediant consists of what tones ? " Cl. " Mi Sol Ti."

§ 566. Tr. " The chord of the Sub-Dominant consists of what tones ? " Cl. " Fa La Do."

§ 567. Tr. " The chord of the Dominant consists of what tones ? " Cl. " Sol Ti Re."

§ 568. Tr. " The chord of the Sub-Mediant consists of what tones ? " Cl. " La Do Mi."

§ 569. Tr. " The chord of the Sub-Tonic consists of what tones ? " Cl. " Ti Re Fa."

§ 570. Tr. " What name shall we now give to the four-fold chord founded upon Sol ? " Cl. "The chord of the Dominant Seventh."

§ 571. Tr. " The chord of the Dominant Seventh consists of what tones ? " Cl. " Sol Ti Re Fa."

Note 120.—These chords should be practiced at the opening of every lesson. Five minutes thus spent will be of the utmost advantage to the class.

Each new point should first be illustrated on the blackboard, after which the class should turn quickly to the book and study the exercises which involve it. . .

Eighth Notes.

Note 121.—The teacher writes two double measures of quarter notes each and asks :

§ 572. Tr. " How many measures have I written ? " Cl. " Two."

§ 573. Tr. " Sing the exercise ? " (They sing.)

§ 574. Tr. "Listen while I sing and observe whether I sing correctly." (He sings and divides the first pulse in the second measure into two equal parts.)

§ 575. Tr. "Did I sing correctly or incorrectly?" Cl. "Incorrectly."

§ 576. Tr. "In which measure did the error occur?" Cl. "Second."

§ 577. Tr. "Which pulse was wrong?" Cl. "The first."

§ 578. Tr. "How was it wrong?" Cl. "You sung two Ta's instead of one."

§ 579. Tr. "I wish you to sing two Ta's to that pulse, and I will indicate it by erasing the quarter note and writing two notes which are made with a hook at the end of the stem thus." (Writes two eighth notes.)

§ 580. Tr. "How does this note (pointing to an eighth note) compare in length with the quarter note?" (Pointing to quarter note.) Cl. "It is one-half as long."

§ 581. Tr. "What is one-half of a quarter?" Cl. "An eighth."

§ 582. Tr. "What, then, would be a good name for this note?" Cl. "An eighth note."

§ 583. Tr. "How many eighth notes will we sing to one pulse?" Cl. "Two."

§ 584. Tr. "Sing the exercise?" (They sing.)

§ 585. Tr. "When a pulse is represented by *one* note we call it single ; when it is represented by more than one note we call it divided."

§ 586. Tr. "Is this pulse (pointing to a

quarter note) single or divided?" CL. "Single."

§ 587. TR. "This one?" (Pointing to eighth notes.) CL. "Divided."

§ 588. TR. "Into how many parts is the pulse divided?" CL. "Two."

§ 589. TR. "Are they equal, or unequal?" CL. "Equal."

§ 590. TR. "What kind of notes do we use to divide the pulse into two equal parts?" CL. "Eighth notes."

§ 591. TR. "Look at No. 68. In what kind of measure is it written?" CL. "Double measure."

§ 592. TR. "How do you know?" CL. "The numerator of the fraction is 2."

§ 593. TR. "What is the beat-note?" CL. "A quarter note."

§ 594. TR. "How do you know?" CL. "The denominator of the fraction is 4."

§ 595. TR. "Read the fraction." CL. "Two quarter notes will fill a measure."

§ 596. TR. "Are the pulses in the first measure single, or divided?" CL. "Divided."

§ 597. TR. "Are the pulses in the second measure single, or divided?" CL. "Single."

§ 598. TR. "How many pulses are united in the fourth measure?" CL. "Two."

§ 599. TR. "How many eighth notes will you sing to one beat?" CL. "Two."

NOTE 122.—Have them practice No. 68, being careful that they beat correctly and do *not* give a beat to each eighth note.

Absolute Pitch.

Note 123.—Knowing that many good teachers doubt the possibility of a class, or an individual, ever becoming sufficiently educated to know at all times what tones they are singing, or hearing, we wish to explain still further concerning the subject. During the past few years we have tested the matter thoroughly, in our classes and in private instruction, and we are convinced that children have an intuitive perception of absolute pitch, which, if developed as it may be by the careful teacher, will enable them at all times to determine with absolute precision what tones are being sung or played in their hearing, thereby greatly enhancing their enjoyment, and rendering them more intelligent musicians. We have conversed with hundreds of teachers who have during the past few years been practising this method, and without an exception they inform us that they have succeeded in getting their classes to comprehend, and put in practice, absolute pitch, after the first few lessons.

It is said of Mozart that while yet almost an infant he remarked to his father that he liked his friend's violin better than his own, because it was a " quarter of a tone " higher than his. Upon the instruments being brought together it was found that the child was correct. We have a friend, who will follow the most elaborate and entangling modulations, and not only name the last chord which is played but all those through which the player has passed.

We mention these instances for the purpose of impressing more firmly upon the minds of teachers throughout the country that with them rests the responsibility of developing the talents of the members of their classes, and also to encourage any who may have commenced.

The teacher should frequently review what has been learned.

The Eighth Note as a Beat-Note.

§ 600. Tr.   " We sometimes have the eighth note as the beat-note, in which case the denominator of the fraction will be 8." (Writes the fraction $\frac{4}{8}$.)

§ 601. Tr. "If the eighth note is the beat-note, what note will represent the connecting of two pulses?" Cl. "The quarter note."

§ 602. Tr. "How many beats will you give to the quarter note?" Cl. "Two."

Note 124.—Write as follows and explain that the exercises are the same, only represented differently.

The Eighth Rest.

§ 603. Tr. "We have a rest which occupies as much time as an eighth note; what would be a good name for it?" Cl. "An eighth rest."

Note 125.—The teacher erases an eighth note and writes an eighth rest, and after the usual preliminary questions, practices No. 77.

Legato, Semi-Staccato, and Staccato.

§ 604. Tr. "There are three ways in which tones succeed each other. They may be closely connected thus: Listen!" (Sings the first two measures of No. 83 *legato*, and asks the class to imitate him.)

§ 605. Tr. "This style of singing is called Legato (pronounced lāy-gäh'-tō). What is it called?" Cl. "Legato."

§ 606. Tr. "Legato means smooth and connected. What does legato mean ? " Cl. "Smooth and connected."

§ 607. Tr. "Tones may be disconnected, thus." (Sings the same phrase *staccato,* and asks the class to imitate him.)

§ 608. Tr. "This style of singing is called staccato (pronounced stäh-cäh'-tō). What is it called ? " Cl. "Staccato."

§ 609. Tr. "Staccato means short and distinct. What does staccato mean ? " Cl. "Short and distinct."

§ 610. Tr. "Tones may be short and distinct, but not so short as staccato, thus." (Sings the same phrase semi-staccato, and asks the class to imitate him.)

§ 611. Tr. "This style of singing is called semi-staccato. What is it called ? " Cl. "Semi-staccato."

§ 612. Tr. "Semi-staccato means half-staccato. What does semi-staccato mean ? " Cl. "Half-staccato."

Note 126.—In illustrating these styles care should be taken not to hurry when singing staccato. The pulses should follow each other with the same frequency whether singing Staccato, Semi-staccato, or Legato.

Note 127.—Explain the Staccato and the Semi-staccato marks, and practice No. 83.

Note 128.—Explain that the connecting of the stems of eighth notes frequently takes the place of a slur, and practice No. 76.

Da Capo.

§ 613. Tr. "D. C. are the initial letters of the Italian words Da Capo ; but they are more frequently used as an abreviation of a whole

Italian sentence, namely, *Da capo al fine*—which is freely translated as follows : *Da*, from the ; *capo*, commencement ; *al*, to the ; *fine*, end – Sing 'from the commencement to the end.' " (Practice No. 142.)

SEXTUPLE MEASURE.

§ 614. TR. "Listen !" (Counts *one*, two, three, *four*, five, six.)

§ 615. TR. "How many pulses are there in this kind of measure ? " CL. "Six."

§ 616. TR. "A measure having six pulses is called SEXTUPLE MEASURE. What is it called ? " CL. "Sextuple measure."

§ 617. TR. "Listen while I count again, and observe how many, and which are the strong pulses." (Counts, accenting firmly.)

§ 618. TR. "Which are the strong pulses ? " CL. "One and four."

§ 619. TR. "Listen, and notice while I beat and count." (Beats and counts, making two beats in the measure, downward to the first pulse, and upward to the fourth pulse.)

§ 620. TR. "How many beats did I give ? " CL. "Two."

§ 621. TR. "Were they on strong, or on weak pulses ? " CL. "On strong pulses."

§ 622. TR. "What motion did I give to the first pulse ? " CL. "Downward."

§ 623. TR. "To the fourth pulse ? " CL. "Upward."

§ 624. TR. "How many beats do we give to sextuple measure ? " CL. "Two."

§ 625. Tr. "How many pulses do we reckon to each beat?" Cl. "Three."

Note 129.—The teacher explains that when the movement is slow, each pulse receives a beat, thus:

§ 626. Tr. "What motion do we give to the first pulse?" (Pointing.) Cl. "Down."

§ 627. Tr. "What motion is given to the second pulse?" (Pointing.) Cl. "Left."

§ 628. Tr. "What motion to the third pulse?" (Pointing.) Cl. "Left."

§ 629. Tr. "What motion to the fourth pulse?" (Pointing.) Cl. "Right."

§ 630. Tr. "What motion to the fifth pulse?" (Pointing.) Cl. "Right."

§ 631. Tr. "What motion is given to the sixth pulse?" (Pointing.) Cl. "Up."

Note 130.—As soon as the class can make these motions accurately the teacher should put upon the board diagrams of the four kinds of measure thus:

and have the class practice them alternately as he calls for them. He should always call out the change on the up beat, and point to the diagram as he calls.

§ 632. Tr. "Look at Exercise No. 86."

§ 633. Tr. "In what kind of measure is this written?" Cl. "Sextuple."

§ 634. Tr. "How do you know?" Cl. "The numerator of the fraction is 6."

§ 635. Tr. "What kind of a note do we reckon to each pulse?" Cl. "A quarter note."

§ 636. Tr. "How do you know?" Cl. "The denominator of the fraction is 4."

§ 637. Tr. "Read the fraction?" Cl. "Six quarter notes will fill a measure."

§ 638. Tr. "How is the first measure filled?" Cl. "Six quarter notes."

§ 639. Tr. "How is the second measure filled?" Cl. "Two dotted half notes."

§ 640. Tr. "Two dotted half notes are equivalent to how many quarter notes?" Cl. "Six."

§ 641. Tr. "How many beats do we give to sextuple measure?" Cl. "Two."

§ 642. Tr. "How many pulses do we reckon to each beat?" Cl. "Three."

§ 643. Tr. "Which beat do we give to the first three notes?" Cl. "Downward."

§ 644. Tr. "Which beat do we give to the next three notes?" Cl. "Upward."

Note 131.—Practice all exercises which involve sextuple measure.

Note 132.—Write as follows, and explain that the exercises are the same, only represented differently:

The Hold and Pause.

§ 645. Tr. "Sometimes, in order to produce certain effects, it becomes necessary to prolong a tone beyond its normal length; such prolonged tone is indicated by a character called a HOLD made thus." (Writes the hold.)

§ 646. Tr. "What is it called?" Cl. "A hold."

§ 647. Tr. "Sometimes it is necessary to have a prolonged silence; such an effect is indicated by a character called a PAUSE, written in connection with a rest, thus." (Writes.)

§ 648. Tr. "What is this character called?" (Pointing.) Cl. "A hold."

§ 649. Tr. "What is this character called?" (Pointing.) Cl. "A pause."

§ 650. Tr. "The pause or hold says to the singers, 'Look at the leader;' what does the hold or pause say to the class?" Cl. "Look at the leader."

NOTE 133.—Practice exercises involving the hold and pause.

Sharp Four.

§ 651. Tr. "Sing one by syllable Ta." (They sing.)

§ 652. Tr. "Sing two?" (They sing.)
§ 653. Tr. "Sing three?" (They sing.)
§ 654. Tr. "Sing four?" (They sing.)

NOTE 134.—The teacher requests them to listen, and sings *sharp four*, and asks:

§ 655. Tʀ. "Was the tone I sang higher, or was it lower, than four?" Cʟ. "Higher."

Nᴏᴛᴇ 135.—He then requests the class to sing five, after which he again sings sharp four and asks:

§ 656. Tʀ. "Was the tone which I sang higher or was it lower than five?" Cʟ. "Lower."

§ 657. Tʀ. "You said, a moment since, that it was higher than *four*, and now you say it is lower than *five*. How can this be?" Cʟ. "It is half-way between the two."

§ 658. Tʀ. "Then between what two numerals have we found an intermediate tone?" Cʟ. "Between four and five."

§ 659. Tʀ. "This intermediate tone we call ꜱʜᴀʀᴘ ꜰᴏᴜʀ—the Italian name is Fi (Fee)."

§ 660. Tʀ. "Sharp four is usually followed by five."

Rᴇsᴏʟᴜᴛɪᴏɴ ᴏꜰ Sʜᴀʀᴘ Fᴏᴜʀ.

§ 661. Tʀ. "When a part moves according to its natural tendency, it is said to *resolve*, and the tone to which it moves is said to resolve it; therefore five resolves sharp four."

§ 662. Tʀ. "Sharp four is generally used in one of the following ways. Listen, and imitate the tones you hear."

Nᴏᴛᴇ 136.—The teacher then sings numerous examples, as indicated by the following figures—the class singing each after him (making use of the Italian syllables, of course :)

5, ♯4, 5 | 6, 5, ♯4, 5 | 8, 7, 6, 5, ♯4, 5 | 1, 5, ♯4, 5 |
3, 5, ♯4. 5 | 6, 5, ♯4, 5 | 8, 5, ♯4, 5 | 6, 5, ♯4, 5 |

5, 6, 5, ♯4, 5 | 6, 7, 8, ♯4, 5 | 8, 7, 6, ♯4, 5 | 3, 4, 5, ♯4, 5 | 3, 6, 5, ♯4, 5 | 1, 3, 5, ♯4, 5 | 1, 2, 3, ♯4, 5, etc.—carefully guarding against singing sharp four too low.

How Sharp Four is Represented.

§ 663. Tr. " Sharp four is represented upon the same degree of the staff upon which we represent *four;* and that we may not mistake it for four we place a character before it which we call a sharp (writes) thus."

Note 137.—The teacher then places notes upon the board to represent the examples indicated in Note 136, and requests the class to sing as he points.

Rule for Accidentals.

§ 664. Tr. " Whenever sharps (♯) occur in a tune they are called ACCIDENTALS, and they are subject to the following rule : *Accidentals continue their significance throughout the measure in which they occur.*"*

Note 138.—Practice the exercises which involve sharp four. After which the teacher should introduce the other intermediate tones whose tendency is upward (sharps) exactly as sharp four was introduced ; and practice the exercises which illustrate them. They should be introduced in the order in which they are most frequently used, viz., sharp four, sharp two, sharp one, sharp five, and sharp six.

---

* The additional clause of this rule, as formerly given, namely, " and from measure to measure until cancelled by a note intervening upon another degree of the staff," is very properly discontinued by most of our modern composers, as it is of no benefit and causes great confusion. In all of the author's works, whenever an accidental is required in the following measure it will be placed there.

DOTTED QUARTER NOTES.

NOTE 139.—The teacher writes an exercise like the following :

and after the usual preliminary questions—"What kind of measure ? What is the beat-note ? Read the fraction. Is the first pulse single or divided ? Is the second pulse divided or single ?" etc.—says :

§ 665. TR. "Sing the exercise." (They sing.)

§ 666. TR. "Listen, and observe whether I sing it correctly or incorrectly." (He sings and connects the first pulse with the first half of the second pulse.)

§ 667. TR. "Did I sing it correctly or incorrectly ?" CL. "Incorrectly."

§ 668. TR. "In which measure did the error occur ?" CL. "In the first measure."

§ 669. TR. "How was it wrong ?" CL. "You connected the first pulse with the first half of the second pulse."

NOTE 140.—The teacher may be obliged to repeat the illustration before the class can grasp it. But all will soon comprehend that his object is to attach the first half of the second pulse to the first pulse.

§ 670. TR. "Yes, I connected the first one and one-half pulses, and I wish you to so connect them. I will indicate it by what ?" (Drawing a tie under the two notes.) CL. "A tie."

NOTE 141.—The exercise will appear thus:

§ 671. Tr. "Sing the exercise." (They sing.)

§ 672. Tr. "We have one note which represents the connecting of one and one-half pulses, it is called a DOTTED QUARTER NOTE." (Erases the tie and eighth note and dots the quarter note.)

§ 673. Tr. "What is it called?" Cl. "Dotted quarter note."

§ 674. Tr. "The dotted quarter note represents the connecting of how many pulses?" Cl. "One and one-half pulses."

Note 142.—The exercise will now appear thus:

§ 675. Tr. "Sing the exercise." (They sing.)

§ 676. Tr. "Look at Exercise No. 78. What kind of a note is the first note of this tune?" Cl. "A dotted quarter note."

§ 677. Tr. "A dotted quarter note requires how many beats?" Cl. "One and one-half."

§ 678. Tr. "Sing this tune." (They sing.)

Note 143.—It will be observed that the exercise which was put on the board to illustrate the new idea was a scrap of the tune which followed. This is an important feature and should be followed in all similar instances.

The Half Note as a Beat-note.

§ 679. Tr. "We sometimes have the half note as a beat-note, in which case the denominator of the fraction will be 2."

Note 144.—Write as follows, and explain that the exercises are the same, only represented differently.

§ 680. Tr.   "If a quarter note is the beat-note, what kind of notes will divide the pulse into two equal parts?"   Cl.   "Eighth notes."

§ 681. Tr.   "If a half note is the beat-note what kind of notes will divide the pulse?"   Cl. "Quarter notes."   (Practice exercises involving the half note as a beat-note.)

Sixteenth Notes.

Note 145.—The teacher writes as follows:

§ 682. Tr.   "In what kind of measure is this exercise written?"   (Pointing to the fraction.) Cl.   "Quadruple measure."

§ 683. Tr.   "What is the beat-note?"   Cl. "An eighth note."

§ 684. Tr.   "Sing the exercise?"   (They sing.)

§ 685. Tr.   "Listen!"   (He sings, dividing the second pulse of the first measure.)

§ 686. Tr.   "Did I sing correctly or incorrectly?"   Cl.   "Incorrectly."

§ 687. Tr.   "In which measure did the error occur?"   Cl.   "In the first."

§ 688. TR. "Which pulse was wrong?" CL. "The second."

§ 689. TR. "How was it wrong?" CL. "You divided the pulse."

§ 690. TR. "I wish you to divide the second pulse, and will indicate it by erasing the eighth note and writing two notes instead. Thus." (Writes.)

NOTE 146.—The example will appear thus:

§ 691. TR. "These two notes (pointing) occupy the time of what kind of a note?" CL. "An eighth note."

§ 692. TR. "How does one of these notes (pointing) compare in length with an eighth note?" CL. "It is one half as long."

§ 693. TR. "What is one half of an eighth?" CL. "A sixteenth."

§ 694. TR. "What then would be a good name for these notes." CL. "Sixteenth notes."

§ 695. TR. "Sing the exercise." (They sing.)

§ 696. . TR. "Would you be puzzled if I should divide another pulse thus?" (Writes two sixteenths in place of the eighth note in the first pulse, and asks them to sing the exercise.)

NOTE 147.—The example will now appear thus:

§ 697. Tr. "Look at No. 105. In what kind of measure is it written?" Cl. "Quadruple measure."

§ 698. Tr. "What note is used as beat-note?" Cl. "An eighth note."

§ 699. Tr. "Read the fraction?" Cl. "Four eighth notes will fill a measure."

§ 700. Tr. "Is the first measure full?" Cl. "It is."

§ 701. Tr. "How is it filled?" Cl. "Four sixteenth notes and two eighth notes."

§ 702. Tr. "Is the first pulse single or divided?" Cl. "Divided."

§ 703. Tr. "The second pulse?" Cl. "Divided."

§ 704. Tr. "Third and fourth pulses each?" Cl. "Single."

§ 705. Tr. "The first two pulses in the next measure?" Cl. "Single."

§ 706. Tr. "How many pulses are united in the quarter note?" Cl. "Two."

Note 148.—Practice sixteenth notes. Omit tunes in A minor until the minor scale is introduced. See page 109, § 792.

Permanent Names of Tones.

§ 707. Tr. "Sing the scale ascending." (While they sing he writes the scale on the blackboard.)

§ 708. Tr. "Sing One." (They sing.)

§ 709. Tr. "Sing Two." (They sing.)

§ 710. Tr. "Sing it again and call it Ta." (They sing.)

§ 711. Tʀ. "Where is it represented ?" Cʟ. "Space below." (He writes.)

§ 712. Tʀ. "Sing it again and call it Do." (They sing.)

§ 713. Tʀ. "See if you can sing a scale from that pitch. Begin." (While they sing he writes the scale a little to the right and parallel with the other scale.)

§ 714. Tʀ. "Sing One of this new scale." (They sing.)

§ 715. Tʀ. "What number of the old scale is One of this new scale ?" Cʟ. "Two."

§ 716. Tʀ. "Sing it again and call it Re." (While they sing he draws the pointer across to the corresponding note in the old scale and says :)

§ 717. Tʀ. "Sing as I point." (He points to Two, Three, Two, One, thus bringing them back to the correct pitch of the old scale. Not stopping, however, he points to Two and then to Three and says :)

§ 718. Tʀ. "Sing Three again." (They sing.)

§ 719. Tʀ. "Where is it represented ?" Cʟ. "First line." (He writes.)

§ 720. Tʀ. "Sing it again and call it Ta." (They sing.)

§ 721. Tʀ. "Sing it again and call it Do." (They sing.)

§ 722. Tʀ. "How many can sing a scale from that pitch ? Begin." (While they sing he writes the new scale and says :)

§ 723. Tʀ. "Sing One of this last scale." (They sing.)

§ 724. Tr. "What is its name in the second scale?" Cl. "Re."

§ 725. Tr. "What is its name in the old scale?" Cl. "Mi."

§ 726. Tr. "Sing as I point." (Points to One of the last scale and they sing Do ; points to the corresponding note in the second scale and they sing Re ; points to the corresponding note in the old scale and they sing Mi.)

§ 727. Tr. "Are these different pitches or the same pitch with different names?" Cl. "The same pitch with different names."

§ 728. Tr. "Sing as I point." (Again he leads them down to Do and back up to Fa.)

§ 729. Tr. "Sing Fa again." (They sing.)

§ 730. Tr. "Where is it represented?" Cl. "First space." (He writes and says :)

§ 731. Tr. "Sing a scale from this pitch." (He again writes as they sing and draws them back through the scales and down to Do of the old scale, then up to Sol, where he proceeds to introduce a scale from Sol and writes it as they sing, when the blackboard will present the picture as follows :)

Note 149.—The class is now requested to follow the pointer while they are led through a short exercise in the lowest four or five tones of the last scale, when he finally points to Re, and while they sing he slowly draws the pointer across to the corresponding note in the next scale to the left and asks :

§ 732. Tr. "What is it called in this scale ?'
Cl. "Mi."

§ 733. Tr. "Sing it and call it Mi." (While they sing he slowly draws the pointer across to the corresponding note in the next scale to the left, and asks :)

§ 734. Tr. "What is it called in this scale ?"
Cl. "Fa."

§ 735. Tr. "Sing it and call it Fa." (While they sing he again draws the pointer across to the corresponding note in the next scale to the left, and asks :)

§ 736. Tr. "What is it called in this scale ?"
Cl. "Sol."

§ 737. Tr. "Sing it again and call it Sol." (While they sing he again draws the pointer slowly across to the corresponding note in the old scale and asks :)

§ 738. Tr. "What is it called in the old scale?"
Cl. "La."

§ 739. Tr. "Sing as I point, giving the tones their correct names." (He points to the notes on the second space successively, beginning at La of the old scale and ending at Re of the last scale, and asks :)

§ 740. Tr. "Do these notes on the second space (drawing the pointer through all the notes on that space) indicate different pitches or the same pitch with different names?" Cl. "The same pitch with different names."

§ 741. Tr. "Yes, the pitches never change, and inasmuch as they are permanent they should have permanent names. The names of the first seven letters of the alphabet are used as the names of the pitches, viz.: A, B, C, D, E, F, and G."

§ 742. Tr. "The names of what letters are used as permanent names of pitches?" Cl. "A, B, C, D, E, F, and G."

§ 743. Tr. "Repeat them backward."

Note. 150.—These letter names should be practiced until the pupils can repeat them backward as rapidly as forward.

§ 744. Tr. "In applying these pitch names to the lines and spaces we go upward on the staff as we go forward in the alphabet, and downward on the staff as we go backward in the alphabet. Beginning with this space and naming it A (pointing to the second space) what will we call this line?" (Pointing to the third line.) Cl. "B."

§ 745. Tr. "This space?" (Pointing to the third space.) Cl. "C."

Note 151.—The teacher proceeds in this manner up to the space above and says:

§ 746. Tr. "We only use the names of the first seven letters, so if we wish to go higher, we must repeat them. What name shall we give to the first short line above?" Cl. "A."

§ 747. Tr. "Name the pitches as I point." He points from A above down to A second space, and asks:)

§ 748. Tr. "If we wish to go farther down what will this line be named?" (Pointing to the second line.) Cl. "G."

Note 152.—The teacher points to the degrees down as far as C, then up through the entire staff, backward and forward until the pitch names are quite familiar, then turn to some of the simple exercises in the first part of the book and request all to read by letters. Hereafter every exercise should be read, not sung, by letters before reading by syllables.

The Key of G.

§ 749. Tr. "A scale is named from the letter name of the tone which forms its tonic."

§ 750. Tr. "What is the name (pointing) of this first scale?" Cl. "The scale of C."

§ 751. Tr. "How do you know?" Cl. "Because C is Do or tonic."

§ 752. Tr. "What is the name (pointing) of this second scale?" Cl. "The scale of D."

§ 753. Tr. "How do you know?" Cl. "Because D is Do or tonic."

§ 754. Tr. "What is the name (pointing) of this third scale?" Cl. "The scale of E."

§ 755. Tr. "What is the name (pointing) of this fourth scale?" Cl. "The scale of F."

§ 756. Tr. "What is the name (pointing) of this last scale?" Cl. "The scale of G."

§ 757. Tr. "How do you know?" Cl. "Because G is Do or tonic."

§ 758. Tr. "The tones which group themselves around a tonic form what is called a key, and a key, like a scale, is named from its tonic."

§ 759. Tr. "What are the permanent names of the tones which form the key of C?" (Pointing on modulator across to the right hand margin.) Cl. "C, D, E, F, G, A, and B."

§ 760. Tr. "How high on the C key shall we go to find Do of the G key." (Pointing from Do to Sol, in C column, on modulator.) Cl. "To Sol."

§ 761. Tr. "Sing Do." (Points to Do in C column.)

Note 153.—Always compare their Do with the instrument.

§ 762. Tr. "Sing as I point." (Points from Do to Sol on modulator, and slowly going across to the G column, says :)

§ 763. Tr. "Sing this tone Sol again, but call it Do." (They sing.)

§ 764. Tr. "Sing as I point." (By his pointing they are made to sing "Old Hundred.")

Note 154.—The teacher should quickly erase the first four scales on the board and repeat this exercise of "Old Hundred" by pointing to the notes.

§ 765. Tr. "We would not have this grand old tune if we had not this G Key. Listen ! (Sings the first line of the "Old Oak Tree.") All who recognize this tune raise their hands. (Of course all hands are raised.) We would be deprived of very many beautiful tunes if we had not this G key. Let us learn a little more about this new key. We will compare its tones with those in the C key. (Pointing to C column.) All characters on this modulator that are printed in black ink represent diatonic tones, *i.e.*, the tones that are not intermediate ; the characters printed in carmine (red) ink represent intermediate tones whose tendency is upward, called sharps ; and all characters which are printed in gas-light green represent intermediate tones whose tendency is downward, called flats, and which will be more fully explained in a future lesson. Now let us compare the diatonic tones of this new key with the diatonic tones of the model key. (Pointing.) If both are black they agree, if not they disagree."

§ 766. Tr. " Do, agree or disagree?" (Pointing to Do in G column and drawing the pointer across to Sol in C column.) Cl. " Agree."

§ 767. Tr. " Re, agree or disagree?" (Pointing to Two in G column and drawing pointer across to La in C column.) Cl. " Agree."

§ 768. Tr. " Mi, agree or disagree?" (Pointing to Three.) Cl. " Agree."

§ 769. Tr. " Fa, agree or disagree?" (Pointing to Four.) Cl. " Agree."

§ 770. Tr. " Sol, agree or disagree? (Pointing to Five.) Cl. " Agree."

§ 771. Tr. " La, agree or disagree?" (Pointing to Six.) Cl. " Agree."

§ 772. Tr. "Ti, agree or disagree?" (Pointing to Seven.) Cl. " Disagree."

§ 773. Tr. " Let us go to the margin and find what this disagreement is." (Drawing pointer slowly across to F♯ in right hand margin of modulator.)

§ 774. Tr. " What is this disagreement?" Cl. " F sharp."

§ 775. Tr. " Let us record it." (Goes to the board and writes a sharp on fifth line following the clef.)

§ 776. Tʀ. "This sharp (pointing) is called a
sɪɢɴᴀᴛᴜʀᴇ, and is the sign of the G key. It also
shows that these two keys have all tones in common except one."

§ 777. Tʀ. "What tone has the G key that is
not common to the C key?" Cʟ. "F sharp."

Nᴏᴛᴇ 155.—Explain that all degrees whose names are
G now represent Do. Place a note upon the second line
and space above of Soprano staff, and first line and fourth
space of Bass staff, and mark them Do, thus:—

§ 778. Tʀ. "Turn to Exercise No. 118. In
what key is this tune written?" Cʟ. "In the
G key."

§ 779. Tʀ. "How do you know?" Cʟ. "The
signature is One sharp."

§ 780. Tʀ. "What syllable is first in Soprano?" Cʟ. "Do."

§ 781. Tʀ. "How do you know?" Cʟ. "Because the tone indicated is G."

§ 782. Tʀ. "How do you know G is Do?"
Cʟ. "The signature is One sharp."

§ 783. Tʀ. "What syllable is first in Alto?"
Cʟ. "Sol."

§ 784. Tʀ. "What syllable is first in Tenor?"
Cʟ. "Mi."

§ 785. TR. " What syllable is first in Bass ? "
CL. " Do."

§ 786. TR. " All read the syllables in the Soprano, speaking together, distinctly and slowly." (They read.)

§ 787. TR. " All read the syllables in the Alto." (They read.)

§ 788. TR. " All read the syllables in the Tenor." (They read.)

§ 789. TR. " All read the syllables in the Bass." (They read.)

NOTE 156.—It will be found an excellent device for the teacher to commit to memory the different parts of this piece, and, closing his book, repeat the syllables after the class has read them, asking the singers to watch the notes, and if he makes a mistake, to say *" Wrong ;"* by purposely making a mistake occasionally, he can test their watchfulness. For those who have studied the principles of Thorough-bass and Harmony * it will be comparatively easy to read these parts from memory, as the chord will almost surely indicate the progressions.

§ 790. TR. " Sing Do of the C key—the old Do." (They sing, and the teacher compares their pitch with the instrument.)

§ 791. TR. " Ascend the C scale as far as Sol, which will become Do, and then go to your places through the chord of this new Do." (They sing.)

NOTE 157.—The class should be required to repeat this exercise until they can go solidly from C to their places in the first chord of the piece, and hereafter they should

---

* A careful study of *Palmer's Theory of Music* (The John Church Co., price $1.00) will prove an excellent investment of time and money.

always be required to go from the pitch C to their places in the first chord of the new tune, whatever the key may be. This point cannot be emphasized too strongly.

NOTE 158.—Practice exercises in the G key, always beginning with the preliminary questions, "What is the key?" "How do you know?" "What kind of measure?" "Read the fraction." "Are the pulses single or divided?" "With which beat do we begin to sing?" etc.

THE MINOR SCALE AND KEY.

§ 792. TR. "Sing the C scale, ascending and descending, by the syllable Ta." (They sing).

NOTE 159.—The teacher asks them to listen and sings a minor scale by syllable Ta from the same starting-point, C, as follows :

§ 793. TR. "Is this the scale you sung or a new one?" CL. "A new one."

§ 794. TR. "Let us learn this new scale. We are already familiar with most of its intervals. Listen and sing after me." (He sings as follows, and the class imitates him.)

La Ti Do Re Mi.

§ 795. TR. "Again listen and imitate." (Sings slowly and distinctly as follows :

La Ti Do Re Mi Fa Mi.

Note 160.—While the teacher sings he holds his left hand before the class with the second and third fingers apart, thus:

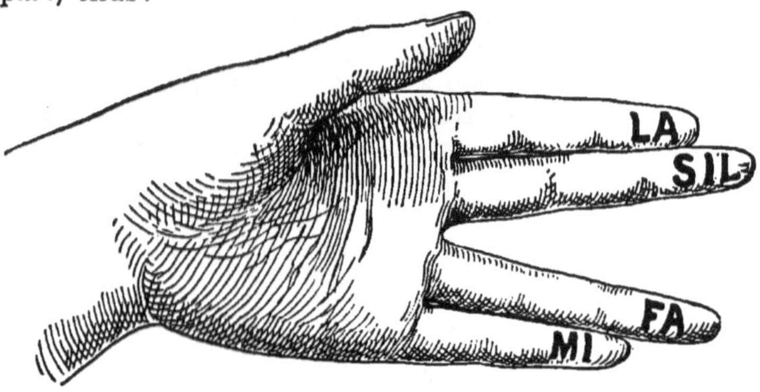

As he sings Mi Fa he points with the index finger of the right hand to the third and fourth fingers, respectively, of the left hand, and continues pointing to the fingers which represent Mi Fa, La Sil the class singing after him until he has firmly established the pitches of these four tones in the minds of his class, after which they may be taken over the large second, with perfect intonation by always coming to an abrupt stop upon approaching the large second both in ascending and descending, thus:

After sufficient practice, as indicated above, the class may sing this scale in regular rhythm thus:

Give extra stress where the accent mark (>) occurs.

The teacher calls attention to the modulator and proceeds as follows:

§ 796. Tr. "What kind of a second is La Ti?" (Pointing to the central column.) Cl. "A major second."

§ 797. Tr. "What is the second Ti Do?" (Pointing.) Cl. "A minor second."

§ 798. Tr. "What is the second Do Re?" (Pointing.) Cl. "A major second."

§ 799. Tr. "What is the second Re Mi?" (Pointing.) Cl. "A major second."

§ 800. Tr. "What is the second Mi Fa?" (Pointing.) Cl. "A minor second."

§ 801. Tr. "Look at the second Fa Sil, (Pointing.) Is it larger, or is it smaller than the major second?" Cl. "Larger."

Steps and Half-Steps.

§ 802. Tr. "For the first time in this course of lessons the necessity has now arisen for some means of measuring intervals; this is done by Steps and Half-steps. A half-step being equal to a minor second and a step being equal to a major second, we can now measure this second Fa Sil, (pointing), which is larger than a major second. How large is the second Fa Sil?" (still pointing). Cl. "A step-and-a-half."

§ 803. Tr. "A second which is as great as a step-and-a-half is called an Augmented Second. What is it called?" Cl. "An Augmented

§ 804. Tr. "How much larger is an augmented second than a major second?" Cl. "A half-step larger."

Note 161.—The teacher should be careful to use the term "step-and-a-half" when applied to the measurement of the augmented second. It is not correct to say an augmented second is as great as one step and one half-step, for while the augmented second is a single unit, the terms a *step* and a *half-step* form two units.

The E Minor Key.

§ 805. Tr. "Turn to No. 133. What is the signature?" Cl. "One sharp."

§ 806. Tr. "One sharp is the sign of what key?" Cl. "The G key."

§ 807. Tr. "Any key whose scale consists of the syllables Do Re Mi Fa Sol La Ti Do is called a Major key, and any key whose scale consists of the syllables La Ti Do Re Mi Fa Sil La is called a Minor key. Hence a signature always indicates two keys, a major key and what is called its *relative minor* key. The pitch which is Do gives us the name of the major key and the pitch which is La gives the name of the relative minor key. In the signature of One sharp what pitch becomes Do?" (Pointing to modulator.) Cl. "G."

§ 808. Tr. "Hence what major key is indicated by the signature of One sharp?" Cl. "G major."

§ 809. Tr. "What pitch becomes La in this signature?" (Pointing.) Cl. "E."

113

§ 810. Tr. "Hence what minor key is indicated by the signature of One sharp?" Cl. "E minor."

§ 811. Tr. "One sharp is the sign of what keys?" Cl. "G major and E minor."

§ 812. Tr. "The first chord in a major tune is the chord of Do. What syllables form it?" Cl. "Do Mi Sol."

§ 813. Tr. "The first chord in a minor tune is the chord of La. What syllables form it?" Cl. "La Do Mi."

§ 814. Tr. "In this exercise what syllable is first in Soprano?" Cl. "La."

§ 815. Tr. "What syllable is first in Alto?" Cl. "Mi."

§ 816. Tr. "What syllable is first in Tenor?" Cl. "Do."

§ 817. Tr. "What syllable is first in Bass?" Cl. "La."

§ 818. Tr. "What syllables form the first chord in this tune?" Cl. "La Do Mi."

§ 819. Tr. "Is this tune major or minor?" Cl. "Minor."

§ 820. Tr. "How do you know?" Cl. "Because the first chord is the chord of La."

§ 821. Tr. "Spell the chord of La and pronounce as in the first chord of this exercise." They sing.)

Note 162.—Practice all the exercises in the E minor key, and then return to No. 110 and practice the A minor exercises which were omitted, being careful to ask the preliminary questions "Is this tune major or minor?" "How do you know?" etc.

The D Key.

§ 822. Tr. "Sing Do of the C key." (They sing, and the teacher compares their pitch with the instrument.)

§ 823. Tr. "Sing Re." (They sing.)

§ 824. Tr. "Sing it again and call it Do." (They sing.)

§ 825. Tr. "Where shall I place a note to indicate it?" Cl. "Space below." (Teacher writes, and says :)

§ 826. Tr. "Sing a scale from that pitch." (They sing.)

Note 163.—While they sing the teacher writes the scale rapidly, when it will appear thus :

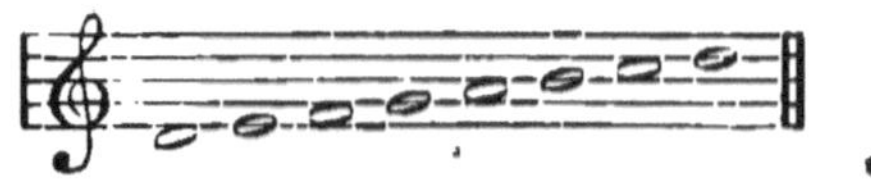

§ 827. Tr. "What is the name of this scale?" Cl. "D scale."

§ 828. Tr. "How do you know?" Cl. "Because D is Do or tonic."

§ 829. Tr. "Let us go to the modulator and compare this D scale with our model, the C scale."

§ 830. Tr. "Does Do agree or disagree?" (Pointing to Do in D column, and drawing the pointer across to Re in C column.) Cl. "Agree."

§ 831. Tr. "Re, agree or disagree?" (Pointing to Re in D column, and drawing pointer across to Mi in C column.) CL. "Agree."

§ 832. TR. "Mi, agree or disagree?" (Pointing.) CL. "Disagree."

§ 833. TR. "Let us go to the margin and find what this disagreement is." (Drawing pointer slowly across to F♯ in right-hand margin.)

§ 834. TR. "What is the name of this point of disagreement?" CL. "F sharp."

§ 835. TR. "Let us record it." (Goes to the board and writes a sharp on fifth line following the clef.)

§ 836. TR. "Continuing our comparisons, Fa (pointing), agree or disagree?" CL. "Agree."

§ 837. TR. "Sol (pointing), agree or disagree?" CL. "Agree."

§ 838. TR. "La (pointing), agree or disagree?" CL. "Agree."

§ 839. TR. "Ti (pointing), agree or disagree?" CL. "Disagree."

§ 840. TR. "What is the name of this disagreement?" (Pointing to C♯ in margin.) CL. "C sharp."

§ 841. TR. "Let us record it." (Writes a ♯ on third space.)

§ 842. TR. "These two sharps are placed here (pointing) to record the difference between the D key and our model, the C key, and thus form the signature of the D key."

§ 843. TR. "All the D's in this key are Do." (Writing notes on fourth line and space below of Soprano staff, and third line of Bass staff, when the exercise will appear thus :)

§ 844. Tʀ. "Turn to No. 131. In what key is it written?" Cʟ. "D key."

§ 845. Tʀ. "How do you know?" Cʟ. "The signature is two sharps."

§ 846. Tʀ. "Is the tune major or minor?" Cʟ. "Major."

§ 847. Tʀ. "How do you know?" Cʟ. "Its first chord is the chord of Do."

§ 848. Tʀ. "If the tune were minor, what would be its first chord?" Cʟ. "The chord of La."

§ 849. Tʀ. "What syllable is first in Soprano?" Cʟ. "Mi."

§ 850. Tʀ. "What syllable is first in Alto?" Cʟ. "Do."

§ 851. Tʀ. "What syllable is first in Tenor?" Cʟ. "Sol."

§ 852. Tʀ. "What syllable is first in Bass?" Cʟ. "Do."

§ 853. Tʀ. "All read the syllables in Soprano." (They read.)

§ 854. Tʀ. "All read the syllables in Alto." (They read.)

§ 855. TR. "All read the syllables in Tenor." (They read.)

§ 856. TR. "All read the syllables in Bass." (They read.)

NOTE 164.—See Note 156 for suggestions in memory exercises.

NOTE 165.—It is an excellent plan, when reading the first time in a new key, for *all* not only to read each part in concert, but to sing each part in unison before singing the several parts together.

NOTE 166.—Practice exercises in two sharps as far as No. 136.

THE DEGREES OF POWER.

§ 857. TR. "Close your books. Bass and Alto sing Do ; Soprano sing Mi ; and Tenors sing Sol." (Giving the pitch D.)

§ 858. TR. "Take a deep breath and sing the chord again, don't restrain your voices, neither use any undue effort, but let the tones flow out easily and naturally." (They sing.)

§ 859. TR. "Repeat the chord with some vocal restraint, giving me a softer degree of power." (They sing.)

§ 860. TR. "Repeat the chord again with great vocal restraint, giving me the softest tone you can produce." (They sing.)

§ 861. TR. "Sing the chord again with the power you gave it first." (They sing.)

§ 862. TR. "Now with a little vocal effort, give me a louder degree of power." (They sing.)

§ 863. TR. "With great vocal effort, give me the loudest degree of power consistent with pure tone ; don't let the voice become harsh and unmusical, but up to that point give me all the power you can." (They sing.)

§ 864. Tr. "Sing the chord again with the power you gave it first." (They sing.)

§ 865. Tr. "How many degrees have we had that were softer than this ?" Cl. "Two."

§ 866. Tr. "How many louder?" Cl. "Two."

§ 867. Tr. "This, then, is the *middle degree of power*, there being as many degrees softer as there are louder."

§ 868. Tr. "How many degrees of power have we had altogether?" Cl. "Five."

§ 869. Tr. "These degrees are numbered from the softest, and their technical names are taken from the Italian language. The first dedegree is called *Pianissimo,* which means *very soft,* and is indicated thus : (writing) *pp.* The second degree is called *Piano,* which means *soft,* and is indicated thus : (writing) *p.* The third or middle degree is called *Mezzo,** which means *medium,* and is indicated thus : (writing) *m.* The fourth degree is called *Forte* † which means *loud,* and is indicated thus : (writing) *f.* The fifth degree is called *Fortissimo,* which means *very loud,* and is indicated thus : (writing) *ff.*"

Note 167. The teacher takes a walking-stick, and, holding it in the middle with the left hand, points with the right hand to the small end and says :

§ 870. Tr. "Let this point represent the

---

* Pronounced Măt'-zo.   † Pronounced fŏr'-tĕ.

first degree of power—what is its technical name?" Cl. "*Pianissimo.*"

§ 871. Tr. "What letters stand for it?" Cl. "*pp.*"

§ 872. Tr. "Let this point (pointing half-way between the hand and the small end of the stick) represent the second degree of power; what is its technical name?" Cl. "*Piano.*"

§ 873. Tr. "What letter stands for it?" Cl. "*p.*"

§ 874. Tr. "Let this point (pointing to the stick at the hand) represent the third or middle degree of power; what is its name?" Cl. "*Mezzo.*"

§ 875. Tr. "What letter stands for it." Cl. "*m.*"

§ 876. Tr. "Let this point (pointing half-way between the hand and the large end of the stick) represent the fourth degree of power; what is its name?" Cl. "*Forte.*"

§ 877. Tr. "What letter stands for it?" Cl. "*f.*"

§ 878. Tr. "Let this point (pointing to the large end of the stick) represent the fifth degree of power; what is its name?" Cl. "*Fortissi-no.*"

§ 879. Tr. "What letters stand for it?" Cl. "*ff.*"

§ 880. Tr. "Sing as I point."

Note 168.—The teacher points to different parts of the stick which represent the different degrees, skipping round until their judgment is well formed as to the relative powers of the different degrees. He will find the

greatest difficulty in getting the proper difference between the first and second degrees. This may be corrected by skipping from the fourth degree to the second,
which will be almost as soft as the first degree. then by
immediately calling for the first degree they will see that
their second degree was too near the first. After a little
practice he will have the satisfaction of hearing them
sing with an intelligent idea of these different degrees of
power.

Degrees of Power Illustrated.

Note 169.—These five degrees of power are sufficient
for all practical purposes, and if composers would grade
them in this way performers would soon learn to use
them so. That there is an innumerable number of degrees of power between pianissimo and piano must be ad-
mitted, otherwise no such effect as crescendo could be
produced, but like the innumerable number of pitches
which, all must admit, lie between C and C♯, the human
mind cannot classify or analyze them.

After many years' experience in conducting large
bands of performers, both vocal and instrumental, the
writer is prepared to assert, without fear of contradiction, that no performer can produce a degree of power
between *piano* and *mezzo*, or between *mezzo* and *forte*
(any more than he can produce a pitch between C and
C♯): hence the terms *mezzo-piano* and *mezzo-forte*, with
their abbreviations *m.p*, and *m.f.*, are nonsensical,
and should be thrown out of our nomenclature. We
might as well say *mezzo-pianissimo* or *mezzo-fortissimo*.
The bad effects which have arisen from a lack of a classification of these degrees of power are shown by the fact
that when our modern composers wish a passage to be
performed *pianissimo*, they mark it with three or even
four *p's*. Now, as *pianissimo* means that the tone or

passage shall be as soft as possible we cannot make it softer with a dozen *p's ;* and if *fortissimo* means all the power of which the performer is capable (consistent with pure tone) a thousand *f's* would not make it louder.

CRESCENDO.

§ 881. TR.   "Commence at the first degree, and slowly increase the power as I point, being careful to arrive at the different degrees as I pass their representatives."   (Passes his finger slowly along the stick from the small end to the large end, when he suddenly withdraws his hand and the class will cease the chord abruptly.)

CRESCENDO ILLUSTRATED.

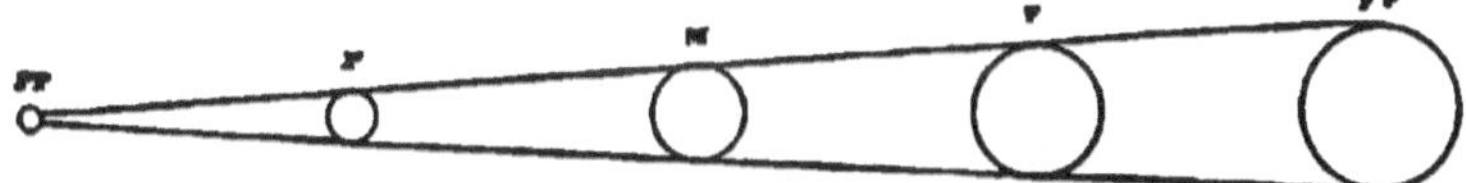

§ 882. TR. "When the power of a tone or passage is gradually increased, the effect produced is called *Crescendo.*   What is it called ?" CL. "Crescendo."

§ 883. TR.   "It is indicated by the word *crescendo,* or by the abbreviation *cres.,* or by two diverging lines, thus : <———— ." (Writing.)

DECRESCENDO OR DIMINUENDO.

§ 884. TR.   "Sing as I point, being careful to arrive at the proper degrees as I pass their representatives." (Passes his finger slowly from the large end of the stick to the small end.)

DECRESCENDO OR DIMINUENDO ILLUSTRATED.

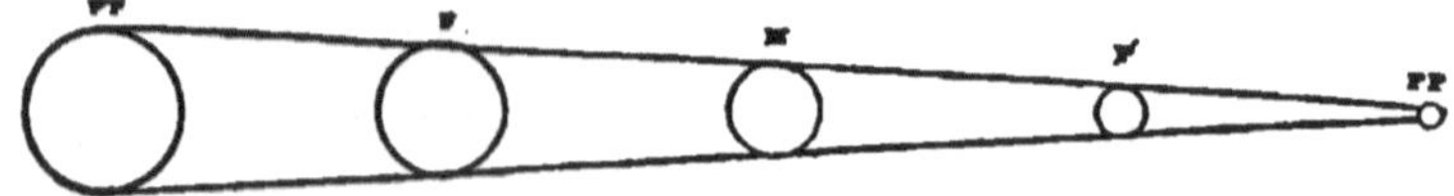

§ 885. Tr. "When the power of a tone or passage is gradually decreased the effect produced is called *Decrescendo* or *Diminuendo*.* What is it called?" Cl. "*Decrescendo* or *diminuendo*."

§ 886. Tr. "It is indicated by either of those terms or their abbreviations (*decres.* or *dim.*) or by two converging lines, thus : ⟩." (Writing.)

THE SWELL.

§ 887. Tr. "Take a deep breath and sing as I point."

Note 170.—He passes his finger slowly from the small end of the stick to the large end, and as slowly returns; upon their return they will probably jump back from the fifth degree to the second, instead of gradually decreasing through the fourth and third degrees. After their attention has been called to this defect, and they have practised several times, they will be able to produce a beautiful combination of *crescendo* and *decrescendo*.

---

* Pronounced dĭm-ĭn-ōō-ăn'-do.

The Swell Illustrated.

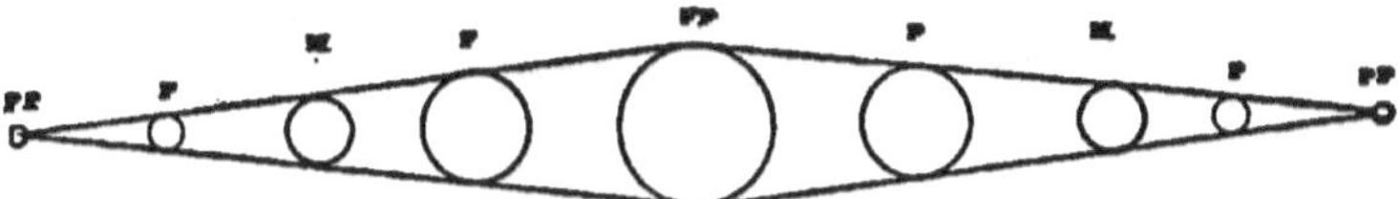

§ 888. Tr. "A proper union of *crescendo* and *diminuendo* produces an effect which is called a *Swell*. What is it called?" Cl. "A Swell."

§ 889. Tr. "It is indicated by diverging and converging lines, thus : ⟨⟨⟩⟩." (Writing.)

Sforzando.

§ 890. Tr. "Sing as I point." (Pointing to the large end of the stick and moving his fingers rapidly down to the point representing the second degree, and then more slowly on to the first degree.)

Sforzando Illustrated.

Note 171.—On the pianoforte the pure sforzando is impossible, but the *mental desire* to attain it produces a special attack, which is accepted in the place of the effect.

§ 891. Tr. "When the power is *instantly* diminished and the tone held in a low degree of power, the effect is called *Sforzando*. What is it called?" Cl. "*Sforzando*."

§ 892. Tr. "It is indicated by suddenly converging marks thus : >." (Writing.)

Note 172.—Other ways of indicating sforzando are *f*, *fz*, and *fp*. The last is much used in music for orchestra and military band.

§ 893. Tr. "Turn to No. 136. In which degree of power does it begin?" Cl. "The second degree."

§ 894. Tr. "Is the first line to be sung with increasing or decreasing power?" Cl. "Increasing power."

§ 895. Tr. "To what degree do we increase in singing that line?" Cl. "To the fourth degree."

§ 896. Tr. "In singing the second line should we diminish or increase?" Cl. "Diminish."

§ 897. Tr. "To what degree do we diminish?" Cl. "To the second degree."

§ 898. Tr. "With which degree does the third line begin?" Cl. "The third degree."

§ 899. Tr. "How is the third line to be sung?" Cl. "*Crescendo.*"

§ 900. Tr. "It increases to what degree?" Cl. "To the fifth."

§ 901. Tr. "How is the fourth line to be sung?" Cl. "*Diminuendo.*"

§ 902. Tr. "From which degree to which degree?" Cl. "From the fifth to the first."

§ 903. Tr. "How is the last chord to be sung?" Cl. "With a *swell.*"

Note 173.—The teacher should insist upon the correct use of these degrees of power, not permitting them

to sing with the third degree when they should be singing with some other degree, etc.

NOTE 174.—When they reach the last chord, a uniform
swell may be produced by requesting the class to be
guided by the leader's hands. He should hold his hands
high so all may see them. At *pianissimo* the hands
should touch each other ; when the hands separate the
power should increase, and diminish when they approach
each other.

NOTE 175.—Practice exercises in the D key. At No.
141 explain BIS, (pronounced bēse). The passage so
marked must be sung twice.

DOTTED EIGHTH NOTES.

NOTE 176.—The teacher writes a measure on the board
thus :

After the class has sung it, he says :

§ 904. TR. "Is the first pulse single or divided ? " CL. " Single."

§ 905. TR. "Is the second pulse single or
divided ? " CL. " Divided."

§ 906. TR. "Into how many parts is it divided ? " CL. " Into two parts."

§ 907. TR. " Are the two parts of the second
pulse equal or unequal ? CL. " Equal."

§ 908. TR. "Listen and observe while I sing
the exercise." (He sings and prolongs the first
eighth note.)

§ 909. TR. " Did I sing correctly or incorrectly ? " CL. " Incorrectly."

§ 910. Tr. "Which pulse was wrong?" Cl. "The second pulse."

§ 911. Tr. "How was it wrong?" Cl. "The first part was too long, and the second too short."

§ 912. Tr. "Yes, I held the first part of the pulse three times as long as the second. I wish you to do the same, and will indicate it by dotting the first note, and making the second into a sixteenth note." (He dots the first eighth-note, and adds a second hook to the other, when the exercise appears thus :)

Note 177.—The teacher should sing the exercise correctly and have the class imitate him, after which he asks:

§ 913. Tr. "Is the first pulse single or divided?" (Pointing.) Cl. "Single."

§ 914. Tr. "Is the second pulse single or divided?" (Pointing.) Cl. "Divided."

§ 915. Tr. "Into how many parts is it divided?" Cl. "Two."

§ 916. Tr. "Are the two parts equal or unequal?" Cl. "Unequal."

§ 917. Tr. "An eighth note equals how many sixteenths?" Cl. "Two."

§ 918. Tr. "A dotted eighth note equals how many sixteenth notes?" Cl. "Three."

§ 919. Tr. "How does this note (pointing to the dotted eighth) compare in length with that one?" (pointing to the sixteenth note.) Cl. "It is three times as long."

§ 920. Tr. "Turn to No. 142. What is the key?" Cl. "D key."

§ 921. Tr. "How do you know?" Cl. "Signature is two sharps."

§ 922. Tr. "Is the exercise major or minor?" Cl. "Major."

§ 923. Tr. 'Read the Fraction." Cl. "Four quarter notes will fill a measure."

§ 924. Tr. "Is the first pulse single or divided?" Cl. "Single."

§ 925. Tr. "Second pulse?" Cl. "Divided."

§ 926. Tr. "Into how many parts is it divided?" Cl. "Two."

§ 927. Tr. "Are they equal or unequal?" Cl. "Unequal."

§ 928. Tr. "Is the next pulse single or divided?" Cl. "Single."

Note 178.—The teacher should continue questioning as above, and then practice all exercises in two sharps, both major and minor.

Flats.

§ 929. Tr. "All our intermediate tones thus far (pointing to modulator) tend upward and are called sharps, here shown by carmine ink. Observe that each of these intermediate tones has a corresponding tone (pointing), shown here by gaslight green, whose tendency is downward, which is called a Flat. These flats take their syllable names from above, changing the vowel to long e. Thus (pointing) flat Ti is called Te (tay) ; flat La is Le (lay) ; flat Sol is Se (say) ; flat Mi is Me (may) ; but Re having long e already, the vowel is changed to the broad sound of ä—so flat Re is Rä (rah)."

§ 930. TR. "What is the name of the flat (pointing) which corresponds to sharp La ?" CL. "Te" (tay).

§ 931. TR. "What flat corresponds to sharp Sol ?" CL. "Le" (lay).

§ 932. TR. "What flat corresponds to sharp Fa ?" CL. "Se" (say).

§ 933. TR. "What flat corresponds to sharp Re ?" CL. "Me" (may).

§ 934. TR. "What flat corresponds to sharp Do ?" CL. "Rä" (rah).

NOTE 179.—That the teacher may obtain a clearer comprehension of these intermediate tones, their tendencies and resolutions, he is referred to Remark 7, page 188.

NOTE 180.—It will be observed that we use the terms *sharp Do, sharp Sol, flat La, flat Mi*, etc. If the teacher prefers *sharp One, sharp Five, flat Seven, flat Three*, etc., he can, of course, use them. although there is not one well-founded reason why the intermediate tones should not be called *sharp Do, sharp Re*, etc., while there are several excellent reasons why they *should* be so named.

THE F KEY.

§ 935. TR. "Sing Do of the C key." (They sing, and the teacher compares their pitch with instrument.)

§ 936. TR. "Sing Re." (They sing.)
§ 937. TR. "Sing Mi." (They sing.)
§ 938. TR. "Sing Fa." (They sing.)
§ 939. TR. "Sing Fa again, and call it Do."
(They sing.)

§ 940. TR. "Where shall I place a note to indicate it?" CL. "First space." (He writes and says :)

§ 941. TR. "Sing a scale from that pitch."

NOTE 181.—While they sing the teacher writes the scale rapidly, when it will appear thus:

§ 942. TR. "What is the name of this scale?" CL. "The F scale."

§ 943. TR. "How do you know?" CL. "Because F is Do or Tonic."

§ 944. TR. "Let us compare this F scale with our model scale of C. Does Do agree or disagree?" (See §§ 766 and 777 inclusive.) CL. "Agree."

§ 945. TR. "Re, agree or disagree?" CL. "Agree."

§ 946. TR. "Mi, agree or disagree?" CL. "Agree."

§ 947. TR. "Fa, agree or disagree?" CL. "Disagree."

§ 948. TR. "Let us go to the margin and find what this disagreement is." (Drawing the pointer slowly across to the left-hand margin.)

§ 949. TR. "What is the name of this point of disagreement?" CL. "B flat."

§ 950. TR. "Let us record it." (Goes to the board and writes a flat on the third line, following the clef, thus :

§ 951. TR. "Let us continue our comparisons. Sol, agree or disagree?" CL. "Agree."

§ 952. TR. "La, agree or disagree?" CL. "Agree."

§ 953. TR. "Ti, agree or disagree?" CL. "Agree."

§ 954. TR. "How many points of disagreement have we found?" CL. "One."

§ 955. TR. "What is the disagreeing point?" CL. "B flat."

§ 956. TR. "A flat placed on the B degree at the commencement forms a signature or sign of the F key, and also shows that the F key differs from our model, the C key, only in one point."

§ 957. TR. "All the Fs of the staff have now become Do." (He writes notes on first space and fifth line of Soprano staff, and fourth line of Bass staff, thus :)

§ 958. TR. "Turn to No. 159. What is the key?" CL. "The F key."

§ 959. TR. "How do you know?" CL. "Signature of One flat."

§ 960. TR. "In what variety of measure is it written?" CL. "Quadruple measure."

§ 961. TR. "What is the first syllable?" CL. "Do."

NOTE 182.—The teacher should ask the preliminary questions as at §§ 780 and 789 inclusive.

§ 962. TR. "What tone of the C key becomes Do of the F key?" CL. "Fa."

§ 963. TR. "All sing Do of C key." (They sing, and their pitch is compared with instrument.)

§ 964. TR. "Go from Do in the C key to your several places in the F key." (They sing Do Re Mi Fa, in C key, and, taking this Fa as their new Do, spread out to their several parts in the chord of F.)

NOTE 183.—Too much stress cannot be laid upon having the class *always* get their several pitches from Do. They should *always* go from Do through the Tonic chord to their places.

NOTE 184.—The particular attention of the teacher is called to Note 105.

THE CANCEL.

§ 965. TR. "Sometimes we wish to discontinue the effect of a sharp or flat, in which case we use a character called *cancel*, made thus: ♮." (Writing.) When a cancel occurs, it shows that a sharp or a flat was previously used, either in the signature or as an accidental, the effect of which is now discontinued or cancelled."

Note 185.—The old-fashioned name of this character "*Natural*" should be discontinued. No doubt many things are better for being old-fashioned, but in the case of this term, the fact of its age and prevalence does not in the least do away with its pernicious tendencies. It is *never used except to cancel the effect of a previous flat or sharp*, hence the new name Cancel is a thousand times better than the old-fashioned term "*Natural*" which does not even hint at its office. Besides, the term *Natural* will always carry with it the idea of something easier or more natural than some other thing with which it is contrasted, for instance, "*B Natural*," as it is so often called, is thought to be in some way more natural than *B flat*, etc.

But the most pernicious influence of the term *Natural* is felt when it is applied to the C key (the *Natural Key* as it is commonly called), and after the teacher has wasted much valuable time in explaining that the term *Natural* is used in its technical sense, he will be met with the assertion that "I can read in the *Natural Key* but can't read in the other keys," thus showing that, owing to the misleading influence of this pernicious term, all keys except the C key are considered *un-natural*, whereas all keys are equally natural, and a child is as like to sing its little song in the C sharp key as in the C key.

Nearly four thousand teachers of music have promised the writer that they will adopt the name Cancel, and judging from their letters, they are among the most intelligent music-teachers of our land.

Some, however, are bothered by the superfluous use of the term, *e.g.*, one superior teacher of the piano says that he likes the term Cancel, and will adopt it, but has difficulty in throwing out the term *Natural*, and asks "What do you say when you wish to tell a pupil to play '*B natural*' instead of '*B flat*?' it sounds badly to say 'Play *B cancel*.'" My reply is that either term is superfluous in such connection. It is like saying "a wet rain," or "a widow woman," rain is always wet and who ever heard of widow who was not a woman? Tell your pupils to play B and teach them that B is as unlike B flat as daylight is unlike darkness.

If teachers would throw out of the nomenclature all ambiguous and useless terms, and substitute correct names, our loved science would soon take its place among the accurate sciences, and its devotees would be accorded a high rank instead of being relegated to the list of insipid, long haired men, and short haired women, as they sometimes are nowadays.

NOTE 186.—A very common use of the cancel should be explained to the class and their attention called to it whenever it occurs, viz., when the cancel is used as an accidental in keys which have sharps for signature, it always *acts as a flat*, as follows:

THE CANCEL ACTS AS A FLAT.

and when it is used as an accidental in keys which have flats for signature, it always *acts as a sharp*, e.g.:

THE CANCEL ACTS AS A SHARP.

Note 187.—Practice exercises which involve the cancel.

Complementary Signatures.

Note 188.—It now becomes necessary to explain Complementary Signatures, which may be done as follows:

§ 966. Tr. "Complementary signatures are those which indicate two different keys that are represented by the same degrees of the staff, as F one flat and F♯ six sharps."

§ 967. Tr. "Sharp signatures always have their complements in flat signatures, and *vice versa*, the united number of signs being *seven*, thus:

Sharps	1	2	3	4	5	6
Flats	6	5	4	3	2	1
	7	7	7	7	7	7

§ 968. Tr. "To find the complement of any given signature, subtract the number of its signs from *seven*, and the remainder (in the opposite kind of signs) will be the desired complement."

§ 969. Tr. "What is the complementary signature of one flat?" Cl. "Six sharps."

Note 189.—The teacher writes the signature of one

flat with all its Do's indicated, and the signature of six
sharps with its Do's thus:

§ 970. Tr. "What is the complementary signature of two flats?" Cl. "Five sharps."

§ 971. Tr. "What is the complementary signature of three flats?" Cl. "Four sharps."

§ 972. Tr. "What is the complementary
signature of four flats?" Cl. "Three sharps."

§ 973. Tr. "What is the complementary signature of five flats?" Cl. "Two sharps."

§ 974. Tr. "What is the complementary signature of six flats?" Cl. "One sharp."

§ 975. Tr. "What is the complementary signature of one sharp?" Cl. "Six flats."

§ 976. Tr. What is the complementary signature of two sharps?" Cl. "Five flats."

§ 977. Tr. "What is the complimentary signature of three sharps?" Cl. "Four flats."

§ 978. Tr. "What is the complementary signature of four sharps?" Cl. "Three flats."

§ 979. Tr. "What is the complementary signature of five sharps?" Cl. "Two flats."

§ 980. Tr. "What is the complementaty signature of six sharps?" Cl. "One flat."

Note 190.—Practical teachers will at once see the usefulness of this with classes—for having once learned to read, for instance, in F (one flat), they can read equally well in F sharp (six sharps). The fact, however, should not be lost sight of, that the two keys involved by complementary signatures are not alike in anything except the representation, and that the doctrine of complementary signatures is only useful while learning to read.

Note 191.—Practice exercises in six sharps, followed by exercises in one flat, explaining D minor in its proper place.

The B Flat Key.

§ 981. Tr. "Sing Do in C key." (They sing, and their pitch is compared with the instrument.)

§ 982. Tr. "Sing it again and call it Re." (Pointing on modulator across to the second column to the left of C column.)

§ 983. Tr. "How far down will you go to get the new Do?" Cl. "A major second."

§ 984. Tr. "Sing the new Do (pointing) and then spell and pronounce a tonic chord from there." (They sing.)

§ 985. Tr. "Sing the scale ascending from this new Do." (They sing.)

Note 192.—While they sing the teacher writes the scale on the board, thus:

§ 986. Tr. "Let us compare this new scale with our model, the C scale. Does Do (pointing) agree or disagree?" Cl. "Disagrees."

§ 987. Tr. "Go to the margin and see what the point of disagreement is. (Pointing to the margin of the modulator.) What is the name of this point of disagreement?" Cl. "B flat."

§ 988. Tr. "We will record it." (Writing a flat on the second line in the signature place.)

Note 193.—The teacher proceeds as in the introduction of the scales of G, D, and F, and then says:

§ 989. Tr. "How many points of disagreement did we find?" Cl. "Two."

§ 990. Tr. "What are the names of the disagreeing points?" Cl. "B flat and E flat."

§ 991. Tr. "These two flats form the signature or sign of the B flat key, and also show that this key differs from the C key, in two points."

§ 992. Tr. "By virtue of this signature (pointing) all degrees which formerly represented B and E now represent B flat and E flat, and all the B flat degrees represent Do.

Note 194.—The teacher writes the Do's thus:

§ 993. Tr. "Turn to No. 167. What is the key?" Cl. "The B flat key."

§ 994. Tr. "How do you know?" Cl. "Signature of two flats."

§ 995. Tr. "Is the piece major or minor?" Cl. "Major."

§ 996. Tr. "How do you know?" Cl. "The first chord is the chord of Do."

Note 195.—The teacher should ask questions as at § 780 to § 789, after which he will proceed thus:

§ 997. Tr. "Do in C key is what tone of B flat key?" (Pointing.) Cl. "Re."

§ 998. Tr. "Sing Do in C key." (They sing.)

§ 999. Tr. "Sing it again and call it Re, and drop down to the new Do." (They sing.)

§ 1000. Tr. "Spell and pronounce a Tonic chord from there." (They sing.)

§ 1001. Tr. "Take your places in the first chord of this piece from lower Do." (They sing.)

Note 196.—Practice exercises in two flats as far as triplets.

Triplets.

Note 197.—The teacher writes a measure of quarter notes, thus:

and requests the class to sing it, after which he says:

§ 1002. Tr. "Listen and beat while I sing the exercise. If I make a mistake, be prepared to say wherein it was wrong."

Note 198.—He sings and divides the first pulse into three equal parts and says:

§ 1003. Tr. "Did I sing the exercise correctly or incorrectly?" Cl. "Incorrectly."

§ 1004. Tr. "Which pulse was wrong?" Cl. "The first pulse."

§ 1005. Tr. "How was it wrong?" Cl. "You sung three Ta's instead of one."

§ 1006. Tr. "Yes, I divided the pulse into three parts, and I wish you to do the same. I will indicate it thus:"

Note 199.—The teacher erases the first quarter note, and writes three eighth notes, and marks them with a figure 3, thus:

§ 1007. Tr. "Is the first pulse single or divided?" Cl. "Divided."

§ 1008. Tr. "Into how many parts is the pulse divided?" Cl. "Three."

§ 1009. Tr. "When a pulse is divided into three equal parts such parts are called *Triplets*. What are they called?" Cl. "Triplets."

§ 1010. Tr. "What are triplets?" Cl. "A pulse divided into three equal parts."

§ 1011. Tr. "When a pulse is divided into two equal parts, such parts are called *Doublets*. What are they called?" Cl. "Doublets."

§ 1012. Tr. "What are Doublets?" Cl. "A pulse divided into two equal parts."

§ 1013. Tr. "Turn to 172. What is the key?" Cl. "B flat."

§ 1014. Tr. "How do you know?" Cl. "Signature is two flats."

§ 1015. Tr. "Is the piece major or minor?" Cl. "It begins in unison, so we can't tell."

§ 1016. Tr. "Look at the last chord. What chord is it?" Cl. "The chord of Do."

§ 1017. Tr. "If the beginning will not decide the mode the final chord usually will. The last chord of this piece being major, we will expect to find it a major tune."

§ 1018. Tr. "Is the first pulse single or divided?" Cl. "Divided."

§ 1019. Tr. "How is it divided?" Cl. "Into triplets."

§ 1020. Tr. "What are triplets?" Cl. "A pulse divided into three equal parts."

Note 200.—Practice exercises involving triplets, after which practice all exercises in two flats, explaining the G minor key at its proper place.

§ 1021. Tr. "What is the complementary signature of two flats?" Cl. "Five sharps."

§ 1022. Tr. "Turn to No. 174. What is the key?" Cl. "The B key."

§ 1023. Tr. "How do you know?" Cl. "Signature of five sharps."

§ 1024. Tr. "All the B degrees represent Do. You will read the notes exactly as you did in two flats."

Note 201.—Practice all exercises in five sharps.

The E Flat Key.

§ 1025. Tr. "Sing Do in C key, our old friend." (They sing.)

§ 1026. Tr. "Sing it again and call it La." (Pointing on modulator across to the third column on the left of C column.)

§ 1027. Tr. "Sing as I point." (Pointing to La Ti Do in E flat column.)

§ 1028. Tr. "Sing a scale ascending from this new Do."

Note 202.—While they sing the teacher writes the scale thus:

§ 1029. Tr. "Let us compare this new scale with our model, the C scale. Does Do (pointing) agree or disagree?" Cl. "Disagrees."

§ 1030. Tr. "What is the name of the disagreeing point?" (Pointing to the margin.) Cl. "E flat."

§ 1031. Tr. "Let us record it." (Writes a ♭ on fourth space in signature place, being careful to leave room for another ♭ between it and the clef.)

Note 203.—The teacher proceeds as in the introduction of the scales G, D, F, and B flat, and says:

§ 1032. Tr. "How many points of disagreement have we found?" Cl. "Three."

§ 1033. Tr. "What are the names of the disagreeing points?" (Pointing to the signature on the board.) CL. "B flat, E flat, and A flat."

§ 1034. TR. "These three flats (pointing) form the signature of the E flat key, and also show that this key differs from the C key in three points."

§ 1035. TR. "By virtue of this signature (pointing) all degrees which formerly represented E, now represent E flat, and notes on these degrees will represent Do."

NOTE 204.—The teacher adds the Bass staff to the exercise already on the board and writes the Do's, when the whole will appear thus:

§ 1036. TR. "Turn to No. 176. What is the key?" CL. "E flat."

§ 1037. TR. "How do you know?" CL. "Signature of three flats."

§ 1038. TR. "In what variety of measure is it written?" CL. "Quadruple measure."

§ 1039. TR. "What is the first syllable?" CL. "Do."

NOTE 205.—The preliminary questions should follow as at § 780 to § 789, after which proceed as follows:

§ 1040. TR. "The tone Do in the C key is what tone in the E flat key?" (Pointing across to the third column to the left of C column.) CL. " La."

§ 1041. TR. "Sing Do in C key." (They sing.)

§ 1042. TR. "Sing it again and call it La, and ascend to the new Do." (They sing.)

§ 1043. TR. "Spell and pronounce a tonic chord from there." (They sing.)

§ 1044. TR. "Go from Do to your several places in the first chord of this piece." (They sing.)

NOTE 206.—Practice exercises in E flat major and C minor.

CHANTING.

NOTE. 207.—The correct style of chanting differs so broadly from what is usually accepted as chanting throughout our country, even in our metropolitan churches, that a few words in explanation of the priniples which underlie this arm of the church service seem necessary.

First. Chanting *is not singing*, and should not be confounded with singing. Chanting is *speaking in tune*, while singing is the art of prolonging vowels according to a given notation.

Second. Notes have no rhythmic value in a chant. The chanting tone is continued until certain words are spoken, and its continuance depends entirely upon the number of words to be spoken. Thus far there is little or no difference of opinion; it is when we come to the cadences that we hear the dreadful prolonging of tones which takes the performance out of the realm of chanting and carries it into the most disagreeable form of *singing*, by drawing the tones out to an interminable length. Another bad and exceedingly objectionable feature of chanting as it is usually performed is that of prolonging the last emphatic syllable before a cadence. It is illogical and disagreeable, and while it is *very prevalent* it is not less unpleasant on that account.

Correct chanting consists of a deliberate and steady speaking of the words of the chanting-tone, about as rapidly as a good reader would read them, without undue haste, but especially without dragging, and the cadences only slightly slower, and somewhat measured.

In introducing this subject to a class the teacher should select some simple chant and, having committed both tones and words, should have the class learn the music by syllables, then request them to close their books and listen and imitate him. After chanting it through in good style he begins at the commencement and chants the first sentence, and the class imitate him, then the second sentence, etc., going back frequently to connect two or more sentences, and so on through to the end. This practice should be continued until the principles of chanting are thoroughly established, when they will be able to perform any simple chant at sight.

The teacher should insist upon all starting together, and that all should come together at the punctuation marks. These two points are most important, and large bodies of singers, or even large congregations, may chant well if these suggestions are carried out by the leader.

Frequently chants will be found which are made up of chanting and singing alternately, in which case the parts which are rhythmical should be sung as usual, but the chanting parts *should not be sung,* speak them in tune.

Note 208.—Practice the exercises in chanting, also the remaining exercises in three flats, introducing the C minor key in its proper place.

The E Key.

§ 1045. Tr. "What is the complementary signature of three flats?" Cl. "Four sharps."

§ 1046. Tr. "Turn to No. 186. What is the key?" Cl. "E key."

§ 1047. Tr. "How do you know?" Cl. "Signature four sharps."

§ 1048 Tr. "All E degrees represent Do. You read the notes exactly as you did in three flats."

Note 209.—Practice all exercises in four sharps.

The A Flat Key.

§ 1049. Tr. "Sing Do in C key, our old Do." (They sing, and their pitch compared with the instrument.)

§ 1050. Tr. "Sing it again and call it Mi." (Pointing across to fourth column to the left of the C column.)

§ 1051. Tr. "Sing as I point." (Pointing to Mi Fa Sol La Ti Do in that column.)

§ 1052. Tr. "What is the name of this scale?" (Pointing from Do across to the left-hand margin.) Cl. "A flat."

§ 1053. Tr. "Let us compare this scale with our model, the C scale."

Note 210.—The teacher proceeds as in the introduction of the other scales, ascertaining what the differences are, and recording them for a signature of the A flat key.

Note 211.—Practice No. 188, after asking the preliminary questions as at § 778 to § 789.

§ 1054. Tr. "Sing Do in C key." (They sing.)

§ 1055. Tr. "Sing it again and call it Mi. Pointing across to the A flat column.) Ascend to the new Do, and spell and pronounce the tonic chord." (They sing.)

Dal Segno ('D. S.).

§ 1056 Tr. "When we wish to repeat a portion of a composition which is not designated by a double-bar or other general division, a sign (:§:) is placed at the beginning of the portion to be repeated, and at the end of the portion to be repeated are the letters D. S., which stand for the Italian words Dal Segno (pronounced *dähl-sayn'-yō*), and which, translated literally, mean *Dal* from the, *segno* sign—*repeat from the sign.*"

Note 212.—Practice all exercises which involve *Dal segno*, and follow with all exercises in four flats. The complementary signature of four flats (three sharps) may be introduced, following the order previously given, with all exercises in that key.

The D Flat Key.

Note 213.—The signature of five flats can best be introduced as complementary of two sharps. It is advisable to review a few exercises in two sharps and then introduce the five flat key as complementary, following the order already given, viz., compare it with the C key, the record of the differences becoming the signature.

Before practicing No. 195, the teacher should explain double flats.

Double Flats.

§ 1057. Tr. "Whenever a diatonic tone is represented by a degree which is flatted by the signature, and we wish to flat that diatonic degree, we indicate it by a character called a *Double flat*, thus : (Writing.)

Here La is B flat, so if we wish flat La (Le) we must still further flat the La degree a half-step, which is done by means of the *double flat*."

The Cancel-Flat.

§ 1058. Tr. "Whenever we wish to discontinue the effect of a *double flat*, and restore the degree to its diatonic condition, we indicate it by a character called a *Cancel flat*, thus :" (Writing.)

Note 214.—Practice exercises involving the Double flat and the Cancel flat together with all exercises in five flats.

The Key of G Flat.

Note 215.—The signature of six flats can best be introduced as complementary of *one sharp*. The teacher is advised to review a few of the exercises in one sharp, and then introduce this key of six flats as complementary, following the order previously given, the differences between it and the model C key forming the new signature.

Note 216.—It will be observed that the keys of five flats and six flats could not have followed the introduction of the keys of One sharp and Two sharps, although they are complementary, for the reason that at that stage of progress *flats* had not been mentioned.

Practice exercises in G flat key.

END OF JUNIOR GRADE.

PALMER'S CLASS METHOD.

SENIOR GRADE.

Note 217.—Throughout the Senior Grade every piece should be practiced by syllables until all its tones are sung in time and in tune, and all modulations well understood. Less haste will bring greater speed, for every piece which is well learned imparts an added strength to the learner, which will be of great assistance in overcoming the obstacles of all future efforts.

Note 218.—The writer is of the opinion that the entire Grade should first be sung by syllables, all being obliged to beat, then return and apply the words, with expression, etc. There is great danger in abandoning syllables and beating too soon, as all are apt to blunder through once, and, with quick ears, catch their several parts by rote, and sing very well the second time, thus passing for readers, whereas, if left to their own powers, unsustained by an instrument, they would make sorry work of reading.

Note 219.—When the syllable names are thoroughly impressed upon the mind as names of *tone-relations*, the learner has progressed a long way toward an intelligent knowledge of tone-combinations, without which no one can be called a good reader, for a good reader should always know what relation the tone which he is singing sustains to the Tonic. Two terms of lessons cannot be called a long time to be confined to the practice of syllables and beating, if, in those two terms, the pupils shall have acquired a perfect knowledge of tone-relationships.

Note 220.—In all cases in this grade (as in the junior grade) the study should be without instrumental accompaniment, the teacher merely giving them the pitch C, and obliging the class to go from that pitch to their Tonic, spell the tonic chord and at once spread out to their several pitches in the first chord of the piece they are about to study; and after going through with the piece once or twice, require them to spell and pronounce the Tonic Chord then compare the pitch with the correct tone on the instrument, thus clearly showing any deviation from pitch while studying. This plan, persistently adhered to in the study of every piece, will have a telling effect upon the intelligence of the singers, the almost immediate results of which will be extremely satisfactory.

Note 221.—The first few minutes of each lesson should be spent in Practicing Scales and Chords. The following plan may be of use to teachers:

1st. Call on the class to sing Do. (pitch C, compare their pitch with the instrument.)

2nd. The Diatonic Major Scale ascending and descending.

3rd. The Diatonic Minor Scale (Harmonic) from same pitch, up and down.

4th. The Melodic Minor up and down (always starting on C.)

5th. Up with major and down with harmonic minor.

6th. Up with harmonic minor and down with major.

7th. Up with major, down with melodic minor.

8th. Up with melodic minor and down with major.

9th. Up with harmonic minor and down with melodic minor.

10th. Up with the melodic minor and down with harmonic minor.

11th. Spell and pronounce the Tonic Chord, it should be spelled both forward and backward.

12th. Spell and pronounce the Super-Tonic Chord, spell it both forward and backward.

13th. Spell and pronounce the Mediant Chord, spell it both forward and backward.

14th. Spell and pronounce the Sub-Dominant Chord, spell it both forward and backward.

15th. Spell and pronounce the Dominant Chord, spell it both forward and backward.

16th. Spell and pronounce the Dominant Chord in the lower octave, spell both forward and backward.

17th. Spell and pronounce the Sub-Mediant Chord in the lower octave, spell both forward and backward.

18th. Spell and pronounce the Sub-Tonic Chord (resolving it into the Tonic Chord).

19th. Spell, pronounce and resolve the Dominant 7th chord, major. (In the F key.)

20th. The same spelled backward.

21st. Spell and pronounce the Dominant 7th of the minor key (mi, sil, ti, re) resolving it into the minor Tonic.

22d. Again spell, pronounce and resolve the major Dom. 7th. (These dominant 7th chords should always begin with the pitch C, as Sol.)

23d. Spell, pronounce and resolve the Diminished 7th chord after its introduction at §§ 1209 to 1212 inclusive, (always spelling it backward, fa, re, ti, sil). At first this Diminished 7th chord should follow the Dominant 7th chord; its tones being the same (with one exception), it will be much more easily comprehended.

The practice of the above schedule will require only about 8 minutes, and should be strictly adhered to at the opening of each lesson. After which—

24th. Turn to Exercises in Rhythmics, page 106, and sing Nos. 257, 258 and 259; omit No. 260 until Syncopation has been explained (See § 1281 to Note 339 inclusive). At each lesson begin with No. 257 and add one new number. After having practiced all the numbers on this page, (which will be at about the eighth or ninth lesson) :—

25th. Turn to the Cadences, page 107, and sing three or four numbers each lesson until all are familiar with them. (For the best way to introduce the study of these cadences, see Notes 481 to 486 inclusive.)

Thus the first 16 or 20 minutes of each lesson will be spent in the most profitable manner possible.

NOTE 222.—The first few lessons of this Senior grade should be devoted to a rapid review of all the work which has been gone over in the Junior grade, begining with No. 66, page 19 ; read by syllables after asking the preliminary questions as follows :

§ 1059. TR. "In what key is this piece written?" CL. "The C key."

§ 1060. TR. "How do you know?" CL. "Because the clef stands without flats or sharps." or "Because it has no signature."

§ 1061. TR. "When there is no signature, what keys have we?" CL. The C major key, and the A minor key."

§ 1062. TR. "What pitches form the C major key?" CL. "C D E F G A and B."

§ 1063. TR. "What pitches form the A minor key ?" CL. "A B C D E F and G♯."

NOTE 223.—The Harmonic form of the minor will be given unless the Melodic form is especially mentioned.

§ 1064. TR. "What kind of measure is this piece written in ?" CL. "Quadruple measure."

§ 1065. TR. "How do you know?" CL. "The numerator of the fraction is 4."

§ 1066. TR. "What is the beat-note?" CL. "A quarter note."

§ 1067. TR. "How do you know?" CL. "The denominator of the fraction is 4."

§ 1068. Tr. "Read the fraction." Cl. "Four quarter notes will fill a measure."

Note 224.—The above ten questions should precede the study of each piece during the first and second review lessons.

Note 225.—Go thoroughly over the entire Junior grade practicing each number once only, unless some great blunder is made. Call attention to each new point by way of refreshing their memories, and dash along as rapidly as possible.

Note 226.—Two or three times during each lesson, the teacher should go to the other end of the room while they are singing an exercise, so as not to lose (any time) and, standing on a chair or bench, request the class to rise, face him, and repeat the exercise, or ing the next exercise. In this way he can keep in touch with those in the rear seats. He should return to the platform while they are singing.

Note 227.—Until the Junior work has been thoroughly reviewed, the class should be kept singing the syllables Do Re Mi etc. and beating, for they cannot be merely guessing so long as they give the correct syllable and the correct beat.

Note 228.—An excellent plan is to frequently practice reading a piece by letter names.

Note 229.—A thorough review of the Junior grade will occupy the first five or six lessons.

Remark 2.—If the teacher prefers, he may review only the pieces in the Junior grade which serve to introduce a key, and then turn at once to the more difficult exercises in the Senior grade, thus doing review work together with the Senior work at each lesson. If this plan is followed the teacher should be guided by the Notes which precede each new key in the Senior grade, as for instance, on page 83, preceding exercise No. 225, the suggestion for the review work is as follows:— "Note —— Before studying the three following pages, review all the four part pieces on pages 19 to 34 inclusive." These suggestions are so explicit that the teacher cannot go far astray so long as he follows the course thus mapped out for him.

It remains for us to indicate the best way of introducing the more advanced points, which we will now proceed to do.

CLEFS AND THEIR SIGNIFICANCE.

NOTE 230.—The teacher explains that the G clef is so called, not because it fixes G somewhere, but because it fixes MIDDLE C somewhere, hence a better name would be "Treble clef" or "Violin clef."

§ 1069. TR. "When the Treble or G clef is used, the pitches are so arranged that MIDDLE C is represented by the first added line below, thus:"— (writes)

§ 1070. TR. "What is the name of the pitch thus represented?" (pointing.) CL. "C."

§ 1071. TR "What particular C?" CL. "MIDDLE C."

§ 1072. TR. "Hereafter, when we speak of this pitch we will call it MIDDLE C. It is the tone which lies in the middle of the great vocal and instrumental compass."

§ 1073. TR. "Ladies sing MIDDLE C." (pointing to the note on the board. They sing and their pitch is compared with the instrument.)

§ 1074. TR. "Are the most of your tones above MIDDLE C, or below?" CL. "Above."

§ 1075. Tr. "You will observe that all the degrees of the staff are above Middle C, thus making it easy to represent your tones."

§ 1076. Tr. "Basses sing Middle C." (pointing to the board.)

Note 231.—Most will sing an octave too low. They can be brought to the correct pitch as follows:

§ 1077. Tr. "Does this note (pointing) indicate your lower Do, or your upper Do?" Cl. "Upper Do."

§ 1078. Tr. "Sing your lower Do, and go up through the Tonic chord to your upper Do." (They sing).

§ 1079. Tr. "Are the most of your tones below Middle C, or above?" Cl. "Below."

§ 1080. Tr. "We must, then, arrange the staff so as to bring all its degrees below Middle C. This is done by the Bass clef thus:— (writing)

which makes it easy to represent your tones."

§ 1081. Tr. "Tenors sing Middle C." (They sing.)

§ 1082. Tr. "Do you frequently sing below Middle C?" Cl. "We do."

§ 1083. Tr. "Do you frequently sing above Middle C?" Cl. "We do."

§ 1084. Tr. "Then the degrees should be so arranged as to bring Middle C nearly in the middle of the staff; this is done by the Tenor clef, thus :—(writing)

so that the tones of your voices may be represented easily, whether above MIDDLE C or below."

§ 1085. TR. "Ladies sing as I point." (pointing to the first example on the board, and they sing).

§ 1086. TR. "What tone did you sing?" CL. "MIDDLE C."

§ 1087. TR. "Gentlemen sing as I point." (points to the second example, and they sing).

§ 1088. TR. "What tone did you sing?" CL. "MIDDLE C."

§ 1089. TR. "All sing as I point." (points to the third example, then to either indiscriminately, and they sing).

NOTE 232.—The class should now be asked to name the degrees of each of the three staffs, up and down from MIDDLE C until all are familiar with the pitch names of the degrees, and should hereafter read each new exercise by letter before singing it.

---

*This new and beautiful Tenor clef was invented for, and was first used in THE PALMER-CURTIS SERIES OF MUSIC READERS FOR SCHOOLS, issued by the publishers of the CLASS METHOD. It was just too late to be incorporated among the many good features of GRADED STUDIES, and is mentioned in the present work with the desire that it may be generally adopted. It will not be copyrighted, so all may use it at pleasure, but it is hoped that credit will be given to the Palmer-Curtis Series, for its first use. All will at once concede its superiority over other forms of the Tenor clef; the T being the initial of the word "Tenor" and the C having a double meaning, 1st, as the initial of the word "clef," and 2d, being the letter whose name is given to the pitch represented by that degree.

Major and Minor Thirds.

§ 1090. Tr. " The second, Do Re (pointing on C column of the modulator) is what kind of a second?" Cl. " A major second."

§ 1091. Tr. "The second, Re Mi is what kind of a second?" Cl. "A major second."

§ 1092. Tr. "The third, Do Mi consists of how many and what kind of seconds?" Cl. "Two major seconds."

§ 1093. Tr. "Look at the third, Me Sol, of how many and what kind of seconds does it consist?" Cl. "One major second and one minor second."

§ 1094. Tr. "Is the third, Do Mi larger or smaller than the third, Mi Sol?" Cl. "Larger."

§ 1095. Tr. " A large third is called a MAJOR THIRD, what is it called?" Cl. "A major third."

§ 1096. Tr. "A small third is called a MINOR THIRD, what is it called?" Cl. "A minor third."

§ 1097. Tr. "Let us now examine the thirds in the chord of Do. You will observe that the chord consists of two thirds, one above the other (pointing), what kind of a third is the lower third?" Cl. "A major third."

§ 1098. Tr. "What kind of a third is the upper third?" Cl. "A minor third."

§ 1099. Tr. "This is a rule, viz: If the lower third of a chord be a major third, the upper third will be a minor third."

§ 1100. Tr. "Let us now examine the chord

of Re (pointing on the modulator), is the lower third major or minor?" CL. "Minor."

§ 1101. TR. "What kind of a third is the upper third?" CL. "A major third."

§ 1102. TR. "This is also a rule, viz: If the lower third be minor, the upper third will be major."

MAJOR AND MINOR CHORDS.

§ 1103. TR. "As regards their character, chords are named from their lower thirds: if the lower third of a chord be major, the chord is a MAJOR CHORD, and if its lower third be minor, the chord is a MINOR CHORD."

§ 1104. TR. "What kind of a chord is the chord of Do?" (pointing to the lower third). CL. "A major chord."

§ 1105. TR. "How do you know?" CL. "Because its lower third is major."

§ 1106. TR. "What kind of a chord is the chord of Re?" (pointing to the lower third). CL. "A minor chord."

§ 1107. TR. "Why?" CL. "Because its lower third is minor."

§ 1108. TR. "What kind of a chord is the chord of Mi?" (pointing to the lower third). CL. "A minor chord."

§ 1109. TR. "What kind of a chord is the chord of Fa?" (pointing to the lower third). CL. "A major chord."

§ 1110. TR. "What kind of a chord is the chord of Sol?" (pointing to the lower third). CL. "A major chord."

§ 1111. Tr. "What kind of a chord is the chord of La?" (pointing to the lower third). Cl. "A minor chord."

§ 1112. Tr. "Let us now examine the chord of Ti; its lower third is what kind of a third?" Cl. "A minor third."

§ 1113. Tr. "According to our rule, its upper third should be a major third: what kind of a third is it?" (pointing). Cl. "A minor third."

§ 1114. Tr. "Here then we find an exception to our rule. The chord of Ti consists of two minor thirds. This peculiarity necessitates a peculiar name for this chord."

§ 1115. Tr. "Thus far we have named our chords from their thirds, but as the thirds of the chord of Ti are not different from the minor thirds of other chords, it is evident that we cannot name it from its thirds."

Perfect Fifths and Diminished Fifths.

§ 1116. Tr. "Let us now examine the fifths of all the chords; perhaps we may find some peculiarity in them which we may adopt to distinguish this chord from the others."

§ 1117. Tr. "Look at the fifth, Do Sol, (pointing), of how many and what kind of thirds does it consist?" Cl. "Two, a major third and a minor third."

§ 1118. Tr. "A fifth which consists of one major third and one minor third is a Perfect Fifth."

§ 1119. Tr. "What kind of a fifth is Do Sol?" (pointing). Cl. "A perfect fifth."

§ 1120. Tr. "How do you know?" Cl. "Because it consists of a major third and a minor third."

§ 1121. Tr. "What kind of a fifth is Re La?" (pointing). Cl. "A perfect fifth."

§ 1122. Tr. "Yes, it makes no difference which third is higher, or which is lower, the fifth is the same."

§ 1123. Tr. "What kind of a fifth is Mi Ti?" (pointing). Cl. "A perfect fifth."

§ 1124. Tr. "What kind of a fifth is Fa Do?" (pointing). Cl. "A perfect fifth."

§ 1125. Tr. "What kind of a fifth is Sol Re?" (pointing). Cl. "A perfect fifth."

§ 1126. Tr. "What kind of a fifth is La Mi?" (pointing). Cl. "A perfect fifth."

§ 1127. Tr. "Let us now examine the fifth, Ti Fa. (pointing.) It consists of how many and what kind of thirds?" Cl. "Two minor thirds."

§ 1128. Tr. "A perfect fifth consists of how many and what kind of thirds?" Cl. "Two, a major third and a minor third."

§ 1129. Tr. "Is the fifth Ti Fa, smaller or larger than a perfect fifth?" Cl. "Smaller."

§ 1130. Tr. "How much smaller?" Cl. "A half-step smaller."

§ 1131. Tr. "A fifth which is a half-step smaller than a perfect fifth is called a Diminished fifth, what is it called?" Cl. A "diminished fifth."

§ 1132. TR. "We can now give a name to the chord of Ti; the only difference between it and the other chords is in its diminished fifth, hence we will call it a DIMINISHED CHORD. What is it called?" CL. "A diminished chord."

§ 1133. TR. "How many kinds of three-fold chords have we found?" CL. "Three."

§ 1134. TR. "What are they called?" CL. "Major chords, minor chords and diminished chords."

NOTE 233.—The following order of practicing thirds is recommended.

MANNER OF PRACTICING THIRDS.

§ 1135. TR. "This is Do, (any convenient pitch, the pitch A will be good), sing a major third up and back." (They sing Do—Mi, Mi—Do.)

§ 1136. TR. "This is Fa, (same pitch as their last Do), sing a major third up and back, and end by singing Mi." (They sing Fa—La, La—Fa, Mi.)

§ 1137. TR. "This is Sol, (starting at the same pitch as the others), sing a major third up and back and then sing Do." (They sing Sol—Ti, Ti—Sol, and end with upper Do.)

§ 1138. TR. "This is Re, sing a minor third up and back and end with Do." (They sing Re—Fa, Fa—Re, Do.)

§ 1139. TR. "This is Mi, sing a minor third up and back and then sing Do." (They sing Mi—Sol, Sol—Mi, Do.)

§ 1140. Tʀ. "This is La, sing a minor third up and back and end with Do." (They sing La—Do, Do—La, Do.)

§ 1141. Tʀ. "This is Ti, sing a minor third up and back and then sing Do." (They sing Ti—Re, Re—Ti, Do.)

Nᴏᴛᴇ 234.—The teacher should frequently reverse this order of practicing, *e. g.* Tʀ. "This is Ti, sing a major third down and up, and then sing Do." (They sing Ti—Sol, Sol—Ti, Do,) etc., through all the thirds used above. Too much importance cannot be attached to this feature, as all progress and musical development depend upon a thorough knowledge of tone relationship, and in no way can these be better gained than by this work on intervals.

Nᴏᴛᴇ 235.—Many good teachers still follow the old plan of *speaking* of tones by their *numeral* names; why? There is not one good reason why tones should not be called by their syllable names, both in speaking and singing, and many reasons why they should be so called. I was taught the old way, and have squandered much valuable time in trying to compel pupils to "always *speak* of tones by their numeral names." I now throw the numeral names overboard after the syllables are once learned. Syllable names are especially powerful in teaching harmony. I always failed to satisfy myself in explaining the augmented 6th chords, until I adopted the plan of calling the tones by their syllable names. Now when I tell a class that the tones Le-double-do-fi always form the the Italian 6th chord, and that Le-do-ri-fi always form the American 6th chord, and that Fa-la-do-ri always form the German 6th chord (minor), they not only know the key these chords are in but they also know their resolutions. Teachers who prefer to use numeral names in *speaking* of tones will simply substitute them for the syllable names, being careful, however, that the pupils never sing tones by numeral names.

Note 236.—The teacher should form the habit of never giving the class the pitch until they have tried to get it without help. If this plan is persistently followed, they will soon be able to sing the "old Do" (pitch C) perfectly. Observe also that we always go from the "old Do" to each new Do. If this plan is carried out through the lower grades, the pupils will be able, when they arrive at the higher grades, to give the correct pitch of any key without help. This *seems* impossible to those who have never seen it tried, but it has been done in hundreds of cases, so there is no further doubt about it. The writer's adult classes, when first called to order, are requested to " spell and pronounce the Tonic chord in the E Flat Key," (or any other key), and, without the least hesitation, they give the correct pitch of the key called for. Their mental process is to take the pitch C, which they are perfectly sure of, call it " La," and ascend to Do in E Flat, and spell and pronounce the Tonic chord.

For explanation in detail, see page 200.

Note 237.—The different parts should always get their proper pitch in the first chord from Do—singing through the Tonic chord to their several places. This serves two important ends, viz. : 1st, The voices are brought into *tune* quickly and effectively; and, 2nd, it is a continual reminder that the Tonic governs everything tonal.

Remark 3.—An important change has been adopted in the present work, for which we would respectfully and earnestly ask the aid of all thinking teachers, viz: the change of the name of sharp Sol from Si to Sil (Seel). It is an ugly fact that we have permitted three different things to be called by the same name, the letter name of a certain pitch (C), seven of the major scale (Si), and sharp Sol (Si). By almost universal consent Si, seven of the major key, has been changed to Ti, which has done much to rid us of the difficulty, but two different things are still called by the same name, which is an abomination in any exact science. With the proposed change the difficulty wholly disappears, and teachers can speak of sharp Sol (Seel) without fearing it will be confounded with C. It was formerly most confusing when speaking of the minor dominant 7th chord, for instance, to call its tones Mi-si-si-re. Some may object that the two l's coming together (Sil-la) make it a little difficult to prononnce, but this difficulty vanishes under the rule for pronunciation which tells us that when a word ends with a consonant, and the next word begins with the same consonant, one utterance of the mutual conso·nant sufficies for both words, as in "let *us sing*," one s does for both *us* and *sing;* or in *with thee,* one vocal lisping *th* is sufficent for both words; so with *sil-la* one l only is required to be sounded.

The Minor Scale, Melodic Form.

§ 1142. Tr. "The form of the minor scale which we have studied thus far is called the HARMONIC FORM ; it ascends and descends with the same order of intervals. We have another minor form which ascends with one order of intervals and descends with another order. Listen."

NOTE 238.—The teacher sings thus:

and the class imitates him.

§ 1143. Tr. " Again listen and imitate."

NOTE 239.—The teacher sings slowly and distinctly as follows :

The pupils will get these tones in their minds better by singing them with the following syllables:

The teacher sings Do Re Mi Fa and the class imitates him, then Mi Fi Sil La, same pitches, they singing after him; then Sol La Ti Do, same pitches, they repeating, then Mi Fi Sil La, they imitating in quick succession. The teacher holds his left hand before the class with the fingers so separated as to show equal distances between the second and third, and fourth and third, thus:

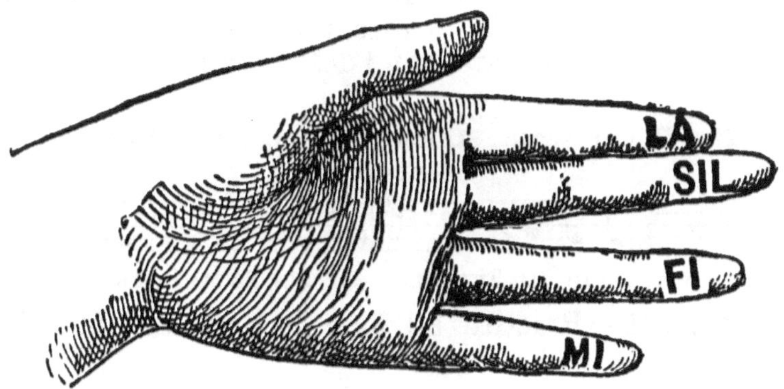

As the teacher sings these highest four syllables he points with the index finger of the right hand to the fingers of the left hand, the class singing after him, until he has established the relative pitches of these four tones in the minds of the class, after which he sings the scale from La to La, thus:

the class singing after him. He should show on the
Modulator that the second, Mi Fi, is a major second
and that the second, Fi Sil, is a major second. He explains that this scale differs from the Harmonic scale
in that the awkward *augmented second* is done away
with, thus making this scale more melodious, hence
it is called the MELODIC FORM of the minor scale.

NOTE 240.—After practicing the ascending scale
many times, especially the highest four tones, the
teacher should explain that this scale descends with
a different order of intervals, and sings, thus:

emphasizing *sol* particularly. After practicing this
descending scale a few times, the teacher writes the
Melodic Form ascending and descending on the board,
thus:

**The Minor Scale, Melodic Form, Ascending and
Descending.**

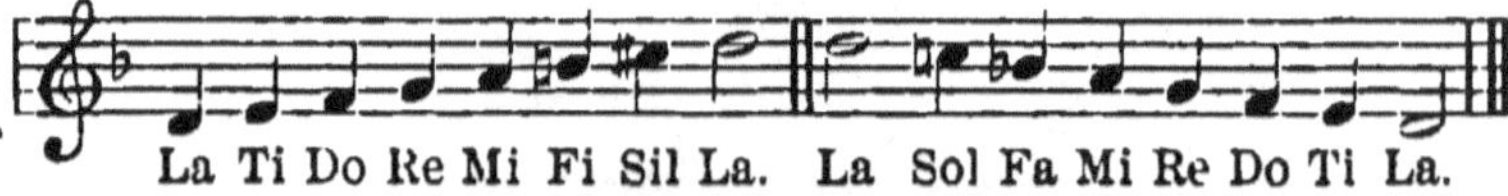

NOTE 241.—Practice all exercises in the Melodic
form.

MIXED SCALES.

NOTE 242.—An excellent practice is to mix the
scales; *e. g.*, taking the pitch D, sing the major scale
up and down; the minor scale, harmonic form, up
and down (same pitch); the minor scale, melodic
form, up and down (same pitch); the major up and

the harmonic down ; the harmonic up and the major down ; the major up and the melodic down ; the melodic up and the major down ; the harmonic up and the melodic down ; the melodic up and the harmonic down. A few minutes spent in this practice at each lesson will impart to pupils a correct idea of a subject which has been unfortunately mystified by a popular piano instruction book, published upwards of thirty years ago, in which the minor scales were *mixed* for the purpose of saving space, but without mentioning that they were mixed; thus page after page of exercises for daily practice consists of the melodic up and the harmonic down, until many good teachers throughout our country have come to regard these *mixtures* as "*the real minor scale.*"

NOTE 243.—All exercises may first be read (not sung) by letter names, then sung by syllables, then with words.

NOTE 244.—The teacher should require the class to give the letter names of the pitches which form the several major and minor keys, thus:

THE C MAJOR KEY AND ITS RELATIVE, A MINOR.

§ 1144. TR. "What pitches form the C major key?" CL. "C, D, E, F, G, A and B."

REMARK 4.—It may be well to state here, that a key really consists of all the tones which the ear can detect, having a certain fixed relation to each other; for example, all possible tones whose names are C, D, E, F, G, A and B with their intermediates constitute the key of C. The key may be manifested, however, by the seven tones.

NOTE 245.—The teacher rests the pointer on the syllable and tells the pupils to glance across to the margin of the Modulator and give the letter name of the pitch, and thus proceeds slowly from Do to Do.

Note 246.—The teacher writes the scale in C major on the board with syllables and letters, thus:

The Scale in C Major.

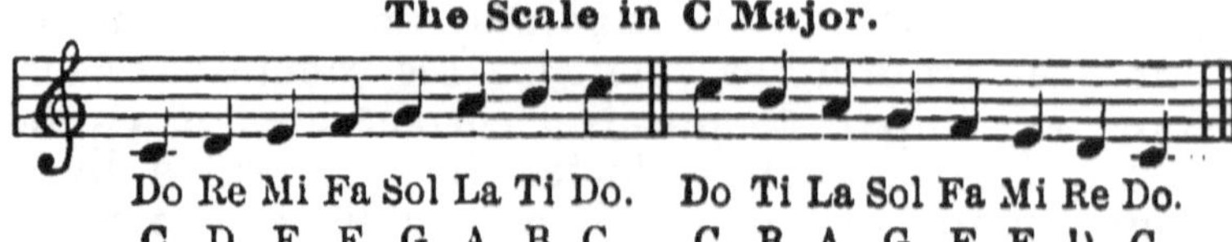

and after a thorough drill proceeds to the relative minor as follows.

§ 1145. Tr. "What is the relative minor key of C major?" (pointing to La in the C column of Modulator while the pupils glance across to the margin.) Cl. "A minor."

§ 1146. Tr. "Name the pitches of the A minor key, harmonic form." Cl. "A, B, C, D, E, F and G♯."

Note 247.—The teacher writes the scale in A minor, harmonic form, on the board, thus:

The Scale in A Minor, Harmonic Form.

§ 1147. Tr. "Name the pitches of the A minor key, melodic form, ascending." Cl. "A B C D E F♯ and G♯."

§ 1148. Tr. "Name the pitches of the A minor key, melodic form, descending." Cl. "A G F E D C B A."

Note 248.—The teacher writes the scale in A minor, melodic form, thus:

The Scale in A Minor, Melodic Form.

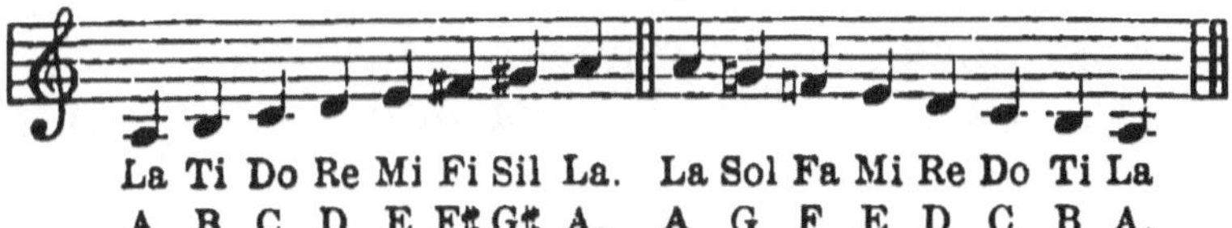

NOTE 249.—The teacher should not fall into the error of calling this the *Melodic Minor Key;* there is no such key. The avoidance of the augmented second between 6 and 7, by "raising 6," gave rise to the "Melodic Minor Scale." But the law which provides that all dominant chords shall have major thirds, and thus fixes 7 of the minor key a half-step below 8, is no more binding than the law which says that the sub-dominant chord of a minor key shall always have a minor third, and so establishes the interval of an augmented second from 6 to 7. It is absolutely impossible to harmonize the melodic form in any acceptable manner; and while all the classical composers frequently gave that form in melodic passages, they invariably wrote the sub-dominant chord with a minor third. Most of the old theorists pass over this striking inconsistency in silence; probably recognizing the fact that any attempt to reconcile such palpable contradictions would be utterly useless. Richter says that "The sixth degree of the minor scale (key) is not capable, *in a harmonic sense*, of any such chromatic alteration;" also, that the sub-dominant chord with a major third, (in the minor key,) "cannot be conceived of." In other words, we have but one minor *key*, that which is known as the *Harmonic Minor* (the order of intervals of which is given at ¶¶ 796 to 804 inclusive; and while we frequently form a *scale*, called the Melodic Minor, there *never was a Melodic Minor Key.* Whenever such passages occur, they can easily be accounted for as passing tones or appoggiaturas.

See remark on page 68 of Palmer's Theory of Music, published by the John Church Co., Cincinnati, Ohio, price $1.

§ 1149. Tr. "How are the C major and A minor keys distinguished from the other keys?" Cl. "By the clef and the absence of flats or sharps."

Note 250.—The teacher should remember that *signature* is defined by Webster as "The designation of the key (when not C major or A minor) by means of one or more sharps or flats immediately after the clef," so without flats or sharps at the beginning there is no signature, and the facts prove this idea to be correct; *e. g.*, the G key differs from the C key in a single point, namely F sharp, and this difference is recorded near the clef at the beginning, and such record (one sharp), together with the clef, becomes the sign or signature of the G key; and while it is not necessary for pupils in sight-reading to know more than that a given signature shows that Do is in a certain position, the scientific fact remains that a signature is simply a record, showing which tones in a given key are not diatonic in the C key.

Note 251.—The pupils should be drilled on these keys and scales, until they are thoroughly understood.

The G Major Key, and its Relative, E Minor.

§ 1150. Tr. "What pitches form the G major key?" Cl. "G A B C D E and F♯."

Note 252.—The teacher writes the scale in G major on the board with syllables and letters, thus:

The Scale in G Major.

and after a thorough drill introduces the relative minor, as follows:—

§ 1151. Tr. "What is the relative minor key of G major?" (pointing to La in the G column of the Modulator, while the pupils glance across to the margin.) Cl. "E Minor."

§ 1152. Tr. "Name the pitches of the E minor key, harmonic form." Cl. "E, F♯, G, A, B, C and D♯."

Note 253.—The scale in E minor, harmonic form, should be written on the board, thus:

Scale in E Minor, Harmonic Form.

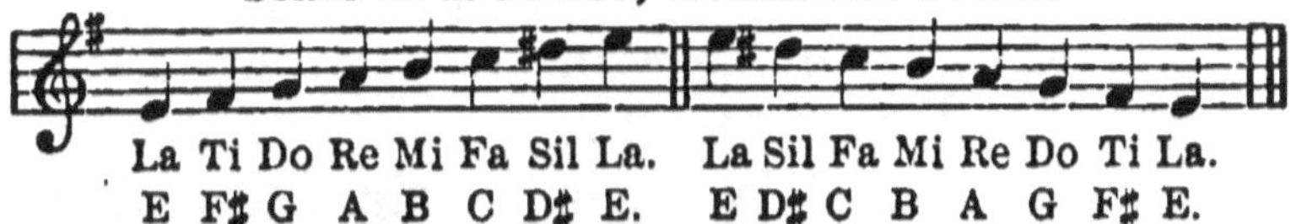

After thorough drill introduce the melodic form, thus:

§ 1153. Tr. "What pitches form the E minor key, melodic form, ascending?" (pointing slowly to the syllables in G column of Modulator, while the pupils glance across to the margin and give the letter names.) Cl. "E, F♯, G, A, B, C♯ and D."

§ 1154. Tr. "Name the pitches of the E minor key, melodic form, descending." (pointing to syllables.) Cl. "E, D, C, B, A, G, F♯, E."

Note 254.—The teacher should write the scale in E minor, melodic form, thus:

The Scale in E Minor, Melodic Form.

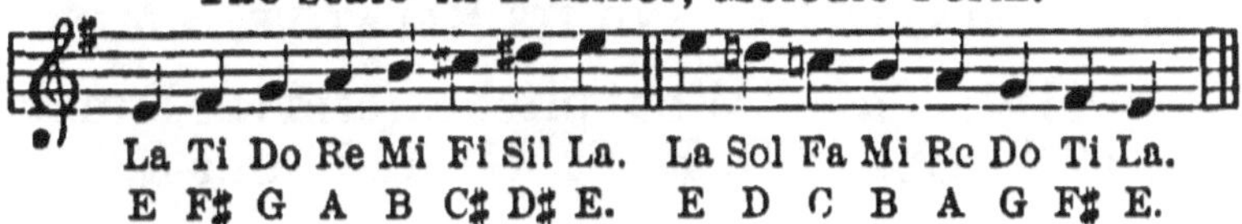

§ 1155. TR. "What is the signature of the
G major and E minor keys?" CL. "The clef
and one sharp."

§ 1156. TR. "The clef and one sharp form
the signature of what keys?" CL. "G major
and E minor."

NOTE 255.—While asking this last question, the
teacher should point first to Do, then to La in the G
column of the Modulator, the pupils glancing across
to the right-hand margin for the key names.

NOTE 256.—Practice Exercises No. 118 to 130 inclusive, always beginning with the following formula:
(taking No. 118, for example.)

§ 1157. TR. "What is the signature of this
piece (or exercise)?" CL. "The clef and one
sharp."

§ 1158. TR. "The clef and one sharp form
the signature of what keys?" CL. "G major
and E minor."

§ 1159. TR. "In what key is this piece (or
exercise) written?" CL. "G major."

§ 1160. TR. "What pitches form the G major key?"

NOTE 257.—The pupils recite the names of the
pitches of G major as at § 1150. If the exercise be
minor they should be questioned accordingly and
made to recite the pitches of the minor key, both harmonic form (as at § 1152) and melodic form (as at §§
1153 and 1154).

THE D MAJOR KEY AND ITS RELATIVE, B MINOR.

§ 1161. TR. "What pitches form the D major
key?" CL. "D, E, F♯, G, A, B and C."

Note 258.—The teacher writes the scale in D major, thus:

The Scale in D Major.

and after thorough drill introduces the relative minor as follows:

§ 1162. Tr. "What is the relative minor key of D major?" (pointing to La in the D column, while the pupils glance across to the margin.) Cl. "B minor."

§ 1163. Tr. "Name the pitches of the B minor key, harmonic form." Cl. "B, C♯, D, E, F♯, G and A♯."

Note 259.—The scale in B minor, harmonic form, should be written on the board, thus:

The Scale in B Minor, Harmonic Form.

Drill thoronghly; then introduce the melodic form as follows:

§ 1164. Tr. "Name the pitches of the B minor key, melodic form, ascending." (pointing slowly to the syllables in the D column of the Modulator, while the pupils glance across to the right hand margin and give the letter names.) Cl. "B, C♯, D, E, F♯, G♯ and A♯."

§ 1165. Tr. "Name the pitches of the B

minor key, melodic form, descending." (pointing to the syllables.) CL. "B, A, G, F♯, E, D, C♯, B."

NOTE 260.—The teacher writes the scale in B minor, melodic form, thus:

The Scale in B Minor, Melodic Form.

§ 1166. TR. "What is the signature of the D major and B minor keys?" CL. "The clef and two sharps."

§ 1167. TR. "The clef and two sharps are the signature of what keys?" (pointing to Do and then to La in the D column, while the pupils will glance across to the margin.) CL. "D major and B minor."

NOTE 261.—Practice all exercises in the B minor key, always beginning with the four questions as at §§ 1157 to 1160 and Note 257.

THE F MAJOR KEY AND ITS RELATIVE, D MINOR.

§ 1168. TR. "What pitches form the F major key?" CL. "F, G, A, B♭, C, D and E."

NOTE 262.—The Teacher writes the scale in F major, thus:

The Scale in F Major.

After drilling thoroughly, introduce the relative minor, as follows:

§ 1169. TR. "What is the relative minor key of F major?" (pointing to La in the F column, while the pupils glance across to the left-hand margin.) CL. "D minor."

§ 1170. TR. "Name the pitches in the D minor key, harmonic form." CL. "D E F G A B♭ and C♯."

NOTE 263.—The teacher writes the scale in D minor, harmonic form, as follows:

The Scale in D Minor, Harmonic Form.

§ 1171. TR. "Name the pitches of the D minor key, melodic form, ascending." (pointing slowly to the syllables in the F column, while the pupils glance across to the left-hand margin and give the letter names.) CL. "D E F G A B and C♯."

§ 1172. TR. "Name the pitches of the D minor key, melodic form, descending." (pointing to the syllables.) CL. "D C B♭ A G F E and D."

NOTE 264.—The teacher writes the scale in D minor, melodic form, thus:

The Scale in D Minor, Melodic Form.

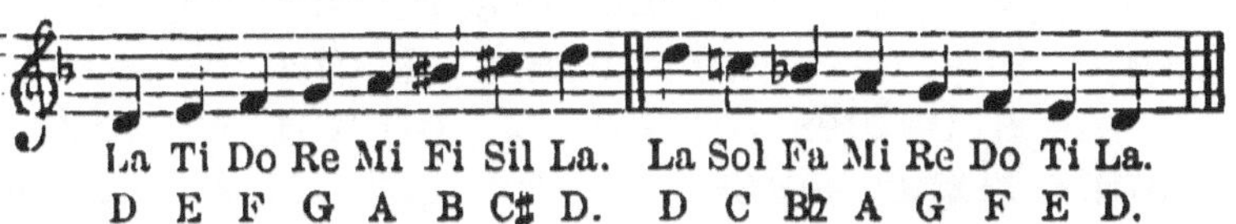

§ 1173. Tr. "What is the signature of the F major and the D minor keys?" Cl. "The clef and one flat."

§ 1174. Tr. "The clef and one flat form the signature of what keys?" Cl. "F major and D minor."

Note 265.—Practice all exercises in D minor, always questioning the class as at §§ 1157 to 1160 and Note 257 inclusive.

The B Flat Major Key and its Relative, G Minor.

§ 1175. Tr. "What pitches form the B flat major key?" Cl. "B♭ C D E♭ F G and A."

Note 266.—The teacher writes the scale in B♭ major, thus·

The Scale in B♭ Major.

Do Re Mi Fa Sol La Ti Do.   Do Ti La Sol Fa Mi Re Do.
B♭ C D E♭ F G A B♭.   B♭ A G F E♭ D C B♭.

and, after drilling sufficiently, introduces the relative minor, as follows:

§ 1176. Tr. "What is the relative minor key of B♭ major?" (pointing to La in the B♭ column, while the pupils glance across to the left-hand margin.) Cl. "G minor."

§ 1177. Tr. "Name the pitches in the G minor key, harmonic form." (pointing slowly to the syllables in the B♭ column, while the pupils glance across to the left-hand margin

of the Modulator and give the letter names.)
CL. "G A B♮ C D E♮ and F♯."

NOTE 267.—The scale in G minor, harmonic form, should be shown on the board thus:

The Scale in G Minor, Harmonic Form.

After thorough drill, introduce the melodic form thus:

§ 1178. TR. "Name the pitches of the G minor key, melodic form, ascending." (pointing slowly to the syllables in the B♮ column, while the pupils glance across to the margin and give the letter names.) CL. "G A B♮ C D E and F♯."

§ 1179. TR. "Name the pitches of the G minor key, melodic form, descending." (pointing to the syllables as before.) CL. "G F E♮ D C B♮ A G."

NOTE 268.—The teacher writes the scale in G minor, melodic form, thus:

The Scale in G Minor, Melodic Form.

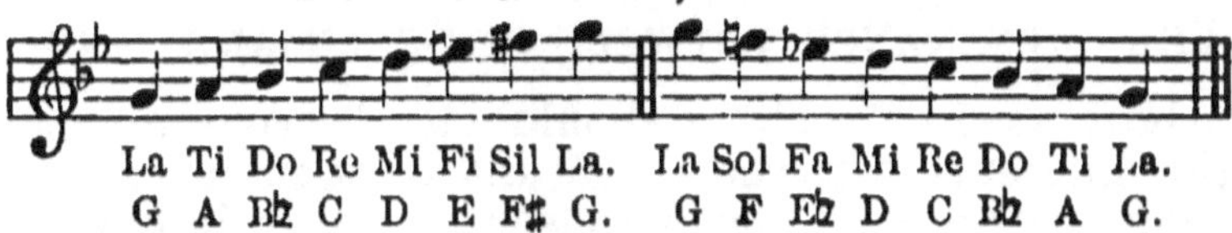

§ 1180. TR. "What is the signature of the B♮ major and G minor keys?" CL. "The clef and two flats,"

§ 1181. TR. " The clef and two flats are the signature of what keys?" CL. " B♭ major and G minor."

NOTE 269.—Practice all exercises in G minor, questioning the class according to the formula given at §§ 1157 to 1160 and Note 257.

NOTE 270.—Whenever it is desirable to introduce any other minor key, the teacher should proceed as above, through the relative major; *e. g.*, through A major to F♯ minor; E major to C♯ minor; B major to G♯ minor; F♯ major to D♯ minor; E♭ major to C minor; A♭ major to F minor; D♭ major to B♭ minor; and G♭ major to E♭ minor. A table of major and minor keys and scales will be found, beginning on page 180, Note 271, showing the relatives and their signatures, together with their syllable and letter names.

TECHNICAL NAMES IN MINOR, FOLLOW THE SAME ORDER AS IN MAJOR.

REMARK 5.—The technical names in the minor are applied exactly on the same plan as in the major; *i. e.*, *One* (La) is Tonic, *Two* (Ti) is Super-Tonic, *Three* (Do) is Mediant, etc. The chord of La is Sub-Mediant in major and Tonic in minor. The chord of Do is Mediant in minor and Tonic in major.

THE DIFFERANCE BETWEEN A SCALE AND KEY.

REMARK 6.—Teachers should clearly comprehend the difference between a *scale* and a *key*, in order that their instructions may be clear. A scale implies a certain invariable order of succession, (the tones from Do to Do in the major, and the tones from La to La in the minor, for example), while the tones which group themselves around the Tonic (key-tone) either major or minor, are called a *key*, and may be used in any possible order of succession. Again, a *scale* must have eight tones, while a *key* may be manifested by seven. A *scale* is a very simple melody written in a *key*.

This may be made clear to the pupils as follows :—

§ 1182. TR. " Name the pitches in the C major key." CL. "C D E F G A and B."

§ 1183. TR. " How many pitches did you mention ? " CL. " Seven."

§ 1184. TR. " What syllables form a diatonic major scale ? " CL. " Do Re Mi Fa Sol La Ti and Do."

§ 1185. TR. " How many tones did you mention ? " CL. " Eight."

§ 1186. TR. " What number of tones are required for a diatonic scale ? " CL. " Eight."

§ 1187. TR. " What is the least number of pitches that will manifest a key ? " CL. " Seven."

§ 1188. TR. " Yes, a scale requires eight tones, while a key may be manifested by seven. The tones which group themselves around a Tonic form a key, and a key, like a scale, is named from the tone which is taken as One, or Tonic. Scale and key differ further in that a scale implies a certain unvaried order of succession, while the group of tones of which it is formed, called a key, may be used in any possible order. A scale, then, is the simplest melody that can be written in a key."

Relative Major and Minor Modes.

Note 271.—The following tables are simply intended to show the teacher at a glance the relative major and minor modes in the several keys. In case it becomes necessary for the teacher to write a particular scale, he will find it here. Lack of space prevents us from showing these scales descending. Bear in mind, that in the major modes the scales ascend and descend with the same order of intervals. This is also true of the Harmonic form of the minor scale. In the Melodic form of the minor, however, the scale ascends and descends with the differing orders of intervals, inasmuch as the accidentals of the ascending scale are not used in descending.

Relative Modes.

Relative Modes.

Relative Modes.

Relative Modes.

Relative Modes.

Relative Modes.

Relative Modes.

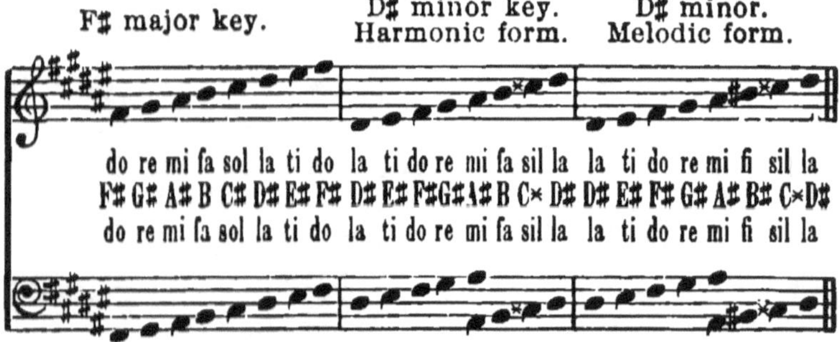

Relative Modes.

Relative Modes.

Relative Modes.

Relative Modes.

Relative Modes.

Relative Modes.

The Chord of the Dominant Seventh, Minor.

§ 1189 Tr. "The dominant seventh chord in the minor is formed of the same intervals as the dominant seventh chord in the major, but it resolves differently and consequently its tones require different syllable name; thus, the dominant seventh chord in the major has the syllables Sol Ti Re Fa (pointing to those syllables in the G column) and resolves to the chord of Do. You will notice that while the tones of the minor dominant seventh chord are exactly the same as those of the major dominant seventh chord, the syllable names are different, and it resolves to the chord of La."

Note 272.—The teacher points to Sol in the G column, and draws the pointer slowly across to Mi in the B flat column, while he asks :—

§ 1190. Tr. "Sol in the major chord becomes what in the minor chord?" Cl. "Mi."

§ 1191. Tr. "Ti in the major chord becomes what in the minor chord?" (pointing from Ti in the G column, across to Sil in the B flat column.) Cl. "Sil."

§ 1192. Tr. "Re in the major chord becomes what in the minor chord?" (pointing from Re across to Ti.) Cl. "Ti."

§ 1193. Tr. "Fa in the major chord becomes what in the minor chord?" (pointing from Fa across to Re.) Cl. "Re."

§ 1194. Tr. "What syllables form the minor dominant seventh chord?" (pointing to Mi Sil Ti Re in the B flat column.) Cl. "Mi Sil Ti Re."

Note 273.—The pupils should get their pitch in the G key from the "old Do."

§ 1195. Tr. "Spell the major dominant seventh chord." (pointing in the G column while they sing Sol Ti Re Fa, thus :—)

§ 1196. Tr. "Sing the same tones but give them the syllables Mi Sil Ti Re, as I point." (points in the B flat column, and they sing thus :—

Note 274.—The pupils should practice these two chords alternately several times, so as to thoroughly comprehend that the tones are the same.

§ 1197. Tr. "In the resolution of the minor dominant seventh chord, the Re resolves downward a major second to Do. Sopranos spell, pronounce and resolve your part of this chord."

Note 275.—They will sing thus :—

§ 1198. Tr. "The Ti in this chord resolves downward a major second to La. Tenors spell, pronounce and resolve your part of this chord."

Note 276.—They will sing thus :—

§ 1199. Tr. "The Sil in this chord resolves upward a minor second to La. Altos spell, pronounce and resolve your part of this chord."

NOTE 277.—They will sing thus:—

§ 1200. TR. "The Mi in this chord resolves upward a perfect fourth to La. Basses spell, pronounce and resolve your part of this chord."

NOTE 278.—They will sing thus:—

§ 1201. TR. "Now all together, spell, pronounce and resolve the chord of the dominant seventh in the minor."

NOTE 279.—The result should be thus:—

Probably the Sopranos will fail, in the resolution, to sing Do. If so, they should go over their part alone as indicated at §1197, and Note 275, until they can feel the minor effect.

NOTE 280.—The two dominant seventh chords should now be practiced alternately, thus:—

The Major Dominant 7th.   **The Minor Dominant 7th.**

until the class can sing either without hesitancy whenever called upon.

Note 281.—Intelligent teachers will appreciate the advantage of our changing the names of 7 (Si) to Ti and of sharp Sol (Si) to Sil, thus avoiding the confusion which arises from calling three different things by the same name, viz: C, the letter name of a pitch; Si, 7 of the key, and Si, sharp Sol. The old names appear in all their confusion in the chord of the dominant seventh, minor, thus:—(observe the Si Si C).

Already a host of teachers throughout the country have written that they are delighted with the change (Sil for Si) and will hereafter teach it. To all who are now in the ranks and to all who will come into the ranks we extend a hearty "Thank you."

The Tendency of Tones.

Remark 7.—A forceful demonstration of the fact that tones have no progressive tendency in and of themselves, *i. e.*, apart from their immediate surroundings, may be given as follows:—The teacher gives the pitch between G and A (G♯ or A♭,) and says:—

¶ 1202. Tr. "All sing this tone by the syllable Ta." (They sing.)

¶ 1203. Tr. "Sing it again and notice that it seems as restful as if it were the Tonic, *i. e.*, it does not tend either up or down." (They sing.)

¶ 1204. Tr. "I will now surround it with certain tones; sing it again, and if you see that it has a tendency either up or down, follow that tendency and resolve it accordingly."

NOTE 282.—He plays the full chord of the dominant seventh in the A key, thus:

§ 1205. TR. "You see that its associate tones pushed it upward, so to say. Now sing the same tone again, unaccompanied, and notice that it is as restful as the Tonic." (They sing.)

§ 1206. TR. "I will now surround it with other certain tones; sing it again, and if you feel that it has a tendency either up or down, resolve it accordingly."

NOTE 283.—He first strikes the tone alone, to fix their attention upon it, then plays the full chord of the dominant seventh in the E flat major key. They sing, and feeling the downward tendency, resolve thus:

§ 1207. TR. "Thus you see that a tone may be drawn down, or pushed up, so to say, by its companions. If an intermediate tone tends upward, it is represented by the lower of two degrees, and called *sharp*. If it tends downward, it is represented by the higher of two degrees, and called *flat*."

NOTE 284.—The teacher writes A♭ and G♯ on the board, with their respective resolutions, thus:—

and says:—

¶ 1208. TR. "Our notation is such that we must represent an intermediate tone by different degrees of the staff, according as it resolves upward or downward, but on the modulator they appear to the eye as having the same pitch, which is the fact." (Points to Sil, and draws the pointer slowly across to Le.)

THE DIMINISHED 7TH CHORD.

NOTE 285.—The diminished 7th chord is so nearly like the major dominant 7th chord, that it is best introduced after practicing the dominant 7th chord, as follows;

§ 1209. TR. "Spell, pronounce and resolve the dominant 7th chord." (They sing.)

§ 1210. TR. "Spell it backwards, pronounce and resolve it as usual." (They sing thus :—

NOTE 286.—While they spell the chord the teacher points to the several notes, and when they pronounce the chord he draws the pointer quickly down through all the notes of the chord, and removes the pointer; as they resolve the chord the pointer should rest on the final chord.

NOTE 287.—The teacher sings thus :—

and the class imitate him. After which he sings thus :—

and they imitate.   He then sings thus;—

and, finally he sings:—

and the class imitate him.

§ 1211. TR.   "This fourfold chord is called a Diminished 7th chord.   What is it called?" CL.   "A diminished 7th chord."

§ 1212. TR.   "It always consists of the syllables Fa Re Ti Sil, and is spelled backward, but is pronounced and resolved as we pronounce and resolve all 7th chords.   Thus:—

NOTE 288.—Practice In Heavenly Love Abiding, page 162, calling particular attention to the diminished 7th chords in the first, fifth, sixth and fourteenth measures.

TABLE SHOWING ALL THE COMPLEMENTARY SIGNATURES.

NOTE 289.—The following table, showing the various complementary signatures, may be found useful to the teacher. They can be placed on the board if thought best, one at a time, in the order in which they are reached in the course.

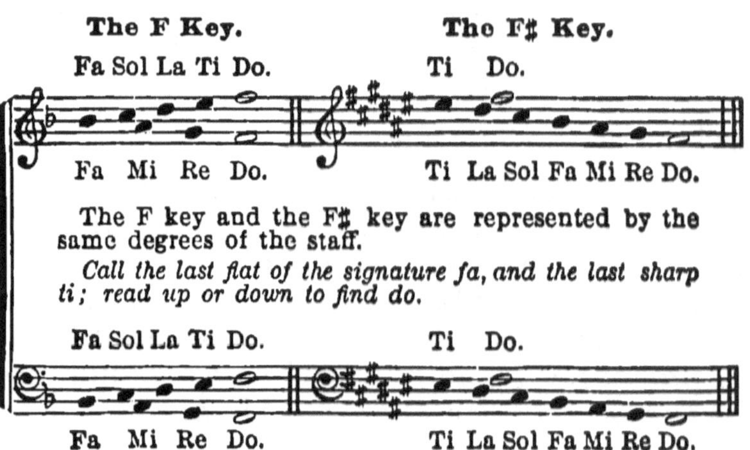

The F key and the F♯ key are represented by the same degrees of the staff.

Call the last flat of the signature fa, and the last sharp ti; read up or down to find do.

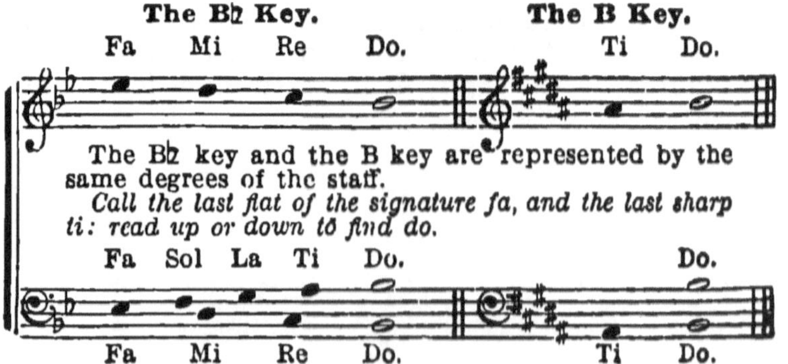

The B♭ key and the B key are represented by the same degrees of the staff.

Call the last flat of the signature fa, and the last sharp ti: read up or down to find do.

The Eb key and the E key are represented by the same degrees of the staff.

Call the last flat of the signature fa, and the last sharp ti; read up or down to find do.

The Ab key and the A key are represented by the same degrees of the staff.

Call the last flat of the signature fa, and the last sharp ti; read up or down to find do.

The Db key and the D key are represented by the same degrees of the staff.

Call the last flat of the signature fa, and the last sharp ti: read up or down to find do.

The G♭ key and the G key are represented by the same degrees of the staff.

Call the last flat of the signature fa, and the last sharp ti; read up or down to find do.

NOTE 290.—We have now gone over the whole ground of the complementary signatures, with the exception of the extreme keys of seven sharps and seven flats; and here we would remark that if there ever was any doubt in the minds of teachers or pupils that *the C key has no signature*, the next illustrations will probably settle the question for them.

§ 1213. TR. "What is the complement of seven sharps?" CL. "No flats."

§ 1214. TR. "What is the complement of seven flats?" CL. "No sharps."

§ 1215. TR. "Yes, the seven signature-flats of the C flat key leave no signature-sharps for the C key, and the seven signature-sharps of the C sharp key leave no signature-flats for the C key, hence *the C key has no signature.*

NOTE 291.—Indicate the C key with the C sharp key before it, and the C flat key following it, with their Do's, thus:

The Effect of Complementary Signatures upon Accidentals.

Note 292.—In going from a signature of sharps to a flat complementary, a sharp (♯) is turned into a cancel (♮), a cancel is turned into a flat (♭), a double-sharp (♯♯ or ✕) into a sharp (♯), and a flat (♭) into a double-flat (♭♭).

In going from a signature of flats to a sharp complementary, the above order is reversed, viz: a cancel (♮), is turned into a sharp (♯), a flat (♭) is turned into a cancel (♮), a sharp (♯) into a double sharp (♯♯ or ✕) and a double flat (♭♭) into a flat (♭).

How to Find Any Key-Tone (Tonic) From Our Old Do.

Note 293.—The teacher who has no instrument in his class-room must get the correct pitch of an exercise or song from a pitch-pipe. One should be obtained which will give the pitch C an octave above middle C, thus:

From this, any key-tone or Tonic (Do major, or La minor) can readily be found as follows:

To Find Do in the G Major Key.

Note 294.—Call the pitch-pipe tone Do, sing down to Sol and call that Do, thus:

For the relative minor, sing the new Do, and go down to La.

To Find Do in the D Major Key.

Note 295.—Call the pitch-pipe tone Do, sing up to Re and call that Do, thus:

For the relative minor, sing the new Do and go down to La.

To Find Do in the A Major Key.

Note 296.—Call the pitch-pipe tone Do, sing down to La, and call that Do, thus:

For the relative minor, sing the new Do and go down to La.

To Find Do in the E Major Key.

Note 297.—Call the pitch-pipe tone Do, sing up to Mi and call that Do, thus:

For the relative minor, sing the new Do and go down to La.

To Find Do in the B Major Key.

Note 298.—Call the pitch-pipe tone Do, sing down to Ti and call that Do, thus:

For the relative minor, sing the new Do and go down to La.

To Find Do in the F Sharp Major Key.

Note 299.—Call the pitch-pipe tone Do, sing down to Fi, and call that Do, thus:

For the relative minor, sing the new Do and go down to La.

To Find Do in the F Major Key.

NOTE 300.—Call the pitch-pipe tone Do, sing down to Fa and call that Do, thus:

For the relative minor, sing the new Do, and go down to La.

To Find Do in the B Flat Major Key.

NOTE 301.—Call the pitch-pipe tone Do, repeat it and call it Re, and descend to the new Do, thus:

For the relative minor, sing the new Do and go down to La.

If the class find difficulty in descending at once from Re to the new Do, let them sing Re Mi two or more times until they feel the new key, thus:

To Find Do in the E Flat Major Key.

NOTE 302.—Call the pitch-pipe tone Do, repeat it and call it La, and ascend to the new Do, thus:

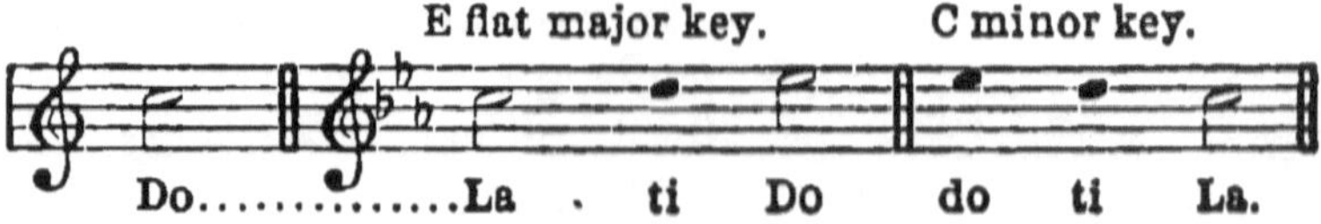

For the relative minor, sing the new Do and go down to La.

To Find Do in the A Flat Major Key.

NOTE 303.—Call the pitch-pipe tone Do, repeat it and call it Mi, and sing down to the new Do, thus:

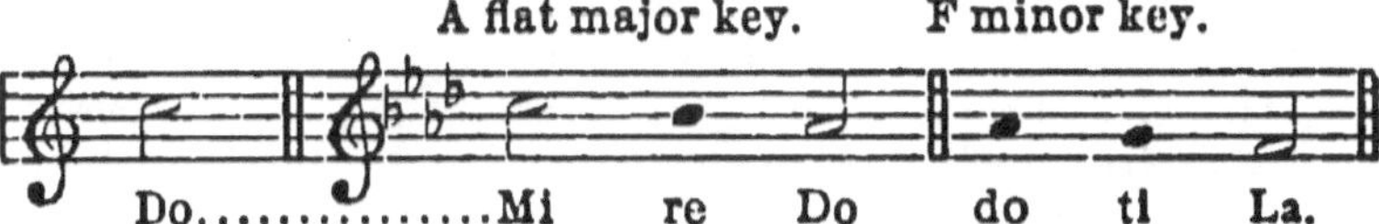

For the relative minor, sing the new Do and go down to La.

To Find Do in the D Flat Major Key.

NOTE 304.— Call the pitch-pipe tone Do, repeat it and call it Ti, and sing up to the new Do, thus:

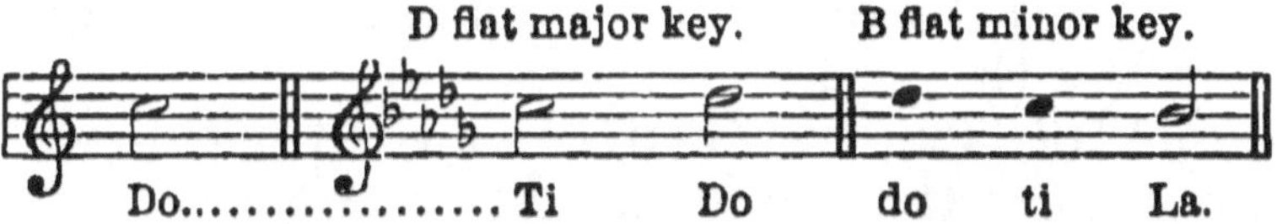

For the relative minor, sing the new Do and go down to La.

To Find Do in the G Flat Major Key.

NOTE 305.—Call the pitch-pipe tone Do, sing down to Fa, call that Ti and sing up to the new Do, thus:

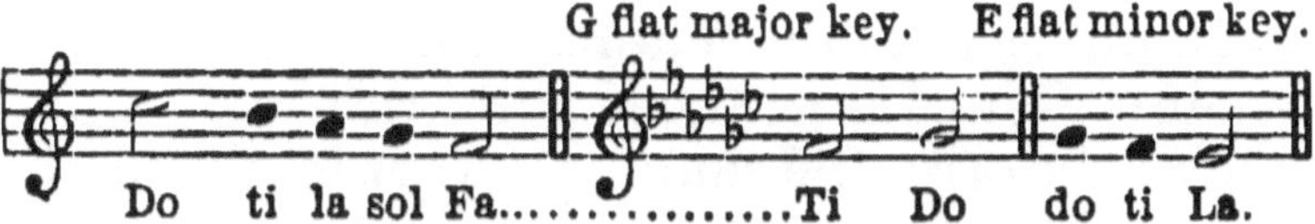

For the relative minor, sing the new Do and go down to La.

Process by which the class can learn to sing the Tonic chord in any given Key, at the correct pitch, without the aid of an instrument.

Note 306.—The pupils having become so familiar with the pitch C that they can sing it correctly at any time, it is only necessary to show them a Mental Process by which they can go from that pitch to any required pitch. The following plan has proved successful in hundreds of cases.

From C Major to F Major.

§ 1216. Tr. "I am about to ask you to spell and pronounce the Tonic chord in the F major key. Look at the modulator. What tone of the C key becomes the Tonic of the F major key?" Cl. "Fa."

§ 1217. Tr. "When I ask you to spell and pronounce the Tonic chord in the F key, your mental process will be to ascend the C scale to Fa, call that tone Do, and spell and pronounce the chord from that pitch."

§ 1218. Tr. "Sing our old Do." (They sing).

§ 1219. Tr. "Follow my pointer mentally, and when we arrive at the new Do, spell and pronounce a Tonic chord from that pitch." (points from Do in the C column slowly up to Fa, and draws the pointer across to Do in the F column, thus :)

NOTE 307.—The first effort may not be entirely satisfactory. If so, let the class *sing* the mental process a few times until the teacher is sure it is understood, after which it should always be taken silently.

FROM C MAJOR TO B FLAT MAJOR.

§ 1220. TR. "I will now ask you to sing the Tonic chord in B flat major. Our old Do becomes what tone in the B flat key?" (pointing across from Do in the C column to Re in the B flat column.) CL. "Re."

§ 1221. TR. "Sing our old Do, pitch C." (They sing.)

§ 1222. TR. "Follow my pointer mentally, and when we arrive at the new Do, spell and pronounce a Tonic chord from that pitch." (Points from Do in the C column, slowly across to Re in the B flat column and descends to the new Do, thus:)

NOTE 308. If the class have trouble with this, it may be well to try the following:

FROM C MAJOR TO E FLAT MAJOR.

§ 1223. TR. "I shall now call for the Tonic chord in E flat major. Do in the C key becomes what syllable of the E flat key?" (pointing from Do in the C column across to La in the E flat column.) CL. "La."

§ 1224. TR. "Sing our old Do." (They sing.)

§ 1225. TR. "Follow my pointer mentally, and when we arrive at the new Do, spell and pronounce a Tonic chord from that pitch." (Points from Do in the C column slowly across to La in the E flat column, and ascends to the new Do, thus :)

FROM C MAJOR TO A FLAT MAJOR.

§ 1226. TR. "I shall now call for the Tonic chord in A flat major. Our old Do (C) becomes what syllable in the A flat key?" (pointing from Do in the C column slowly across to Mi in the A flat column.) CL. "Mi."

§ 1227. TR. "Sing our old Do." (They sing.)

§ 1228. TR. "Follow my pointer mentally, and when we arrive at the new Do, spell and

pronounce a Tonic chord from that pitch."
(Points from Do in the C column, slowly
across to Mi in the A flat column, and
ascends to the new Do, thus:)

NOTE 309.—The teacher may find it necessary to
have the class *sing* the mental process at first, but
should take it silently as soon as possible.

FROM C MAJOR TO D FLAT MAJOR.

§ 1229. TR. "I will now ask you to sing
the Tonic chord in D flat major. Our old Do
becomes what syllable in the D flat key?"
(pointing slowly across from Do in the C column to 7 in the D flat column.) CL. "Ti."

§ 1230. TR. "Sing our old Do." (They sing.)

NOTE 310.—The teacher should constantly bear in
mind that after every effort of the class to sing the
pitch C from memory, he should compare their pitch
with the instrument, and call their attention to any
deviation. One of the many causes for flatting the
pitch is bad ventilation in the class-room. The room
should be well ventilated before the class convenes,
and the air kept pure if possible.

§ 1231. TR. "Follow my pointer mentally,
and when we arrive at the new Do, spell and
pronounce a Tonic chord from that pitch."
(Points from Do in the C column slowly across
to 7 in the D flat column, thus :)

FROM C MAJOR TO G FLAT MAJOR.

§ 1232. TR. "I will now call for the Tonic chord in the G flat key.   What tone of the C key is diatonic in the G flat key?" (pointing from Fa in the C column across to Ti in the G flat column.)   CL. "Fa."

§ 1233. TR. "Sing our old Do." (They sing.)

§ 1234. TR. "Follow my pointer mentally, and when we arrive at the new Do, spell and pronounce a Tonic chord from that pitch." (Points from Do in the C column up to Fa, then slowly across to Ti in the G flat column, and ascends to Do, thus :)

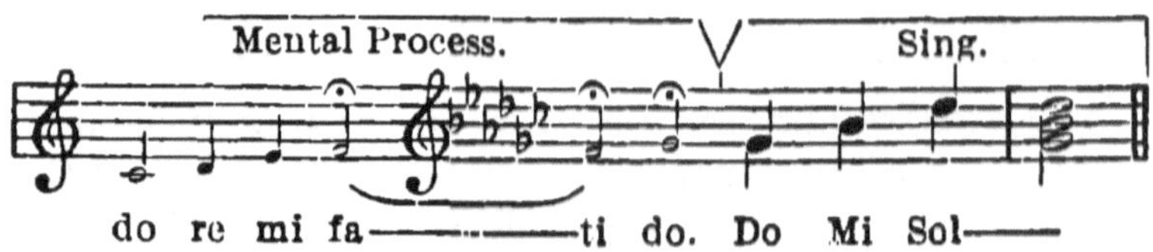

FROM C MAJOR TO G MAJOR.

§ 1235. TR. "I am about to call for the Tonic chord in G major.   What tone of the C key becomes Tonic in the G major key?" CL. "Sol."

§ 1236. TR. "When I ask you to spell and pronounce the Tonic chord in the G key, your mental process will be to ascend the C scale to

Sol, call that tone Do, and spell and pronounce a Tonic chord from that pitch."

§ 1237. "TR. "Sing our old Do, pitch C."
(They sing.)

§ 1238. TR. "Follow my pointer mentally,
and when we arrive at the new Do, spell and
pronounce a Tonic chord from that pitch."
(points from Do in the C column slowly up to
Sol, and draws the pointer across to Do in the
G column, thus:)

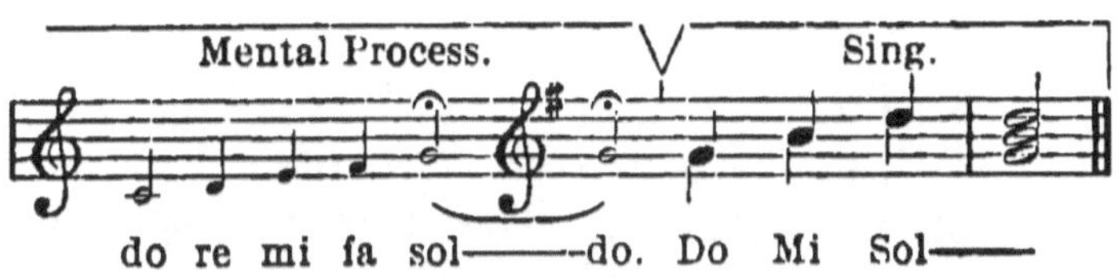

NOTE 311.—Again their first effort may not prove
satisfactory. If so, let them *sing* the mental process
once or twice, and then try it silently.

FROM C MAJOR TO D MAJOR.

§ 1239. TR. "I shall now call for the Tonic
chord in D major. What tone of the C key
becomes Tonic in the D key?" CL. "Re."

§ 1240. TR. "Sing our old Do, pitch C."
(They sing.)

§ 1241. TR. "Follow my pointer mentally,
and when we arrive at the new Do, spell and
pronounce a Tonic chord from that pitch."
(Points from Do in the C column, slowly up
to Re, and draws the pointer across to Do in
the D column, thus:)

FROM C MAJOR TO A MAJOR.

§ 1242. TR. "I shall now call for the Tonic chord in A major. What tone in the C key becomes Tonic in the A key?" (pointing from Do in the A column across to La in the C column.) CL. "La."

§ 1243. TR. "Sing our old Do." (They.sing.)

§ 1244. TR. "Follow my pointer mentally, and when we arrive at the new Do, spell and pronounce a Tonic chord from that pitch." (Points from Do in the C column up to La, then across to Do in the A column, thus:)

FROM C MAJOR TO E MAJOR.

§ 1245. TR. "I am about to call for the Tonic chord in E major. What tone in the C key becomes Tonic in E major?" (pointing from Do in the E column across to Mi in the C column.) CL. "Mi."

§ 1246. TR. "Sing our old Do." (They sing.)

§ 1247. TR. "Follow my pointer mentally, and when we arrive at the new Do, spell and

pronounce a Tonic chord from that pitch."
(Points from Do in the C column up to Mi,
and thence across to Do in the E column,
thus :)

FROM C MAJOR TO B MAJOR.

§ 1248. TR. "I will now call for the Tonic
chord in B major. What tone in the C key
becomes Tonic in B major?" (pointing from
Do in the B column across to 7 in the C
column.) CL. "Ti."

§ 1249. TR. "Sing our old Do." (They sing.)

§ 1250. TR. "Follow my pointer mentally,
and when we arrive at the new Do, spell and
pronounce a Tonic chord from that pitch."
(Points from Do in the C column down to 7
(Ti·, and thence across to Do in the B
column, thus :)

FROM C MAJOR TO F SHARP MAJOR.

§ 1251. TR. "I shall now call for the Tonic
chord in F sharp major. What tone in the C
key becomes Tonic in F sharp major?" (point-

ing from Do in the F sharp column across to Fi in the C column. CL. "Fi."

§ 1252. TR. "Sing our old Do." (They sing.)

§ 1253. TR. "Follow my pointer mentally, and when we arrive at the new Do, spell and pronounce a Tonic chord from that pitch." (Points from Do in the C column up to Fi, and thence across to Do in the F sharp column, thus :)

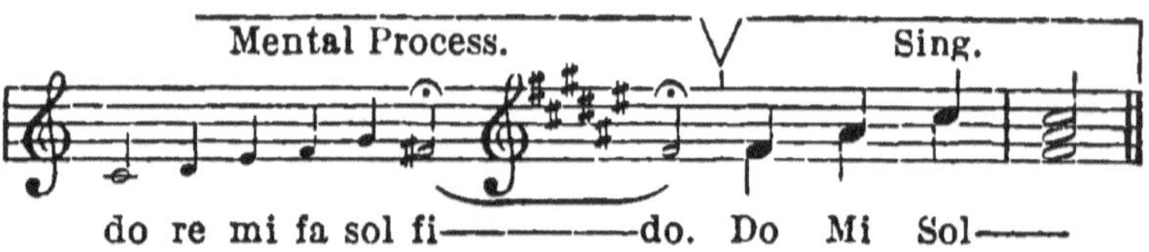

RULES FOR FINDING DO IN ANY SIGNATURE.

NOTE 312.—As pupils are liable to forget where Do is in the various signatures, the teacher should give them the following simple rules, viz: If the signature is one sharp, that sharp is always Ti, and the next degree above it is always Do. If the signature consists of two or more sharps, the last sharp (the sharp farthest to the right) is always Ti, the next degree above being always Do.

If flats form the signature, the last flat (the flat farthest to the right) is always Fa, read up or down to find Do. In signatures of more than one flat, the next to the last flat is always Do.

THE DOUBLE SHARP.

§ 1254. TR. "When we wish to sharp a degree which is already sharped by the signature, we indicate it by a character called a *Double sharp* (×) thus: (writes.)

Here (pointing to the last note in the first measure) Ri (sharp Re) is wanted, and as Re is F sharp by virtue of the signature, we can only get sharp Re (Ri) by still further sharping the Re degree; hence the necessity of the Double sharp. The degree now presents the pitch F double sharp, which is produced on the piano or organ by pressing the G· key."

Note 313.—The teacher should explain that it will not do to write it on G, for that degree is already monopolized by Mi (G sharp); and that while a degree may be made to represent five different tones (as G, G flat, G double flat, G sharp, and G double sharp), it can not be made to represent two tones which are a second apart as are Ri-Mi. Practice all exercises which involve the double sharp.

The Cancel-Sharp.

§ 1255. Tr. "Whenever we wish to discontinue the effect of a *double sharp*, and restore the degree to its diatonic condition, we indicate it by a character called a *cancel-sharp* (♮♯) thus: (writing.)

Here (pointing to second pulse) F sharp is Re by virtue of the signature, and as we want sharp Re (Ri), we must double-sharp the Re degree, which makes it represent F *double-sharp*. At the fourth pulse (pointing) we want Re instead of Ri, and so must cancel the double-sharp and thus restore the degree to its diatonic condition, which is F sharp (Re), using the cancel-sharp (♮♯) for that purpose."

NOTE 314.—Practice all exercises which involve the cancel-sharp.

THE WHOLE REST.

NOTE 315.—The teacher writes two measures on the board, the second being filled with two half rests, and after the class have sung the exercise, says:

§ 1256. TR. "We have a rest which indicates a silence of four pulses, called a *whole rest*. I will place it here instead of these two rests." (erases the half rests and writes a *whole rest*.) "It is a square block below a line. What is it called?" CL. "A whole rest."

§ 1257. TR. "How many beats do we give the whole rest?" (pointing.) CL. "Four."

§ 1258. TR. "Sing the exercise." (They sing.)

§ 1259. TR. "Rests correspond with notes of the same duration, *i. e.*:—A whole rest corresponds to a whole note; a half rest (our former *long rest*), corresponds to a half note; and a quarter rest (our former *short rest*), corresponds to a quarter note."

NOTE 316.—The teacher writes as follows:

Quarter note and rest.   Half note and rest.   Whole note and rest.

and questions concerning the duration of each note and rest.

§ 1260. Tr. "Turn to page 36 and look at No. 116. What kind of a rest fills the fifth measure?" Cl. "A whole rest."

§ 1261. Tr. "What does the whole rest mean?" Cl. "That we are to remain silent during four pulses."

§ 1262. Tr. "Sing the exercise." (They sing.)

The Whole Rest as a Measure Rest.

Note 317.—Irrespective of its absolute value—as equaling four quarter notes—the whole rest is arbitrarily used as a *measure rest* (filling the measure, whether more or less), in any of the following measures: $\frac{2}{4}$, $\frac{3}{4}$, $\frac{6}{4}$, $\frac{4}{8}$, $\frac{6}{8}$, $\frac{9}{8}$, $\frac{12}{8}$.

Note 318.—While on the subject of the Measure rest, it may be well to mention the

Double Whole Note and Double Whole Rest.

This note is much used in the better class of church music, and is an absolute necessity in $\frac{4}{2}$ measure; while the rest, in vocal or instrumental music published in separate parts, is also continually used to mark a pause of two measures, thus :—

Double Whole Note.   Double Whole Rest.

The four measure rest, thus :    is also in continual use. All pauses of more than four measures are indicated by groups of four, two and one measure rests, thus :—

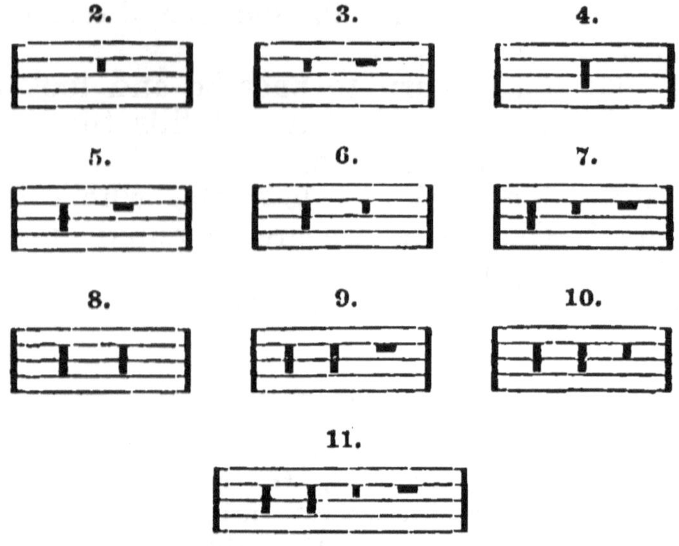

When large numbers of measures are to be passed in silence, it is indicated thus :—

NOTE 319.—When a measure begins with a rest, it may be well for the teacher to mark the downward beat by a slight tap with pencil or baton on the desk. It is also a good plan sometimes, for the class to speak in a soft tone, or a whisper, the word "rest" exactly in time.

1ST TIME AND 2ND TIME.

NOTE 320.—The teacher explains that the words "1st time," and "2nd time," or "*1mo*" and "*2do*," or the figures "1" and "2," refer to the first ending and second ending of a repeated passage. Study No. 84, page 25.

Exceptional Uses of the Tie and Slur;
(a) as used for Differing Words.

Note 321.—It frequently occurs when two or more stanzas are sung to the same music, that there may be two syllables in one stanza where there is only one syllable in another stanza, in which case two notes are written separately and joined with a tie or slur.

(b) The Slur as a Legato Mark.

Note 322.—The slur in frequently used as a Legato mark. It then becomes a species of mark for phrasing, as the singer is supposed to sing with one breath all that such slur encloses.

Grace-Notes.

Note 323.—Grace-notes are small notes used to indicate ornamental tones. They are used for the purpose of adding grace and beauty to the melody. They are usually performed independently of the main melodic tones, and also of the rhythm. The following bit from the old song "The Last Rose of Summer" will illustrate grace-notes. These notes sometimes receive their full value in addition to the time given to the other notes in the measure.

The Appoggiatura.*

Note 324.—The teacher explains the Appoggiatura as a melodic ornament. It is a tone which suspends or delays the melodic tone before which it occurs. The time of the appoggiatura is always taken from the principal tone. The long appoggiatura takes half the time of the following note. It is expressed by a grace-note, thus:—

---

*Pronounced Ăp-poj-jä-tŏo′rä.

Other forms of the appoggiatura need not be mentioned here, as they rarely occur in vocal music. The short appoggiatura has no time of its own, but is crushed, so to say, against the following tone. It is expressed by a grace-note, an eighth or a sixteenth, with an oblique dash through the stem, thus :—

This grace-note is commonly called an

ACCIACCATURA.†

and is more frequentlly used in instrumental music than in vocal.

NOTE 325.—Practice the exercises which involve the Appoggiatura and the Acciaccatura.

DOUBLE FRACTION.

§ 1264. TR. "Sometimes a composition requires two kinds of measure to express the sentiment, or rhythm, of the words to good advantage, in which case a *double fraction* is used. The kind of measure which predominates, or that which is used first will be indicated by the first fraction." (See page 163.)

NOTE 326.—Question the class concerning the double fraction, and practice beating, being very careful that the pupils change their beat with each

---

† Pronounced Ă-tchäk-kä-tŏo′rä.

change of measure. If the teacher can play, (piano or organ) it would be an excellent plan to have the class beat while he plays the piece. When they can beat it correctly, let them try to sing it and beat.

SUSPENSION.

§ 1265. TR. "Turn to page 106, look at exercise No. 264. In thirteenth and fourteenth measures you will observe that the voice lags behind the beat, so to say. When the voice thus delays and follows the pulse, the effect is called Suspension."

NOTE 327.—Practice the exercise, taking particular care to mark the entrance of the beats by a sharp click of stick or pencil.

ANTICIPATION.

§ 1266. "Look at No. 266 and notice that here the voice precedes the beat. Such effect is called Anticipation."

§ 1267. TR. "Anticipation is directly the opposite of Suspension, but they are very similar in effect."

NOTE 328.—Practice the exercise, being careful to indicate the entrance of the pulses by sharp stroke of stick or pencil.

§ 1268. TR. "When does suspension occur?" CL. "When the voice is delayed and follows the pulse."

§ 1269. TR. "When does anticipation take place?" CL. "When the voice precedes the pulse."

§ 1270. Tr. " The important thing in sing-ing Suspension and Anticipation is to keep a firm mental grasp on the pulses. The voice should be carried smoothly past the pulse-point, for nothing in singing can be more crude than "beating time" with the voice.

DISSONANCES AND SUSPENDED TONES.

Note 329.—The pupils should commit to memory the following rule, viz: " All dissonances and sus-pended tones should be forcibly struck and their resolutions clearly marked." An instance of a disso-nance by suspension with a free resolution, which comes under this rule, will be found on page 132 in the second, fourth and sixth measures of the refrain. The first chord in each of these measures should be sung with *pressure accent*, so to say.

MODULATION.

Note 330.—Modulation takes place when the tones of a composition group themselves around a new Tonic. The process of finding a new Do having been followed from the earliest lessons in this series, the task of teaching Modulation is thereby greatly simpli-fied, it being only necessary to determine which tone of the present key becomes the new Do. At first this must be decided for the pupils. In exercises Nos. 230 and 231 the syllables show where and what the change is. If the new key is retained long enough to establish itself in the mind, *i. e.*, if it con-tains the chords of the Tonic, Dominant and Sub-Dominant of that key, it becomes a modulation; but if it is only of short duration, one or two chords, it is called a *digression;* and while a digression is really a modulation, it is so short as to make it scarcely worth while to give it so dignified a name.

In studying this subject the following plan should be pursued :—

§ 1271. TR. "Turn to page 87, first piece. What key does it begin in?" CL. "The G key."

§ 1272. TR. "Read the soprano to the end of the fourth measure." (They read.)

§ 1273. TR. "What tone is last in the fourth measure?" CL. "Re."

§ 1274. TR. "What is the letter name?" CL. "A."

§ 1275. TR. "A is what tone of the D key?" CL. "Sol."

§ 1276. TR. "Sing Re again, repeat it and call it Sol, and sing on through the new key." (They sing.)

§ 1277. TR. "Through how many measures does the new key continue?" CL. "Four."

§ 1278. TR. "What is the last tone of the new key?" CL. "Do."

§ 1279. TR. "This Do is what tone in our original key?" CL. "Sol."

§ 1280. TR. "Now sing the soprano from the beginning to the end." (They sing.)

NOTE 331.—Proceed in the same way with each of the other parts. It may be necessary to go over the parts where the key changes several times, but "Slow and sure" should be the motto of the successful teacher. Be certain that the pupils understand the exercise thoroughly before leaving it.

Practice all other exercises which involve Modulation.

Melody and Harmony.

(Supplementary to Note 84, Page 51.)

Note 332.—The teacher should explain that when four parts are sung simultaneously, it is called four-part harmony or Quartet; that three-part harmony is called a Trio; and two-part harmony, a Duet; while a melody sung by a single voice is called a Solo. When a number of voices are combined on the same part in any of the above forms, the effect is called a Chorus. Choruses are classified as Unison, Two-part, Three-part, etc.

SYNCOPATION.

Note 333. The teacher writes two quadruple measures, thus:

§ 1281. Tr. "How many measures have I written?" Cl. "Two."

§ 1282. Tr. "What kind of measures?" Cl. "Quadruple measures."

§ 1283. Tr. "How many strong pulses has quadruple measure?" Cl. "Two."

§ 1284. Tr. "Which are the strong pulses?" Cl. "The first and third."

§ 1285. Tr. "After beating the silent measure, sing the exercise by the syllable Ta, making the strong pulses prominent." (They sing.)

§ 1286. Tr. "Count and beat while I sing, and observe whether I sing correctly."

Note 334.—The teacher sings and connects the second and third pulses and asks:—

§ 1287. Tr. " Did I sing correctly, or incorrectly ? " Cl. " Incorrectly."

§ 1288. Tr. " In which measure did the error occur ? " Cl. " In the first measure."

§ 1289. Tr. " How was it wrong ? " Cl. " You connected the second and third pulses."

§ 1290. Tr. " I wish you to connect the second and third pulses, and will indicate such connection (writes the tie) by what character ? " Cl. " The tie."

Note 335.—The exercise will now appear as follows :

§ 1291. Tr. " Sing the exercise as it now stands, making the strong pulses particularly prominent." (They sing, and of course fail to accent the third pulse in the first measure.)

§ 1292. Tr. " How many strong pulses has quadruple measure ? " Cl. " Two."

§ 1293. Tr. " Did you accent the two strong pulses in the first measure ? " Cl. " We did not."

§ 1294. Tr. " Which strong pulse did you pass without accent ? " Cl. " The second strong pulse."

§ 1295. Tr. " Why did you not accent it ? " Cl. " Because it is tied to the preceding weak pulse."

§ 1296. Tr. " How long did you sustain the tone ? " Cl. " Two beats."

§ 1297. Tr. " Does the tone begin on a weak

pulse, or on a strong pulse?" CL. "On a weak pulse."

§ 1298. TR. "And continues through what kind of a pulse?" CL. "It continues through a strong pulse."

§ 1299. TR. "When a tone begins on a weak pulse and continues through a strong pulse, the accent which is usually given to the strong pulse is thrown back, so to say, upon the weak pulse, and greatly exaggerated. Such a tone is called a

SYNCOPATED TONE,

or a *Syncope*** and the note which indicates it is called a *Syncopated Note*. Sing the exercise (pointing to the blackboard) and accent the second pulse strongly. (They sing.)

§ 1300. TR. "Such effects are usually indicated thus:"—

NOTE 336.—The teacher erases the exercise and writes:—

§ 1301. TR. "The accent mark (pointing) is used to call special attention to the accent, and for the purpose of indicating the necessity of giving extra accent to the syncope. However it is generally understood that the syncope should receive extra stress, whether marked or not."

---

* Pronounced Sin'ko-pee.

§ 1302. Tr. "Sing the exercise again." (They sing).

§ 1303. Tr. "A syncope may begin on the last pulse of a measure and continue through the first strong pulse in the following measure, in which case it would be indicated thus:—" (writes).

§ 1304. Tr. "Sing this exercise, being careful to accent the last pulse of the first measure strongly, and hold the tone smoothly over the bar, and through the first pulse in the following measure." (They sing).

§ 1305. Tr. "Passages frequently occur in which several syncopes follow each other in succession. In such cases great care must be taken not to lose the mental grasp of the pulses."

Note 337.—The teacher writes the following examples on the board, at first requiring the pupils to beat while he sings, and then to sing and beat, proceeding from the simpler to the more elaborate without stopping (*i. e.*, as though they were all one exercise), unless mistakes occur, in which case the particular exercise which bothers them should be repeated until the class have mastered it; then commence again at the beginning. This should be continued until they can sing all the exercises without a mistake.

If two or three exercises are written on each staff, as below, there will be ample room on the board.

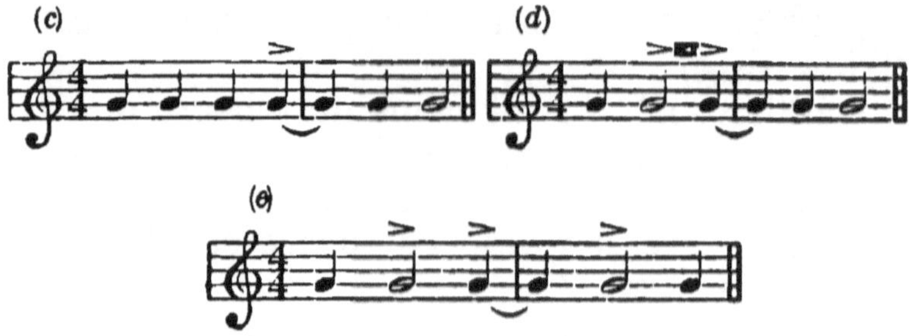

§ 1306. Tr. "A syncope frequently enters after a rest, thus: (writes).

§ 1307. Tr. "Syncopes are frequently formed by uniting the last half of a pulse with the first half of the following pulse, thus:—

Note 338.—The above exercise may be still further syncopated as follows:—

Note 339.—The teacher should make an audible beat with stick or pencil, while the pupils are becoming familiar with syncopation, to assist them in retaining their mental grasp on the pulses. Practice all exercises involving syncopation.

COMPOUND MEASURES.

NOTE 340.—Compound measures, such as $\frac{6}{8}$, $\frac{9}{8}$, $\frac{12}{8}$, etc., are often misunderstood, and consequently wrongly explained. Pulses group themselves either into twos or threes, (double and triple) and these two groupings are the fundamental forms of rhythm. For convenience in reading we unite two double measures and make what we call quadruple measure. By uniting two triple measures we form a sextuple (six pulse) measure, thus:

This would have the same effect on the hearer if written thus:

Slow movements like the above require six beats in a measure. (See Note 129 to § 644 inclusive. p. 90.)

If we quicken sextuple, we have simply double measure with the pulses divided into triplets instead of into doublets, thus:

If this were written as follows, the effect on the hearer would be quite the same, thus:

Instruct the pupils to give two beats to a measure, comprehending three pulses to each beat.

NOTE 341.—In $\frac{9}{8}$ measure (compound triple measure) we have simply triple measure with the pulses divided into triplets, thus:

This would have the same effect on the hearer if written thus:

The pupils should be taught to give three beats to a measure (Down, Left, Up) comprehending three pulses to each beat. Practice all exercises which involve $\frac{9}{8}$ measure.

NOTE 342.—In $\frac{12}{8}$ measure (compound quadruple measure) we have simply quadruple measure with the pulses divided into triplets, thus:

Give four beats to a measure (Down, Left, Right, Up,) comprehending three pulses to each beat. Practice all exercises which involve $\frac{12}{8}$ measure.

THE CHROMATIC SCALE.

NOTE 343.—Before the lesson hour, the teacher should write the chromatic scale ascending on the board, thus:

§ 1308. TR. "The normal tones of a key, those whose names are Do, Re, Mi, Fa, Sol, La and Ti, are called Diatonic tones. What are they called?" CL. "Diatonic tones."

§ 1309. TR. "The intermediate tones of a key are called Chromatic tones. What are they called?" CL. "Chromatic tones."

§ 1310. TR. "When the diatonic and chromatic tones of a key occur in this order, (pointing to the example on the board,) they form what is called the chromatic scale. What is it called?" CL. "The chromatic scale."

§ 1311. TR. "In the chromatic scale ascending (pointing to the board) you will observe that each intermediate tone is indicated by a sharp and resolves to the next diatonic tone above."

§ 1312. TR. "Our notation is not capable of showing the exact position of these intermediate tones. Give attention to the modulator; you will notice that sharp Do (Di) is just half way between Do and Re, (pointing to those syllables in the central column) while on the staff Do and Di are represented by the same degree, (pointing to C and C sharp on the blackboard) the only difference being that a sharp is placed before the note which represents the intermediate tone."

Note 344.—The teacher should now write the chromatic scale descending on the board, thus:

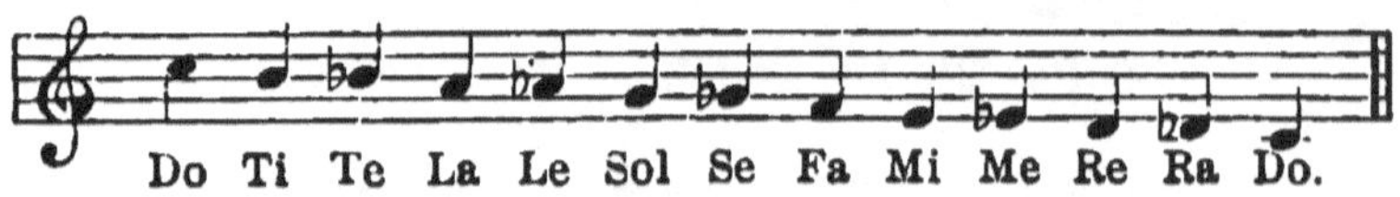

§ 1313. Tr. "In the chromatic scale descending (pointing to the last example on the board,) you will observe that each intermediate tone is indicated by a flat and resolves to the next diatonic tone below."

§ 1314. Tr. "The chromatic scale, as such, is of very little use to singers; but it is highly important that we should be able to sing its intermediate tones and resolve them correctly."

§ 1315. Tr. "In studying the sharps we first sing the diatonic tone above, then descend to the sharp and return Listen and imitate." (Sings thus:)

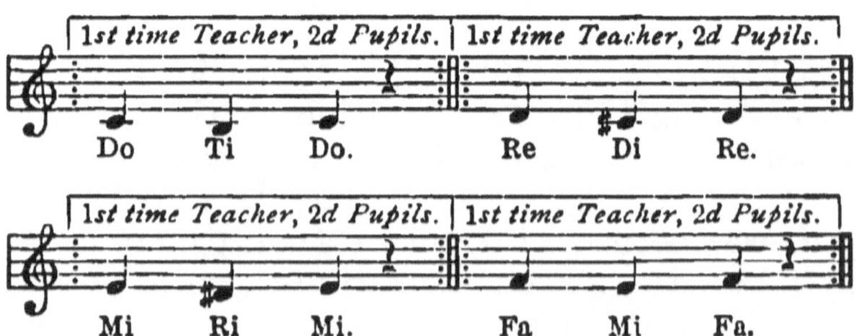

§ 1316. TR. "In studying the flats we first sing the diatonic tone below, then ascend to the flat and return; Listen and imitate." (Sings thus :)

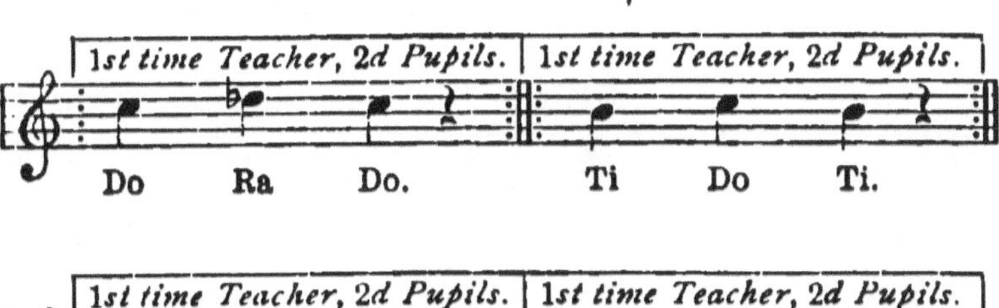

§ 1317. Tr. "These minor seconds are exactly like Mi Fa, and Do Ti, with which we are so familiar; in studying the sharps, we may substitute Do Ti Do, for any of the formulas; Listen and imitate." (Sings thus:)

§ 1318. Tʀ. "In studying the flats we may substitute Mi Fa Mi, for any of the formulas ; Listen and imitate." (Sings thus :)

* Draw attention to the absolute similarity of Mi Fa Mi, and Ti Do Ti.

Remark 8.—The above exercises are not to be written on the board, neither will they be found in the Reader. The teacher is expected to commit them to memory, requiring the pupils to repeat each formula in exact time after he has sung it. These formulas are so written that the rhythm need not be interrupted from the beginning to the finish. They do not require an accompaniment, but if the teacher has an instrument, he should play with his own voice when giving out the formula, thus ensuring more accurate intonation than most teachers are able to give without such assistance; but in no case should he play while the pupils repeat the formula.

Remark 9.—The following "study" is a very important one; and if the teacher has an instrument and can play, he should commit the accompaniment to memory and play with eyes on the class. Observe that the "study" has the form of, and if sung without accompaniment, is virtually the chromatic scale; the harmony, however, is so arranged that every tone is broadly diatonic. In ascending, each tone begins as Tonic, and in the fourth pulse is changed to the third of the dominant seventh chord, thus becoming the *leading tone* of a new key. In descending, this order is reversed; each tone after the first begins as the third of the dominant chord, and through the influence of the augmented sixth chord, is changed, and in the third pulse becomes a new Tonic. The voice part should be written on the board, in large characters so as to be distinctly visible from the farthest seat in the school-room. If the teacher cannot play, he may request a friend to come in occasionally to play the accompaniment for him. If there is no instrument in the school-room, the " study " must be omitted.

Each tone should be commenced with a deep breath, and sustained with a slow, steady swell, regardless of the exact time required.

Copyright 1896, by The John Church Co.

* If this accompaniment is played on a piano the ties should be disregarded.

Ta
Ta
Ta

Ta
Ta
Ta

Ta
Ta
Ta

NOTE 345.—Practice all exercises which involve the chromatic scale.

Reasons for using E♯ instead of F.

Note 346.—Review the pitch-names of the several keys as follows:

§ 1319. Tr. "What pitches form the D major key?" Cl. "D, E, F♯, G, A, B, and C♯."

§ 1320. Tr. "What pitches form the E major key?" Cl. "E, F♯, G♯, A, B, C♯, and D♯."

§ 1321. Tr. "What pitches form the B major key?" Cl. "B, C♯, D♯, E, F♯, G♯, and A♯."

Note 347.—The teacher should point to the syallable names on the modulator, asking the class to glance across to the margin and give the letter names which are printed nearest the vertical line, explaining that the other letters indicate the enharmonic alternates of the several pitches, as F, which they will see is the same as E♯; thus preparing for the explanation of the 7th degree of F♯ key. He then writes on the blackboard, thus:

§ 1322. Tr. "What degree is made to represent 6?" (pointing.) Cl. "The fourth line."

§ 1323. Tr. "What degree represents 8?" Cl. "Fifth line."

§ 1324. Tr. "If the 6 is represented by the fourth line and 8 by the fifth line, what degree must represent 7?" Cl. "The fourth space."

Note 348.—The teacher writes a # before D and F, when the exercise will appear, thus:

§ 1325. "Tr. "What kind of a second must we have between 6 and 7?" Cl. "A major second."

§ 1326. Tr. "Is the example correct as it stands?" Cl. "It is not."

§ 1327. Tr. "How is it incorrect?" Cl. "The interval between 6 and 7 is a minor second instead of a major second, and the interval between 7 and 8 is a major second instead of a minor second."

§ 1328. Tr. "How can I correct the example?" Cl. "By placing a # before E."

Note 349.—The teacher writes a # before the note on the fourth space, when the example will appear thus:

§ 1329. Tr. "What is the distance from E to F?" Cl. "A half-step."

§ 1330. Tr. "What is the distance from E to E#, which is the alternate of F?" (pointing to F and E# on the margin of the modulator). Cl. "A half-step."

§ 1331. Tr. "What is the difference between E# and F?" Cl. "They differ only in representation."

ENHARMONIC CHANGE.

§ 1332. TR. " Changing the representation without changing the tone is called an enharmonic change. What is it called?" CL. "An enharmonic change."

§ 1333. TR. " Why can I not represent 6, 7 and 8 thus?" (writes on another part of the board.)

CL. "Because the interval from 6 to 7 is a third while it should be a second."

AN AUGMENTED PRIME.

§ 1334. TR. " Another reason why the example is wrong is because from 7 to 8 should be a second, while here it is what we call an *augmented prime.*"

PRIMES EXPLAINED.

NOTE 350.—The teacher explains that where two tones are represented by the same degree the interval is called a *prime*. There are two kinds of primes, viz: (*a*) *perfect prime*, which is a unison, *i. e.*, when two parts sing the same tone, and (*b*) *augumented prime* when two parts sing tones a half-step apart, but which are represented by the same degree, thus:— (writes on another part of the board.)

§ 1335. Tr. "Another reason why the example (pointing) is wrong is that 6 being represented by the fourth line, and 7 by the fifth line, leaves the fourth space out of the count entirely. So it becomes clear that the only way to properly represent 7 in this example is to write E♯."

§ 1336. Tr. "Name the pitches in the F♯ major key." Cl. "F♯, G♯, A♯, B, C♯, D♯, and E♯."

Note 351.—Practice all exercises in the key of F♯ major.

Reasons for Beating.

Remark 10.—It is manifestly the teacher's business to guide the *thoughts* of pupils in right channels; to do this, he should in some way be able at all times to know just how they are thinking, and to correct any slip of the mind from right mental processes. Now it is desirable in the extreme for pupils to know exactly on which pulse of a measure they are singing. The pulse, as a ruler, is so tyrannical that the least loss of mental grasp on it marks the entrance of guess work. How are the teachers to *know* that pupils are thinking correctly? A tap of their finger on book or hand will not convey to him their thought. They may be mentally wrong from first to last without the possibility of his knowing it. No way has ever been devised for indicating the individual pulses of a measure *while singing*, except by distinct motions, and there is no way whereby the teacher may absolutely *know* that pupils are mentally right or wrong unless they indicate their thought in some *visible* manner, so that at a glance he can ascertain their mental process. This can be done by beating, and in no other way which has been invented. The ta-te-fe system of Chevet, (which the Tonic-Sol-Fa people have incorporated into their system without giving M. Chevet the credit), cannot be used *while singing.* A bright pupil will catch the general drift of a piece, and sing it correctly *without knowing* it, but no one can beat correctly and not know it. The instant he loses his mental grasp of the pulse, a wrong motion shows the teacher his difficulty, but by the *tap* or *pressure* system, the teacher is as ignorant of the pupil's mental slip as the pupil himself. The teacher who uses the tap or pressure plan would make sorry work of leading a large body of singers, or especially an orchestra by such means. Teachers, don't give up the old orthodox beating and singing by syllables; their fruits make for the healing of the multitudes.

Note 352.—An excellent way to explain the dividing of pulses is as follows:

DOUBLETS.

§ 1337. Tr. "Listen and imitate," (at the rate of about 60 to the minute, one in a second, he beats and describes, thus:)

Down | Left | Right | Up. ||

Note 353.—They imitate. The pulses should recur with the precision of clock-work.

§ 1338. Tr. "Again listen and imitate." (counts 1, 2, 3, in even, exact rhythm, so timing the 1 and 2 that they will come on the down beat, the 3 falling with extra accent on the next pulse, thus:

1—2—|3———||
Down | Left. ||

They imitate, after which the teacher asks:

§ 1339. Tʀ. " Into how many parts did you divide the first pulse ? "   Cʟ. " Into two parts."

§ 1340. Tʀ. " When a pulse is divided into two equal parts, such parts are called Doublets. What are they called ? "   Cʟ. " Doublets."

§ 1341. Tʀ. " What are doublets ? "   Cʟ. " A pulse divided into two equal parts."

§ 1342. Tʀ. " Beat and count one measure, dividing the first and third pulses into doublets."   (They beat and count, thus :)

$$1\text{—}2\text{—}\mid\overset{>}{3}\text{————}\mid 1\text{—}2\text{—}\mid\overset{>}{3}\text{————}\mid\mid$$
$$\text{Down} \mid \text{Left} \mid \text{Right} \mid \text{Up.}$$

Tʀɪᴘʟᴇᴛs.

§ 1343. Tʀ. " A pulse may be divided into three equal parts, in which case we count 1, 2, 3, $\overset{>}{4}$; the 4 falling with extra accent on the next pulse, thus : "

$$1\text{—}2\text{—}3\text{—}\overset{>}{4}\text{————}\mid 1\text{—}2\text{—}3\text{—}\mid 4\text{————}\mid\mid$$
$$\text{Down} \mid \text{Left} \mid \text{Right} \mid \text{Up.}$$

Nᴏᴛᴇ 354.—Remember that these pulses should recur with great precision. After the class has imitated the above example, the teacher asks:

§ 1344. Tʀ. " Into how many parts did you divide the first and third pulses ? "   Cʟ. " Into three parts."

§ 1345. Tʀ. " When a pulse is divided into three equal parts, such parts are called Triplets. What are they called ? "   Cʟ. " Triplets."

§ 1346. Tʀ. " What are Triplets ? "   Cʟ. "A pulse divided into three equal parts."

§ 1347. Tr. " Beat and count two measures, in the first measure, divide first and third pulse into doublets, and in the next measure, divide the first and third pulses into triplets." (The result should be as follows :)

```
               >                    >
1———2——|3————————|1——2——|3————————||
 Down  |  Left   | Right |  Up.   ||

            >                 >
1—2—3—|4————————|1—2—3—|4————————||
 Down |  Left   | Right |  Up.  ||
```

§ 1348. Tr. " Reverse the exercise, let the Triplets come first." (Their effort should be as follows :)

```
            >                 >
1—2—3—|4————————|1—2—3—|4————————||
 Down |  Left   | Right |  Up.  ||

               >                    >
1———2——|3————————|1——2——|3————————||
 Down  |  Left   | Right |  Up.  ||
```

QUADRULETS.

§ 1349. Tr. " Sometimes a pulse is divided into four equal parts, in which case we count 1, 2, 3, 4, $\bar{5}$; the 5 falling with extra accent on the next pulse, thus : "

```
               >                   >
1—2—3—4—|5————————|1—2—3—4—|5————————||
 Down   |  Left   | Right  |  Up.  ||
```

Note 355.—The class imitate; after which the teacher asks:

§ 1350. Tr. " Into how many parts did you divide the first and third pulses? " Cl. " Into four parts."

§ 1351. TR. "When a pulse is divided into four equal parts, such parts are called Quadrulets. What are they called?" CL. "Quadrulets."

§ 1352. TR. "What are Quadrulets?" CL. "A pulse divided into four equal parts."

§ 1353. TR. "Beat and count three measures; in the first measure give me Doublets; in the second, give me Triplets; and in the third, Quadrulets." (They should proceed as follows:)

1—2— 3————	Left	1—2— 3————	Up.	1—2—3— 4————	Left
Down		Right		Down	

1—2—3— 4————	Up.	1—2—3—4— 5————	Left	1—2—3—4— 5————	Up.
Right		Down		Right	

NOTE 356.—From beginning to the end the pulses should recur with the same frequency.

§ 1354. TR. "Reverse the order, let the Quadrulets come first." (Their effort should result as follows:)

1-2-3-4- 5————	Left	1-2-3-4- 5————	Up.	1-2-3— 4————	Left
Down		Right		Down	

1-2-3— 4————	Up.	1—2— 3————	Left	1—2— 3————	Up.
Right		Down		Right	

QUINTOLETS.

§ 1355. TR. "A pulse is sometimes divided into five equal parts; in which case we count to 6, letting the 6 fall with extra accent on the next pulse, thus:"

```
        >                        >
1-2-3-4-5-|6————————|1-2-3-4-5-|6————————||
  Down    |  Left   |  Right   |  Up.   ||
```

NOTE 357.—After the class imitate the exercise the teacher says:

§ 1356. TR. "Into how many parts did you divide the first and third pulses?" CL. "Into five parts."

§ 1357. TR. "When a pulse is divided into five equal parts, such parts are called Quintolets. What are they called?" CL. "Quintolets."

§ 1358. TR. "What are Quintolets?" CL. "A pulse divided into five equal parts."

§ 1359. TR. "Beat and count Quintolets, Quadrulets, Triplets, Doublets, and return to Quintolets (they recite as follows:)

```
         >                          >
1-2-3-4--5-|6————————|1-2-3-4-5-|6————————||
  Down     |  Left   |  Right   |  Up.   ||

         >                        >
1—2—3—4—|5————————|1—2—3—4—|5————————||
  Down   |  Left   |  Right  |  Up.   ||

       >                      >
1—2—3—|4————————|1—2—3—|4————————||
  Down  |  Left   |  Right |  Up.   ||

      >                    >
1——2——|3————————|1——2——|3————————||
  Down |  Left   | Right  |  Up.   ||

       >                      >
1—2—3—|4————————|1—2—3—|4————————||
  Down  |  Left   |  Right |  Up.   ||

        >                        >
1-2-3-4-|5————————|1-2-3-4-|5————————||
  Down   |  Left   |  Right  |  Up.   ||

         >                          >
1-2-3-4-5-|6————————|1-2-3-4-5-|6————————||
  Down     |  Left   |  Right   |  Up.   ||
```

Note 358.—If the teacher desires, Sextolets, Septolets, and Octolets may be added, each introduced in the same way.

§ 1360. Tr. "Turn to page 106, No. 261. Is the first pulse single, or divided?" Cl. "Single."

§ 1361. Tr. "Is the second pulse single, or divided?" Cl. "Divided."

§ 1362. Tr. "How is it divided?" Cl. "Into doublets."

Note 359.—The teacher should go through to the end of the exercise. He can make the questions move along rapidly by making them brief, thus:

§ 1363 Tr. "First pulse in next measure?" Cl. "Single."

§ 1364. Tr. "Second pulse?" Cl. "Doublets."

§ 1365. Tr. "First?" Cl. "Doublets."
§ 1366. Tr. "Second?" Cl. "Single." (etc. to the end.)

Note 360.—Call attention to the *rit.* in the last three measures of No. 261, and teach the class that the first tone of the *rit.* should not be slower than *a tempo*, (*i. e.*, the general movement of the piece); the second tone should be slower than the first; the third slower than the second, and so on slower and slower until the last tone, which is prolonged almost as if marked with a hold (⌒).

Remark 11.—The term *A tempo* is defined as *in equal time*, but it has come to mean the general movement of a composition. Whenever the composer wishes the time to be slackened or to become *gradually slower*, he marks the passage *rit.*, which is the abbreviation of *Ritardando*, meaning *slower and slower*. The general movement is restored by the term *A tempo*. If the composer wishes the movement quickened, he marks the passage *Accel.*, which is the abbreviation of *Accellerando*, meaning *faster and faster*. Again the general movement of the piece is restored by the term *A tempo*. Practice all exercises which involve *rit.*, *accel.* and *a tempo*.

Note 361.—No. 263 should now be studied in the same way No. 261 was studied, thus:

§ 1367. Tr. " Is the first pulse single or divided?" Cl. " Single."

§ 1368. Tr. " Second pulse?" Cl. " Triplets." Tr. " Third and fourth each?" Cl. " Doublets." Tr. " First?" Cl. " Single." Tr. " Second?" Cl. " Triplets." (etc. to the end.)

Unequal Doublets.

Note 362.—The teacher writes an exercise on the board, thus:

and proceeds as follows:

§ 1369. Tr. " All sing this exercise." (They sing.)

§ 1370. Tr. " Is the first pulse single, or divided?" Cl. " Single."

§ 1371. Tr. " Is the second pulse single, or divided?" Cl. " Divided."

§ 1372. Tr. " How is it divided?" Cl. " Into Doublets."

§ 1873. Tr. " Are these doublets equal, or unequal?" Cl. " Unequal."

§ 1374. Tr. " When a pulse is divided into two unequal parts, such parts are called un-equal doublets."

§ 1375. Tr. " Turn to page 106, look at No. 262. Is the first pulse single, or divided ? " Cl. " Single."

§ 1376. Tr. " Second pulse ? " Cl. " Triplets."

§ 1377. Tr. " Third and fourth pulses each ? " Cl. " Unequal doublets." (etc. to the end.)

§ 1378. Tr. " Read exercise No. 263, pulse after pulse, from the beginning to the end." (They begin thus : " Single, triplets, doublets, doublets, single, triplets, doublets, single," etc., continuing to the end.)

Absolute and Relative Pitch.

Remark 12.—Absolute Pitch is a term used to describe the unalterable highness or lowness of tones. Each tone has a fixed pitch which is the result of a certain number of vibrations in a given length of time. Thus, according to American standard pitch 435 vibrations in a second, result in the tone A, first above middle C. Tones with reference to *absolute pitch* are named after the first seven letters of the alphabet.

Relative Pitch is a term used to describe the relationship which tones bear to their Tonic. With reference to *relative pitch*, tones are named Do Re Mi Fa Sol La Ti, major, La Ti Do Re Mi Fa Sil, minor, and One Two Three Four Five Six Seven Eight.

Note 363.—The teacher should explain that the accent mark (>) is used to call special attention to the accent, and for the purpose of indicating the necessity of giving extra accent to certain tones.

Note 364.—In introducing the

Rules for Taking Breath

(See §§ 140 to 144 inclusive, page 31), an excellent way to impress them on the memory is as follows:

As the teacher speaks the words "*two positive*," in § 140, he should lift his left hand with the first and second fingers open and spread apart, and as he speaks the words "*two negative*," he should withdraw his left hand and lift his right hand with the first and second fingers open; as he gives the *first positive* rule he lifts his left hand *with the first finger open*, and says, "The *first positive* rule, we *may* do something," and gives the rule. As he gives the *second positive* rule, he shuts his first finger and opens his second finger, and says, "The *second positive* rule," and gives the rule. As he gives the first negative rule he lifts his right hand with the first finger open and says, "The *first negative* rule, we may *not* do something," and gives the rule; as he gives the *second negative* rule he shuts the first finger and opens the second finger and says, "The *second negative* rule," and gives the rule.

The pupils should be required to repeat these rules frequently as they proceed with the following lessons. The finger illustrations will help to recall the different rules to mind, *e. g.* the first finger of the left hand will recall the first positive rule; the second finger will recall the second rule, and so on with the right hand and the negative rules.

The Round.

Note 365.—At No. 52, page 16, explain that the Round is a short vocal composition so constructed that its several numbered parts may be sung in harmony. It is performed as follows:

One division of the class begins alone; the second division begins at the beginning when the first division has reached the figure 2; the third division begins when the second reaches the figure 2, etc. Each division should continue to repeat the round until signaled by the teacher to stop.

This form of composition is technically called a Canon in the Unison.

THE METRONOME.

REMARK 13.—From this time onward all exercises the exact speed of which is important, will have that speed indicated by Metronome Marks.

The Metronome is an instrument which was invented for the purpose of giving the exact movement of any piece of music. It consists of a pendulum to which is attached a movable weight, and which is made to vibrate by machinery resembling that of a cylinder escapement watch. Behind the pendulum is fixed a column of figures from 40 upward, and when the weight on the pendulum is placed at any of these figures, they indicate the number of vibrations to the minute; thus $\quarternote = 60$ means that the weight being placed at 60, there will be 60 distinct ticks or vibrations in a minute, each tick or vibration indicating the time of a quarter note. It is recommended that teachers procure a pocket metronome, which is more accurate than machine metronomes and only costs fifty cents. For sale by the publishers of this work.

PREPARING LESSONS.

REMARK 14.—All blackboard exercises should be written plainly, with the notes far enough apart, and large enough to be easily read from the most distant point in the room. In preparing a lesson the teacher should go to the class-room, write an exercise on the board, and examine it from the farthest seat. It is not probable that the exercise will be too plainly written, or too large. Inexperienced teachers usually write their exercises so small that those who sit on the rear seats cannot read them. An excellent plan, in preparing lessons, is for two friends to work together, one to listen from the most distant seats, while the other explains a point, and then change, each suggesting to the other in turn.

Da Capo.

(Supplementary to ? 613, page 88.)

Note 366.—Draw attention to the fact that the close is put where the word "Fine" occurs, though it be in the middle of the music as printed; only a double bar being put at the *apparent* end of the piece, where the D. C. stands. (Observe No. 159, page 57.

Male and Female Voices.

(Supplementary to Note 86, page 51, and following.)

Note 367.—If the teacher be a woman, she should select a gentleman, whom we will call Mr. X, and, having drilled him previously, let him sing the low tones for her, while she commences the lesson with ? 302, and makes such changes thereafter as will correspond with the beginning of the lesson, somewhat as follows:

§ 1379. Tr. "Gentlemen remain silent (She requests Mr. X. to sing Do, pitch C, second space of the Bass staff, and says :)

§ 1380. Tr. "Ladies sing that tone." (They sing a tone just an octave too high, of course.)

§ 1381. Tr. "You did not sing the tone Mr. X. sang. I will ask him to repeat it and you may try again. (etc., etc., as given on page 52, § 305, and following.)

Phrasing.

Remark 15.—Phrasing is defined by Webster as "The act or method of grouping the notes so as to form distinct musical phrases." But this definition is incomplete. Phrasing, in its broadest sense, covers everything necessary to the correct expression of a musical thought, either in the writing, or the rendering, of a musical composition.

NOTE 368.—The foundation principle of Phrasing, from the vocal view-point lies in the obvious fact that in singing a low tone less effort is necessary than in singing a high tone. It follows as a matter of course, that in progressing from a low tone which requires less effort, to a high tone which requires greater effort, we must increase our power, and *vice versa*. We thus establish two general rules, viz:

§ 1382. TR. " Ascending passages should be sung with increasing power."

§ 1383. TR. " Descending passages should be sung with decreasing power."

NOTE 369.—The exceptions to these fundamental rules are so numerous as to render necessary a careful study of the structure and aim of the composition which may be under consideration.

THE STRUCTURE OF A COMPOSITION.

THE PERIOD.

NOTE 370.—Expressing thought in music may be compared to the expression of thought in language. In writing an article for the press, for example, when we have used words enough to make complete sense, we call such grouping of words a SENTENCE. So, in writing music, as soon as we have expressed complete sense we call such portion of our work a PERIOD.

THE SECTION.

NOTE 371.—As the Sentence is divided into clauses, so our Period is divided into *Sections*. A section is usually one half of a Period.

THE PHRASE.

Note 372.—As the clauses of a Sentence are divided into smaller portions by commas, so our Sections are divided into smaller portions called *Phrases*.

THE GERM.

Note 373. The smallest divisions of a Sentence consist of words and syllables, so the smallest portion of a Phrase is a *Germ*.

Note 374.—A musical Germ consists of two or more tones, thus, for example:

The Germ.

THE PASSAGE.*

These two tones alone seem to have no meaning whatever, but if we repeat them, thus:

The Germ repeated.

they begin to awaken an interest, and if we repeat them at a lower pitch, thus:

The Passage.

or at a higher pitch, thus:

The Passage.

---

*A passage is a portion of a phrase which begins satisfactorily and ends unsatisfactorily, or *vice versa*.

they form a *passage*, which excites expectation in the mind of the listener, and so leads on to the phrase, thus:

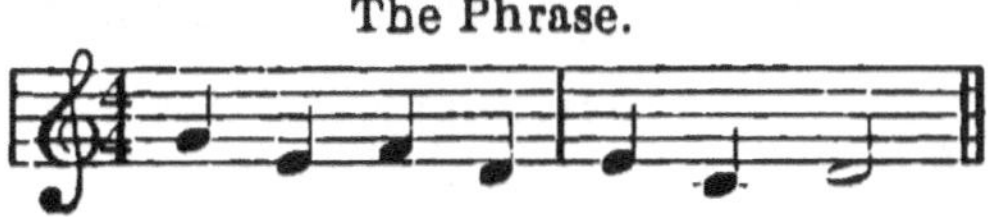

or thus:

NOTE 375.—A Phrase is that part of musical composition which expresses sense, but not complete sense.

EXPANSION.

NOTE 376.—A germ may not only be repeated at the same pitch, or at a higher, or a lower pitch, but it may be *Expanded, i. e.*, made up of larger intervals, thus:

CONTRACTION.

NOTE 377.—A germ may also be *Contracted*, thus:

AUGMENTATION.

NOTE 378.—A germ may be *Augmented, i. e.*, made to occupy twice as much time, thus:

DIMINUTION.

NOTE 379.—A germ may be *Diminished, i. e.,* made of notes one half as long as those of the original, thus:

The Germ Diminished.

NOTE 380.—Two of these treatments may be combined, for example, we may expand and diminish the germ at the same time, thus:

The Germ Expanded and Diminished.

NOTE 381.—The germ may be Contracted and Diminished at the same time, thus:

The Germ Contracted and Diminished.

NOTE 382.—The germ may be Expanded and Augmented, thus:

The Germ Expanded and Augmented.

NOTE 383.—The germ may be contracted and augmented, thus:

The Germ Contracted and Augmented.

NOTE 384.—One of the members of a germ may be divided equally, thus:

A member of the Germ divided
equally.

NOTE 385.—One of the members of **a germ may** be
divided **unequally, thus:**

A member of the Germ divided
unequally.

THESIS.

NOTE 386.—A passage may be so constructed as to
excite expectation and so become *Thesis*, or the question asked, thus:

Thesis.

ANTITHESIS.

NOTE 387.—The above requires an answering passage which is called *Antithesis*, or the question answered, thus:

Antithesis.

NOTE 388.—The question may be extented so as to
require the whole Phrase, thus:

The whole Phrase as Thesis.

MOZART.

NOTE 389. — The above requires an answering
Phrase, thus:

TONE-CHAIN.

NOTE 390.—A well defined melody may be called a *Tone-chain*.

ASCENDING TONE-CHAIN.

NOTE 391.—Passages or Phrases which progress from low to high, are called *Ascending Tone-chains*, thus:

According to our first general rule, this passage should take the *crescendo*.

DESCENDING TONE-CHAINS.

NOTE 392.—Passages or phrases which progress from high to low are called *Descending Tone-chains*, thus:

According to our general rule, this should take the *diminuendo*.

VAGUE TONE-CHAINS.

NOTE 393.—Tone-chains which ascend and descend irregularly are called *Vague Tone-chains*, thus:

Note 394.—A vague Tone-chain may, however, belong to an ascending series, thus:

Vague Tone-Chain, ascending.

and so take the *crescendo.*

Note 395.—A vague Tone-chain may belong to a descending series, thus:

Vague Tone-Chain, descending.

and so require the *diminuendo.*

THE PHRASE-MARK.

Note 396.—In the following example, the phrase should receive the *crescendo,* for although it is a vague Tone-chain, it progresses from low to high, and there is no intimation from the author to the contrary. It should be sung with one breath, as indicated by the curved line which is called a *Phrase-mark.*

Note 397.—The following phrase, though vague, is so decidedly an ascending one as to leave no doubt as to its requiring the *crescendo.*

Note 398.—So the answering phrase, as decidedly requires the *diminuendo*, for a similar reason, thus:

Note 399.—The two following phrases are both Ascending, but, as the author has indicated that they should each be sung with the *Swell*, the general rules must yield to the arbitrary marking, thus:

Note 400.—This leads us to another *general rule*, viz:

§ 1384. Tr. " All well defined phrases should, as a general thing, begin softly, increase, decrease, and end softly, unless the author has for special reasons marked them otherwise, in which case all rules that conflict must be set aside for the time being; an author is supposed to know best how his composition should be performed."

§ 1385. Tr. " A long, slow tone, unless it belongs to an ascending, or a descending phrase, should take the *swell*."

§ 1386. Tr. " All dissonances and suspended tones should be forcibly struck and their resolutions clearly marked."

Note 401.—Thus far we have considered this subject with direct regard to solo, or one voice work.

Our teachers throughout the country are more generally connected with four-voice work, or chorus singing, and will naturally ask "How can I adapt this instruction to my choir or chorus practice?" The reply is: In most four-part compositions which are written by musical scholars there will be an artistic portent, so to say, in the chief melody, which may be treated according to the foregoing remarks. The leader must study the composition beforehand and determine exactly how the musical thought may be best brought out. He will arrive at his decision by studying the melody—keeping in mind that the other parts are intended as aids in the expression of the thought contained in the melody, *i. e.*, if the melody requires a *cres.* all parts must unite in such *cres.*, etc., etc., whether they ascend and descend with the melody or not.

NOTE 402.—No. 138, page 49, is an illustration of the principle that all parts should unite with the melody (which is in the soprano in this case), to produce the required effect.

NOTE 403.—Every instant of a *crescendo* should be louder than the preceding instant, in other words, every tone should end louder than it begins, instead of making a *crescendo* by jumps, so to say, that is: holding a tone from beginning to end with the same power, and then beginning the next tone louder and sustaining it with one degree of power, etc., which cannot be called a *crescendo*. Pure *crescendo* is a *growth*, *i, e.*, a gradual but continued increase. So also is *diminuendo* a gradual but continual decrease.

NOTE 404.—The teacher will meet with numerous instances where the melody will be transferred to some other part, but the expression must be governed by the melody, and other parts must be willing to be subservient to the part which carries the melody for the time being.

Note 405.—Many compositions are not intended to be rendered with reference to light and shade. Pieces like Coronation ("All hail the power,") cannot be made more expressive by singing some tones loud and others soft; neither can the phrases be made with the *crescendo* or *diminuendo;* the firm on-marching of the rhythm is mostly relied upon to give expression to the words.

Note 406.—Again, some music will require the study of the complete harmonic effects; its interweaving harmonies, its sequences, its interesting progressions, its smooth modulations, must all be regarded. Each important element must be recognized, and all should be so brought out as to produce a symmetrical and artistic whole

Note 407.—Other important factors enter into the perfect rendering of a vocal composition, viz : proper breathing, the correct "placing" of the voice, the best quality of tone to express the required emotion, neat enunciation (utterance of consonant and vowel sounds), effective articulation (joining of vowel and consonant sounds), self-control, mental grasp of the idea to be brought out, etc., etc.

Note 408.—To discuss all these points would far transcend the limit set for the present volume, but the writer cannot drop this subject without a few hints concerning the production of the articulate sounds of our language, and a few words with regard to the fundamental principle of breathing, the combination of sounds such as those of the double vowels, double consonants, etc.

POSITION.

Note 409.—The best position for singing is the standing posture, but as it would be tiresome to stand throughout a long lesson, the next best position, sitting, may be taken. The class, however, should frequently be requested to stand during the practice of an exercise. Whether sitting or standing, let the body be erect, the chest well forward, and the chin slightly elevated. While explanations are being given, or while the teacher is lecturing, pupils may rest against the backs of the seats, but when engaged in singing they should invariably straighten up, put their feet back under the chair, or seat (noiselessly, of course), so as to assist in retaining an erect position of the body.

BREATHING.

NOTE 410.—The following exercises are recommended. First: Stand on both feet with the weight of the body a little more on the balls of the feet than on the heels, let the arms hang limp by the side, (imagine them attached to the shoulders by a leather string), chest well forward.

NOTE 411.—Second: Close the lips and inhale a deep breath; after the lungs are inflated ask yourself the question, mentally, "Can I force another atom of air into my lungs," do so if possible.

NOTE 412.—Third: Open the mouth and let the breath flow out slowly, holding it back with an aspirate (whispered "h" as in "ha"), until the lungs are empty. This we will call DEFUSIVE BREATHING. Practice three times deliberately.

NOTE 413.—Fourth: Position as given at Note 410, close the lips and inhale a deep breath, ask yourself the mental question (Note 411);

NOTE 414.—Fifth: Open the mouth and throat and allow the breath to pass out without restraint, but also without effort to expel it. Simply let the lungs collapse; in other words "let go." This we will call EXPULSIVE BREATHING. Practice three time deliberately.

Note 415.—Sixth: Position as given at Note 410, close the lips and inhale deeply, ask yourself the mental question (Note 411);

Note 416.—Seventh: Open the mouth and expel the breath with greath effort, empty the lungs in a half-second. This we will call Explosive breathing. Practice three times deliberately.

Note 417.—It will be observed that in practicing these exercises we are educating the muscles which are brought so prominently into action in controlling the breath. The Defusive gives exercise to the muscles which *hold back* the breath. In the Expulsive we learn to *let go*. In the Explosive we bring into action the muscles which *push the breath forward*.

Note 418. — These exercises are most beneficial if practiced in the morning immediately upon rising. The chest and abodomen are then untrammeled and consequently the muscles will have free play.

Note 419.—Eigth: Position (Note 410), deep breath, sing with syllable "Ta" (pitch about D), and sustain the tone eight seconds. The teacher may hold his watch, or count two quadruple measures, giving one second to each pulse (Met. 60). At the end of the first measure he speaks the word "four" distinctly and on the last pulse of the second measure he says "stop."

Note 420.—Ninth: Same again and sustain the tone twelve seconds (three quadruple measures). On the fourth pulses of the measures say distinctly "four," "eight," "stop."

Note 421.—Tenth: Same again and sustain the tone sixteen seconds (four measures). On the fourth pulses say "four," "eight," "twelve," "stop."

. Note 422.—Eleventh: Same again and sustain the tone twenty seconds (five measures). Announce the fourth pulses by saying distinctly "four," "eight," "twelve," "sixteen," "stop."

NOTE 423.—Twelfth: Same again and sustain the tone twenty-four seconds (six measures). Announce the fourth pulses by saying "four," "eight," "twelve," "sixteen," "twenty," "stop."

NOTE 424.—Ladies should, as a rule, be able to sustain a good pure tone twenty-eight or thirty seconds, and gentlemen should, as a rule, be able to sustain a good tone forty seconds.

NOTE 425.—Pupils may determine, with tolerable accuracy, whether the breath is all being converted into tone by holding the back of the hand within four inches of the lips while sustaining the tone. If any warmth is felt, some of the breath is being allowed to pass out without being converted into tone; in other words the tone is too breathy, not pure.

NOTE 426.—Another way to discover whether or not the tone is too "breathy" is to stand before a mirror, and hold a lighted candle within three inches of the lips, and sing a steady tone. If the blaze flares, the breath is not well "husbanded," and the singer should obtain a firmer mental grasp on the muscles.

NOTE 427.—An excellent exercise for educating and developing the muscles which control the lungs is as follows:

NOTE 428.—Stand erect (Note 410), with hands behind you; put the backs of the hands together, interlock the fingers and turn them upward and over toward the body; keep turning the hands at the wrists until the elbows are thoroughly straighened; this will pull the shoulders back, and draw the lungs open, so to say. Keep the head well back and the chin slightly elevated. Take a deep breath as explained at Note 411. Children and young people will have no difficulty in practicing this exercise. Some adults who are broad between the shoulders may, perhaps, find it too difficult.

Vowel Sounds.

Note 429.—By giving particular attention to certain six of our vowel sounds we develop not only these six, but at the same time gain control of the muscles which are brought into action in the formation of all the sounds of our language, whether vowels or consonants.

Note 430.—The six most prominent vowel sounds in our language are ē, ā, ä, a̤, ō and o͞o. The following rules for the proper production of these six sounds will be found practicable :

Note 431.—First, ē (as in *meet*): In producing this sound the mouth should be opened just enough to admit the end of the fourth finger between the teeth. Its shut position prevents the forming of a voice-chamber in the mouth, and renders necessary the protruding of the lips, which thus rounds the edges of the tone, so to say, and thereby takes away the sharp buzzing sound which is the peculiar characteristic of this vowel unless so modified. Short ĭ and short y̆ are so closely related to long ē that they must be treated similarly.

Note 432.— Second, ā (as in *lay*): Long ā is a double vowel, the radical sound of which requires that the mouth should be open sufficiently to insert the end of the thumb between the teeth. As this sound vanishes in long ē the lips have much to do with its purity. Even in giving the radical sound the mouth is too much closed to admit of a full resonant tone, and so must have the aid of the lips. These should be slightly protruded, and as the sound vanishes, should assume the form for long ē (see Note 431). Bear in mind that the vanish and cessation of tone should be nearly simultaneous.

Note 433.—Third, ä (as in äh): This is a single vowel, *i. e.*, has no vanish. The mouth should be opened sufficiently to admit the ends of the first and second fingers between the teeth. The lips should remain passive, neither protruded nor drawn back.

Note 434.—Fourth, a̤ (as in a̤wl): This is also a single vowel. The mouth should assume about the same position as for ä (see Note 433), perhaps a little wider open; the cheeks slightly compressed, the lips thrown forward and the aperture rounded, but kept as large as possible.

Note 435.—Fifth, ō (as in gō): This is a double vowel. The radical sound is produced with the teeth separated nearly as much as for a̤ (see Note 434). The cheeks should be slightly more compressed, the lips still more protruded and drawn together to form a smaller aperture. It vanishes into long double o͞o, which is described in the following:

Note 436.—Sixth, o͞o (as in bo͞ot): This is a single vowel, and should be studied in connection with long ō, of which it forms the vanish. The cheeks are more compressed than for ō, the teeth are brought nearer together (to about the width of the end of the thumb), and the lips are more tightly puckered. While this is a smothered tone, so to say, it is much used and should be carefully studied.

Note 437.—The study of these six vowel sounds will greatly facilitate the production of all the other vowel sounds, many of which are formed by combining some of these, thus, ī is a union of ä and ē; oy and oī (as in *boy, boil*), are formed by uniting a̤ and ĕ, etc.

How to teach the Proper position of the lips in singing long ē, short ĭ and short y̆.

Note 438.—Call attention to page 161 by questions which will lead them to observe the different movements. Practice by syllables first, then with words, the pupils beating, of course. After singing several times through, and the piece has become quite familiar, draw the attention of the singers to the vowel ē somewhat as follows:

§ 1387. Tr. "In which word do you find the first long ē?" Cl. "In the first word."

§ 1388. Tr. "All parts sing that word and prolong the ē until I withdraw my hand." (They sing.)

Note 439.—While they sing the teacher holds his open hand high, with the palm towards the class, when he wishes them to cease the tone he suddenly withdraws his hand.

§ 1389. Tr. "Sing the word again, being particular to make the ē distinct." (They sing.)

Note 440.—The thin, ready quality which is natural to this vowel will thus be made prominent.

§ 1390. Tr. "Sing the same chord again, with the words ' *even me* ', being careful to give a pure long ē." (They sing.)

§ 1391. Tr. "Sing the same chord again to the syllable mōo." (They sing.)

§ 1392. Tr. "Sing the same again and change the ōo into ēē, without changing the position of the lips, when I close my hand, sustain the long ē until I withdraw my hand." (They sing.)

Note 441.—The teacher holds his hand open about three seconds and then closes it with the middle finger resting on the thumb, when the effect will be mōo........ēē. After they have held the last sound three or four seconds the teacher withdraws his hand and the tone ceases.

§ 1393. Tr. " Spell and pronounce the word 'me,' thus: Moo.........ee.........me; be careful not to change the position of the lips in going from oo to ee." (They sing.)

§ 1394. Tr. "Sing the words ' even me,' beginning with moo, thus :"

Note 442.—The teacher sings moo.........e....ven me...... and the class imitate.

§ 1395. Tr. "Now sing the word me, with the lips drawn back, being particular to make the ē prominent, as you did awhile ago." (They sing.)

Note 443.—The effect will be so thin, disagreeable and even ludicrous that usually a spontaneous laugh will follow.

§ 1396. Tr. "The tone at which you laugh is no worse than the one you sung when we first begun this drill, but now that your attention has been called to it, you see how disagreeably thin and buzzing the vowel ē is unless it is modified by the lips. This is the case with all voices until they have passed under the hand of the master. Moreover, when I tell you that long ē is the ·most frequently used vowel in our language, and that short y̆ and short ĭ are closely related to long ē, you will comprehend how important it is that they should be modified by the lips."

§ 1397. Tr. "Now let us sing this piece again, with particular reference to all words which contain the vowel ē."

Note 444.—Practice first for all the long ē's, then ĭ's, and again for the short ĭ's, somewhat as follows:

§ 1398. Tr. " Sing as far as the second word which contains long ē, and prolong ē regardless of the exact time, then return to the beginning and go to the third word having long ē," etc.

Note 444.—In each instance the teacher should question the class as to "which is the next word that has long ē ? " and then commence at the beginning, go to that word and hold the ē, etc., until they have practiced all the long ē's and short y̆'s and short ĭ's in the piece.

Note 445.—A most excellent exercise for the control of the muscles of the face, and the muscles which open and shut the mouth, etc., is as follows :
The teacher makes a triangle on the board with the letters written at the angles, thus:

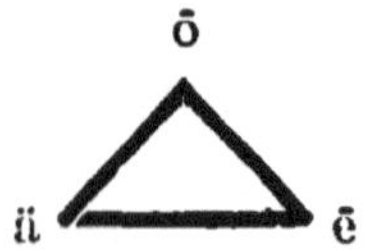

and then, requesting them to sing as he points, he begins with ō and points to one after the other, slowly at first, but increases the speed until their mouths are opened and shut with great rapidity. Then beginning with ē, he repeats the process, after which he begins with ä, etc.

Note 446.—The following exercise is intended for every-day practice. The teacher should commit the accompaniment to memory and drill with his eyes on the class. An excellent plan is for the teacher to get some one to play the accompaniment, thus enabling him to go back and forth among the singers, correcting here and there, giving each person at least a glance. By a nod of approval, or a negative shake of the head and a motion of the hand he can keep their attention upon the position of the lips, the teeth, the cheeks, the breathing, etc.

EXERCISE FOR THE PRACTICE OF THE SIX VOWEL SOUNDS.

NOTE 447.—The following study should be preceded by the careful practice of each of the vowel sounds as given in Notes 431 to 438 inclusive.

all sō cōōl. Thēse dăys ăre all sō cōōl.

Thēse dăys ăre all sō cōōl. Thēse dăys ăre

all sō cōōl. Thēse dăys ăre all sō cōōl.

Thēse dāys äre all sō cōōl.
Thēse dāys äre

all sō cōōl.
Thēse dāys äre

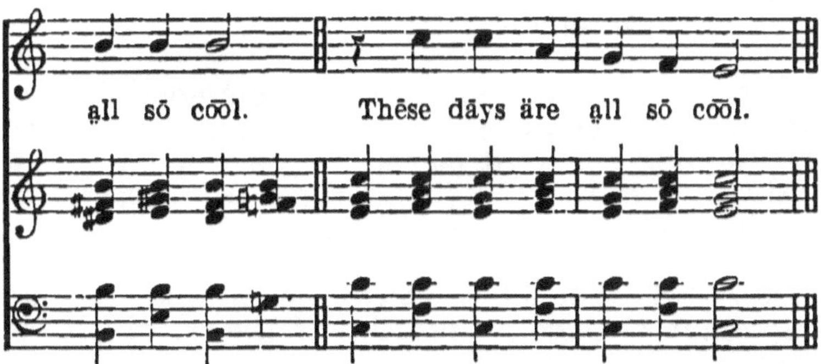
all sō cōōl.
Thēse dāys äre all sō cōōl.

Note 448.—The following table showing the various vowel sounds may be useful:

TABLE OF SINGLE VOWELS.

ä, as in fär.	ĭ, as in hĭt.
a̤, " " bạll.	ŏ, " " nŏt.
ă, " " hăt.	ô, " " fôr.
ē, " " mēet.	o͞o, " " mo͞on.
ĕ, " " mĕt.	w, prefixed by o͞o.
ê, " " hêr.	y, prefixed by ē.

Note 449.—The following table shows the various double vowels:

TABLE OF DOUBLE VOWELS.

ā vanishes into ē.
ī   "   "   ē.
ō   "   "   o͞o.
oi and oy vanish into ē.
ou vanishes into o͞o.

Note 450.—In uttering these double vowels the radical sound should be prolonged as much as possible, leaving the least possible time for the vanish and consonant combinations.

Note 451.—A fault more or less common is that of prolonging a sound on its vanish instead of its radical sound, thus, the word *hate* would be sung hā-ē....t, instead of hā........ēt, and the word *light* would be sung lī-ē......t, instead of lī .....ēt.

Note 452.—The following exercise will be found an important one for the practice of the various vowel sounds.

EXERCISE WITH SINGLE VOWELS. H. R. P.

*If this accompaniment is played on a piano the ties should be disregarded.

Note 453.—After practicing the vowel sounds as set forth in the foregoing pages, it remains to study the consonant sounds, which we now proceed to do. We can only hope to block out a plan of study which the student will follow as far as it leads in his direction.

The Consonant Sounds.

Note 454.—A plan of study which has proved successful is to take the consonants in the order in which they occur in our alphabet.

Note 455.—B. This labial sonant mute has but one sound. It is made by compressing the lips and producing as much tone as possible at the larynx, thus: (The teacher gives the element twice, and the pupils imitate.)

Note 456.—The teacher may connect this element with the six vowel sounds given in Note 430, thus: Bĕ, Bā, Bä, Bạ, Bŏ, Bōō, and sing them to the exercise under Note 447, either carrying it through the whole octave or stopping at the end of the first phrase, according to the amount of time which he may have at his disposal.

Note 457.—C. Stands for four sounds. (1) Its name sound as in the word *city*. This is made by placing the tip of the tongue near the roots of the upper teeth, and forcing the breath through. The teacher gives the element twice, sharp and short, and the pupils imitate him. He then pronounces the word *city*, giving the sound of c with energy, and the pupils repeat it. S sometimes stands for this sound. (2) The sound that c stands for in the word *suffice*. In making this sound, the position of the tongne, teeth, and lips are the same as in giving the first sound, the only difference being that the breath is vocalized. The teacher gives the element twice, and the pupils imitate. He then pronounces the words *suffice*, *sacrifice*, etc., the pupils repeating each in its turn. (3) The sound that c stands for in the word *come*. This sound is made by placing the middle of the tongue firmly against the roof of the mouth, and suddenly forcing them apart, so to say, with the breath. The teacher gives the element twice, and the pupils imitate. He then pronounces the words *come, came, cold*, etc., the pupils repeating them. K sometimes stands for this sound. (4) The sound that c stands for in the word *ocean*. It is made by protruding the lips and rolling them outward slightly, thickening the tongue and turning the tip downward, and forcing the breath through. The teacher gives the element twice, sharp and short, and the pupils imitate him. He then pronounces the words *ocean, concience, associate*, etc., the pupils repeating each in its turn. Sh. sometimes stands for this sound.

Note 458.—D. This dental sonant mute has two sounds. (1) Its name sound as in the word *did*. This is made by placing the tip of the tongue firmly against the roof of the mouth near the front teeth, and vocalizing the breath with energy. The teacher gives the element twice, and the pupils imitate. He then pronounces the words *did, dido, daddy*, etc., the pupils repeating them after him. (2) The sound of T as in the word *vexed*. It is made by placing the tip of the tongue firmly against the roof of the mouth near the teeth, the same position as for the first or name sound of this letter, and suddenly forcing the breath through ; a sound which resembles a slight explosion. The teacher gives the element twice, and the pupils imitate. He then pronounces the words *vexed, mixed, helped*, etc., the pupils repeating them after him. T sometimes stands for this sound.

Note 459.—D always takes its second sound when it is preceded by a surd in the same syllable. As *kissed, looked, dipped*, etc.

Note 460.—F. This labiodental consonant has two sounds. (1) A surd fricative, as in the word *fife*. It is made by placing the under lip against the upper teeth, and forcing the breath through. The teacher gives the element twice, and the pupils imitate him. He then pronounces the words *fife, fame, foam*, etc., the pupils repeating them after him. (2) A sonant fricative, as in the word *of*. It is made by placing the under lip against the upper teeth, as in the first sound of this letter, the only difference being that the breath is now vocalized. The teacher gives the element twice, the pupils imitating him. He then pronounces the words *of, thereof, hereof*, and *whereof* (the only words in our language in which f takes its second sound), and the pupils repeat them. V sometimes stands for this sound.

Note 461.—G has three sounds. (1) A guttural sonant mute as in the word *go*. This sound is made by injecting vocalized breath into the pharyngeal cavity, which is closed by pressing the middle of the tongue up against the roof of the mouth. The teacher gives the element twice, and the pupils imitate him. He then pronounces the words *go, gewgaw, rugged*, etc., and the pupils repeat them. (2) A compound consonant, as in *gem*. This sound is made by injecting vocalized breath into the mouth, the position of which is nearly the same as for the first sound of *d*. The teacher gives the element twice, and the pupils imitate him. He then pronounces the words *gem, rage, ginger*, etc., the pupils repeating them. (3) A sonant fricative, as in the word *rouge*. The position of the mouth is like that described under *sh* (see exercises for vigorous enunciation No. 20), the principal difference being that here the breath is vocalized. The teacher gives the element twice, the pupils imitating him. He then pronounces the words *rouge, cortege, menagerie*, etc., and the pupils repeat them.

Note 462.—H. This is a simple aspirate. Send the breath ahead of the vowel, so to say, as in *hate, here, hard, hit, home*, etc,

NOTE 463.—J. This is a diphthongal consonant compounded of *d* and *zh*. Place the mouth, tongue, etc., in position for *ch* in *church*, and then vocalize the breath. The teacher gives the element twice, and the pupils imitate. He then pronounces the words *join*, *jury*, *jest*, etc. The pupils repeating them.

NOTE 464.—K. This guttural surd mute (as in *kind*) agrees with the sonant *g*, see Note 461 (1). The sound is made by pressing the back of the tongue up against the soft palate and forcing them apart by the breath. The teacher gives the element twice, and the pupils imitate, after which he pronounces the words *kill*, *elk*, *milk*, etc., and the pupils repeat them. C sometimes stands for this sound. See Note 457 (3).

NOTE 465.—L. This palatal sonant fricative consonant is made by placing the tip of the tongue against the roof of the mouth near the front teeth, but with the sides of the tongue free for the passage of the breath, as in the word *low*. The teacher gives the element twice, the pupils imitating. He then pronounces the words *low*, *hole*, *all*, etc., and the pupils repeat them.

In *battle*, *bridle*, etc., "the *l* in an unaccented following an accented syllable fulfills the office of a vowel," hence *noble* should not be sung no-*bul*, *people* should not be sung peo-*pul*, etc., although the same authority suggests that "the voice-glide (by which is meant the minute connection between the *b* and *l* in the above words), naturally intervenes in making a separate syllable with the *l*."

NOTE 466.—M is the labionasal consonant, as in *me*. The sound is made by closing the lips and collecting the vocalized breath in the open oral passage, which being cut off by the compressed lips the sound is sent through the open nasal passages. The teacher gives the element twice, and the pupils imitate him. He then pronounces the words *my*, *may*, *him*, etc., and the pupils repeat them. *M* serves as a vowel in *ism*, *schism*, *chasm*, etc.

Note 467.—N is the dentonasal, or linguanasal consonant, as in *no*. The oral passage is stopped by gently pressing the edges of the tongue against the upper part of the mouth, thereby throwing the vocalized breath through the nasal passages which are left open. The teacher gives the element twice, the pupils imitating. He then pronounces the words *no, none, ten*, etc., and the pupils repeat them. In *even, often, maiden*, etc., *n* serves as a vowel.

Note 468.—P is the labial surd mute, as in *pay*. It is made by the sudden release of the breath accumulated within the distended walls of the mouth. The teacher gives the element twice, and the pupils imitate. He then pronounces the words *pay, pen, cup, pup*, etc., and the pupils repeat them.

Note 469.—Q is always followed by *u*, and will be considered among the double consonants later in this article.

Note 470.—R. The limits that the writer has set for this article precludes the possibility of a very full description of this much abused consonant. Speaking in general terms this sound may be said to be made with the edges of he tongue resting against the roof the mouth (the hard palate) near the teeth, the middle depressed somewhat giving a slightly cylindrical passage between the tongue and the hard palate. Then by raising the point of the tongue, we get the *r* sound. Some authorities approve of a slight trilling of the *r* when it occurs before a vowel in the same syllable. The sound of *r* bears a close relation to vowels of the mixed order. Such as ŭ in *cup*, û in *ûrn*, ê in *fêrn*, etc. "In New England a usage has prevailed, not approved or used by well educated people, of dropping the *r*" in all such words as *war, far, more, here, farm*, etc. But generally throughout the United States, the *r* takes a more or less clear sound as a consonant in all situations.

Note 471.—S. This is a sibilant, and has four sounds. (1) Its name sound as a surd sibilant, in such words as *yes, hiss, kiss, see*. It is made by placing the edges of the tongue against the upper teeth, the point depressed and the breath forced through the small passage between the tongue and the roof of the mouth near the front teeth. (2) A sonant as in *is, as, was*, etc. This sound differs from the surd, as described above, in that the breath is vocalized. (3) The sound of *sh* as heard in *mission, excursion, passion*, etc., in which the breath is forced through the almost closed teeth, and (4) the sound of *zh*, heard in the words *fusion, vision, explosion*, etc. Practice as was suggested with the previous consonants.

Note 472.--T is the dental surd mute, as in *tot, ten, tie, tone*, etc. The position is exactly the same as for the dental sonant mute *d*. (See Note 458.) Practice as before.

Note 473.—V is a labiodental fricative element (sonant correlative of the surd *f*), as in *vain, vivid, vast*, etc. The position for this sound is precisely the same as for the surd *f*. (See Note 460.) Practice as before.

Note 474.—W is a labial sonant fricative, always beginning with $\bar{oo}$ or $\breve{oo}$, as in *we, went, away*, etc. The position of mouth, lips, etc., is exactly the same as for $\bar{oo}$. (See Note 436.) Practice as with the previous consonants.

Note 475.—X has three sounds. (1) A surd like *ks* as in *fix, wax*, etc., and (2) a sonant, like *gz* as in *exalt, exert*, etc.; (3) like *z* at the beginning of a syllable, as in *Xenia, Xerxes*, etc. Practice as before.

Note 476.—Y is a consonant (palatal sonant fricative) only when it begins a word or a syllable. It is always a vowel at the end or in the middle of a word or a syllable. It commences with a brief sound of long $\bar{e}$ or short $\breve{i}$. The position of the tongue, etc., s nearly the same as that for long $\bar{e}$, only slightly farther back. The teacher gives the element twice, and the pupils imitate him. He then pronounces the words *you, yet, yield*, etc., the pupils repeating them. This sound is frequently represented by *i* as in *senior, junior, familiar*, etc.

NOTE 477.—Z is ordinarily a sonant fricative, as in *zero, zest*, etc. It is the cognate of the surd *s*, being made by nearly the same position of the mouth, tongue and teeth, except that the tongue is pressed closer to the hard palate. The teacher gives the element twice, the pupils imitating him. He then pronounces the words *zero, zest, zeal*, etc., and the pupils repeat them. This sound is represented by *s* as in *is, has, his, business*, etc. See Note 471 (2). And by *c* as in the word *suffice, sacrifice*, etc. See Note 457 (2).

DOUBLE AND TRIPLE CONSONANTS.

NOTE 478.—After the vowels and single consonants, it remains to mention the double and triple consonants.

NOTE 479.—There are less than fifty instances in our language wherein two or more consonants combine to begin a word or a syllable. In the following list will be found examples of most of these so arranged as to bring them in connection with the tones of a simple melody.

NOTE 480.—The practice of a few of these exercises at each lesson, or choir rehearsal, will work wonders in a short time. The immediate and permanent effects of such practice will be exceedingly gratifying. They should be committed to memory, the teacher singing a phrase, and the class imitating.

EXERCISES FOR VIGOROUS ENUNCIATION.

The following exercises should be sung to the melody on page 279 :

2. Br—Brē, brā, brạ, brō, brōō.

  ‖: Brake, brush and bramble crown the brook's bright brow. : ‖

3. Ch—Chē, chā, chä, chạ, chō, chōō.

  ‖: Chase, chime and chanting have no charms for a churl, : ‖

4. Ch—(*as in chord*, like k, see Note 464).

5. Cl—Clē, clā, clä, clạ, clō, clōō.

  ‖: Click, clamor, click clack clangs the clashing old mill. ; ‖

6. Cr—Crē, crā, crä, crạ, crō, crōō.

  ‖: Crisply the water-cresses creep by the creek. : ‖

7. Cz—(as in czar, *zär*, like z, see Note 477).

8. Cz—(as in czech, *chĕk*, like *ch*, see No. 3).

9. Dr—Drē, drā, drä, drạ, drō, drōō.

  ‖: Drink not the dreadful dram, its dregs are drear. : ‖

10. Dw—Dwē, dwā, dwä, dwạ, dwō, dwōō.

  ‖: Dwindled and dwarfish are the dwellings where they dwelt. :

11. Fl—Flē, flā, flä, flạ, flō, flōō.

  ‖: Flocks flying, flitting, fleetly flitting in their flight. : ‖

12. Fr—Frē, frā, frä, frạ, frō, frōō.

  ‖: Frank, Fred and Fritchie frisk and frolic, frown and fret. : ‖

13. Gl—Glē, glā, glä, glạ, glō, glōō.

  ‖: Gladly we're gliding, glancing o'er the glassy glare. : ‖

14. Gr—Grē, grā, grä, grạ, grō, grōō.

  ‖: Green grows the grass upon the graded ground. : ‖

15. Kr—(as in krä, an ape, like *cr*, see No. 6).

  Ph—(as in *phase*, like *f*, see Note 460.)

16. Pl—Plē, plā, plä, plạ, plō, plōō.

  ‖: Plowing, planting, plodding, pleasant plan for the wise. : ‖

17. Pr—Prē, prā, prä, prạ, prō, prōō.

  ‖: Prim, proud and pritty, prattlen Poll, prince of pets. : ‖

18. Qu—Quē, quā, quä, quạ, quō, quōō.

  ‖ : Quaint, queer quiver, quoth the quack to the Queen. : ‖

19. Sc—Scē, scā, scä, scạ, scō, scōō.

  ‖ : Scudding from the scaffold, 'scaped the sly, scheming scamp. : ‖

20. Sh—Shē, shā, shä, shạ, shō, shōō.

  ‖ : Sharp, short and shocking shot the shell from the shore. : ‖

21. Sk—(like *sc*, see No. 19).

22. Sl—Slē, slā, slä, slạ, slō, slōō.

  ‖ : Sleighs slipping, sliding, slant and slew, slip and slide. : ‖

23. Sm—Smē, smā, smä, smạ, smō, smōō.

  ‖ : Smack, smatter, smashing, smites the smart small smith. : ‖

24. Sn—Snē, snā, snä. snạ, snō, snōō.

  ‖ : Snapping, snarling, sniv'ling sneers the sneezing, snoring snob. : ‖

25. Sp—Spē, spā, spä, spä, spō, spōō.

  ‖ : Speed the spying Spartan, spare his spattered, spangled spurs. : ‖

26. Sq—Sqē, sqā, sqä, sqạ, sqō, sqōō.

  ‖ : Squalling in their squalor, how they squabble, squeeze and squirm.: ‖

27. St—Stē, stā, stä, stạ, stō, stōō.

  ‖ : Still Stanley stumbles as he staggers through the storm. : ‖

28. Sw—Swē, swā, swä, swạ, swō, swōō.

  ‖ : Swell, swing, swagger, sweat and swelter, swash and swim. : ‖

29. Th—(lisping) Thē, thā, thä, thạ, thō, thōō.

  ‖ : Thousands of thistles through the thatcher's thick thumb. : ‖

30. Th—(vocal lisping) Thē, thā, thä, thạ, thō, thōō.

  ‖ : This, that, the other, hither, thither, there they go. : ‖

31. Tr—Trē, trā, trä, trạ, trō, trōō.

  ‖ : Try tripping trampping, tracing traffic, truck and trade. ; ‖

32. Tw—Twē, twā, twä, twạ, twō, twōō.

  ‖ : Twice twenty twisters, each a twine doth entwist. : ‖

33. Wh—Whē, whā, whä, whạ, whō, whōō.

  ‖ : Whack, whang, whopper what a whirling, whistling whale. : ‖

34. Chr—(as chromo, like *cr*, see No. 6).

35. Phl—(as in phlox, like *fl*, see No. 11).

36. Phr—(as in phrase, like *fr*, see No. 12).

37. Sch—(as in school, like *sc*, see No. 19).

38. Scr—Scrē, scrā, scrä, scrạ, scrō, scrōō.

  ‖ : Scribes without scruple scratch and scribble o'er the scroll. : ‖

39. Sph—Sphē, sphā, sphä, sphạ, sphō, sphōō.

  ‖ : Sphere, spherics, spheroid, sphingid, sphex, sphinx, sphene. : ‖

40. Sphr—Sphrē, sphrā, sphrä, sphrạ, sphrō, sphrōō.

  ‖ : Sphragide, sphragistics. sphragide, sphrigosis, sphragide. : ‖

41. Spl—Splē, splā, splä, splạ, splō, splōō.

  ‖ : Splice followed splitting with a splutter and a splash. : ‖

42. Spr—Sprē, sprā, sprä, sprạ, sprō, sprōō.

  ‖ : Sprightly they're springing through the spray so spry. : ‖

43. Squ—Squē, squā, squä, squạ, squō, squōō.

  ‖ : Squeezed by their squalor how they squabble, squirm and squall. : ‖

44. Str—Strē, strā, strä, strạ, strō, strōō.

  ‖ : Strength comes from striving, strongly striving in the strife. : ‖

45. Thr—Thrē, thrā, thrä, thrạ, thrō, thrōō.

  ‖ : Thrice thirty thrushes thrill'd the throng through and through. : ‖

46. Thw—Thwē, thwā, thwä, thwạ, thwō, thwōō.

  ‖ : Thwack, thwaite and thwittle thwarts the thwite thwartly thwack. : ‖

47. Tsch—(as Tschego—an ape, like *ch*, see No. 3).

Variations of the Perfect Cadence.

Note 481.—Introduce this subject somewhat as follows. Play the Perfect Cadence, thus:

Call attention to its familiar sound and say:

§ 1399. Tr. "You would recognize it if I should play it, thus:" (Plays it as written at top of the first column, page 107.)

§ 1400. Tr. "You see that I varied it by repeating each chord. You will still recogni⁻ it if I play it like this:" (Plays the melody of No. 270 with the right hand, and the accompanying harmony with the left hand.)

§ 1401. Tr. "Turn to page 107 and sing No. 270 by syllables." (They sing.)

Note 482.—Great care must be taken to make the sixteenth notes smooth and even, *i. e.*, neither slighted. Don't hurry. There never was a tone so short but there was ample time for its performance.

Note 483.—Practice No. 271. Then divide the class and let Sop. and Tenor sing No. 271, while the Alto and Bass sing No. 270, and *vice versa*.

Note 484.—Call attention to the syncopation in No. 272 and see if the class has profited by the provious study of the Syncope. Practice No. 272 and No. 273 separately, after which let Sop. and Tenor sing No. 273 and Alto and Bass sing No. 272, then change parts. Nos. 274, 275, 276 and 277 involve the syncope, but while attention is drawn to the syncopated tones, the teacher should keep in mind that the sixteenth notes must be carefully and smoothly performed.

NOTE 485.—At 280 the practice of triplets is reviewed. Divide the class into two equal divisions, and let one division sing 280, the other 281, and then change parts.

NOTE 486.—A very important exercise is to have one division sing triplets (No. 280) and the other division sing quadrulets (No. 282), and then change parts. First, all sing 280 and go to 282, in exact time, then without stopping sing 280 again. After a few times through in this way, the two numbers may be sung together.

Always begin this part of the work with 270, adding one or two new numbers at each lesson until the class can sing the whole page without stopping.

MOVEMENT.

§ 1402. TR. "The most accurate way of showing how fast a piece of music should be performed is the Metronome mark. There are also certain technical terms taken from the Italian language, which are used for the same purpose by musicians of all languages."

NOTE 487.—Some German musicians, with Schumann at their head, have refused to fall into the general custom, and put nearly all their directions in their own language. Certain English and American church writers have feebly attempted to follow this unwise custom; unwise, because it would necessitate the learning of all languages by every broad-minded musician.—C. F.

NOTE 488.—In the following table the terms which refer to the movement or *tempo* have been graded, so as to form a scale of degrees from slow to fast. It is only approximately correct in *grading*, for, unfortunately, different composers use the same term differently, e. g., *Andantino* and *Larghetto*.

For pronunciation of these terms see GLOSSARY, page 287.

FIRST CLASS. — From 50 to 60 beats per minute.	*Adagio.* *Grave.* *Lento.* *Largo.*	Very slow.
SECOND CLASS.— From 56 to 76 beats per minute.	*Larghetto.* *Andante.* *Andantino.* *Moderato.*	Gentle and distinct; somewhat less slow than the first class.
THIRD CLASS.— From 72 to 104 beats per minute.	*Maestoso.* *Allegretto.* *Tempo giusto.* *Con commodo.*	This is the middle class, and indicates a brisk, but serious and dignified movement.
FOURTH CLASS.— From 100 to 132 beats per minute.	*Allegro.* *Vivace.* *Con spirito.* *Spiritoso.*	Brilliant and spirited.
FIFTH CLASS. — From 126 to 160 beats per minute.	*Con brio.* *Con fuoco.* *Presto.* *Prestissimo.*	This class indicates the utmost degree of rapidity.

NOTE 489.—These are the principal words which are used for the purpose of indicating movement; their meaning, however, is frequently modified and intensified by the use of other words, such as the following:—

Assai, very; as, *Adagio assai,* very slow; *Allegro assai,* very brisk, very lively; *Moderato assai,* very moderately.

Meno, less; as, *Meno adagio,* less slow; *Meno allegro,* less fast; *Meno mosso,* less motion.

Molto, much, very; as, *Molto allegro,* very lively; *Molto adagio,* very slowly. This word is more frequently used for the purpose of modifying terms which indicate expression and style. *Molto crescendo,* increase greatly; *Molto diminuendo,* decrease greatly.

Mossa, motion (this word is almost universally written *mosso,* which is a participle, and means changed, moved, affected).

Più, more; as, *Più adagio,* more slowly; *Più allegro,* more lively; *Più mosso,* more motion (faster).

Poco, a little, slightly, somewhat; as, *Poco adagio,* somewhat slow; *Poco lento,* a little slow. *Poco* is the opposite of *Molto.* The signification of *Meno* (less) and *Più* (more), is often modified by *Poco,* as *Poco più mosso,* a little more motion; *Poco più presto,* a little more rapidly.

Quasi, as, like, almost; as, *Largo quasi andante,* in a broad, large style, but somewhat less slowly; almost *andante.*

Troppo, too much; as a musical term it is generally used with *Non* (not) and *Ma* (but); as, *Ma non troppo,* but not too much; *e. g., Adagio ma non troppo,* slow, but not too much so; *Allegro ma non troppo,* fast, but not too much so.

Tempo, time; as, *Tempo primo,* in the original time.

STYLE AND EXPRESSION.

§ 1403. Tr. "Expression and style are indicated by certain words from the Italian language, which, like those indicating movement, are understood and employed by musicians of all languages."

Note 490.—The following Glossary includes the principal terms which are used for the purpose of indicating the style and expression of musical compositions.

Note 491.—The terms in the Glossary are taken from **Palmer's New Pronouncing Pocket Dictionary of Musical Terms,** which was copyrighted in 1889. Publishers are hereby warned that hundreds of these terms are defined in such a way that the author's copyright will enable him to hold all imitators to strict liability for infringement.

GLOSSARY

OF

ONE THOUSAND MUSICAL TERMS,

TOGETHER WITH THEIR DEFINITIONS AND
PRONUNCIATION.

The vowels in this Glossary are marked as follows: āte, äh, ăt;
ēke, ĕnd; īre, ĭt; ōde, ŏn, ōōze; lūte, hŭt; ü French
sound; French n like n in bank.

E. English; *F.* French; *G.* German; *Gr.* Greek; *H.* Hebrew;
I. Italian; *L.* Latin; *S.* Spanish; *W.* Welsh.

By H. R. Palmer, *Mus. Doc.*

Abbreviation marks. (1) An oblique stroke across the stem
of a half-note shows that as many 8th notes are to be played as
equal a half-note: Two strokes indicate 16th notes, etc.; (2) A
diagonal mark with a dot either side denotes a repetition of
the previous group or measure; (3) Figures in or over a measure show the number of measures rest or silence.

Ä cä-pel′lä. (*I.* päl′.) See *Alla capella.*

Äc-cĕl-e-rän′dō. (*I.* tchĕl-ā.) Accelerating the time.

Accent. A stress given to a pulse to mark its position in the
measure.

Accessory notes. Notes a degree from the principal note of a
turn.

Accessory parts. Accompaniments.

Accessory tones. Harmonics.

Äc-ciäc-cä-tu′rä. (*I.* at-tchak-a-tōō′rä.) From *acciaccare*, to
crush. A short *appoggiatura* crushed against the principal
note, but instantly released.

Accidentals. Occasional flats, sharps, and cancels (naturals).

Accompaniment. The subordinate parts accompanying the
voice or principal instrument.

Ä cem′bä-lō. (*I.* tchäm.) For the piano.

Acoustics. (kow.) The science of sounds.

Added lines. Short lines that enlarge the staff.

(287)

Added sixth. A sixth added to the sub-dominant chord. It forms the first inversion of the super-tonic seventh.

Ad lib´i-tum. (*L.*) At will, performed at pleasure.

Æsthetics. (*Gr.*) The theory or philosophy of taste; the science of the beautiful in nature and art, or that which treats of the principles of *belles lettres* and the fine arts; in music, that which relates to sentiment, expression, and the power of music over the soul.

Äf-fet-tu-ō´sō. (*I.* tōō-ō´zŏ.) Affectionately; tenderly; with feeling.

Äf-fli-zi-ō´ne. (*I.* flēt-sĕ.) Affliction, sadness, sorrow.

Ä-ge´vō-lĕ. (*I.* jă´.) With facility and lightness.

Ä-gil´i-tä. (*I.* jĕl.) Agility, lightness.

Äg-i-tä´tō. (*I.* äj-ē.) Agitated; implies hurrying.

Ag´nus De-i. (*L.* ag´nōōs dä´ē.) Lamb of God. See *Mass*.

A in alt. First added line above, of the treble staff.

A in altissimo. Octave above A in alt.

Air. A musical thought expressed by a pleasing succession of single tones; a melody, tune, aria.

Äl fi´nĕ. (*I.* fē´nĕ.) To the end.

Äl. (*I.*)
Äl´lä. (*I.*) } In the, to the, in the manner of, in the style of.

Äl´lä bre´vĕ. (*I.* brä´.) Originally a measure filled by a double-whole note, *a breve*, hence the name; found in old church music; modern *alla-breve* measure has two half-notes, usually quick, indicated by 2-2, or the letter C with a stroke through it.

Äl´lä cä-pel´lä. (*I.* päl´.) (1) In church style; (2) voices unaccompanied; (3) if accompanied play in unison with voices; (4) equivalent to *alla breve*.

Äl-lĕ-grä-men´tĕ. (*I.* män´.) Joyfully, gaily.

Äl-lĕ-gret´tō. (*I.* grä´.) Slower than *allegro*.

Äl-le´grō. (*I.* lä´.) Quick, lively; a quick movement.

Äl´ lō´cō. (*I.*) To the previous position or place.

Äll´ ot-tä´vä. (*I.*) At an octave (higher or lower).

Äll´ ot-tä´vä äl´tä. (*I.*) An octave above.

Äll´ ot-tä´vä bäs-sä. (*I.*) An octave below.

Äll´ u-ni´sō-nō. (*I.* ōō-nē´sō-nŏ.) In unison.

Äl pi-ä-ce´rĕ. (*I.* pē-ä-tchä.) At pleasure.

Äl segn´ō. (*I.* sän´yō.) Return to the sign.

Ält. (*I.*) } All notes in the octave above fifth line,
Al-tis´si-mō. (*I.* tēs´ē.) } treble staff, are *in all*; those in the next octave are *in altissimo*.

Äl´to. High; the part formerly sung by high male voices, now sung by low female voices.

Älto clef. The C clef on the third line.

A-mä′bi-le. (*I.* bē-lā.) Lovely, gentle, tender, amiably.

Ambrosian chant. A system introduced by Ambrose, Bishop of Milan, in the 4th century, out of which grew the Gregorian system.

Ambrosian Hymn. The Te Deum, attributed to Ambrose.

Ä-men. (*H.*) Be it so.

American fingering. The thumb is marked ✕, the fingers 1, 2, 3, 4; see under *Fingering*.

American Sixth. An augmented sixth chord consisting of le, do, ri, fi, and resolving to sol, do, mi, sol; for the origin of Augmented 6th chords, see *Palmer's Theory of Music*, pp. 93 to 97.

Ä mez′zä vō′ce. (*I.* mät′sä vō′tchĕ.) Soft; with half voice.

Ä-mō′rĕ. (*I.*) Love, affection, ardor.

Än-cō′rä. (*I.*) Again, once more; see *encore*.

Än-cŏr pi′u mōs′so. (*I.* pe′o͞o.) Quicker, more motion.

Än-dän′tĕ. (*I.*) Going moderately, a moderate movement.

Än′ĭ-mä. (*I.*) } Life, animation, spirit; with courage, dash,
Än-ĭ-mä′tō. (*I.*) } and fire; lively and energetic.

Antecedent. The phrase which is imitated; (2) the passage which is answered; (3) the subject of a fugue.

Anthem.
Anthem, double.
Anthem, full.
Anthem, soli.
Anthem, verse. } A composition usually set to Bible words; *full*, for chorus only; *verse*, for quartet and chorus; *soli*, for solos and chorus; *double*, for two choirs singing antiphonally.

Anticipation. The entrance of one or more tones before they are expected, thus causing a momentary discord.

Ä pi-ä-ce′rĕ. (*I.* pē-ä-tchä′.) At pleasure.

Ä pō′cō. (*I.*) . A little.

Äp-päs-sĭ-ō-nä′tō. (*I.*) With feeling, passion.

Äp-pog-giä-tu′rä. (*I.* podg-ä-to͞o.) From *Appoggiare*, "to lean upon." A melodic ornament. It consists in suspending or delaying a tone by means of a tone introduced before it, the time of the latter being always taken from the principal tone.

Äp-pog-giä-tu′rä, long. (*I.* pŏdg-ä-to͞o′) Takes half the time of the following note; expressed by a grace-note..

Äp-pog-giä-tu′rä, short. (*I.* pŏdg-ä-to͞o′.) Is crushed against the following note; expressed by a grace-note with an oblique dash through the stem; see *Acciaccatura*.

Äp-pog-giä-tu′rä, double. (*I.* pŏdg-ä-to͞o′.) Two short notes, usually one below and one above the principal note.

Är-peg′gio. (*I.* pädg-jō.) The tones of a chord performed in succession instead of simultaneously.

Arrangement. The whole or part of a composition, adapted to uses other than that for which it was written.

Är′sis. (*Gr.*) The up-stroke in beating time.

Äs-sä′i. (*I.* sä′ē.) Very much, enough, copiously.

Ä tĕm′pŏ. (*I.*) In time; (2) a return to the original time after a change.

Ä tĕm′pŏ ru-bä′tŏ. (*I.* rōō.) Robbed time; the time made slightly irregular for better expression.

Ä tre, or ä 3. (*I.* ä trä.) For three performers; a Trio.

Ä tre cor′dĕ. (*I.* trä.) For three strings.

Ät-täc′cä. (*I.*) Attack; the vigorous entry of voices or instruments.

Ät-täc′cä su′bi-tŏ. (*I.* sōō.) Begin at once.

Augmentation. The appearance of the subject of a fugue in notes of double the original value.

Augmented intervals. Those which are a half-step greater than major and perfect intervals.

Augmented prime. A prime a half-step greater than a unison.

Augmented 2d. A 2d a half-step greater than a major 2d.

Augmented 4th. A 4th a half-step greater than a perfect 4th.

Augmented 5th. A 5th a half-step greater than a perfect 5th.

Augmented 6th. A 6th a half-step greater than a major 6th.

Augmented 6th, Chords of the. See *American 6th; French 6th; German 6th; Italian 6th.*

Augmented octave. A half-step greater than a perfect octave.

Ä u′nä cor′dä. (*I.* ōō.) On one string; use soft pedal.

Authentic cadence. Perfect cadence, *q. v.*

B. Sub-tonic in the C key; Tonic in key of five sharps, major mode; Ger. H (hä); in German, B indicates the B flat Key or Tone.

Băg-ä-telle′. (*F.* tĕl.) A short, easy piece; a toy, a trifle.

Băl′lad. Formerly a dance-song, from *Ballare,* to dance. Now used as synonymous with *Song.*

Bäl-lä′dĕ. (*G.*) ⎫ A dance; a ballad; the name of four piano
Bäl-lä′tä. (*I.*) ⎭ pieces by Chopin, viz: op. 23, 38, 47, 52.

Băl-let′. (*F.* lä′.) · A story without words, told by dancing and gesticulation : a pantomime.

Bar. A line drawn across the staff to show the strong pulse of a measure ; erroneously applied to the measure itself.

Bär-cä-rō′lä. (*I.*) ⎫ A boat-song in imitation of the songs
Bär-cä-rōlle′. (*F.* rōl′.) ⎭ of the Gondoliers.

Baritone. The male voice between Bass and Tenor; the bass saxhorn in B flat or C.

Bass clef. Sign of the bass staff; it fixes *middle C* on the first short line above.

Bass, figured. See *Thorough Bass*.

Bäs-soon'. A wood-wind bass instrument.

Bä-tōn'. (*F.* bä-tōn'.) The stick used for beating time.

Beats. The outward manifestations of pulses; motions of the *baton* which indicate the pulses of a measure.

Ben. (*I.* bän.)
Be'nĕ. (*I.* bā'nĕ.) } Well; used to express approval.

Ben mär-cä'tō. (*I.* bän.) Well and clearly marked.

Ben mod-ĕ-rä'tō. (*I.* bän.) Very moderately.

Ben tĕ-nu'tō. (*I.* bän tĕn-noo'.) Well held.

Bind. A tie.

Binding tone. A tone common to two chords.

Bis. (*I.* bĕs.) Twice; repeat the passage so marked; again.

Boc'cä chi-u'sä. (*I.* kĕ-oo'zä.) With mouth closed.

Bouche fer'mé. (*F.* boosh fär-mä.) With mouth closed.

Brace. A mark connecting two or more staffs.

Brä-vu'rä. (*I.* voo'.) Daring: Music written to test the skill and powers of an artist.

Breit. (*G.* brīt.) Broad.

Bre've. (*I.* brä'vĕ. Eng. brēve.) A double whole-note.

Bril-län'tĕ. (*I.* brĕl.) Brilliantly, sparklingly; in a showy style.

Bri'ō. (*I.* brē'.) Vigor, force, animation.

Buf'fä. (*I. fem.* boo'fä.)
Buf'fō. (*I. mas.* boo'fō.) } From *Buffare*, to blow; a comic singer.

Buōn. (*I.* bwōn.) Good.

Bur-let'tä. (*I.* boor-lät'.) A comic operetta, a farce.

C. Tonic of C key; French ut; Italian Do; One in the Ionic mode; the only tone from which a major scale can be formed without sharps or flats. Unfortunately several methods are used to denote the exact octave in which a tone occurs. The following plan is logical, and combines the good features of all the prevailing schemes, viz.:—a small letter denotes the octave which begins with *middle c*; a small letter with one stroke (c') denotes the next octave above; with two strokes (c") the second octave above; with three strokes (c''') the third octave above, etc., always reckoning from *middle c.* So in descending, a capital letter indicates the octave first below *middle c*; a double capital denotes the second octave below, etc.

C. Denotes the octave below *middle c.*

CC. Denote the second octave below *middle c.*

CCC. Denote the third octave below *middle c.*

C C C C. Denote the fourth octave below *middle c.*

Ȼ On the staff following the Signature, denotes quadruple measure, formerly called "common time."

Ȼ Indicates *Alla breve. q. v.*, or *Alla capella, q. v.* Two pulses in a measure.

Cadence. The end of a musical thought or expression.

Cadence, authentic. See *Perfect cadence.*

Cadence, perfect. Ending with the tonic chord, 1st position, preceded by the dominant chord.

Cadence, imperfect. Ending with the tonic chord, 2d or 3d position, preceded by the dominant chord.

Cadence, half. A sub-ending in dominant harmony.

Cadence, plagal. Ending with the tonic chord, preceded by the sub-dominant chord.

Cadence, deceptive. One in which the dominant chord is unexpectedly followed by any other than the tonic chord.

Cadence, suspended. One in which certain tones of the final chord are delayed by tones of the previous chord.

Cä-den′zä. (*I.* dänt′sä.) A flourish preceding the end, or an important section, of a composition.

Cä-län′dō. (*I.*) Diminishing and retarding.

Cäl′mä. (*I.*)
Cäl-mä′tō. (*I.*) } With calmness, tranquillity, repose.

Cä-lō′rĕ. (*I.*) With heat, warmly, full of passionate feeling.

Cancel. A sign (♮) used to cancel the effect of a previous flat or sharp, unfortunately called a *Natural.*

Căn′on. A rule; an imitation; a piece in which one part is imitated by another, note for note.

Căn-tä′bi-le. (*I.* bē-lä.)
Căn-tän′dō. (*I.*) } In a melodious, singing style.

Căn-tä′rĕ. (*I.*) To sing.

Căn-tä′tä. (*I.*) A short oratorio without action.

Căn′tō. (*I.*) The upper voice part; the melody.

Căn′tus fir′mus. (*L.* tōōs, mōōs.) Tenor or chief melody, now given to *soprano,* hence called *canto;* (2) a subject to which counterpoint is added.

Căn-zō′nä. (*I.* tsō′.) A short song with unimportant words.

Cä-pĕll-meis′ter. (*G.* mīs.) See *Maestro di cappella.*

Cä′pō. (*I.*) Head, commencement.

Cä′pō däs′trō. (*I.*) A nut used for the purpose of shortening guitar strings.

Cä-pric′ciŏ. (*I. n.* prē-tchŏ.)
Cä-pric-ciŏ′sō. (*I. a.* prē-tchŏ′zō.) } A freak, whim, fancy; a composition irregular in form; in a free, fantastic style.
Caprice′. (*E. n.* ka-prēs′.)

Cä-ril-lons. (*F*. kä-rŭ-yŏng.) A peal or set of bells.

Carol. (*E*.) A song of joy for Christmas or Easter.

Catch. (*E*.) A humorous round so written that the singers catch each other's words and pervert them.

Catgut. (*E*.) Strings made of the intestines of sheep.

Cä-vä-ti′nä. (*I*. tĕ′.) A smooth and melodious air, frequently preceded by a recitative.

C clef. The clef which fixes *middle C* on whatever degree it is placed upon; formerly used for alto and soprano, now used principally in orchestral music, or for the tenor part in vocal music.

Ce-le-ri-tä′. (*I*. tchä-lä-rĕ.) Celerity, velocity.

Cel′lo. (*I*. tchäl′.) Violoncello, *q. v*.

Chä-conne′. (*F*. shä-cŏne.) A slow dance in 3-4 measure.

Changing tones. Passing tones occurring on the accent.

Chant. A musical recitation.

Chant, double. A chant extending through two verses.

Chant, single. A chant extending through one verse.

Che. (*I*. kä.) That, than, which.

Chest tones.
Chest voice. } The lowest register of the voice.

Chi-ä′rō. (*I*. kĕ.) Clear, pure, brilliant tone.

Chi-ä-rō-scu′rō. (*I*. kĕ skōō.) Light and shade, expression.

Chi-ä′vĕ. (*I*. kĕ.) Key or clef.

Chi-u′sō. (*I*. kĕ-ōō-zō.) Close, hidden, concealed.

Choeur. (*F*. kur.) The chorus or choir.

Chō-rä′lĕ. (*G*.) A slow hymn tune.

Chord. A combination of tones.

Chord, characteristic. The dominant chord.

Chord, common. See *Common chord*.

Chord, dominant. See *Dominant chord*.

Chor′dä sep′ti-mä. Chord of the seventh.

Chord, equivocal. See *Diminished seventh chord*.

Chorus. A band of singers; a composition for a number of voices; the refrain or *Burden* of a song.

Chromatic. By half-steps.

Chromatic half-step. An augmented prime, *q. v*.

Chromatic scale. One that consists of half-steps.

Chromatic signs. Accidentals; sharps, flats, and cancels (naturals).

C in alt. Second added line above, of the treble staff.

C in altissimo. The octave above C in alt.

Classical music. Music which is chaste, pure, and refined, and conforms to the best authority in art.

Cla-vi-chord. The forerunner of the piano.

Cläv-ier. (*F. ẽr.*) The old name for the *clavichord*.

Clĕf. (*F.*) A sign which determines the pitch of tones as represented by the degrees of the staff.

Clef, alto. Fixes middle C on the third line.

Clef, bass. Fixes middle C on the added line above.

Clef, C. Fixes middle C on whichever degree it is placed on.

Clef, F. See *Clef, bass*.

Clef, G. Fixes middle C on the added line below.

Clef, tenor. Fixes middle C on fourth line; in most modern
American music it fixes middle C on the third space.

Close harmony In which the parts are kept close together.

Cō (*I.*)
Cō´i. (*I.* kō-ĕ.) } With, at the same time with.

Cō´dä. (*I.*) A few measures added for a more effective close.

Col. (*I.*)
Col´lä. (*I.*) } With.
Col´lō. (*I.*)

Col´lä vŏ´ce. (*I.* tchē.) With the voice.

Coll' ōt-tä´vä. (*I.*) With the octave

Cō´mĕ. (*I.*) As, like, the same as.

Com-mō´dō. (*I.*) Quietly, easily, without haste.

Common chord. A chord with a fundamental, third and fifth.

Common measure. A measure with any multiple of two
pulses: its signs are ²⁄₂, ²⁄₄, ⁴⁄₄, ⁴⁄₈, etc.

Common metre. A four-line stanza (8, 6, 8, 6).

Compass. The whole range of tones capable of being produced
by a voice or an instrument.

Complementary interval. One which, added to any other,
completes the octave.

Complementary signatures. Signatures that denote those
different keys which are represented alike on the staff, as
4 sharps and 3 flats; sharp signatures have their complements
in flat signatures and *vice versa*, the united number of signs
being seven, thus:

Sharps,	0	1	2	3	4	5	6	7
Flats,	7	6	5	4	3	2	1	0
	7	7	7	7	7	7	7	7

Compound intervals. Intervals greater than an octave.

Compound measures. Measures of two, three, or four *groups
of threes*, as 6-4; 6-8; 9-4; 9-8; 12-4; 12-8.

Cōn. (*I.*) With.

Cōn bri´ō. (*I.* brē´ō.) With life.

Concerted music. Music for several performers.

Con-cer′tō. (*I.* tchär′.) A composition in Sonata form for solo instrument with orchestra.

Concert pitch. Standard pitch ; various pitches have prevailed during the past 200 years, viz : French, 1699=404 vibrations per second ; Handel's, 1740=416 ; French, 1858=448 ; London, 1859=455 ; the French " Diapason Normal "=435, is now coming into general use, for pitch A, first above middle C.

Conductor. A leader of chorus and orchestra.

Cŏn e sĕn′zä strō-mĕn′tē. (*I.* ā sĕn′tsü.) With and without instruments.

Cŏn ĕs-prĕs-si-ō′nĕ. (*I.* ē.) With expression.

Cŏn fōr′zä. (*I.* fōrt-sü.) With force.

Cŏn fu-o′cŏ. (*I.* fōō.) With fire.

Cŏn gli. (*I.* glē.) With the.

Cŏn gräz′i-ä. (*I.* grät′sē-ü.) With grace.

Cŏn mō′tō. With motion, spirited.

Connecting tone. A tone common to two chords.

Cŏn ot-tä′vä. (*I.*)
Cŏn 8vä. (*I.*) } With the octave ; to be played in octaves.

Cŏn prĕ-ci-si-ō′nĕ. (*I.* tchē-zē.) With precision and exactness.

Consecutive fifths. Perfect fifths progressing in similar motion.

Consecutive octaves. Octaves progressing in similar motion.

Con′sō-nance, perfect, in which the interval is invariable, as fifths, fourths, and octaves. As inversion does not change their characteristics, they are called *Perfect intervals.* Other intervals change their characteristics by inversion ; thus major intervals become minor when inverted, and *vice versa ;* augmented intervals, inverted, become diminished, and *vice versa.*

Con′sō-nance, imperfect, in which the interval varies, *e. g.,* thirds and sixths may be either major or minor.

Cŏn sor-di′ni. (*I.* dē′nē.) (1) With mutes, violin ; (2) With soft pedal, piano.

Cŏn spi′ri-tō. (*I.* spē′rē.) With spirit.

Con′trä. (*I.*) Against ; with other words it means below, under.

Con-träl′tō. (*I.*) The lowest female voice.

Con-tra-pun′tal. Pertaining to, or according to the rules of counterpoint.

Con-träp-pun′tō. (*I.* pōōn.) Counterpoint.

Con′trä-punt-ist. (*E.*) One skilled in Counterpoint.

Contrary motion. Proceeding in opposite directions.

Con-trä-sōg-get′tō. (*I.* sōd-jät′tō.) Counter subject of a fugue.

Cŏn 8va, ad. lib. With octaves at pleasure.

Cor. (*F.*) A horn ; usually a French horn.

Copyright. The right of an author to control his works during a certain term of years.

Cor Anglaise. (*F.* äng-gläs.) ⎱ English horn: the alto of the
Cor-nō In-gle′sĕ. (*I.* glä′zĕ.) ⎰ oboe family.

Cor′dä. (*I.*) A string, as *Una corda*, one string, *i. e.*, use the soft pedal of the piano.

Cornet. A small brass wind instrument; an organ stop

Cor′ni. (*I. pl.* nē.) Horns.

Cor′nō. (*I.*) A horn.

Cō′rō. (*I.*) A chorus; a choir.

Cō-rō′nō. (*I.*) A hold; a pause.

Couac. (*F.* quăk.) The false, quacking sound made by bad blowing of a clarinet, oboe, or bassoon.

Counterpoint. Notes were formerly called *points*, or *pricks*, hence *contrapunctum*, or counterpoint, meaning note against note; the art of harmonizing a theme by adding parts which shall be in themselves melodious. C. may be either *single* (*plain*), *double, triple* or *quadruple*.

Counterpoint, double, is one which may be inverted without faulty progressions.

Counterpoint, plain, is divided into five species: (1) note against note ; (2) two against one; (3) four against one ; (4) syncopated ; (5) florid.

Counterpoint, quadruple. In four parts, which may be inverted.

Counterpoint, single. Counterpoint not intended for inversion ; see counterpoint, *plain*.

Counterpoint, triple. In three parts, which may be inverted.

Counter-subject. The principal counterpoint to a *subject* in fugue.

Crĕs-cen′dō. (*I.* shän′.) Gradually increasing in force or power.

Crotch-et. A quarter-note.

Cue. A word or phrase used as a guide to singers, indicating when to begin.

Cus-tō. (*I.* kōōs.) *A direct*, ∿. The sign placed at the end of a line or page to show the position of the next note.

Cym-bals. Circular concave disks made of brass, set in vibration by being clashed together.

D. First tone of Dorian, mode; (2) super-tonic in C key; (3) tonic in key of two sharps; (4) third string of violin, second of viola and cello; (5) *Abb.* for *Discantus, Dissus, Destra*, etc.

Dä cä′pō. (*I.*) From the beginning ; first used about 1696.

Dä cäp′ō äl fi′nĕ. (*I.* fē′.) From the beginning to the word *fine*.

Dä cäp′ō äl segn′ō. (*I.* sän′yō.) Repeat from the sign.

Däl. (*I.*)
Däl´lä. (*I.*) } By the ; of the ; from the, etc.

Däl segn´ō. (*I.* sän´yō.) From the sign.

Damper pedal. Improperly called "loud pedal;" the piano pedal which raises the dampers from the strings.

Dampers. The felt cushions which rest on piano-strings to prevent undesirable vibration.

Dé´but. (*F.* dā´bu.) The first appearance.

Dĕ-cä´nĭ (*L.*) The singers on the Dean's side of the choir; those on the Cantor's side are "*Cantoris.*"

Dĕ-cĭ´sŏ. (*I.* dā-tchĕ´zŏ.) Boldly; decidedly.

Dĕc-lä-män´dŏ. (*I.*) In declamatory style; see *Recitative.*

Decorative notes. Embellishments.

De-cre-scen´dŏ. (*I.* dā-krā-shän´.) Gradually decreasing in power.

De-gree. A line or a space of the staff.

Dĕl. (*I.*) Of the.

Dĕl-ĭ-cä-tez´zä. (*I.* tāt´sa.)
Dĕl-ĭ-cä-tŏ. (*I* dĕl-ē-cä´tŏ.) } Delicately, smoothly.

Del´lä. (*I.* däl.) By the, of the, etc.

Dĕm-i. (*I.* dĕm´ē.) Half.

Dĕm-i-sem-i-qua-ver. A 32d note.

Des-cant. (*L.*) The addition of one or more parts to a subject: the forerunner of modern counterpoint.

Dĕs trä. (*I.*) Right.

Dĕ-tĕr-mi-nä´tŏ. (*I.*) Resolute, determined.

De-vò-zi-ŏ´ne. (*I.* tsĕ.) Devout, religious feeling.

Dĕx-trä. (*L.*) The right hand.

Di. (*I.* dē.) With, for, of, etc.

Di-ä-ton´ic. (*Gr.*) Through the tones of the key, *i. e.*, with no chromatic tones.

Di-ä-ton-ic half-step. A minor second.

Diatonic scale. The tones of a key in successive order, from one tonic to the next, inclusive.

Di brä-vu´rä. (*I.* vōō.) Brilliantly.

Di-es´trä. (*I.* dĕ-äs´.) The right hand.

Dign-i-tä´tĕ. (*I.* dĕn-yĕ.) Dignity, grandeur.

Di grä´dŏ. (*I.* dē.) By degrees; opposed to *Di salto, q. v.*

Dil-ĕt-tan´tĕ. (*I.*) See *Amateur.*

Dil-ĭ-gen´zà. (*I.* jän´tsa.) Diligence.

Dil-u-en´dŏ. (*I.* ōō-än´.) See *Morendo.*

Diminished intervals Those which are a half-step less than minor and perfect intervals.

Dĭm-ĭn-u-en dō. (*I.* ŌŌ-ăn′.) Diminishing; softer and softer.

Dĭ mōl′tō. (*I.* dē.) Very much.

D in ält. Four degrees above A in alt, *q. v*

D in al-tĭs′sĭ-mō. Octave above D in alt.

Dĭ qui-e′tō. (*I.* dē quē-ā′.) Quietly.

Direct. A sign (⌁) used to indicate the next note.

Direct motion. Similar motion, *q. v.*

Dĭ säl-tō. (*I.* dē.) By skips, opposed to *Di grädo, q. v.*

Dis-diäpāson. (*Gr.*) Two octaves; a 15th.

Dis-ĭn-vŏl′tō. (*I.* dēz.) Free, off hand, bold.

Dispersed harmony. Harmony in which the chord tones are widely separated.

Dissonance. A mingling of inharmonious tones.

Distance. The interval between two tones.

Dĭs-tĭn′tō. (*I.* tēn′.) Distinct, clear.

Dĭ tes′tä. (*I.* dē täs′.) Of the head.

Dĭ-vĕr-tĭ-men′tō. (*I.* män′.) ⎫ Light, entertaining music; a

Divertissement. (*F.* mŏng.) ⎭ short ballet; an *Entr'acte.*

Dĭ-vi′si. (*I.* dē-vē′zē.) Divided; the instruments playing from one staff must separate and play in two parts. Their reunion is directed by *unisono.*

Dŏ. (*I.*) The syllable applied to the Tonic of all major modes; most foreigners confine it to the pitch C.

Dŏl′cĕ. (*I.* dŏl-tchĕ.) ⎫

Dŏl-cez′zä. (*I.* tchăt′sä.) ⎬ Delicate, gentle, very soft, sweet.

Dŏl-cis′sĭ-mō. (*I.* tchēs′sē.) ⎭

Dŏ-len′tĕ. (*I.* län.) Sad.

Dŏ-lō-rō′sō. (*I.* zō.) With grief; with sorrow; sadly; mournfully.

Dom′ĭ-nant. The fifth of a key.

Dŏ′pō. (*I.* also spelled doppo.) After.

Dŏp′pĭ-ō mō-vĕ-men′tō. (*I.* män.) Twice as fast.

Dŏp′pĭ-ō tĕm-pō. . (*I.*) Twice as fast.

Dot. Placed after a note adds one half to its value; two dots add three fourths; placed over a note indicates semi-staccato; at the side of a bar they show that the music on that side is to be repeated.

Double bar. A broad bar, or two single bars drawn across the staff, denote (1) the end of the strain; (2) the end of a line in hymn-tunes.

Double flat. Two flats before a note, indicating a tone two half-steps lower; contradicted by a cancel and a flat.

Double measure. A two-pulse measure.

Double sharp. Two sharps before a note, indicating a tone two half-steps higher; contradicted by a cancel and a sharp.

Double suspension. The delaying of two parts; see *Suspension*

Double tonguing. A term applied to rapidly repeated tones in cornet and flute playing.

Doublet. A pulse divided into two equal parts.

Drä′ma-tis pĕr-sō′næ. (*L.*) The characters of an opera or play.

Drit′tō. (*I.* drē.) Right.

Drone. The large tube of the bagpipe.

Drum-major. The director of a drum corps.

Du′ĕ. (*I.* dōō′ĕ.) Two; in two parts. See *Divisi.*

Du′ĕ cŏr-dĕ. (*I.* dōō-ĕ kŏr′dĕ.) Two strings; discontinue the soft pedal.

Due pĕ-dä′lĭ. (*I.*) Use both pedals.

Due vōl′tĕ. (*I.*) Twice.

Du-et′tō. (*I.* dōō-ât′.) ⎫ A composition for two voices or instru-
Du′ŏ. (*I.* dōō′.) ⎭ ments.

Dutch concert. A convivial exercise in which each person sings a different song, all singing at once, some familiar chorus being used after each stanza.

Dynamics. (*Gr.*) Relating to power of tones; the five dynamic degrees are pp, p, m, f, ff.

E. (*I.* ā.) ⎫
Ed. (*I.* äd.) ⎭ And.

Ecclesiastical. Pertaining to the church.

E′cō. (*I.* ä′kō.) An echo.

Eighth. An octave.

Eisteddfod. (*W.* ïs-teth′vōd.) A congress to elect chief bards; a Welsh musical festival.

El-ĕ-gän′tĕ. (*I.* gän′tĕ.) Elegant, graceful.

El-ĕ-gän′zä. (*I.* gänt′sä.) Elegance, grace.

El-ĕ-gi′ä. (*I.* jĕ′.) A mournful poem; a funeral song; a monody.

Em-bou-chure. (*F.* ŏng-bōō-shōōr.) The mouth-piece of a wind instrument; position of the lips in playing such instruments.

En-cōre′. (*F.* ŏng-kōr′.) Again; more.

En-er′gi-cō. (*I.* ĕn-är′jĕ.) Energetic; vigorous.

Enharmonic change. A change of notation without change of tone, as A flat and G sharp.

En-sem′-ble. (*F.* ŏng-sŏng-bl.) Together; the general effect; the union of a whole company in a piece.

Entr′acte. (*F.* ŏng-tr′äkt.) Music between the acts of a drama.

En-trä′tä. (*I.* än.) Prelude; entry; introduction.

Episode. A digression, separable from the main subject, but naturally arising from it.

E po'i. (*I.* ǎ pō-ē.) And then.

Equal temperament. A way of tuning whereby the inequalities of the octave are divided equally between all the keys.

Equivocal chord. The Diminished Seventh chord.

Equivocal chords. Chords common to two or more keys.

Es-prĕs-sĭ-ó'nĕ. (*I.*) Expression.

Es-prĕs-sĭ'vŏ. (*I.*) With feeling.

Essential tones. The tones proper to a chord.

Es-tin'tŏ. (*I.* tĕn'.) Dying away; ritard and diminish.

Et'tä. (*I.*)
Et'tō. (*I.*) } Diminutive—as *operetta*, a little opera.

E-tude. (*F.* ă-tüd.) A study; an exercise.

Ex'it. (*L.*) He (or she) goes out.

Ex'eunt. (*L.*) They go out.

Explosive tone. One forcibly struck and suddenly diminished.

Expression. The manner or style which gives life and suggestive force to ideas and sentiments.

Extreme sharp sixth. See *Augmented sixth.*

Fä-ci'lĕ. (*I.* tchĕ.)
Fä-ci-li-tä'. (*I.* tchĕl-ē.) } Easy; an easy arrangement of a difficult passage.

Fä-gŏt'tŏ. (*I.*) A bassoon. Also an organ stop.

Fa lä. The refrain in old songs.

False relation. Is a chromatic contradiction in different voices, either simultaneous or so near that the effect of one has not passed before the other enters.

Fäl-set'tŏ. (*I.* săt'.) That part of a male voice that is above its natural compass.

Fän-färe. (*F.*) A flourish of trumpets.

Fän-tä'si-ä. (*I.* tä-zē.) A composition without regular form.

F clef. Bass clef. It fixes middle C on first added line above.

Fĕr-mä'tä. (*I.*) A pause or hold.

Fe-rō'ce. (*I.* fä-rŏ-tche.) Wild, fierce.

FF. *Abb.* of fortissimo.

Fĭ-äs'co. (*I.* fē.) A miserable failure.

Fĭ-ä'tŏ. (*I.* fē.) (1) Wind. (2) Breath in singing.

Fifth, augmented. A fifth one half-step greater than a perfect fifth. See under *fifth, perfect.*

Fifth, consecutive. See *Consecutive fifths.*

Fifth, diminished. A fifth one half-step smaller than a perfect fifth. See under *fifth, perfect.*

Fifth, perfect. An interval of three steps and one half-step; the ancient *diapente*.

Fifth, sharp. See *Augmented fifth*.

Figured bass. See *Thorough-bass*.

Fi-nä′lĕ. (*I.* fē.) The final movement.

Fi′ne. (*I.* fē′nĕ.) The end.

F in alt. An octave above F on the fifth line.

F in altissimo. An octave above F in alt.

Fingering. The art of using the fingers properly.

Fingering, American. See *American fingering*.

Fingering, foreign. Indicating the thumb and fingers by the figures 1, 2, 3, 4, 5, as opposed to the American plan of ×, 1, 2, 3, 4.

Finite canon. A canon not repeated.

Fi′nŏ äl. (*I.* fē.) End at; stop at.

Fin qui. (*I.* fēn quē.) To this place.

Fi-ō-ri′to. (*I.* fē-ō-ri′.) Florid.

First inversion. The form of a chord when the bass takes the third.

Fixed Do. } Syllables used as names of pitches (so used in
Fixed syllables. } foreign countries), as opposed to our American *movable Do*, in which Do is always applied to the major tonic. See *Guidonian syllables*.

Flat. (1) A sign denoting a tone a half-step lower; (2) below pitch; (3) minor, as a flat 3d, a flat 5th, etc.

Florid. Embellished, figured.

Fork, tuning. A fork which gives a certain pitch.

Form. The shape and structure of a composition; the union of its chief elements into phrases, sections, periods, etc.

Fôr′te. (*I.* fôr′tĕ.) Loud, strong; fourth degree of power.

Fôr-tis′si-mŏ. (*I.* tēs′sē.) Very loud; fifth degree of power.

Fôr′zä. (*I.* fôrt′sä.) Force, power.

Fourth, augmented. A fourth a half-step larger than a perfect fourth.

Fourth, diminished. A fourth a half-step smaller than a perfect fourth.

Fourth, perfect. An interval of two steps and one half-step.

French sixth. An augmented sixth chord, always consisting of the syllables *le do re fi* resolving to *sol do mi sol*. For the origin of the augmented 6th chords see Palmer's "Theory of Music," pp. 93 to 97.

Frĕs′cō. (*I.* frĕs′kō.) Fresh; lively; vigorously.

Fu′gä. (*I.* fōō′.) A flight; a chase. See *Fugue*.

Fugue. (fūg.) From *Fugare*, to fly. A polyphonic composition developed from a subject which each voice takes in turn, according to the laws of counterpoint.

Fugue, counter. In which the subjects move in contrary motion

Fugue, double. Which has two subjects.

Fugue, free. One in which the rules are not strictly obeyed.

Fugue, ren-ver-see. (*F.* füg rŏng-vĕr-sä.) An inverted fugue.

Fugue, strict. In which the laws are strictly observed.

Fugue, simple. Has but a single subject.

Full. For all performers.

Full anthem. An anthem without solos. See *Anthem.*

Full cadence. See *Perfect cadence.*

Full chord. A chord, some of whose tones are doubled; (2) a chord for the full power of all performers.

Full organ. Implies the use of all the stops at once.

Full score. A score in which all parts are separately displayed.

Full service. A service in which music is used to the fullest extent allowable.

Fundamental tone. The tone on which a chord is founded.

Fu-ō′cō. (*I.* fōō.) Fire, passion, spirit.

Fu-ō-cō′sō. (*I.* zō.) Vehemently, passionately.

Fu′ri-ä. (*I.* fōō-rĕ.) Fury, rage.

Fu-ri-ō′sō. (*I.* zō.) Furiously.

Gäm′bä, vi′ol di. (*I.* vĕ′ōl dē.) An instrument of the violin family, with 5, 6, or 7 strings, tuned in thirds and fourths; an organ stop.

Gäm′mä. (*I.*) The scale; gamut.

Gamut. The scale in any key.

Gär′bō, con. (*I.*) With grace.

Gauche. (*F.* gōsh.) Left.

Gauche, main. (*F.* gōsh, mäng.) Left hand.

Gä-vōtte. (*F.* vŏt.) From *Gavoto*, the people of a district in France, called *Gap;* a brisk dance of two strains, each repeated.

G clef. A sign combining G and S (Sol). It so fixes the pitches that middle C is on the added line below.

Gĕn-ti-lez′zä. (*I.* lät′sä.) Elegance; grace.

Ge-nus. (*L.*) Sort or class, especially of scales.

German fingering. See under *Fingering.*

German sixth. An augmented sixth chord always consisting of the syllables *fa la do ri*, resolving to *mi la do mi*. This chord should be used only in the minor. When used in major, the American sixth (*q. v.*) would give better voice-leading.

Gigue. (*G.* jĕg. from *Geige*, a fiddle.) A jig; a lively dance.

Giō-cō′sō. (*I.* jō-kō′zō.) Jocose, merry, cheerful, gay, sportive.

Giō-jō′sō. (*I.* jō-yō′zō.) Glad, blithe, gay.

Giu′bi-lō. (*I.* jōō′bē-lō.) Jubilant, rejoicing.

Gius′tō. (*I.* jōōs′.) Just, strict, correct.

Glee. A composition for voices in harmony; originally one voice to a part, the subject either grave or gay.

Gli. (*I.* l′ē.) The.

Glis-sän′dō. (*I.* glēs.) Sliding the tips of the fingers over the piano keys; (2) a slur in violin playing.

Gloriä. (*L.*) A movement of the mass.

Glō′ri-ä Pä′tri. (*L.*) Glory be to the Father, etc. Sung at the end of a psalm.

Glottis. The narrow opening in the upper part of the wind-pipe.

Grace notes. Ornamental notes.

Grän′dĕ. (*I.*) Grand, great.

Grän cäs′sä. (*I.*) The great drum.

Grän-di-ō′sō. (*I.* dē-ō′zō.) Grandeur, dignity.

Grand opera. A full opera, with full cast of performers.

Grä′vĕ. (*I.*) Slow, solemn.

Grä-vĕ-men′tĕ. (*I.* män′.) Heavily, grievously.

Grä′zi-ä. (*I.* grät′sē-ä.) Grace, charm, beauty.

Grä-zi-ō′sō. (*I.* grät-sē-ō′zō.) Graceful, agreeable,

Great organ. Usually the middle key-board of the organ.

Gre-gō′ri-an Chant. Choral music, according to the eight church modes, as arranged by Pope Gregory I.

Gre-gō′ri-an modes. The scales as set in order by Pope Gregory I. (A. D. 590.)

Gre-gō′ri-an tones, or tunes. The Plain Song established by Pope Gregory I. (A. D. 590.)

Grôsse caisse. (*F.* grōs käs.) Big drum.

Grôs′sō. (*I.*) Great, full, grand.

Ground-bass. A short bass phrase, repeated to varied melodies.

Group. A series of short notes grouped.

Grup-pet′tō. (*I.* grōōp-pät′.) "A little group," a turn.

G string. 1st string of double-bass; 3d of cello, viola, and guitar; and 4th of violin.

Gui′dà. (*I.* gwĕ′.) A guide; a direct.

Gui-dō′ni-an syllables. The syllables *ut, re, mi, fa, sol, la,* used by Guido d'Arezzo (gwĕ′dō dä-rät′sō, A. D. 1020), taken from a Latin hymn to St. John, viz:

<table>
<tr><td>*Ut* queant laxis,</td><td>*Fa*muli tuorum,</td></tr>
<tr><td>*Re*sonare fibris,</td><td>*Sol*ve polluti,</td></tr>
<tr><td>*Mi*ra gestorum,</td><td>*La*bia reati,</td></tr>
</table>

*Sa*ncte Johannes.

The *Sa* was added and changed to *Si* to mark the half-step (like *mi*); *ut* became *do*, and all used as *names of tone-relationships*. Americans have always thus used them; European nations having lost sight of this use, employ them *as names of pitches*. As a protest against this narrow use of the syllables, the American plan was introduced into England some forty years ago, resulting in what is known as Tonic Sol Fa; with this difference, however, that Tonic Sol Faists do away with the staff, using a letter notation. In all other respects the Tonic Sol Fa is our American plan of sol-fa-ing from the Tonic.

Gus'tō. (*I.* gōōs'tō.) Expression; taste.

Half-cadence. See under *Cadence*.

Half-step. A term of measurement, smallest in use; equals an augmented prime or a minor second.

Half-tone. An undesirable name for a half-step.

Harmonics. Overtones heard with any simple tone; (2) the soft tones of a string when touched at given points.

Harmony. The science of chords, their construction and progression.

Hemidemisemiquaver. A 64th note. (*Obs. except in England.*)

Hexachord. A scale of six tones.

Hold. A character placed over a note, denoting prolongation. See *Pause*.

Holding-tone. A tone held while others move.

Horn, French. An important brass orchestral instrument. See *Corno*.

Hornpipe. A rude old instrument; (2) a lively dance.

Il. (*I.* ēl.) The.

Imitation. The repetition of a short subject by another part.

Im'měr. (*G.*) Always; ever.

Imperfect cadence. See under *Cadence*.

Im-pe-tu-ō'so. (*I.* ĕm-pä-tōō-ō'zō.) Impetuous.

Im-prŏmp'tu. (*I.* ēm-prŏmp-tōō.) An extensive production without set form.

Im-pre-sä'ri-ō. (*I.* ēm-prĕ-zä-rĕ.) A manager, conductor.

In. (*I.* ēn.) In, in the, into.

In alt. The first octave above fifth line.

In äl-tis'si-mō. (*I.* ēn, tēs'sē.) The next octave above *Alt*.

In-dĕ-ci'sō. (*I.* ēn-dĕ-tchē'zo.) Undecided.

In-fi-ni'tō. (*I.* ēn-fē-nĕ'.) Continual.

In-nō-cen'tĕ. (*I.* ēn-nō-tchän'.) Innocent.

In-nō-cen'zä. (*I.* ēn-nō-tchän'tsä.) Artlessness.

In tem'pō. (*I.* ēn tăm'.) In time; *i. e.,* resume strict time after a *rit.,* etc.

Interlude. } A short passage between stanzas;
In-ter-mez'zō. (*I.* mãt'sō.) } (2) a brief musical number played between the acts of an opera, or drama.

Intermediate tones. Those tones which occur between the diatonic tones of the key.

Interrupted cadence. See under *Cadence.*

Interval. The difference of pitch between two tones-; also their effect when performed simultaneously.

Intervals, perfect. Primes, octaves, 4ths, and 5ths; so called because inversion does not change their characteristics, as is the case with all other intervals.

Intervals, major. 2ds, 3ds, 6ths, 7ths, and 9ths, from the major Tonic.

Intervals, minor. 2ds, 3ds, 6ths, 7ths, and 9ths, a chromatic half-step smaller than the major intervals of the same name.

Intervals, augmented. A chromatic half-step larger than major and perfect intervals.

Intervals, diminished. A chromatic half-step smaller than perfect and minor intervals.

In'ti-mō. (*I.* ēn'tē.) With inward emotion.

Intonation. Correctness of pitch.

In-trä'dä. (*I.* ēn.) An interlude. (From *intra*, between.)

In-tre'pi-dō. (*I.* ēu-trä'pē.) Boldly.

Introduction. A preparatory movement.

In-trō'ĭt. (*E.*) Formerly a psalm sung while the priest was entering within the rails of the altar; now any piece appropriate to opening service, or church service in general.

Invention. The gift of finding new melodies, also a composition in free imitative style.

Inversion. Has five significations—viz: (1) In counterpoint it signifies the repetition of a phrase or passage with reversed intervals. (2) In double counterpoint it indicates that the upper part is placed below the lower, or *vice versa.* (3) Intervals are inverted when the lower tone is so changed as to become the higher. (4) A chord is inverted when any tone other than its fundamental is taken in the lowest part. (5) Pedal point (*organ point*) is inverted when the sustained tone is transferred from the bass to an upper part.

Inverted turn. A turn beginning with the lowest note instead of the highest.

Is-tes'sō. (*I.* tãs'.) The same.

Italian sixth. An augmented 6th chord, always consisting of the syllables *Le, double Do, Fi*, resolving to *Sol, Ti, Re, Sol.* For the origin of the augmented 6th chords see Palmer's "Theory of Music," pp. 93 to 97.

Just intonation. In perfect tune.

Kettle-drum. See under *Drum.*

Key. A family of tones having a fixed relationship: (2) the lever which is pressed by the fingers on keyed instruments.

Key-chord. The tonic chord.

Key, major. A key whose 3d and 6th are major.

Key, minor. A key whose 3d and 6th are minor.

Key, normal. The key which requires no signature, C major or A minor.

Keys, authentic. The five principal Greek modes.

Keys, parallel. The major and minor modes of any given signature.

Keys, plagal. The five Greek modes which began a fourth below their principals.

Keys, relative. Keys having the most tones in common, as C and F; C and G; C maj. and A mi., etc.

Keys, remote. Keys having few tones in common.

Key-tone. The tonic; Do of any major key; La of any minor key.

L. Left. See *L. H.*

Lä. (*I.* and *F.*) The; (2) minor tonic; (3) major submediant.

Lä-cri-mō′so. (*I.* zō.) Mournfully, sadly. A part of *Dies Irae* in the requiem mass.

Lä-gri-mō′so. (*I.* grē-mō′zō.) Weeping, mournful, tearful, sad.

Lä-měn-tō′sō. (*I.* zō.) Mournful, lamentable.

Län-guen′dō. (*I.* gwän′.) }
Län-gui′dō. (*I.* gwē.) } Languor; in a languishing style.

Lär-gä-men′tĕ. (*I.* män′.) Slowly, widely, freely, fully.

Large. *Maxima.* A note equal to eight whole-notes. (*Obs.*)

Lär-ghet′tō. (*I.* gät′.) Slow, but less slow than *largo.*

Lär′gō. (*I.*) Slowly, broadly.

Larynx. The upper part of the *trachea.*

Lä stret′tä. (*I.* strä′.) In quicker time.

Leading tone. Sub-tonic; 7 of any key.

Lě-gä′tō. (*I.*) Connected, close, bound, tied.

Leger lines. Short lines above and below (of the staff).

Leg-gen′dä. (*I.* lěd-jän.) A tale, a legend.

Lěg-giä′drō. (*I.* lěd-jä′.) Handsome, elegant.

Lěg-gie′rō. (*I.* lěd-jä′rō.) Easily, lightly, swift, delicate.

Leit-motif. (*G.* līt-mō-tēf.) Guiding theme, leading motive.

Lěn-tä-men′tĕ. (*I.* män′.) Slowly.

Len′tō. (*I.* län′tō.) Slow.

Lěs-tis′si-mō. (*I.* tēs′sō.) Lively, nimble; quickness.

L. H. Left hand.

Li-bret′tō. (*I.* lĕ-brăt′.) The book of an opera.

License. A deviation from the rules.

Lied. (*G.* leed.) A song.

Lied′ĕr. (*G.* lēd′ĕr.) Songs.

L'is-tes′sō. (*I.* l'ĕs·tăs′.) } The same; in the same time as
L'is-tes′sō tem′po. (*I.* tăm′.) } the previous movement.

Lō′cō. (*I.*) As written.

Long. A note equal to four whole notes.

Lō stĕs′sō. (*I.*) The same.

Long metre. A stanza of four lines of 8s.

Lun′-gä pä-u′-sä. (*I.* lōōn′gü pä-ōō′zä.) Long rest.

Lu-sin-gän′dō. (*I.* lōō-zēn.) Caressingly; in a coaxing manner.

Lyric drama. Opera; acting with singing.

Lyric tragedy. Tragic opera.

Mä. (*I.*) But.

Madrigal. An elaborate vocal piece in three or more parts; it
preceded the modern glee.

Mä-ĕs-tō′sō. (*I.* zō.) Stately; dignified; majestic

Mä-es′trō. (*I.* äs′.) A master.

Main. (*F.* măng.) The hand.

Main droite. (*F.* măng drwät.) Right hand.

Main gauche. (*F.* măng gōsh.) Left hand.

Major. Larger, as regards intervals.

Major diatonic scale. The scale with major 3d and 6th.

Major fourth. See *Perfect fourth.*

Major key. }
Major mode. } The mode in which the 3d and 6th are major.

Major seventh. A seventh as great as two major thirds and
one minor third.

Major sixth. A 6th as great as a major 3d and a perfect 4th.

Major third. A 3d as great as two major seconds.

Major tonic. The first tone of a major key.

Major triad. A chord with major 3d and perfect 5th.

Mä′nō. (*I.*) The hand.

Mä′nō des′trä. (*I.* däs.) }
Mä′nō drit-tä. (*I.* drēt.) } The right hand.

Mä′nō si-nis′trä. (*I.* sē-nēs.) The left hand.

Manual. The key-board.

Mär-cän′dō. (*I.*) }
Mär-cä′tō. (*I.*) } Marked; accented, prominent.

March. A piece of martial music in 4–4 measure.

Mär'ci-ä. (*I.* tchē.) A march.

Martial music. Music adapted to military use.

Mär-zi-ä'lĕ. (*I.* märt-sē.) Martial; warlike.

M. D. The right hand. See *Main droit, Mano destra.*

Measure. A group of strong and weak pulses.

Mĕ-de'si-mō. (*I.* dä'zē.) The same.

Mē'dĭ-ănt. (*L.*) The third above the tonic.

Mē-dĭ-ănt, sub. The third below the tonic.

Medley. A mixture consisting of detached parts from several pieces; a *Pot-pourri,* (*q. v.*) Medley is applied to vocal, *Pot-pourri* to instrumental compositions.

Melodics. A department of musical science which treats of the pitch of tones and the laws of melody.

Mĕl'ō-drä-mä. A dramatic performance intermixed with songs; (2) Music accompanying speech or action on the stage.

Melody. A pleasing succession of tones.

Me'nō. (*I.* mä'nō.) Less.

Met. *Abb.* of *metronome, q. v.*

Meter or **metre.** A rhythmical arrangment of syllables into verses, stanzas, strophes, etc.

Metrical. Pertaining to measure.

Met-rō-nōme. A clock-work which gives a certain number of ticks per minute; ♩=60, shows that if the sliding weight is set at 60, it will give the time of a half-note. An expensive machine. A simple metronome is now made, which can be carried in the vest-pocket, is more accurate, and only costs fifty cents.

Mez'zō. (*I.* mät'sō.) Half, medium, middle, the third degree of power.

M. G. *Abb. Main Gauche, q. v.*

Middle C. The C between the Bass and Treble staffs.

Min-ĭm. A half-note. (*Obs. except in England.*)

Minor. Smaller, as regards intervals.

Minor key. } A mode whose third and sixth are minor.
Minor mode. }

Minor second. A second as small as a half-step.

Minor seventh. A 7th a half-step smaller than a major 7th.

Minor sixth. A 6th a half-step smaller than a major 6th.

Minor third. A 3d a half-step smaller than a major 3d.

Minor triad. A chord with minor 3d and perfect 5th.

Minuet. A stately dance in triple measure.

Mĭs-sä sol-ĕn-nĕlle. (*L.* nĕl'.) A solemn mass.

Mis-te-ri-ō'sō. (*I.* mĕs-tĕ-rē-ō'zō.) Mysteriously.

Mod-ĕ-rä′tō. (*I.*) Moderately.

Modulation. A change of key; (2) a gradation of tone.

Modulation, abrupt. Sudden change to remote keys.

Modulation, enharmonic. A modulation effected by altering the notation of a tone or tones, thus changing the resolution of the chord.

Modulation, note of. A note introducing a new key.

Modulation, passing. } A modulation in which the new key
Modulation, transient. } is left nearly as soon as heard.

Mōl′tō. (*I.*) Much, extremely.

Mŏ-nŏ-phō′nic. (*Gr.*) Single voiced, having one part only.

Mor-ceau. (*F.* sō.) A morsel; a little composition.

Mor-den′tĕ. (*I.* dān.) A short trill of two notes preceding the principal note.

Mŏ-ren′dō. (*I.* rän.) Gradually decreasing; dying away.

Mŏr-mŏ-rän′dō. (*I.*) } In a gentle, murmuring, whispering
Mŏr-mŏ-rō′sō. (*I.* zō.) } manner.

Mŏs′sō. (*I.*) Motion, movement.

Mŏ-tĕt′. An anthem. Formerly it signified a composition more elaborate than an anthem.

Mŏ-tif′. (*F.* mŏ-tēf.) Motive, subject, theme.

Motion, contrary. In which one part ascends while another part descends.

Motion, oblique. In which one part moves while another remains stationary.

Motion, direct. }
Motion, parallel. } In which two or more parts move in the same direction.
Motion, similar. }

Motive. A musical figure or germ; the theme.

Mŏ′tō. (*I.*) Motion, movement.

M. S. (Mä′nŏ sĭ-nĭs′trä.) The left hand.

Musicale. (*F.* mu-si-cäl.) An informal concert; a recital.

Music grammar. The rules of composition.

M. V. *Abb.* of *mezza voce, q. v.*

Natural. A character used to cancel the effect of a previous sharp or flat; hence *cancel* is rapidly supplanting *natural* as the name of the character.

Natural keys. Keys which require no signature. Thinking people now call these *primary keys*, thereby curtailing the word *natural*, which is the most pernicious term in our nomenclature.

Ne′gli. (*I. pl.* näl-ye.) }
Nel. (*I.* näl.) } At the; in the.

Ninth. An octave and a second.

Nŏc-turne′. (*E.*) ⎱ Originally a serenade, now a gentle, quiet,
Not-tur′nŏ. (*I.*) ⎰ elegant and song-like composition.
Nōn. (*I.*) No, not.
Nōn mōl′tō. (*I.*) Not much.
Nōn tän′tō. (*I.*) Not too much.
Nōn trōp′pō. Moderately, not too much.
Notation. The signs which represent musical tones.
Note. A sign for the pitch and duration of a tone.
Notes, accessory. Notes one degree above or below the princi-
pal note of a turn.

O. (*I.* ō before a consonant.) ⎱
Od. (*I.* before a vowel.) ⎰ As, either, or.
Ob-li-gä′tō. (*I.* ōb-lē.) Indispensable; must not be omitted.
Oblique motion. One part is stationary and another moves.
Octave. The interval of an eighth, above or below.
Octave, augmented. A half-step greater than a perfect octave.
Octave, diminished. A half-step smaller than a perfect octave.
Octave, perfect. An interval of five steps and two half-steps.
Oc-tet. A composition for eight voices, or instruments.
Olio. A miscellaneous collection of musical pieces.
Open diapason. The most important organ stop.
Open harmony. See *Dispersed harmony.*
O-pĕ-rä. (*I.* ō′.) A lyric drama for solo, chorus, and orchestra.
Opera libretto. The text of an opera.
Operatic. In the style of an opera.
Operetta. A little opera.
O′pus. (*L.*) Work, labor; as, Op. 1, the first work.
Oratorio. A composition on a Scriptural subject for solos,
chorus, and orchestra, without action.
Orchestra. A band of instrumental performers in a theater or
hall; (2) the space occupied by the band.
Organ. A compound wind-instrument used in churches and
halls, of surpassing grandeur and dignity.
Organ-point. A passage in which the tonic or dominant is
sustained while other parts move; pedal-point.
Os′si-ä. (*I.*) Or else, or, otherwise.
Os′siä pi′u fä′ci-lĕ. (*I.* pē′ōō fü-tchĕ-lĕ.) Or in this easier way.
Overture. An introduction to an oratorio, opera, etc.

P. *Abb.* of *piano.* Second degree of power.
Parallel keys. The maj. and mi. modes of the same signature.
Parallel motion. Two parts moving together.
Pär-län′dō. (*I.*) In declamatory style.

Partial turn. Three small notes before the main note.

Participating tones. Accessory tones, *q. v.*

Pär-ti-tur'. (*G.* tĕ-tōōr'.) ⎫ A full score; the entire draft of a
Pär-ti-tu'rä. (*I.* tĕ-tōō'.) ⎬ composition for voices and in-
Pär-ti-zi-ō'nĕ. (*I.* tĕt-sē.) ⎭ struments.

Part songs. Ballads in four or more parts; glees.

Passing tones. Tones foreign to the harmony, used in passing from one chord-tone to another.

Päs-si-ō-nä'tä. (*I.*) Passionate, fervent.

Passion music. Music written for Passion Week.

Pastoral. ⎫ A rural lyric drama; an instrumental
Päs-tō-rä'lĕ. (*I.*) ⎭ piece in pastoral style.

Pä-te'ti-cŏ. (*I.* tä'tĕ.) Pathetic.

Pause. A sign over a rest to lengthen its duration. See *Hold.*

Pedals. Levers worked by the feet.

Pedal, damper. A lever by which the foot raises the dampers from contact with the strings.

Pedal, soft. A foot lever for diminishing the tone of a piano.

Pedal-point. See *Organ-point.*

Period. A complete musical sentence.

Pe-sän'tĕ. (*I.* zän'.) Ponderous, heavy.

Phrasing. The art of grouping tones into phrases so as to clearly express the musical idea.

Pi-ä-ce'rĕ. (*I.* pĕ-ä-tchä'rĕ.) Pleasure, delight.

Pi-ä-ce'vō-lĕ. (*I.* pĕ-ä-tchä'.) Pleasing, affable, agreeable.

Pi-än-is'si-mō. (*I.* ĕ-sĕ.) Very soft; the first degree of power.

Pi-ä'nō. (*I.*) Soft; gentle; the second degree of power.

Piano-forte. A stringed instrument with key-board. Its name, *Soft-loud*, indicates its capabilities.

Piano-forte, grand. The largest piano-forte made.

Pi-ät'ti. (*I.* pĕ-ä'tĕ.) Cymbals.

Pic'cō-lō. (*I.* pĕ.) Little; small; a small flute.

Pi-e'nō. (*I.* pĕ-ä'.) Full; as a *piena orchestra*, for a full band.

Pi-e-tä'. (*I.* pĕ-ä.) Pity.

Pi-e-tō'sō. (*I.* zō.) Tenderly; rather slow and sustained.

Pitch-pipe. A pipe which gives a certain pitch.

Pi'u. (*I.* pĕ-ōō.) More.

Piz-zi-cä-tō. (*I.* pĕt-sē.) Pinched; a direction to violinists, etc., to pluck the strings with the finger.

Plä-ci-dä-men'tĕ. (*I.* tchĕ-dä-män.) Placidly.

Plä'ci-dō. (*I.* tchĕ.) Placid; pleasant; tranquil; gentle; calm.

Plagal. Church modes beginning a fourth below the authentic, and distinguished by the word Hypo.

Plagal cadence. See under *Cadence*.

Plain song. A solemn, unisonous music believed to have been sung by the earliest Christians.

Pŏ-cō. (*I.*) A little.

Pŏ'i. (*I.* pŏ'ë.) Then ; see *Poi segue*.

Point of repose. A pause ; the tonic.

Pō-i se'guĕ. (*I.* pō-ē sŭ'guĕ.) Then follows ; here follows.

Pŏl-ŏ-naise. (näz.) A Polish dance in 3–4 measure, with rhythmical cæsura on the last pulse.

Pol-y-phon'ic. For many voices.

Pom-pŏ'sō. (*I.* zŏ.) Pompous, grand.

Pon-dĕ-rō'so. (*I.* zŏ.) Ponderously.

Pŏr-tä-men'tō. (*I.* män.) A gliding of the voice.

Pŏst-lude. (*L.*) } A concluding voluntary ; a piece played
Post-lu'di-um. (*L.*) } at the end of service.

Pot-pour-ri. (*F.* pŏ-pōōr-rĕ.) See *Medley*.

Precentor. A leader of the *Cantoris* (*see Decani*) ; a leader of church music.

Pre-ci-pi-tä'tō. (*I.* prä-tchĕ-pĕ.) Precipitous ; hurrying.

Prelude. } An introduction to a musical work ; an introduc-
Preludium. } tory voluntary.

Preparation. The introduction, as a concord, of a tone which is subsequently to become a discord.

Prĕs-tis'si-mō. (*I.* tēs'sĕ.) As fast us possible.

Pres'to. (*I.* präs'.) Quick ; rapid.

Pri'mä. (*I.* prē'.) First.

Pri'mä Don'nä. (*I.* prē'.) First lady singer.

Pri'mä vis-tä. (*I.* prē-mä vĕs'.) At first sight

Pri'mä vŏl'tä. (*I.* prē'.) The first time.

Primes. Two tones represented by the same degree.

Primes, perfect. Two tones in unison, represented by the same degree of the staff.

Primes, augmented. Two tones represented by the same degree, which are a half-step apart, as C and C sharp.

Pri'mō. (*I.* prē'.) First.

Progression. The movement of parts in harmony.

Promenade concert. A concert during which the audience promenade instead of being seated.

Quä-drille. (*F.* kä-drĭl.) A set of five dance movements connected, viz. : *Le Pantalon, La Poule, L'Eté, La Trenise* (or *La Pastourelli*), and *La Finale.*

Quäd'ru-lets. A pulse divided into four equal parts.

Quä-si. (*I.* zē.) In the style of.

Quadruple measure. A measure having four pulses.

Quarter note. A note a quarter as long as a whole note.

Quä'tu-or. (*L.*) A quartet.

Quät'trō mä'nī. (*I.*) Four hands.

Ques'ti. (*I.* quãs'.) These.

Ques'tō. (*I.* quäs'.) This.

Qui-e'tō. (*I.* quē-ä'tō.) Quiet; calm.

Quintet. A piece for five performers

Räl-lĕn-tän'dō. (*I.*) Gradually slower and softer.

Rä'pi-dō. (*I.*) Rapid.

Rap-so-di'ä. (*I.* dē'.) ⎫
Răp-sō-dĭe. (*F.*) ⎬ A composition in a wild, irregular form.
Rhăp'so-dy. (*E.*) ⎭

Räv-vĭ-vän'dō. (*I.*) Again becoming animated; hurrying.

Rĕ-ci-tä-ti've. (*I.* tchē-tä-tē'vĕ.) A musical declamation.

Re'qui-ĕm. (*L.* rä'.) A mass or service for the dead.

Resolution. Occurs when a part or chord moves according to its natural tendency.

Retard. See *Ritard.*

R. H. *Abb.* of *right hand.*

Rhythm. See *Meter.*

Rĭn-fōr-zän'dō. (*I.* tsän'.) Reinforcing; more energy.

Rĭ-sō-lu'tō. (*I.* rĕ-zō-loo'.) Resolute; bold.

Rit., ritard. (*I.*) *Abb.* of *Ritardando, q. v.*

Rĭ-tär-dän'dō. (*I.* rē.) Slower and slower.

Rĭ-te-nu'tō. (*I.* rĕ-tĕ-noo'tō.) Kept back. It differs from *rallentando* in that it calls for a sudden change to a slower movement instead of a gradual change.

Rĭ-tor-nel'lō. (*I.* rĕ-tōr-näl'.) Chorus, refrain, burden.

Rō-man'zä. (*I.* tsä.) A Roman dialect in which Troubadour love-songs were recited; hence "Romance" applies to music suggestive of a tender love-story.

Rōn-dō. (*I.*) A round; a movement, the distinguishing characteristic of which is the continual reappearance of the first musical section.

Rondo form. In the style of a rondo.

Root. The fundamental tone of a chord.

Rou-läde. (*F.* roo-läd.) A running passage of short tones.

Roundelay. A poem with certain lines frequently repeated: also the tune to which it is sung.

Ru-bä'tō. (*I.* roo.) Robbed; stolen; *i. e.,* some tones held beyond their true length and others shortened in proportion.

Run. A rapid flight of tones, a *Roulade, q. v.*

Scale. A graded series of tones.

Scale, chromatic. A scale of half-steps.

Schĕr-zän′dŏ. (*I.* skĕr-tsän′) Jokingly, playfully, merrily.

Schĕr′zō. (*I.* sker′tsō.) A lively droll movement; a jest.

Schnell. (*G.* shnĕl.) Quick, rapid.

Score. A copy of a work in which all parts are shown.

Scotch snap. The peculiarity of Scotch tunes in which a pulse consists of a short tone preceding a longer one.

Se. (*I.* sä.) As if.

Se bi-sō′gnä. (*I.* sä bē-zōn′yä.) If required.

Second. An interval involving two degrees in representation.

Se-con′dä. (*I.*) } Second; as, *seconda volta*, second time; *vio-*
Se-con′dō. (*I.*) } *lino secondo*, second violin.

Second, augmented. A second as great as a step and a half.

Second inversion. The form of a chord when its fifth is lowest.

Second, major. A second as great as one step.

Second, minor. A second as small as a half-step.

Se′gno. (*I.* sän′yŏ.) Sign; as, *al segno*, return to the sign.

Se′gue. (*I.* sä′gwĕ.) } Follows; as, *segue il coro*, the chorus
Se-gui′tō. (*I.* sä-gwē′.) } follows.

Selah. A term supposed by many to indicate the interlude during which the priests blew the trumpets.

Semi-quaver. A sixteenth note. (*Obs. except in England.*)

Semi-tone. A half-step. A bad term; *half-step* is better.

Sem-pli′cĕ. (*I.* säm-plē′tchĕ.) Pure, plain, simple.

Sem′prĕ. (*I.* säm′.) Always, ever.

Sentence. A short anthem.

Sĕn-ti-men′tō. (*I.* tē-män′.) Sentiment, feeling.

Sen′zä. (*I.* sän′tsä.) Without.

Septet. A composition for seven parts.

Septolet. A pulse divided into seven equal parts.

Sequence. A series of similar progressions.

Sĕr-e-nāde′. (*E.* näd.) } Music performed at night by gentle-
Sĕr-ĕ-näde. (*F.* näd.) } men, in a spirit of gallantry, under
Sĕr-ĕ-nä′tä. (*I.*) } a lady's window; (2) music on an
amorous subject; (3) an instrumental piece of several movements.

Sestet. (*E.*) A composition for six parts.

Seventh, diminished. A seventh a half-step smaller than a minor seventh, *q. v.*

Seventh, major. A seventh a half-step smaller than an octave.

Seventh, minor. A seventh a half-step smaller than a major seventh, *q. v.*

Sextolet. A pulse divided into six equal parts.

Sex'tu-ple measure. A six-pulse measure.

Sfŏr-zän'dō. (*I.* tsän'.) ⎫ Forced, *i. c.*, the tone or chord must
Sfŏr-zä'tŏ. (*I.* tsä'.) ⎭ receive extra power.

Shake. See *Trill.*

Sharp. Above the true pitch; (2) a character which makes a degree stand for a tone a half-step higher than would be indicated without the sharp; as, G and sharp G.

Sharp, double. See *Double sharp.*

Sharp sixth. See *Augmented sixth.*

Short appoggiatura. See *Appoggiatura.*

Signature. "Sharps or flats at the beginning of a composition which indicate the key." See *Webster's Dictionary.*

Similar motion. See under *Motion.*

Simple intervals. Intervals within an octave.

Sin. (*I.* sēn.) As far as.

Si-nis'trä. (*I.*) Left.

Si'nō. (*I.* sēn'.) To, until.

Sixth. An interval involving six degrees of the staff.

Sixth, augmented. See *Augmented sixth.*

Sixth, diminished. A 6th a half-step less than a minor sixth.

Sixth, major. See major sixth.

Sixth, minor. See minor sixth.

Slĕn-tän'dō. (*I.*) Becoming gradually slower.

Slur. A curved line showing that certain notes must be played *legato;* in singing, it shows that one syllable is applied to all the notes it connects. It is also used as a phrase mark.

Small octave. The first seven tones above middle C.

Smor-zän'dō. (*I.* tsän.) Gradually fading away.

Sō-ä'vĕ. (*I.*) Sweetly, softly, gently, delicately, agreeably.

Sō'li. (*I.* lē.) One performer on each part.

Sō'lō. (*I.*) For one voice or instrument alone.

Sō-nä'tä. A strict instrumental piece in 3 or 4 movements.

Song-form. A form of one, two, or three periods.

Sō'prä. (*I.*) Above, before, over, upon.

Sō-prä'nō. (*I.*) The highest female or boy's voice.

Soprano clef. The G clef, which fixes *middle* C on the added line below; in old music, the C clef on the first line.

Soprano, mez'zo. (*I.* mät'sō.) A voice between soprano and alto.

Sor-di'ni. (*I. pl.* dē-nē.) ⎫ Mute; a small metal instrument used
Sor-di'nō. (*I.* dē.) ⎭ to muffle the tones of a violin.

Sor-di′ni, con. (*I.* côn sŏr-dĕ′nĕ.) With mutes.

Sor-di′ni, sen-zä. (*I.* sänt′zä sŏr-dĕ′nĕ.) Without mutes.

Sŏs-pĭ-rō′so. (*I.* zō.) Sighing, subdued, wretched, doleful.

Sŏs-tĕ-nu′to. (*I.* nōō′.) Sustain the tones their full duration.

Sŏt′tō. (*I.*) Below, under.

Sŏt′tō vō′ce. (*I.* vō′tchĕ.) Softly, in an undertone.

Spi′ri-tō. (*I.* spĕ′rē.) Spirit; life; animated; in a brisk manner.

Stä. (*I.*) As it stands; played as written.

Stäc-cä′tō. (*I.* stäk-kä′tō.) Short and distinct; detached.

Stäc-cä′tō touch. A light, airy effect produced by suddenly lifting the fingers from the keys.

Staff. A character by which tones are represented; it usually consists of five lines with the spaces which belong to them, and is frequently enlarged by short added lines above and below.

Stave. The name formerly given to the *Staff*.

Stĕn-tä′tō. (*I.*) Forced; emphasized.

Step. A term of measurement equal to a major second.

Stes′so. (*I.* stäs′sō.) The same, as *Lo stesso tempo*, the same time.

Stop. Finger pressure on stringed instruments; (2) a guitar fret; (3) a row, register, or collection of organ-pipes.

Strain. A particular portion of a tune, especially one of peculiar interest; in hymn-tunes and church-music, strains are usually divided by double-bars.

Strä-sci-cän′dō. (*I.* shĕ-kän′.)
Strä-sci-nän′dō. (*I.* shĕ.)
Strä-sci-nä′tō. (*I.* shĕ.)
Dragging; drawling; slurring from tone down to tone, while the time is slightly slackened.

Stre′pi-tō. (*I.* strä′pĕ.)
Stre-pi-tō′sō. (*I.* strä-pĕ-tō-zō.)
Noise; noisily, impetuous.

Stret′tō. (*I.* strät′tō.) Close; contracted; the subject and answer of a fugue brought closely together. The rapid *finale* of a movement in a Sonata, overture, or symphony.

Strin-gen′dō. (*I.* strĕn-jän′.) Pressing; hastening the time.

Style. Character, form, or individuality of music.

Suä-vi′tō. (*I.* swä-vĕ.) Sweet, pleasant, agreeable.

Sub. (*L.*) Below; under.

Sub-diăpĕntĕ. (*Gr.*) The fifth below the tonic; the sub-dominant. *Fa* in the major, and *Re* in the minor.

Sub-dominant. Four of a key (*Fa* in major, *Re* in minor).

Su′bi-to. (*I.* sōō′bi-tō.) At once; quickly.

Sub-mediant. Six of a key (the third below the tonic).

Sub-tonic. Seven of a key (the minor 2d below the tonic).

Sull'. (*I.* sōōl.) On the; upon the; by the.

Super. Above.

Super-tonic. Two of a key (the major 2d above the tonic).

Suspended cadence. One in which the chord of the dominant is prolonged or suspended until the bass has taken its final position on the tonic.

Suspension. The withholding of a tone which is proper to a chord, and, in its stead, retaining a tone from the preceding chord, thus producing a momentary dissonance.

Svel′tō. (*I.* svāl′.) Swift; light; quick; free; easy.

Swell. The union of *crescendo* and *diminuendo*.

Symphonic poem. A composition for orchestra in symphonic style, but freer in form than a regular symphony.

Symphony. A sonata for grand orchestra, in several movements.

Syncopation. (*E.*) A displacement of the accent by driving it to an unaccented pulse.

Syn-cō-pĕ. (*L.* sĭnk′ō-pĕ.) To strike; to cut off; the commencing of a tone on a weak pulse, and continuing it into the following strong pulse.

Tā′cĕt. (*L.*) It is silent; a direction that certain instruments shall remain silent; as, *violino tacet*, the violin be silent, etc.

Tän′tō. (*I.*) So much; as, *non tanto*, not so much.

Tä-rän-tel′lä. (*I.* tāl′.) A rapid Italian dance, so called because it is thought to be a remedy for the bite of the tarantula spider.

Täs-tō sō-lō. (*I.*) One key only; without chords; in unison.

Te′mä. (*I.* tā.) A theme or subject; a melody.

Temperament. A system of compromises in tuning the piano, organ, etc., whereby the octave is equally divided into twelve tones; C sharp and D flat becoming the same, etc.

Temperament, equal. That in which the variations of pitch are distributed among all the keys alike.

Temperament, unequal. That in which the variations are thrown into the keys least used.

Tem′pō. (*I.* täm′.) Time; the movement of a piece.

Tem′pō a pi-ä-ce′rĕ. (*I.* pē-ä-tchä′.) Time at pleasure.

Tem′pō prĭ′mō. (*I.* prē′.) In the time of the first movement.

Tem′pō ru-bä′tō. (*I.* rōō.) Robbed time; time occasionally slackened or hastened for the purposes of expression.

Tĕn-ĕ-rez′zä. (*I.* rät′sä.) Tenderness, softness.

Tenor. The highest male chest voice.

Tenor clef. The C clef; used in vocal music to designate the tenor staff.

Te-nō′rĕ rō-bus′tō. (*I.* bōōs.) A tenor with strong, full voice.

Tenth. An interval of an octave and a third.

Te-nu′tō. (*I.* tā-nōō.) Sustained; held the full time.

Ter-zet′tō. (*I.* tär-tsät′.) A piece for three performers.

Third inversion. That form of a chord of the seventh when the bass takes the seventh.

Thorough bass. Indicating the harmony by a figured base.

Tie. A curved line connecting two notes on the same degree.

Tierce. (*F.* tĕrs.) A third.

Tierce de Picardie. (*F.*) A major third in the last chord of a minor composition.

Tĭm-ō-rō′sō. (*I.* zō.) With hesitation; timorous.

Tim-pä′ni. (*I.* tĕm-pä′nĕ.) Kettledrums.

Tōc-cä′tä. (*I.*) A brilliant piece in moderately strict style.

Tone. Any sound in which pitch is perceptible.

Tones, chest. The lowest register of the voice.

Tones, head. The upper tones of the voice.

Tones, passing. Tones foreign to the harmony, used in passing from one chord-tone to another.

Tonic. The point of repose; the tone from which all other tones are reckoned; the key-tone.

Tonic sol fa. The American system of *sol-fa-ing from a tonic*, was carried to England by Dr. Lowell Mason. Its essential principles, viz., *tone-relationship*, were adopted by Rev. John Curwen, and formulated into what is called *tonic sol fa*. It does away with the staff, and substitutes a letter notation, thus antagonizing the universally accepted staff. All its good points were in use in America long before its advent into England.

Tōs′tō. (*I.*) Quick, swift, rapid; as, *piu tosto*, more rapid.

Touch. The manner in which a player presses the key-board, whether light, heavy, pearly, clumsy, firm, etc.

Trä′chē-ä. (*Gr.* kĕ.) The windpipe.

Trän-quil′lō. (*I.* quĕl′.) Tranquilly, calmly.

Transcription. An adaptation.

Transpose. To set or change into another key.

Trä-ves′tie. (*G.* fĕs.) A parody.

Tre. (*I.* trä.) Three; as, *a tre voce*, for three voices.

Treble. The Soprano.

Treble clef. The G clef.

Tre cor′dĕ. (*I.* trä.) Take off the soft pedal (piano).

Tre-män′dō. (*I.* trä.) ⎫ Tremblingly, waveringly; (2) played
Trĕm-ō-län′dō. (*I.*) ⎬ or bowed so rapidly as to produce a
Tre′mō-lō. (*I.* trä.) ⎭   tremulous effect; (3) vibration of the
voice in singing. See *Vibrato*.

Très. (*F.* trä.) Very.

Triad. A chord of three tones.

Triad, augmented. A triad with an augmented fifth.

Triad, major. A triad with a major third.

Triad, minor. A triad with a minor third.

Triad, tonic. A triad founded on the tonic.

Trill. A rapid alternation of two tones; a *shake*.

Trio. A piece for three performers; (2) a part of a minuet, etc.

Triplet. A pulse divided into three equal parts.

Trŏm-bä. (*I.*) A trumpet.

Trŏp′pō. (*I.*) Too much.

Tu′bä. (*L.* tōō′.) A deep bass horn.

Tune. A melody or air; (2) just intonation.

Tuning fork. A two-pronged instrument giving a fixed pitch.

Turn. An ornament formed by taking the tone above and the tone below a principal tone.

Tut′tä. (*I.* tōō.) All, the whole.

Tut′ti. All the performers are to take part.

Un. (*I.* ōōn.) One; as, *una corda*, one string; *una volta*, 'once,' etc.

U′nä cor′dä. (*I.* ōō′nä.) One string; press the soft pedal.

Unison. Having the same number of vibrations.

Un pō′cō. (*I.* ōōn.) A little.

Ve-lō′cĕ. (*I.* tchĕ.) Rapid, swift.

Verse. To be sung by one voice on a part.

Vespers. An evening singing service.

Vi-brä′tō. (*I.* vē.) A tremulous tone; not pure.

Vir-tu-ō′sō. (*I.* vēr′tōō-ō′zō.) A skillful performer.

Vite. (*F.* vēt.) Swiftly, quickly.

Vi-vä cĕ. (*I.* vē-vä′tchĕ.) Lively, quickly, sprightly.

Vi′vō. (*I.* vē′.) Alive, brisk, animated.

Vō′ce. (*I.* tchĕ.) The voice.

Vō′cĕ di pet′tō. (*I.* tchĕ dē pät′.) The chest voice.

Vō′cĕ di tes′tä. (*I.* tchĕ dē täs′.) The head voice.

Vō′cĕ, mez-zä. (*I.* mät-tsä vō-tchĕ.) Half power; subdued.

Voicing. Regulating the tones of organ-pipes.

Voix ce-leste. (*F.* vwä sä-lĕst.) An organ-stop.

Vōl′tä. (*I.*) Time.

Vōl′tä pri′mä. (*I.* prē′.) First time.

Vōl′tä se-con′dä. (*I.* sä.) Second time.

Vōl′ti su′bi-tō. (*I.* sōō′bē.) Turn over quickly.

Vox hu-ma′na. (*L.*) Human voice ; an organ-stop.

Whole note. } A note or rest which equals four quarter notes in
Whole rest. } duration.

Wolf. Cross vibrations heard when two tones are nearly in tune.

Xyl′ō-phōne. (zil′.) An instrument the tones of which are produced by striking pieces of wood.

Zĭth′ĕr. (*G.* tsĭt.) A small flat stringed instrument of limited power and compass.

THE END.

www.ingramcontent.com/pod-product-compliance
Lightning Source LLC
Chambersburg PA
CBHW031153120726
47905CB00006B/1930